~~£12.95~~ £4.95

4.11.89.

Writers in Romney Marsh

This book is for Jane King and
Kitty French with thanks for their
friendship and support.

WRITERS IN ROMNEY MARSH

by IAIN FINLAYSON

SEVERN HOUSE PUBLISHERS

First published in 1986 by
Severn House Publishers of
4 Brook Street, London W1Y 1AA

British Library Cataloguing in Publication Data
Finlayson, Iain
Writers in Romney Marsh
1. Literary landmarks—England—Romney Marsh
I. Title
942.2'395 PR110.R/

ISBN 0-7278-2061-3
ISBN 0-7278-2092-3 Pbk

Typeset by Inforum Limited, Portsmouth.
Printed and bound in England by Oxford University
Press Printing House.

CONTENTS

AUTHOR'S ACKNOWLEDGEMENTS

John and Paddy Aiken; Sarah Anderson of The Travel Bookshop; Geoffrey and Rosemary Bagley; Christopher Bateman; Sir Brian and Lady Batsford; Liz Bland; Patric and Sheila Dickinson; Dion Fielding; May and Beth Finlayson; Kitty French; Lena Frewen; Jane and Linda King; Eric and Joanna Lefevre; Margaret McKechnie; the late Don Moore, and Connie Moore; Dorothy Nicholson; Mary Owen of The Rye Gazette; Molly Parsons; Vera Proctor; Tony and Cynthia Reavell of The Martello Bookshop; John Rice of South East Arts; Mick Rooney; Rosemary Smitherman; Janet and Daniel Thorndike; Graham Watson.

I am indebted, in various ways, to all these generous people whose help, professional and personal, enabled this book to be written. Not least, I am grateful to Deborah Rogers, Lucy Lloyd, and to Julian Mannering and Delia Cooke who nursed this book throughout. I gratefully acknowledge the assistance of a bursary from South East Arts.

PHOTOGRAPHIC ACKNOWLEDGEMENTS

Photographs 1,2,4,8,14 – courtesy of The National Trust.
Photographs 3,5,13,15 – National Portrait Gallery, London.
Photographs 6,7 – BBC Hulton Picture Library.
Photographs 9,10 – Paddy Aiken.
Photograph 12 – Ivy Robbins.
Photograph 11 – taken from 'E.F. Benson' by Cynthia and Tony Reavell.
Photograph 16 – courtesy of Daniel Thorndike.

Cover picture:
Snargate 1982 by John Piper, courtesy of Marlborough Fine Art (London) Ltd.

We gratefully acknowledge the use of the poems 'Rye', 'Tourists of a Sort' and 'Henry James and Lamb House' by Patric Dickinson.

PREFACE

The form and content of this book dictated itself. There have been many critical and biographical studies of the individual writers who lived and worked in Romney Marsh, and I have drawn my material from a good number of these books as well as from the works of the writers themselves and my own experience of living in Romney Marsh. This is not a book of literary criticism, but a domestic literary history of the Marsh and those who, while they lived there, contributed to its importance as a literary centre. There was never a Romney Marsh 'school' of literature, nor any Romney Marsh 'group'. But it is interesting to identify the writers and to give some account of their lives during the periods they lived in Romney Marsh. So far as possible, I have attempted to account for them in their own words and, where possible and appropriate, in the words of their contemporaries, families, friends, neighbours and associates.

Iain Finlayson
Hastings, 1986

ONE

Romney Marsh in Literature

O, I'll be off! I will by Jove!
No more by purling streams I'll ramble,
Through dirty lanes no longer rove,
Bemired and scratched by briar and bramble.

I'll fly the pigsty for the parks,
And Jack and Tom and Ned and Billy
I'll quit for more enlightened sparks,
And Romney Marsh for Piccadilly.

In these affably elated terms, the Reverend Richard Harris Barham signified his overnight decision to quit the curacy of the parishes of Warehorn and Snargate, villages about two miles apart on the north west rim of Romney Marsh, to stand for a minor canonry that had become vacant in St Paul's Cathedral in London. He dashed off ten more verses, bidding a sharp but affectionate farewell to rustic joys, snares, entanglements, and offences, including 'nasty little boys so sweetly in the puddles playing!' and singing 'Adieu, adieu, the cheerful noise of grunting pigs and asses braying!' Some comforts he will regret abandoning, 'gooseberry wine and pear and codling,' but other memories will be less than fond: 'farewell the pimples that illuminate the noses of the squire and vicar.' The fox and partridge will rest easier for his absence, since Barham proposes to renounce his dog and gun and cashier his leather breeches. No more will he tap a clerical shoe at country 'hops' or county balls; not another evening will be lost to games of loo, backgammon and cribbage. Elderly ladies can no more expect Mr Barham for a dish of tea. 'Ye scenes of bliss, ye rural joys, Adieu! and, Bless ye, altogether.' Having given his final benison, satirically but kindly, Mr Barham was confirmed in his metropolitan preferment on 6 April 1821 and took up his residence in London in August the same year in time to witness the funeral procession for the Queen on 14 August. He had spent four years, from 1813, at Ashford and Westwell, and in 1817 had come to Romney Marsh.

'To those who knew Mr Barham only in the latter part of his life,' comments the Reverend RH Dalton Barham in the lively biography of his father which he published in 1880, 'his position in a parish desolate, remote from all educated society, placed, indeed, almost beyond the borders of civilisation, for such the Marsh – or, as the natives called it, the Mesh – really was, must appear about as ill-suited to his character as any that can be well imagined.' To a literate, cultured gentleman, the Marsh might at first sight have appeared (and perhaps may yet seem) unpromising. Romney Marsh did not, in the early years of the nineteenth century, possess any long or distinguished tradition of letters. That it later acquired a literary reputation was – and continues to be – due to incomers who have settled and worked in this apparently improbable outpost of England and the civilisation to which it pretends.

In 'Mrs Botherby's Story. The Leech of Folkestone', one of the tales that make up *The Ingoldsby Legends*, Barham remarks that 'The World, according to the best geographers, is divided into Europe, Asia, Africa, America and Romney Marsh.' Tom Shoesmith, in 'The Dymchurch Flit' from Kipling's *Puck of Pook's Hill*, is inclined to the same view as these eccentric but eminent scholars: 'Won'erful odd-gates place – Romney Marsh . . . I've heard say the world's divided like into Europe, Ashy, Afriky, Ameriky, Australy, an' Romney Marsh.' That the natives of the Marsh were cognizant of the discoveries of

Captain Cook speaks well for their assimilation of the latest intelligence from London, but the addition of Australasia to the store of knowledge of local geographers does not diminish the chauvinism of the men of the Marsh whose important place in the terrestrial cosmography remains undimmed and undisturbed. The claim of Romney Marsh to be a fifth or sixth continent is purely a regional conceit, a Marsh maggot that has wormed its way into the minds of the Marsh folk and resisted, for long ages, any topographical evidence that might tend to confound the notion. It is a faintly sinister little continent. According to Barham, 'a Witch may still be occasionally discovered in favourable, *i.e.*, stormy, seasons, weathering Dungeness Point in an egg-shell, or careering on her broomstick over Dymchurch wall. A cow may yet be sometimes seen galloping like mad, with tail erect, and an old pair of breeches on her horns, an unerring guide to the door of the crone whose magic arts have drained her udder. – I do not, however, remember to have heard that any Conjuror has of late been detected in the district.' There are self-acknowledged witches to this day in Hastings, nevertheless.

With a sure touch for the appropriate adjective, Barham characterises Romney Marsh as 'this recondite region'. It may still be secretive, but it is no longer obscure or secret. It would be difficult to smuggle anything not properly accounted for by the Customs and Excise into the cellars of the Mermaid Inn, in Rye, since Mermaid Street has become one of the most photographed streets in the country, a picture postcard and calendar cliché, smug in its selfconscious picturesqueness. Dr Syn, the romantic fictional cleric-cum-smuggler of Russell Thorndike's imagination, could no longer ride wildly about on the Marsh without being stopped by roaming bands of back-packers asking the way to the nearest bed and breakfast, and his local hostelry, Slippery Sam's, is probably in *The Good Pub Guide*. It is one thing to hold up the coach of a General and a Bishop, quite another to demand their money or their lives of a busload of bemused, camera-clicking Japanese tourists en route from Folkestone to Hastings. Romney Marsh depends largely on sheep and trippers, both of which species can conveniently be herded and left to browse, for its wealth and preservation as a distinct region of the south-east coast of England, on the borderland of East Sussex and Kent. It has long had a doubtful reputation not only for pride, witchcraft and lawlessness, but also for the dangerous, plague-ridden air to which visitors might quickly succumb. In the sixteenth century, Queen Elizabeth travelled across the Weald of Kent to Rye, but took care to avoid 'the dreaded Rumney Marsh'. The Elizabethan topographer, William Lambarde, warned travellers in the Marsh that they 'shall rather find good grasse under foot, than wholesome Air above the head.'

The Marsh people tended to be insular (indeed, the Channel used to wash around villages and towns such as New Romney, Lydd, Rye, and Winchelsea, making islands of what were then important ports and are now cities of the plain) and an expedition to Folkestone or Dover was a tremendous undertaking. Their natural reserve persists, if we are to credit Richard Church who found it 'difficult to recognize the human folk of the Marsh, for they have a technique of invisibility. I have never known such a social reticence. Certainly the flats are sparsely populated, and one would not expect to meet many people in these wide grazing areas; but here and there are cottages, huts, larger settlements that might almost be called farms, and occasionally they coagulate into hamlets and villages. But they appear all to be deserted. Do the natives go indoors and barricade themselves against the passing of a stranger? I suspect that is what happens, for seldom is one of them encountered face to face.' So the Marsh people appeared to the author of *Kent* in the mid-twentieth century. Nigh on forty years later, his impression holds good. Across the county border, in Winchelsea on a summer's afternoon, it is still easy to appreciate Coventry Patmore's description of the village as 'a town in a trance'. It lay as though under an enchantment. To account for the silence and desertion as due to early closing day is inadequate: there is a small general store and post office, selling ices and tinned foods, which had shut its doors against the urgent need of a tourist in search of a packet of cigarettes. The pub had ceased to provide beer and bar snacks by half past two, and the sole sound was a persistent droning, like a hive of harassed bees, which was caused, in fact, by an elderly gardener pushing an electric mower across an impeccable front lawn. The formal rows of white weather-boarded houses, a gleaming tribute to zealous preservation, waited inexhaustibly in the sunlight for the return of their middle-class and elderly owners who had surely deserted the village, for no curtain twitched that dozy afternoon. High and dry, dreaming imperturbably of its long-ago seafaring importance as an Ancient Town of the Cinque Ports, Winchelsea drowsed in its landlocked impotence as though one of the Marsh Pharisees had laid an enchantment upon the hill on which it stands like a citadel.

Down in the Marsh itself, there is more vivacity. Tom Shoesmith in *Puck of Pook's Hill* describes how 'The Marsh is justabout riddled with diks an' sluices, an' tide-gates an' water-lets. You can hear 'em bubblin' an' grummelin' when the tide works in 'em, an' then you hear the sea rangin' left and right-handed all up along the Wall. You've seen how flat she is – the Marsh? You'd think nothin' easier than to walk eend-on acrost her? Ah, but the diks an' the water-lets, they twists the roads about as ravelly as witch-yarn on the spindles. So ye get all turned round in broad daylight.' Richard Church attributes the self-contained, insular character of Romney Marsh to 'the fact that the inhabitants have been working at frantic speed for the last two thousand years building dykes of brushwood and rock, and cutting their way through choking intrusions of sand and shingle in strangled riverbeds. This preoccupation has kept them facing one way – seaward, with their backs to the rest of the land and the community of the Weald. It has made them, perhaps, somewhat impatient of interruption.' The doom of the people of Romney Marsh is an ironic inversion of the tale of the demon set eternally to make ropes of sand – their constant effort is to untangle the land from the choking ropes and drifts of shingle and sand, and lorries may be seen today continually ferrying loads of shingle from one part of the coast to another, in an endless and prodigious labour to thwart the insensible determination of the sea to throw it back where it naturally belongs.

The Sussex Marshes, says Coventry Patmore, stretch in three distinct tracts, the first from Lewes to Newhaven, the second from Eastbourne to St Leonards, and 'the third commences where the Fairlight Downs cease suddenly, about five miles east of Hastings, and is continued to where Sussex ends, a little beyond Rye; where the great plain becomes the Romney Marsh which goes on as far as Hythe, and has a breadth perhaps as great as its length: making in all an almost perfect flat of, I should think, about a hundred square miles.' Patmore, who thoroughly disliked mountains – 'great imposters, claiming and obtaining an amount of admiration to which they have no right. They are petrified catastrophes, stationary tumult, nothing heaped upon nothing, barren bigness that boasts itself more beautiful then life' – discovered in Romney Marsh 'the peaceful and touching charms which render the plain more than a rival to the mountain in the eyes of all who find in human associations, more or less remote, the ground of the truest beauty in landscape.' Year after year, Patmore looked upon Romney Marsh from the walls of Rye 'always with new delight'. It is 'very Dutch in its peculiar beauties,' he declared, but surpasses 'in truly artistic beauty, the scenery alike of Holland, Switzerland and Italy. . . . The plain, in each case [each of the Sussex Marshes], is great enough to expand and satisfy the eye. It is, in each case, set off by the immediate neighbourhood of hills not less than eight hundred feet high – an altitude which, in our atmosphere, is quite as good as three thousand in Italy or the South of France.' He comments favourably on 'the sight of masts and sails at more or less remote distances, impressing us with the presence of the sea even more powerfully than the actual sight of it would.' He remarks the rivers and canals which 'quicken the flats with their lines of light' and is ravished by the old towns, mostly unspoilt by modern building, perched on steep hills, 'as picturesque as those of the Riviera'. The rich, flat sheep pastures are just sufficiently barren as to afford a pleasing contrast with 'well-wooded and populated hills of the fairest English type' which form their northern limits. Of the light, Patmore has never seen it to better effect than from Rye, looking down from the walls 'on something like a hundred square miles without a shadow, except, perhaps, from the dark down of Fairlight; and the endless peaceful glory, organic and alive in every inch of it, is doubled in effect by the continual presence of that other bright, but barren and restless, plain of the sea.' The sun that shines, it is said, with a double lustre upon Rhodes, seems to do so over Romney Marsh, to the immense satisfaction of Mr Patmore and, one supposes, 'the very best of our living English landscape-painters' who, on being introduced to Winchelsea, Rye, and the Pett, Camber and Brede Levels, gratified his cicerone by declaring 'that he had seen there, in our one day's visit, more subjects for pictures than he had ever met with in any other part of Europe in a week.' That artist was Turner.

If the effulgence of the ever-changing light over Romney Marsh is thought to be notable, no less attention should be paid to the sounds of the Marsh. Richard Church, with his ear close to the surface of a site 'often treacherous with bogland', hears a 'subtle wind-music in the Marsh. It comes from the ground, when a smart breeze is leaping over Fairlight, and coming to ground, because it is fresh and cold, over the warmer Marsh. It stoops and runs its fingers through the hairy grasses and weeds, and the result is a steady siffling, sighing rustle, rather like the hum of a swarm of gnats, or a dynamo, with the rhythmic little flick aside that both occasionally give. It is a music that creeps into the mind and gradually hypnotizes it into an indifference to all else in the world. The hills recede, time stands still, and the listener, like John Davidson, finds himself alone "with God and Shakespeare", no other personalities being sufficiently elemental, and at the same time subtle, to bear company in this light-haunted, air-haunted country, through which the water creeps snakelike to the sea, tended by a myriad beetles, sea and land birds, butterflies, and a vast choir of wild flowers and grasses singing an unceasing insectsong; a choir only ankle-high, but faithful and finally dominant over all things foreign to the Marsh.'

'Foreign' – the word rings again, and Church admits it is 'not really easy for the stranger to make close contact with these intimate aspects of the Marsh,' principally perhaps because it is not easy to hunker down or prostrate oneself in a patch of bogland to hear the low music of the Marsh, but also, one feels he implies, because Romney Marsh is a place unto itself, introverted and disinclined to reveal itself immediately, for all its ingenuous flatness, to the casual visitor. The rows of summer houses, bungalows, caravans, chalets, amusement arcades and tea and gift shops that stretch in ribbon development behind Camber Sands seem to have no roots in the soil. They have been put there to be whipped by wind, sand and shingle, and nibbled by sheep, to be weatherbeaten by sun and rain, and given fanciful, evocative names as their only identity. They are not quite real, these shacks, shanties and chalets behind the beach and the golf course. John Piper, who illustrated and described the Marsh in 1950 for Penguin Books, dates them from the nineteen-thirties 'and as a small exhibition of the popular architecture of the period they could not be bettered. . . . A few of their names indicate their character: *Hove To, Windy Cot, Midships, Galleons, Owl's Retreat, Per Mart (Percy, Martha,* perhaps), *Mount Nod, Cooparoo, Linga Longa, Sea Spray, Sea Close, Sea Wynd, Minarest, Thistledome (This'tle do me), Twix Us, Ẹmohruo (Our Home,* backwards), *Ecnamor (Romance,* backwards), *Nelande (Edna, Len* backwards) . . . The romance of this small, blank isolated neck of land is strong,' says Piper of Dungeness, but beyond the shingle of Lydd and the mad Martian figures of the electricity pylons that faintly recall *The War of the Worlds* by HG Wells, a resident of Sandgate, near Folkestone, and the desolation of the flat army firing ranges, fenced in and flying red danger flags, romance by the side of the road from Rye to Lydd is perhaps difficult to find at first sight and the naming of houses in punning, anagrammatical, or onomatopoeic manner is a forgiveable piece of whimsy. The aggrandisement of a holiday house by giving it a name may be necessary in a landscape that tends to swallow the individual. In an autobiographical article, the artist Paul Nash, who painted for a while in Romney Marsh, described how 'I have stayed on Romney Marsh and have watched the eastern sky darken across the dyked flats to Dymchurch and the Channel towards the French coast as the sun set at my back, and have noticed the strange unity of sea, sky and earth that grows unnoticed at this time and place.' In such a place, *Windy Cot* and *Ecnamor* may take confidence from having been named and thus acquiring an identity in an amphibious landscape, where the shingle restlessly moves under one's feet, the wind clatters the windowframes, and the sea appears level with the land.

Piper speaks of the 'flatness and sense of remoteness' of Romney Marsh, 'quite unlike the rest of the beautiful county to which it belongs.' Nash is struck by 'the strange unity of sea, sky and earth,' and Basil Champneys, author of *A Quiet Corner of England*, in 1875 remarks how 'the sense of strangeness and the sense of amphibiousness rush together, and you feel as detached from the ordinary interests of the world and as amphibious as the oldest inhabitant.' To appreciate 'the simplicity and grave harmony of native scenes . . . demands no energy and no effort, but only a little sensitiveness and a little sympathy.'

Nobody was better equipped in these respects than Henry James, the naturalised European who looked upon Romney Marsh and made the point that, 'comparing small things with great – which may always be done when the small things are amiable – if Rye and its rock and church are a miniature Mont-Saint-Michel, so, when the summer deepens, the shadows fall, and the mounted shepherds and their dogs pass before you in the grassy desert, you find in the mild English "marsh" a recall of the Roman Campagna.' There is, in this comparison, a hint of the antique, of the idyll, of the pastoral, of the eclogue, and Coventry Patmore describes Rye as 'a bit of the old world living pleasantly on, in ignorance of the new.' It is not so unconscious of the modern world, however, that it is unaware of the benefits of preserving itself as a minor anachronism in the eyes of the tourist trade. It is a very knowing little town, as set in aspic as the dishes genteelly served at dinner parties behind the net curtains of Church Square and Watchbell Street. It is not improbable that tourists come to feel they are walking around in an alfresco museum, and that it is permissible to knock on doors or simply walk in unannounced to take photographs and admire the quaintly furnished rooms, and the quaint inhabitants, as blatantly picturesque as their surroundings. Here a Fletcher, there a Jeake, perhaps. One does not look in vain for a Miss Mapp, or a Lucia.

Paul Theroux, on his ill-tempered tour of the British coast, was immediately struck by this aspect of Rye: 'the quaintest town in this corner of England, but so museum-like in its quaintness that I found myself walking along the cobblestone streets with my hands behind my back, treating the town in my monkish manner of subdued appreciation like a person in a gallery full of *Do Not Touch* signs. Rye was not a restful place. It had the atmosphere of a china shop. It urged you to remark on the pretty houses and the well-kept gardens and the self-conscious sign painting and then it demanded that you move on.' It is perhaps a place one should come to late in life, with an antiquary's appetite, a curator's connoisseurship.

Rye is determinedly 'homely English', in the view of Henry James who decided that it was just that tone that gave Rye its 'whole pleasant little pathos'. But, still, he regretted Rye's unostentatious refusal to satisfy fully his European taste: 'The best hour is that at which the compact little pyramid of Rye, crowned with its big but stunted church and quite covered by the westering sun, gives out the full measure of its old browns that turn to red and its old reds that turn to purple. These tones of evening are now pretty much all that Rye has left to give, but there are truly, sometimes, conditions of atmosphere in which I have seen the effect as fantastic. I sigh when I think, however, what it might have been if, perfectly placed as it is, the church tower – which in its more perverse moods only resembles a big central button, a knob on a pin cushion – had had the grace of a few more feet of stature. But that way depression lies, and the humiliation of those moments at which the brooding spectator says to himself that both tower and hill *would* have been higher if the place had only been French or Italian.' But it is neither: it is, very firmly, Tourist Board England.

Henry James came to live permanently, at Lamb House, in Rye in 1898 at the age of fifty-five, in the last stage of his wish to turn 'English all over. I desire only to feed on English life and the contact of English minds.' But Romney Marsh has always been threatened by invasion from France, the coast of which may occasionally be observed when conditions are peculiarly clear. The Normans, in 1066, landed just along the coast at Hastings, and Huguenots escaping persecution landed and settled in the area. The novel *Denis Duval* by Thackeray, set in Rye and Winchelsea, deals with this latter period when, as James remarks, the 'south-eastern counties, comparatively at hand, were enriched . . . by a considerable French immigration, the accession of Huguenot fugitives too firm in their faith to have bent their necks to the dire rigours with which the revocation of the Edict of Nantes was followed up. This corner of Sussex received – as it had received in previous centuries – its forlorn contingent; to the interesting origin of which many Sussex family names – losing, as it were, their drawing but not their colour – still sufficiently testify. Portions of the stranger race suffered, struggled, sank; other portions resisted, took root and put forth branches, and Thackeray, clearly, had found his rough material in some sketchy vision of one of these obscure cases of troubled adjustment, which must often have been, for difficulty and complexity, of the stuff of dramas. Such a case, for the informed fancy, might indeed overflow with possibilities of character, character reinforced, in especial, by the impression, gathered and matured on the spot, of the two small ghosts of the Cinque Ports family, the pair of blighted hill-towns [Rye and Winchelsea] that were once sea-towns and that now draw out their days in the dim after-sense of a mere indulged and encouraged picturesqueness.'

'The world knows,' declares Thackeray in the voice of Denis Duval, 'how the bigotry of Lewis XIV drove many families out of France into England, who have become trusty and loyal subjects of the British crown. Among the thousand fugitives were my grandfather and his wife. They settled at Winchelsea, in Sussex, where there has been a French church ever since Queen Bess's time, and the dreadful day of Saint Bartholomew. Three miles off, at Rye, is another colony and church of our people: another *fester Burg*, where, under Britannia's sheltering buckle, we have been free to exercise our fathers' worship, and sing the songs of our Zion.'

Denis Duval attended 'a famous good school, Pocock's grammar-school at Rye,' in the latter part of the eighteenth century. This building, now known as Peacock's School but no longer functioning as a school, may still be seen in the High Street. There, 'I learned to speak English like a Briton . . . I got a little smattering of Latin, too, and plenty of fighting for the first month or two. . . . Whilst I was at Pocock's, I boarded with Mr Rudge, a tradesman, who, besides being a grocer at Rye, was in the seafaring way, and part owner of a fishing boat; and he took *some very queer fish* in his nets, as you shall hear soon.' Augustus Hare, in his late nineteenth-century perambulation of Sussex published in1896, quotes a newspaper, *Once a Week* of 16 September 1865, which describes 'The Romney Marsh men, who attained the most notorious reputation of those lawless days, were mostly natives of Sussex, and made midnight journeys into their native county for the purpose of buying up the flocks of the South Down farmers, and it is stated that these "Owlers", or wool-smugglers, would in a few weeks shear and export 150,000 sheep. So late as 1531, the men of Sussex are supposed to have smuggled upwards of 150,000 packs of wool by the year, and the small landed proprietors whose estates bordered on the sea-coast were too much influenced by a near but false prospect of gain. Large fortunes were accumulated thus in Sussex. Nor did the "free-trading" cease until the war in 1793, existing during its later years contemporary with another and still more disastrous system, namely import smuggling, Romney Marsh still leading the van, the captain of the band being a man named Hunt, who became mixed up in the political disturbances of his time, the smuggling fraternity having none of them any objection to turn a penny in conveying either letters or passengers when the chance offered.'

The old smuggling trade and its legends die hard. The George Hotel in Lydd makes a feature of the running battle that was conducted on the premises in the eighteenth century: a story fit not only for old men by the fire but, nowadays, for readers of beer-mats and souvenir menu cards who like to add a vicarious thrill to a drink or a dinner. To down a pint below a smuggler's bullet hole in the wall, or dine in a room once awash with the blood of a coast-guard is, at least, interesting to the tourist. Smuggling used to be a business, but in the twentieth century its reputation is that of 'an exciting though hazardous game,' or so it was according to EF Benson in his autobiography, *Final Edition*, published in 1940. To the novelist and former Mayor of Rye, familiar with houses that mostly squatted above large cellars, interconnected one with another, 'smuggling was very lucrative'. With civic pride but perhaps less national or Treasury interest, Benson considered that 'to defraud the revenue of the country does not appear as a dirty trick like cheating at cards and defrauding an individual.' Why, Romney Marsh smugglers were, after all, some of them, gentlemen. No gentleman would stoop to palm an ace from his sleeve, but he might have no compunction about running or receiving a barrel of brandy or a peck of snuff. 'Brandy for the parson, baccy for the clerk,' and 'Face the wall, my darling, while the gentlemen go by,' are two familiar lines not only from literature but from social history. Whether the cargoes are now pot for the parson and cocaine for the clerk is neither here nor there – the trade probably still continues. Benson quotes several instances of relatively blameless infractions of the Customs and Excise and remarks, 'The smugglers and their customers were of exactly the same species as the evaders of today and not a whit less respectable' than the ladies who will 'conceal wads of lace and other taxable commodities on their persons when they cross the Channel' or evade income tax, a pastime which 'calls forth high mental qualitites'.

Rye appealed greatly to Benson who found himself, after the death of Henry James and circumstances that appeared to lead ineluctably to his taking on the tenancy of Lamb House, happy to settle into a blameless and quiet middle-aged life. 'I had not come to Rye for any reason except to be there,' and there he discovered 'a stable and solidified sense of home . . . A few months sufficed to convince me that I was not only in Rye, but of it.' This was a subjective view, he admitted, acknowledging that deeply-rooted Ryers might consider him an intruder of the species of Londoner who, enchanted by the quaint, picturesque little town, use the place as a temporary retreat for themselves and their friends. But Benson was permanently hooked. 'To be there made me content: its cobbled ways and its marsh with its huge sky, as at sea, and in particular the house and the garden-room and the garden were making a ferment of their own in my veins, not because they were associated with any cherished and intimate experiences, but because they were themselves.'

But Rye is not the whole of Romney Marsh (some would deny it even a toehold: the citizens of Lydd dread the day when the Rother changes its course and Rye comes again into its vainglory) and Romney Marsh is not Rye which tends to gentility. Romney Marsh, flat and bare, is not gay. Most writers of the region, at a loss for words and keen for lights and commotion, will sooner or later find themselves in Rye which, contrasted with the rest of Romney Marsh, will appear as a glittering centre of civic activity and social excitements. So what, particularly, is the attraction of Rye and the Marsh for writers and artists? For artists, the landscape probably is a reason in itself. For writers, the isolation of the area is possibly the initial allure, but why, then, is the far north-west romantic coast of Scotland, as isolated as one could wish, not equally populated by scribblers? The answer is possibly the perfectly simple fact that Rye is conveniently linked to London by a railway line. One may travel to the metropolis for lunch with a publisher or literary agent, or an early dinner with friends. And the distance is not so great as to impede a constant flow of congenial acquaintances from London who will travel down in tripperish vivacity for a picnic or a weekend in the country. The contact and commerce Henry James maintained with London was considerable. People were quite likely to get on a train at Charing Cross and arrive for lunch, followed by a cheerful chatty walk to Winchelsea, and be home in time for dinner. One may look long and hard for a more comprehensive reason than the railways and the presence of Henry James to account amply for the attraction of Romney Marsh as a suitable literary retreat for his contemporaries and their successors.

However, Ford Madox Ford regarded Romney Marsh as being 'an infectious and holding neighbourhood. Once you go there you are apt there to stay.' To ensure the durability of the charms of Romney Marsh on his friends Henry James, Joseph Conrad, Stephen Crane, and WH Hudson, Ford induced them to drink from the 'spring forming a dip – St Leonard's Well, or the Wishing Well' in the Winchelsea cliff that faces Rye. 'The saying is that once you have drunk of those dark waters you will never rest until you drink again . . . it was perhaps those waters that induced their frequentations of those two towns. But indeed there were sufficient other inducements. An historic patina covers their buildings more deeply than any others, in England at least. Indeed, I know of no place save for Paris, where memories seem so thick on every stone. The climate, too, is very mild. There is practically no day throughout the year on which a proper man cannot eat his meals under a south wall out of doors.' This is a considerable exaggeration, but Ford had in mind less, perhaps, Henry James at his refections than the ideal of the proper man as one who had fathered a child, built a house, planted a tree, and written a book. Henry James conformed to two of these conditions of proper manhood. It is difficult to imagine that paternity or bricklaying skills would have provided him with the additional fortitude to dine in the garden of Lamb House in the depths of winter. It is true to say that Rye and Romney Marsh enjoy a milder climate than many parts of the country (Lydd is reputed to be the dryest place in England), but EF Benson was of the opinion that 'there is no place outside the Arctic Circle so cold as the east end of the High Street when the winter wind blows from that quarter [the east].' Much the same claim is made for the Waverley Station end of Princes Street in Edinburgh, with the additional hazard of winds of considerable velocity, but perhaps each region and town take particular pride in the clemency or disobliging nature of its weather.

Henry James and Ford Madox Ford were contemporaries and neighbours of HG Wells at the turn of this century and, says Ford, 'my friend HG Wells wrote to the papers to say that for many years he was conscious of a ring of foreign conspirators plotting against British letters at no great distance from his residence, Spade House, Sandgate. For indeed, those four men – three Americans and one Pole – lit in those days in England a beacon that posterity shall not easily let die. You have only got to consider how empty, how lacking a nucleus, English literature would to-day be if they had never lived, to see how discerning were Mr Wells's views of that foreign penetration at the most vulnerable point of England's shores.'

Ford referred, of course, to the Americans, Henry James, Stephen Crane, WH Hudson, and the Pole, Joseph Conrad. Of the four, James is best known and his habitation, Lamb House, the most often gazed upon by curious visitors to Rye. There, his memory has been enshrined by the National Trust in rooms and a garden preserved much as he left them, with some of his furniture, books, and a number of contemporary portraits and photographs. No such trouble has been taken with Brede Place, the house Moreton Frewen rented to Stephen and Cora Crane who came to live there in mid-February 1899. On 13 February, the day after their arrival, Cora wrote to Mrs Edward Pease, wife of the secretary of the Fabian Society, to announce that 'we are here. We came yesterday with the dogs and are camping out until our things arrive. . . . This house is more wonderful to us than ever.' The reputation of Brede Place as a haunt of smugglers gives it a lurid and romantic history which is fuelled by the story that the house will tolerate no owners but Frewens, driving out all interlopers by violence and fire.

It was not kind to the Cranes, who experienced some difficult times there, in spite of their enthusiasm for the draughty, inconvenient, ancient, and insanitary house. Brede was 'a pretty fine affair,' wrote Crane to Sanford Bennett, 'and Cora believes that Sir Walter Scott designed it for her. They began one wing in 1378 and somebody kidded it with heavy artillery in Cromwell's time.' Cora, to Edward Garnett, wrote of her hopes 'that the perfect quiet of Brede Place and the freedom from a lot of good, dear people, who take his mind from his work, will let him show the world a book that will live.' Crane did not possess, in Cora's opinion, 'that machine-like application which makes a man work steadily.' Brede, in its isolation, might concentrate his mind. She planted a rose garden, and Crane ran all over the house, quite 'mad' about it. March and early April provided a wild spring, so that in his first enchantment, Crane declared that during 'these late heavy storms the whole house has sung like a harp and all the spouts have been wailing to us. It is rather valkyric.' Opinion was divided as to the suitability of Brede Place for Crane. Ford Madox Ford bewailed it as an 'ill-fated mansion . . . in a damp hollow . . . full of evil influences.' Edith Richie (Mrs I Howland Jones) briskly dismissed any such poetical, gloomy fantasy: 'Rubbish! It stood high, looking down over a little valley where flocks of sheep cropped the good grass.' Some five thousand pounds had been spent on restoring the house by Frewen and his wife, Clara Jerome, sister of Jennie Jerome who had married Lord Randolph Churchill and was the mother of Winston Churchill. The parlous financial state of the Frewens did not stop them patching up the mossy roof or glazing the medieval windows. But 'Mrs Frewen had started renovations with the roof and the garden, not with the plumbing,' states Anita Leslie in *Cousin Clare*, her biography of the artist Clare Sheridan, 'and Moreton considered the sixteenth-century privies perched on the steep slope outside to be an interesting historical feature.' In spite of the antique charm of the place, Ford persisted in his dislike of Brede: 'nothing was more depressing than to drive down into the hollow. In the Middle Ages they built in bottoms to be near the water, and Brede, though mostly an Elizabethan building, in the form of an E out of compliment to Great Eliza, was twelfth-century in site. The sunlight penetrated, pale, like a blight into that damp depression. The great house was haunted. It had stood empty for half a century, the rendezvous of smugglers. On the green banks played fatherless children [Harold Frederic's orphans] – and numberless parasites.' Here, says Ford, 'Crane was the most beautiful spirit I have ever known.' The author of *The Red Badge of Courage* 'was small, frail, energetic, at times virulent. He was full of fantasies and fanaticisms. He would fly at and deny every statement before it was out of your mouth. He wore breeches, riding leggings, spurs, a cowboy's shirt, and there was always a gun near him in that medieval building that he inhabited seven miles from Winchelsea. In that ancient edifice he would swat flies with precision and satisfaction with the bead-sight of his gun. He proclaimed all day long that he had no use for corner lots nor battlefields, but he got his death in a corner, on the most momentous of all battlefields for Anglo-Saxons. Brede Manor saw the encampment of Harold before Hastings.' Crane died, after a terrible journey, a last, mad effort to improve his health, at the Villa Eberhardt, Badenweiler, in the Bavarian Alps, on 5 June 1900. Ford blames Brede for his death: 'The sunlight fell blighted into that hollow, the spectres waved their draped arms of mist, the parasites howled and belched on the banks of Brede.' Crane himself had worked under the most terrible conditions, physical and mental, and 'Death came slowly but Brede was a sure death-trap to the tuberculous.' The Cranes had inhabited Brede Place for not much longer than fifteen months. Perhaps the 'dreaded Romney Marsh' had claimed its latest victim.

But Ford's recollections and reminiscences need to be taken with a considerable pinch of salt. Crane was not the only writer with a head full of 'fantasies and fanaticisms'. We rely on Ford for the spirit of conversations and controversies, of encounters and anecdotes. But truth has to be winnowed from a large field of corn, conjecture and contentiousness. Fact has to be sifted from factitiousness and self-aggrandisement. His dealings with Joseph Conrad are particularly untrustworthy. Nevertheless, it was certainly Ford who was largely responsible for enticing and settling Conrad and his family into Romney Marsh.

David Garnett describes, in *The Golden Echo*, 'staying with Ford and Elsie Hueffer [Ford Madox Ford's original surname was Hueffer] at Aldington Knoll, a little Kentish farmhouse looking out over Romney Marsh . . . There was a stream running through the garden, and Ford had installed a little wooden water-wheel with two brightly painted wooden puppets who seemed to be working very hard as they bent down and straightened up incessantly. Really the water turned the wheel, and the wheel made them move up and down, bending their backs.' It is difficult to resist this image as a description of the joint and individual labours of Ford and his neighbour, Joseph Conrad, both animated and eternally worked by literature's inexorable flow. An introduction, the Conrads to the Hueffers, had been effected by Edward Garnett at his house, The Cearne, at Limpsfield, where the Conrads had set up an unsuitable home at the old Mill-house. Later, at Hueffer's suggestion, they moved to Pent Farm at Aldington which he rented to them with some furniture. The house had once been the habitation of the artist Walter Crane who had painted a crane and inscribed a couplet above the front door: 'Want we not for board and tent, while overhead we keep the Pent.'

Hueffer, in his *Personal Remembrance* of Conrad, a book bitterly resented and criticised by Jessie Conrad in her own book about her late husband, *Joseph Conrad and his Circle*, describes the house: 'The parlour at the Pent was a deep room with a beam across the middle of the low ceiling; small, pink monthly roses always showed insignificant blooms that looked over the window sills. An immense tithe-barn with a great, thatched, black-mossy roof filled in the whole view if you sat by the fireplace; occasionally you would see a rat progressing musingly over this surface. If you approached the window you saw a narrow lawn running to a low brick wall, after which the level dropped to a great stackyard floored usually with straw and not unusually with a bullock or two in it. Conrad and the writer [Hueffer] planted an orange tree, grown from a pip, under the low north wall of this narrow garden. It was still alive in 1917, growing just up to the coping of the low wall where its progress was cut off by the north wind. It was a very quiet, simple room.' Hueffer, in these pleasing surroundings, 'sat in the grandfather's chair, his back to the window, beside the fireplace, reading, his manuscript held up to the light: Conrad sat forward on a rush-bottomed chair listening intently. (For how many years did the writer and Conrad not sit there like that!)' Soon enough, the 'quiet, simple room' began to resound with the groans of Conrad, and Hueffer himself perhaps would begin to roar. Having come 'to the Pent to see what he was in for,' says Hueffer, Conrad 'came in for passion – and suffering.'

Some of that suffering was due to Hueffer, who describes their literary collaboration in vivid, if imaginative terms: 'We would write for whole days, for half nights, for half the day or all the night. We would jot down passages on scraps of paper or on the margins of books, handing them one to the other or exchanging them. We would roar with laughter over passages that would have struck no other soul as humorous; Conrad would howl with rage and I would almost sigh over others that no other soul would have found as bad as we considered them. We would recoil one from the other and go each to our own cottage – our cottages at that period never being further the one from the other than an old mare could take us in an afternoon. In those cottages we would prepare other drafts and so drive backwards and forwards with packages of manuscript under the dog-cart seats. We drove in the heat of summer, through our deluges of autumn, with the winter snows blinding our eyes. But always, always with manuscripts.'

The Marsh flowed with manuscripts, at the turn of the century, and as one flood ceased another gushed forth a few years later from the brothers EF and AC Benson at Lamb House, from Conrad Aiken and his friends at Jeake's House in Mermaid Street, from Radclyffe Hall first at The Black Boy in Rye's High Street and later at The Forecastle in Hucksteps Row, off Church Square. Along the coast, at Folkestone, Jocelyn Brooke was botanising and storing up materials for his post-war novels. Of Sandgate, his memories are 'matutinal . . . bathed in the keen, windy light of spring mornings, a seaside gaiety and brilliance haunted by the thud of waves on the shingle and the tang of seaweed.' He was struck, later, with the curious parallels Sandgate now and again presented with the Mediterranean seaboard: 'Our house was on the Undercliff: behind it, the cliff rose steeply to the Folkestone Leas; below, a garden descended in terraces to the beach. The house, from the road, presented an undistinguished facade of grey cement; at the back, however (on the seaward-facing side), it was faced with white stucco, and the windows were fitted with green *persiennes*, giving to the house an oddly Mediterranean air. The tamarisks in the garden (and an occasional stone-pine) added to this illusion of meridional gaiety.'

Kipps, the eponymous character of HG Well's novel published in 1905, remembers rather similar golden joys: 'glorious days of "mucking about" along the beach, the siege of unresisting Martello towers, the incessant interest of the mystery and motion of windmills, the windy excursions with boarded feet over the yielding shingle to Dungeness lighthouse . . . wanderings in the hedgeless, reedy marsh, long excursions reaching even to Hythe, where the machine guns of the Empire are forever whirling and tapping, and to Rye and Winchelsea perched like dream-cities on their little hills. The sky in these memories was the blazing hemisphere of the marsh heaven in summer, or its wintry tumult of sky and sea; and there were wrecks, real wrecks, in it (near Dymchurch pitched high and blackened and rotting were the ribs of a fishing smack, flung aside like an empty basket when the sea had devoured its crew) and there was bathing all naked in the sea, bathing to one's armpits, and even trying to swim in the warm sea-water (spite of his aunt's prohibition) and (with her indulgence) the rare eating of dinner from a paper parcel miles away from home.'

Romney Marsh is not, perhaps, unique in its suitability as a holiday resort for children who will store it in memory and, one day, remember an idyll. It affects, like any other region of the country, a few who respond to its particular snares and enchantments. The living poet, Patric Dickinson, who has lived much of his adult life in Rye, whispers a clue to the character of Rye and Romney Marsh and suggests that Ford Madox Ford's insistence that his friends should drink from a magic spring might have been unnecessary to keep them glamourised.

But Time is different here.
The streets are full of beggars
You cannot see, who speak
The tongues of centuries
To the deaf tourists.

The town keeps whispering
Its history — fishermen, merchants —
Lifetimes that have been built
From unimportant scraps
To construct a clement

Enclave and sanctuary.
Once you have understood this,
You will feel Rye within,
And be disposed to come back,
If you ever leave it.

This place 'between past and future,' this 'Beautifully jewelled brooch/ Worn at South England's throat,' in Dickinson's words, is a retreat where work may be done. Henry James, in a letter to his sister-in-law, describes the dream fulfilled. 'All the good that I hoped of the place has, in fine, profusely bloomed and flourished here. It was really about the end of September, when the various summer supernumeraries had quite faded away, that the special note of Rye, the feeling of the little hilltop community bound together like a very modest, obscure and impecunious, but virtuous and amiable family began most unmistakeably to come out . . . But the great charm is the simply *being* here, and in particular the beginning of day no longer with the London blackness and foulness, the curtain of fog and smoke that one has each morning muscularly to lift and fasten back, but with the pleasant, sunny garden outlook, the grass all haunted with starlings and chaffinches, and the in-and-out relation with it that in a manner gilds and refreshes the day. This indeed – with work, and a few, a very few people – is the *all.*'

TWO

Henry James at Lamb House

Coincidences do happen, and when they do they are likely to disconcert a sensitive man. In mid-September 1897 Henry James had been discussing Lamb House in Rye with his architect friend, Edward Warren. A day or so later James was informed, by a local ironmonger, that a long lease of the house was available. The news, completing a sequence of events, hit James 'like a blow in the stomach'. He had first seen a watercolour of the house in the winter of 1895, after the failure of his play, *Guy Domville*, on Warren's walls in London. In the summer of 1896, he had lived first at Point Hill, Playden, and then at the Old Rectory, Rye, where he had had daily opportunity to gaze wishfully upon the 'mansion with the garden-house perched on the wall' in West Street. 'The peace and prettiness of the whole land, here . . . has been good to me, and I stay on with unabated relish,' he wrote to Edmund Gosse on 28 August. On 25 September, he signed the lease – not without some qualms – and for twenty-one years at least the 'smallish, charming, cheap old house in the country – down at Rye' was his. 'It is exactly what I want,' he wrote to AC Benson, 'and secretly and hopelessly coveted it (since knowing it) without dreaming it would ever fall. But it *has* fallen.'

It was his intention to retreat there from London, to live half the year in Rye, from May to October. The 'mild, quiet, grey stretch from the mid-October to Christmas' was, for James, the pleasantest part of the London year and he did not propose to give it up for the moment. Lamb House appeared imposing from outside, but its internal economy was small and delightful: to his sister-in-law, Mrs William James, he described 'the little old house . . . the very calmest yet cheerfullest that I could have dreamed – *in* the little old, cobblestoned, grass-grown, red-roofed town, on the summit of its mildly pyramidal hill and close to its noble old church – the chimes of which will sound sweetly in my goodly old red-walled garden. The little place is so rural and tranquil, and yet discreetly animated, that its being within the town is, for convenience and immediate accessibility, purely to the good; and the house itself, though modest and unelaborate, full of a charming little stamp and dignity of its period (about 1705) without as well as within.'

Edward Warren had accompanied James to Rye to inspect and assess the property and the extent of any necessary renovations. The house had been well looked after, so that the only immediate necessity was the installation of sanitation and furniture, and the stripping of paper from 'several roomfuls of pleasant old top-to-toe wood panelling.' Two of these rooms were 'of complete old oak – one of them a delightful little parlour, opening by one side into the little vista, church-ward, of the small old-world street, where not one of the half dozen wheeled vehicles of Rye ever passes; and on the other straight into the garden and the approach, from that quarter, to the garden-house aforesaid, which is simply the making of a most commodious and picturesque detached study and workroom.' The garden, 'about an acre of garden and lawn, all shut in by the peaceful old red wall aforesaid, on which the most flourishing old espaliers, apricots, pears, plums and figs, assiduously grow' was revealed to the professional eye of Alfred Parsons, a landscape gardener, artist, and designer of the sets for *Guy Domville*. Both he and James were delighted with the 'glorious little growing exposure, air, and soil – and all the things that were still flourishing out of doors' as late as 20 November.

To furnish this pretty little paradise, James set about picking up 'a sufficient quantity of ancient mahogany-and-brass odds and ends – a task really the more amusing, here, where the resources are great, for having to be thriftily and cannily performed.' The rent for Lamb House was seventy pounds per annum, inclusive of outside repairs. Ferreting out bits of 'not too-delusive' Chippendale and Sheraton and 'a handful of feeble relics' engrossed James for a winter, but they did not come at bargain prices. It was necessary to establish an adequate income and some cash in hand. *Literature*, a new journal published by *The Times* (later to become the T L S), commissioned a monthly 'American Letter' at forty pounds apiece, and James also undertook to write a life of the sculptor WW Story 'for a definite *fee* on its completion.' William Blackwood, the Edinburgh publisher, paid an advance of two hundred and fifty pounds, offered a further one hundred after the sale of seven thousand copies, and a similar amount for every two thousand copies thereafter. The American magazine, *Harper's Weekly*, agreed to pay three thousand dollars for a serial story that would be the novel known as *The Awkward Age*, and James had already contracted to deliver a serial story to *Collier's* by January – the short novel entitled *The Turn of the Screw*. This activity was designed to provide some security in a life that had come to seem nomadic. 'My love of travel grows smaller and smaller,' he wrote on 7 August to his brother, William James. 'I find it perfectly simple and easy to stick to British soil.' James hoped to move into Lamb House by May 1898, though, in fact, he did not spend his first night there until the end of June.

To AC Benson, James had confided that the merit of Lamb House was 'that it's such a place as I may, when pressed by the pinch of need, retire to with a certain shrunken decency and wither away in – in a fairly cleanly and pleasantly melancholy manner – towards the tomb.' But, for the moment, James was feeling gay and the tomb could wait. A constant to-ing and fro-ing of visitors kept him in a state of high sociability. The procedure for guests travelling from London was of the simplest. Directions to Mrs JT Fields assured her 'that the journey is performed in exceptionally easy conditions. That is, the 11 a.m. from Charing Cross to Rye is a super-excellent train in spite of your having to change at *Ashford* at about 12.30, and have a wait there of twenty-five minutes. But the run, after that, down here, is of the briefest, and places you almost at my very door at about 1.30 – excellent time for luncheon. I meet you at the station, of course, and we are but five minutes from my house. The 4.53 back restores you to Charing Cross at 7.39.' The procedure in reverse, of course, was similarly convenient and ensured that James would not be wholly an exile in Romney Marsh. He still kept up his flat in De Vere Gardens as a guard against feeling quite cut off from the social life of the capital. But more and more he settled into a routine that pleasantly filled his days. The Remington typewriter clicked efficiently in the garden room in the mornings while James fluently dictated to his secretary, McAlpine; then there was lunch; then he might amiably converse with friends on a leisurely walk to Winchelsea or he might go bicycling – twenty-two miles was no great feat. He was still in Rye on Christmas Day, having 'been in this place almost every hour since the end of June.' The autumn was even better than the summer, while Christmas, 'this dreary little festival', was redeemed by being 'still, grey . . . mild and merciful'. Having settled comfortably in, he was proposing even to let the London flat.

He was reluctant to leave Lamb House, and Rye, so much so that a fire in the early hours of the morning in February 1899 caused less damage to James's composure than it did to the house which was saved by the prompt action of local firemen. Amid the charred wood and water, James was able to write to Edmund Gosse: 'Only I don't *want* even *now* to go: this house is so sustained a fit.' Besides, he had a serial to write – *The Awkward Age* – which was not only a job of work but a process of coming to terms with himself and his new situation. Leon Edel, in *The Life of Henry James*, submits that *The Awkward Age* records a great disenchantment. James tells himself that he is well out of London, well out of its lies and camouflage and that the theme of 'his last and greatest works,' to be written at Lamb House, would be 'that civilization and society, forms and manners which ennoble man and make rich his life, would founder without illusions, or artistic lies, the old "suspension of disbelief." In a word, society must have faith in its illusions and yet paradoxically remember they are illusions.' Those last novels, conceived and written at Rye, were to be *The Sacred Fount*, *The Ambassadors*, *The Wings of the Dove*, and *The Golden Bowl*. This great creative period spanned four years, from 1900 to 1904, but first there were two novels in the last years of the nineteenth century, *What Maisie Knew*, completed in 1897, and *The Awkward Age* in the years 1898 and 1899. Later, in 1906 and 1907, James wrote three books of travel observation – *The American Scene*, *English Hours*, and *Italian Hours*.

When he had completed *The Awkward Age*, James went to Italy for a holiday in the spring of 1899. De Vere Gardens had been let for six months and he was feeling so much at home in Rye that visits to town were liable to disconcert him. He wanted to get to work again, begin another novel, and to do so he decided to shake himself up with a tour abroad before re-establishing his daily routine. In Rome, he was introduced to a young American sculptor of Norwegian birth. Hendrik Andersen, from Boston, was as monumental in build and as handsome as one of his own statues. The magnificence of the sculptor did much to atone for the lack of genius in his work. James bought a terracotta bust of Conte Alberto Bevilacqua, which Andersen promised to pack up and ship to Rye, and induced the young man to visit Lamb House. By the end of July 1899 Henry James was back at Lamb House, savouring the charms of the young Count Alberto whose bust was placed in James's dining room, and soon Hendrik followed, equally to be savoured. 'Brave little Bevilacqua and braver still big Maestro Andersen!' Of the bust of little Conte Alberto, James wrote to say, 'I shall have him constantly before me, as a loved companion and friend. He is so living, so human, so sympathetic and sociable and curious, that I foresee it will be a life-long attachment.' He might have been speaking of Andersen.

Andersen stayed only two or three days in Rye before taking off for London and America. He returned, twice, two years later, and in 1905 and 1907 there were further meetings in America and Rome. James's attachment to Andersen lasted a decade in the absence, almost complete, of the beloved. James hoped to make over the studio in Watchbell Street that he had acquired with Lamb House when the freehold of the house was offered to him in July 1899 and accepted. The drawback of this 'little artistic habitation,' he admitted, was that 'Rye, alas, is not sculpturesque, nor of a sculpturesque inspiration,' but perhaps Henry and Hendrik would be 'good for each other; and the studio good for both of us.' But 'our common fate growled out of the harsh false note of whirling you untimely away,' and James began sorely to miss his new friend, that 'most lovable youth', as he described him to friends in Rome.

The American critic Edmund Wilson has pointed to the surfacing of sex in James's last novels. Leon Edel says James had hitherto 'lived with his private sexual life as if he were an anchorite; he attained fame as one of the "monks" of literature who wrote about subjects other than sex . . . He wrote about his own innocence.' But now James 'seems to swim in a sea of erotic promise.' James had had the alarming experiences of encountering a creation of fiction: the character of Roderick Hudson, the sculptor of the novel that bears his name, whose aims and ambitions appeared very similar to those of Hendrik Andersen who also wished to create great works of art, sculptures on abstract themes such as Beauty and Wisdom. Andersen went further: he desired to create a great city, full of monumental sculptures. Andersen was perhaps James's first real love – Lamb House, ardently wished for, had 'fallen' to his wish to possess it: perhaps Andersen, too, might fall within James's grasp. A note of confident intimacy now infects James's letters to young men such as Morton Fullerton, Howard Sturgis, Jocelyn Persse and Hugh Walpole. It must be doubted whether James ever physically seduced Andersen. Edel is of the opinion that love for Andersen opened James up to sensory feeling, to a fuller appreciation of men – and women – as sensual beings. But the inhibitions against physical expression of love, beyond James's amiable and innocent habit of embracing and kissing his friends without erotic intent, remained strong. 'Allowance must be made for James's long puritan years, the confirmed habits of denial, the bachelor existence, in which erotic feeling had been channelled into hours of strenuous work and the wooing of *mon bon*, the available and compliant muse of the writing table.' Then, too, says Edel, James was conscious of his masculinity and feared losing any part of it in his work as much as in his person. And he was constitutionally averse to low life philandering. On and off, he continued to long for the worthless, ambitious, increasingly megalomaniac and inadequate sculptor despite all his conscious distress at Andersen's failure to live up to the highest ideals of art and responsibilities as an artist and as a true friend.

Meanwhile, James had been corresponding with HG Wells at Sandgate – their exchange of letters had begun in 1898 and continued until 1914 – and on 23 May 1900 he is writing to thank young Ford Madox Hueffer for the gift of his 'so curious and interesting book of verses, with so friendly a letter'. James's letter, though genial, is cautious. He commends particularly 'the little rustic lays' in *Poems for Pictures* and wonders, as though pursuing a random line, whether there is still more (he evidently felt there was) the youthful poet can get from the 'poetry of the cold and damp and the mud and the nearness to earth'. James ends by saying he will be glad to see Hueffer should he 'again pass, soon, this way.' It is a vague invitation, but one that Hueffer, with all the confidence of his twenty-seven years and his volume of verse, took up with alacrity. They had, of course, met before. So considerable and masterful a genius could not be ignored. In *Return to Yesterday*, Hueffer concocts a tale that Mrs Clifford, to whom he says James had written to complain about an eye condition, urgently requested him to visit James and report back to her. Whatever the occasion of scraping acquaintance with James, Hueffer made what he could of it. 'On that first occasion he was bearded, composed and magisterial.' James at this point had not yet obtained Lamb House and was living at the Old Rectory in Rye for part of the summer of 1896. 'At lunch he was waited on by his fantastic butler. The fellow had a rubicund face, a bulbous red nose, a considerable paunch and a cutaway. Subsequently he was to become matter for very serious perturbations to his master. His methods of service were startling. He seemed to produce silver entrée dishes from his coat-tails, wave them circularly in the air and arrest them within an inch of your top waist-coat button. At each such presentation James would exclaim with cold distaste: "I have told you not to do that!" and the butler would stand before the considerable array of plate that decorated the side-board.'

James, when living in Lamb House, kept four servants, all of whom were lodged in the top floor attics. A gardener, George Gammon, lived in a nearby cottage conveniently close to the garden. The butler, Smith, performed double duty as James's personal manservant and his wife was employed as the household cook. Additionally, he was served by a parlour maid and a house maid. The Smiths had been with James at the flat in De Vere Gardens, but on 23 September 1901 they departed his service in deep disgrace: 'The tidal wave I had long been expecting and dreading broke just a week ago,' he wrote to Mrs William James on 26 September. 'That is, the tragedy of the Doom of the Smiths has in the course of six or seven days been completely *acted* and is over.' The wretched Smiths had finally gone too far during a visit of various friends who included Hendrik Andersen. 'Smith, who had been more or less drunk and helpless each day and *all* day for many previous, was *most* so on this complicated occasion. . . . Smith was *accumulatedly* so drunk that I got him out of the house – i.e., all Friday Saturday and Sunday – that though I had Skinner [a local doctor] to him to medicate him I could really not communicate with him to the extent of a word, any more than with his wife, whom I made over wholly to her own sister . . . They were, at the end, simply two saturated and demoralized victims, with not a word to say for themselves and going in silence to their doom; but great is the miracle of their having been, all the while, the admirable servants they were and whom I shall unutterably mourn and miss.' The Smiths had drunk all their wages, left James with a bill for more drink, and were hopelessly alcoholic. He paid them a weekly pension for two months and two months' wages 'till they can turn round', though he despaired of their salvation or prospects of employment elsewhere. The episode had been 'a perfect nightmare of distress, disgust and inconvenience. As a climax of the latter I sit tonight without a servant, to call a servant, in the house.' As Hueffer remarks, James was left to the ministrations of the knife-boy, Burgess Noakes, and ate his meals at the nearby Mermaid Inn. The 'gnome', bantam-weight Noakes, was in time promoted to butler-valet and served James with great devotion until the last.

Mrs Smith, despite her disposition to drink, had been a good cook. The search for her replacement was an urgent and anxious business. James had left the kitchen entirely to his cook and 'had not the slightest idea of what foods agreed with him and which did not,' according to Hueffer who gives a comic account of James's domestic exigencies. 'He would pass his time, he said, interviewing ladies all of a certain age, all of haughty – the French would say *renfrongée* – expressions, all of whom would unanimously assure him that, if they demeaned themselves merely by for an instant considering the idea of entering the household of an untitled person like himself, in such a Godforsaken end of the world as the Ancient Town of Rye, they having passed their lives in the families of never anyone less than a belted Earl in mansions on Constitution Hill in the shadow of Buckingham Palace . . . if they for a fleeting moment toyed with the idea, it was merely, they begged to assure him . . . "forthegoodoftheirhealths". Mr James having dallied with this sentence would utter the last words with extreme rapidity, raising his eyebrows and his cane in the air and digging the ferrule suddenly into the surface of the road.' To Agnes Muir Mackenzie, nicknamed 'Hereditary Grand Governess', who had advised him about the garden of Lamb House, James wrote of his travail in the search for a cook-housekeeper: 'I've been up to London over it, and haunted Hastings, and wired to friends . . . and the first thing I think of now when I wake up in the morning is that a "cook-housekeeper" in a Gorringe costume is to arrive next week. I tremble at her.' The replacement for Mrs Smith was ceremonious to the extent of curtseying to James when they encountered one another, bore an expression of irreproachable gravity on her face, dressed respectably (unlike Mrs Smith who had had no money to squander on clothes when there was drink to be bought) – though whether from a London department store cannot be said – and was altogether respectful and competent. The question of a new housemaid was thoroughly vexing: James, according to Hueffer, consulted not only the opinion of the great and the grand but also the humbler, practical expertise of Ford Madox Hueffer's own housemaid. Having satisfactorily engaged a less exceptionable body of servants to replace the unpredictable Smiths, he rejoiced to Hueffer: 'all shall for the future be as I have already adumbrated, not only gas and gingerbread, but cloves and clothespegs and beatitude and bliss and beauty . . .' Mrs Paddington, the cook-housekeeper, was 'a pearl of price; being an extremely good cook, an absolutely brilliant economist, a person of the greatest order, method and respectability, and a very nice woman generally.' Alice Skinner, the parlour-maid was 'a thoroughly respectable, well-disposed and duly competent young woman. And the House-maid is very pretty and gentle – and not a very, *very* bad one. The House-Boy, Burgess Noakes, isn't very pretty, but is on the other hand very gentle, punctual, and desirous to please . . . and makes himself generally useful.' These happy domestic dispositions having been made, James could settle to an ordered life.

In *Henry James at Home*, H Montgomery Hyde recorded the memories of Burgess Noakes about James in Rye: 'We used to call him "The old toff," ' said Noakes, and commented favourably on James's generosity of pocket. That generosity extended not only to Noakes and the other servants, but to a wide range of friends, acquaintances, and colleagues. On 5 June, he wrote, enclosing a cheque for fifty pounds, to Cora Crane at Badenweiler where Stephen Crane was dying. He was annoyed when, on 29 August, he wrote to his agent, James B Pinker, to thank him for a warning about Cora, 'the importunate lady'. 'I sent her a contribution which reached her at the moment of Crane's death and which was really, out of pity for *him*, more substantial than I could afford, and yet I learn that the young local doctor here [Skinner], who gave almost all his time to them, quite devotedly, during all Crane's illness, and took them to the Black Forest, has never yet, in spite of the money gathered in by her at that time, received a penny, and doesn't in the least expect to. It's really a swindle.' His last service to her was a letter of support in favour of her application to the Royal Literary Fund for financial aid. He was careful to make it as brief as possible and to say that 'my note represents the whole connection with it that I shall be able to find possible.' Earlier, to Pinker, he had written, 'my heart, I fear, is generally hard to her.'

He wrote the note at a time when he was feeling depressed. To Morton Fullerton, at this time, in October 1900, he wrote: 'one is face to face, at my age [James was fifty-seven], with every successive lost opportunity . . . and with the steady, swift movement of the ebb of the great tide – the great tide of which one will never see the turn. The grey years gather; the arid spaces lengthen, damn them – or at any rate don't shorten; what doesn't come doesn't, and what goes *does*. . . . The port from which I set out was, I think, that of the *essential loneliness of my life* – and it seems to be the port also, in sooth to which my course again finally directs itself! This loneliness, (since I mention it) – what is it still but the deepest thing about one? Deeper about *me*, at any rate, than anything else: deeper than my "genius," deeper than my "discipline," deeper than my pride, deeper, above all, than the deep countermining of art.' The depth of this feeling had been worked upon in the character of Lambert Strether, in *The Sacred Fount*, the novel which he was at that moment reading in proof. Ageing was difficult, and love, now that it had entered his old soul, was devastating. But this period in his life was crucial to the development of James as an artist: in 'his intellectual power and his new openness to feeling,' says Leon Edel, he showed his readiness for a *vita nuova*. In his "deep well of unconscious cerebration" Henry James had moved slowly from sickness to health. He had taken backward steps into the black abyss in order to discover his power of self-recreation, and now he had emerged again a whole man in spite of assaults and misfortunes . . . the frigid wall of his egotism had been breached to an enlarged vision of the world, and a larger feeling of the world's human warmth.' A few months earlier, he had shaved off his beard, 'unable to bear longer the increased hoariness of its growth: it had suddenly begun these three months since, to come out quite white and made me *feel*, as well as look so old. Now, I feel *forty* and clean and light.' A new century and a new face, says Edel.

Not only did he feel lonely, he began to feel rusticated. He had taken a permanent room at the Reform Club in Carlton House Terrace, but the social snares of London ate up precious time though they provided the necessary mental stimulus he failed to find in Rye. Solitude in Rye was bearable so long as he worked – and he did work, diligently, every day, dictating to a secretary – first Mr McAlpine, who was followed by Miss Weld who was in turn supplanted by Miss Bosanquet, all of them perfectly satisfactory amanuenses. The body and quality of the work was very substantial, and could not otherwise have been achieved in a more socially or intellectually bracing environment. In Rye, he had largely uninterrupted time to write, revise, plan, think, and conduct a copious correspondence that too often plaintively spoke of his need and desire for the company of his friends. Late in 1900, he complained to Edmund Gosse that he had been confined to Rye – 'this hamlet' – for two and a half years, aside from the four months he had spent in Italy, and begged for a trip to Madame Tussaud's. But two trips to London, in March and May 1900, left him replete with the charms of the city and he looked forward to a return to restful Rye. His ambivalence about his country retreat lasted until the beginning of the next decade. Rye was alternately charming and 'slightly grim and nude'. When in London, he thought with benevolence of Rye: when in Rye his cosmopolitan soul longed for London.

What little intellectual and literary companionship there was in Romney Marsh depended in the earlier years on visiting friends and the occasional company of Joseph Conrad and HG Wells. Hueffer was, in James's eyes, negligible, and Crane was soon dead. Wells was a little too remote at Sandgate for constant communion face to face: they visited one another, but letters passed more frequently between them. Contact between James and Conrad was not continuous: they were both busily writing, and Conrad could not afford to entertain or trip around the countryside in lavish style. James, too, was frugal in his habits and understood financial anxieties and pressures. He had supported Cora Crane's appeal to the Royal Literary Fund, and in 1902 took up, also, the cause of Conrad who needed three hundred pounds. He wrote to Edmund Gosse, 'When I think that such completeness, such intensity of expression has been arrived at by a man not born to our speech, but who took it up, with singular courage, from necessity and sympathy, and has laboured at it heroically and devotedly, I am equally impressed with the fine persistence and the intrinsic success. The case seems to me unique and peculiarly worthy of recognition. Unhappily, to be very serious and subtle isn't one of the paths to fortune. Therefore I greatly hope the Royal Literary Fund may be able to do something for him.' Conrad got his three hundred pounds.

On 10 July 1901 James despatched 'the too-long retarded Finis' of *The Ambassadors* to Pinker, his agent, who, on 13 September, was advised that the final revisions to the novel had been completed and sent to him. Meanwhile he was 'well launched into' *The Wings of the Dove* which was published in 1902. The character of Merton Densher in this novel was based on James's friend Morton Fullerton and not, as Hueffer claimed, upon Ford Madox Hueffer.

The ubiquitous Hueffer had presented himself, unbidden, at Lamb House one day a few weeks after publication of this novel. Early in October 1902 he and Conrad had come from Winchelsea to Rye on an errand, and Hueffer had spotted Rudyard Kipling and his wife hurrying down from Lamb

House. They had been to call on Henry James for lunch, driving over from Burwash in a new, grand, expensive motor car. 'In those days,' says Hueffer, 'the automobile was a rapturous novelty.' But the Kiplings, departing, were on foot and appeared perturbed. Hueffer's account of James's subtle delight in the discomfiture of the Kiplings is too good to miss. Adopting the tones and voice of the Master, Hueffer gives a clever pastiche of the Jamesian style of narration:

> 'A writer who unites – if I may use the phrase – in his own person an enviable popularity to – as I am told – considerable literary gifts and whom I may say I like because he treats me – ' and here Mr James laid his hands over his ear, made the slightest of bows and, rather cruelly rolling his dark and liquid eyes and moving his lower jaw as if he were revolving in his mouth a piquant tit-bit, Mr James continued, 'because he treats me – if again I may say any such thing – with proper respect' – and there would be an immense humorous gasp before the word 'respect' – '. . . I refer of course to Mr Kipling . . . has just been to see me. And – such are the rewards of an enviable popularity! – a popularity such as I – or indeed you, my young friend, if you have any ambitions, which I sometimes doubt – could ever dream of, far less imagine to ourselves – such are the rewards of an enviable popularity that Mr Kipling is in possession of a magnificent one-thousand-two-hundred-guinea motor car. And, in the course of conversation as to characteristics of motor cars in general and those of the particular one-thousand-two-hundred-guinea motor car in the possession of our friend . . . But what do I say? . . . Of our cynosure! Mr Kipling uttered words which have for himself no doubt a particular significance but which to me at least convey almost literally nothing beyond their immediate sound . . . Mr Kipling said that the motor car was calculated to make the Englishman . . .' and again came the humorous gasp and the roll of the eyes . . . 'was calculated to make the Englishman . . . think.' And Mr James abandoned himself for part of a second to low chuckling. 'And,' he continued, 'the conversation dissolved

itself, after digressions on the advantages attendant on the possession of such a vehicle, into what I believe are styled golden dreams – such as how the magnificent one-thousand-two-hundred-guinea motor car after having this evening conveyed its master and mistress to Batemans Burwash, of which the proper pronunciation is Burridge, would tomorrow devotedly return here and reaching here at twelve would convey me and my nephew William to Burridge in time to lunch, and having partaken of that repast to return here in time to give tea to my friend Lady Maud Warrender who is honouring that humble meal with her presence tomorrow under my roof . . . And we were all indulging in – what is it? – delightful anticipations and dilating on the agreeableness of rapid – but not, for fear of the police and consideration for one's personal safety, *too* rapid – speed over country roads and all, if I may use the expression, was gas and gingerbread when . . . There is a loud knocking on the door and – *avec des yeux effarés* . . .' and here Mr James really did make his prominent and noticeable eyes almost stick out of his head . . . 'in rushes the chauffeur . . . And in short the chauffeur has omitted to lubricate the wheels of the magnificent one-thousand-two-hundred-guinea motor car with the result that its axles have become one piece of molten metal . . . The consequence is that its master and mistress will return to Burwash, which should be pronounced Burridge, by train and the magnificent one-thousand-two-hundred-guinea motor car will *not* devotedly return here at noon and will *not* in time for lunch convey me and my nephew William to Burwash and will *not* return here in time for me to give tea to my friend Lady Maud Warrender who is honouring that humble meal with her presence tomorrow beneath my roof or if the weather is fine in the garden . . .

'Which,' concluded the Master, after subdued ho, ho hos of merriment, 'is calculated to make Mr Kipling think.'

This extended piece of faintly malicious gossip, travestying James's manner and humour, had clearly been lovingly worked up with enormous pleasure by Hueffer who, no doubt, had rehearsed it in less polished versions to Conrad and other delighted friends and gossips. It is a brilliant, perfectly-timed piece of humorous writing, but it is also useful for giving the flavour of the contemporary gossip retailed among the literary little world of Romney Marsh. James's delight in the seizing up of Mr Kipling's wonderful machine may have been real enough – he had first begun to use a typewriter in 1897, but abandoned it to the fingers of typists employed to transcribe his dictation. Never could he have used it himself. And Edith Wharton, the American novelist and friend of James, wondered that James never possessed a car. She was rich herself, and possessed a very fine car and chauffeur: she did not understand the professed exiguity (however imaginary) of James's purse. He could perhaps very well have afforded a car, but not a chauffeur as well, and it was beyond the bounds of credibility that Henry James could have mastered the internal combustion engine himself. Gas, a dangerous novelty, was confined to the kitchen of Lamb House for cooking purposes. In the public rooms and bedrooms, Henry James preferred oil lamps. Even Kipling, writing to Henry James, confessed that 'It's not as easy as it looks, a sick motor.' The motor, named Amelia, according to an engineer sent from the motor car factory in Birmingham, avowed the accident to the axles to be 'unique in all mechanics and motoring,' which was at least satisfactory for such a magnificent machine. No common mishap had rendered her stationary on the cobbles of Rye.

Lunch for the Kiplings would have been between one o'clock and one thirty. They would not have seen James earlier, since the routine of Lamb House, according to Burgess Noakes, was regular almost to the minute. Henry James was called promptly at eight o'clock, by Noakes, and the process of shaving and bathing and dressing with neat discrimination occupied the next hour. Breakfast was served at nine o'clock, and domestic dispositions for the day were made. At ten o'clock, work began in the garden room, Miss Mary Weld or Miss Theodora Bosanquet, her successor, seated with supple fingers poised over the keys of the Remington. The voice of the Master pronounced the words of his masterpieces until lunchtime when he would stop pacing, and proceed to the dining room. There, he might not, if alone, sit down, but eat on his feet, wandering about the room, looking out at the garden, considering the morning's work and the pleasures of the afternoon ahead: there was a dog to be walked, perhaps friends for tea or dinner; and after dinner there would be the private, personal pleasure of writing long letters in manuscript until he fell asleep, late at night, in the chair in the study.

Lizzie Skinner, the parlour-maid, learned to beware of James when he 'was on a book . . . He was normally very pleasant, but he got irritable when people worried him and he wanted to write; when you lived in the same house with him you got used to it; his work was the one thing he lived for. Sometimes people called when he was like this, and I didn't dare tell him, and I sent them away. When interrupted during his work he would shout.' Miss Weld, the typist who succeeded Mr McAlpine, has her own memories: 'He dictated beautifully. He had a melodious voice . . . Typewriting for him was exactly like accompanying a singer on the piano.'

On 15 April 1903, Henry James was sixty years old. In three years he had published three novels, two volumes of stories, articles, and had completed the life of WW Story for William Blackwood. It had been a prodigious effort, and that summer he acquired Max, a new dog, 'a very precious red Dachshund pup – hideously expensive but eight months old – and undomesticated; but with a pedigree as long as a Remington ribbon', and began a new novel – *The Golden Bowl*, the last of his great novels. Copy had been promised to Methuen for the end of November, and he was, in late October, 'gouging away at it with great constancy' but 'not now as far towards completion as I should like – ' It was published, however, by Scribner's in 1904, 'the best book I have ever done.' It was two hundred thousand words of 'the rarest perfection.' He held 'the thing the solidest, as yet, of all my fictions.' Now that it was over, he felt able to travel again. Substantial fees as a lecturer were dangled before his nose, his fingers twitched in his purse and, letting Lamb House for five pounds a week, he set off for America not only to lecture but to press his publisher, Charles Scribner, about a collected edition of his works – a definitive edition of the James corpus, each volume to contain 'a preface of a rather intimate character' by the author.

He sailed for America in August 1904, and did not return to England – and Rye – until mid-July 1905, eleven months later. He brought back with him a mass of impressions which he distilled into a book, *The American Scene*, published in 1907 and described by Edel as 'written with all the passion of a patriot and all the critical zeal of an intellectual who could not countenance national complacency and indifference.' Simultaneously, he was working on revisions to his work for the *Collected Edition* which, by 1908, consisted of approximately half the final total of twenty-six volumes (two published posthumously). Sales were not encouraging, and James, who had been counting on some profit from this considerable effort, was alarmed. The labour had taken up time he might have better devoted to a new novel – 'out-and-out "creative" work' for which he was 'aching in every bone'. In *Henry James at Home*, H Montgomery Hyde presents the depressing figures for the whole *Collected Edition* late in 1915: and James himself, in a letter that year to Gosse, admits: 'That Edition has been, from the point of view of profit either to the publishers or myself practically a complete failure; vulgarly speaking, it doesn't sell – that is, my annual report of what it does – the whole twenty-four volumes – in this country amounts to about £25 from the Macmillans; and the ditto from the Scribners in the U S to very little more. I am past all praying for anywhere; I remain at my age (which you know), and after my long career, utterly, insurmountably, unsaleable.'

James, in 1909, wrote to Violet Hunt, one of his young (relatively – she was forty-seven) admirers of the new generation. He had known the lively novelist since her childhood. He spoke of Rye ' – where else should I be? For I am here pretty well always and ever' – going on to alert her, should she visit, as to the 'homely and solitary state, my limited resources, my austere conditions, and frugal though earnest hospitality' she should find at Lamb House. These 'meagre terms' being accepted, he would be very glad to see her. James was aware of her association with Ford Madox Hueffer, but it was not an open scandal and therefore could be glossed over. She had stayed at Lamb House on several occasions, since 1903, and James was openly fond of her. She had proposed herself for a visit in November 1909, and he looked forward to seeing her. He had no sooner set himself to issue the invitation she sought than he discovered, from Hueffer, that his wife, Elsie Hueffer, intended to sue for divorce and that he intended to marry Violet Hunt as soon as circumstances made that possible. James was more than disconcerted by this news and he promptly took steps to disassociate himself from any possible unpleasantness and – worse – publicity as a conniving or colluding friend of Hueffer's mistress.

To Violet he wrote: 'I deeply regret and deplore the lamentable position in which I gather you have placed yourself in respect to divorce proceedings about to be taken by Mrs Hueffer; it affects me as painfully unedifying, and that compels me to regard all agreeable and unembarrassed communication between us as impossible. I can neither suffer you to come down to hear me utter these homely truths, nor pretend at such a time to free and natural discourse of other things, on a basis of avoidance of what must now be most to the front in your own consciousness and what in a very unwelcome fashion disconcerts mine. . . . Believe me then in very imperfect sympathy, Yours, Henry James.' A further letter explained that 'I neither knew nor know anything whatever of the matter; and it was exactly because I didn't wish to that I found conversing with you to be in prospect impossible.' He and Violet eventually, after the scandal had died away, continued to be friends and he advised her, 'Well, patch with purple if you must, so long as the piece holds.'

It was important that the social fabric should hold. Hugh

Walpole, a young man of twenty-four in 1909 when, on the literary make in London, he met Henry James, described James acutely as 'curious about everything, he knew everything, but his Puritan *taste* would shiver with apprehension. There was no crudity of which he was unaware but he did not wish that crudity to be named. It must be there so that he might apprehend it, but it must not be named.' Hueffer and Violet Hunt and Elsie Hueffer had named and brought to glaring light their crudities and James recoiled from them, offended by the indiscretion. Walpole's friendship with James admitted him to many intimacies of conversation. Later Walpole recognised James's 'inevitable loneliness'. He did not know, perhaps, of the loneliness James had felt, years ago, at the departure of Hendrik Andersen, and attributed the loneliness to the fact that, as 'an American, he was never really at home in Europe. Nor was he at home in America for when he was there he longed for the age, the quiet, the sophistications of Europe. He was lonely in the second place because he was a spectator of life. He was a spectator because his American ancestry planted a reticent Puritanism in his temperament and this was ever at war with his intellectual curiosity. Sexually also he had suffered some frustration. What that frustration was I never knew . . .' Somerset Maugham used to take deep delight in telling a story that Walpole had made specific sexual advances to James and James had wildly recoiled, crying out, 'I can't, I can't, *I can't*!' There is no saying whether this is true or not, but certainly there existed a deep fondness in James for his young admirer who was often at Lamb House, and perhaps he felt it was now too late to make up for what he had repressed. To Walpole, he wrote, 'I only regret in my chilled age, certain occasions and possibilities I *didn't* embrace.' But the moments, and the opportunities fully to embrace them, for a man approaching seventy, were gone and could not now be redeemed. He advised Walpole, however, to spare no effort, neglect no opportunity: 'We must know, as much as possible, in our beautiful art, yours and mine, what we are talking about – and the only way to know is to have lived and loved and cursed and floundered and enjoyed and suffered.' James had not exactly roistered, he had not made an exhibition of himself in his private life which had been decorous to a degree. But in himself he had lived and loved profoundly and cursed and floundered and enjoyed and suffered. The evidence is there in muffled tones in his work – what he felt intensely he wrote intensely. He had not been afraid.

In August 1910, Henry's brother William died. He had gone to America to be with him at the last, and in his grief James found respite from his own physical troubles. In 1909 he had become worried about his health and had consulted Sir James Mackenzie, a heart specialist, who reassured James about his fear of *angina pectoris*: 'You are sixty-six years of age. You have got the changes in your body which are coincident with your time of life. It happens that the changes in the arteries of your heart are a little more advanced than in those of your brain, or of your legs. It simply follows that if you be more judicious in your living, and give your heart less work to do, there is no reason why you should not reach the ordinary span of human life.' James was very much encouraged by this diagnosis, reported Mackenzie, but his patient continued to feel low-spirited and anxious, and fell into a depression. He suffered attacks of gout, was averse to food, lay humped miserably in bed in the mornings dozing fretfully, and suffered dreadfully from 'the black devils of nervousness, direst damndest demons.' To a friend, he wrote, 'I lie here verily as detached as a sick god on a damp Olympus.' He worried insatiably about his reputation as a novelist and his earnings, neither of which he considered amounted to much. There had been precious little recognition on either score.

On his return to England in August 1911, James recognised that his depression stemmed, in part, from his isolation from London. His secretary, Theodora Bosanquet, was living in Chelsea and she organised two rooms in her Lawrence Street flat as a workroom and a dressing room furnished with a bathroom for his use, since no female visitors, not even respectable secretaries, were admitted to the private apartments of the

Reform Club. Here they worked daily at James's autobiography until June when James returned to Rye for the summer, pleased to 'feel intensely, after so long an absence, the blest, the invaluable little refuge of dear Lamb House.' But Rye had changed: as early as 1908 he had observed, and regretted, that 'Rye is going to the dogs, with increase of population, villas, horrible cheap suburbs, defacements, general ruination.'

Here he again felt that his heart trouble was recurring – there was anginal pain – and later, in October, he suffered an attack 'of the atrocious affliction known as "Shingles".' This complaint kept him in bed for a couple of months, until December 1912. Just before this attack, he had found himself a flat in Cheyne Walk, in Chelsea. Number 21 Carlyle Mansions was suitable in every respect: Miss Bosanquet was within a short walk of the flat which cost only sixty pounds a year more than the rent of his Reform Club apartment, there was a tremendous view of the Thames, there were rooms for his servants, the public salons were sunny, and the literary associations of the neighbourhood were distinguished – Carlyle, George Eliot and Leigh Hunt had all blessed it with their presence at one time or another. Lamb House was reserved solely for the summer. On 5 January 1913 he moved from Rye which had become, 'with its solitude and confinement . . . quite an impossible place for hibernation.'

The move was fretful. As he reported to his sister-in-law, he had tumbled somehow into Carlyle Mansions with the aid of his maidservant's and Miss Bosanquet, suffering horribly from a gastric upset and 'my poor ravaged herpetic tract', and feeling generally debilitated after the attack of shingles. He was pretty much of an invalid, but in April he was able to tell Mrs William James that 'I manage, and have got back to work, and can go about to some extent in the afternoon (to see friends) with the aid of the blest taxis of the low London tariff . . . it is astonishing with how much pain one can with long practice learn constantly and not too defeatedly to live.' There were elaborate celebrations, organised by friends and colleagues for his seventieth birthday on 15 April: they had commissioned a portrait, for which he sat to Sargent, all despite his protests – though, in the event, the marking of the occasion by such a number of distinguished persons reassured him that they did not under-rate him as an artist and as a friend.

When war broke out in 1914, James was in residence at Lamb House. Noakes joined up, and the sound of guns from across the Channel sounded faintly in Rye. Edmund Gosse described how his old friend had 'sat through that gorgeous tawny September, listening to the German guns thundering just across the Channel . . . He used to sally forth and stand on the bastions of his little town, gazing over the dim marsh that became sand-dunes, and then sea, and then a mirage of the white cliffs of French Flanders that were actually visible when the atmosphere grew transparent. The anguish of his execration became almost the howl of some animal, of a lion of the forest with the arrow in his flank, when the Germans wrecked Rheims Cathedral. He gazed and gazed over the sea south-east, and fancied that he saw the flicker of the flames. He ate and drank, he talked and walked and thought, he slept and waked and lived and breathed only the War. His friends grew anxious, the tension was beyond what his natural powers, transfigured as they were, could be expected to endure, and he was persuaded to come back to Chelsea, although a semblance of summer still made Rye attractive.'

'I could no longer endure the solitudinous (and platitudinous) side of my rural retreat,' he said to a friend, Rhoda Broughton, since he was anxious to be where information about the war was most easily to be got – in London, among friends in touch with the grand and the great in the military and the government. He actively wrote and propagandized for the war effort, and on 26 July 1915 took the Oath of Allegiance to the King, George V, before a Commissioner of Oaths, and became a naturalized British subject. At the last, he threw in his lot with Europe and the country he had lived in so long and he was surprised to feel no difference on achieving his new status. To Edmund Gosse, he wrote: 'since 4.30 this afternoon I have been able to say *Civis Britannicus Sum*! . . . the odd thing is that nothing seems to have happened and that I don't feel a bit different; so that I see not at all how associated I have become, but that I was really too associated before for any nominal change to matter.' He was old and tired, and on a visit to Rye, after having been ill in London, he burned some personal papers and found some difficulty breathing. What he took to be gastric upset, he diagnosed and dosed himself. But Skinner, the local doctor, took the view that he was suffering from intermittent tachycardia and prescribed digitalis. He returned promptly to London where, on 2 December 1915, his house-maid discovered him in his bedroom having 'a sort of stroke'. He was calm enough, but a second stroke paralyzed his left side. He recovered a little, but delusions followed – he began to live somewhat in the past and dictated letters in the person of Napoleon Bonaparte. Though he now and again fancied himself to be at sea, he never returned to the landlocked ancient port of Rye, to Lamb House. After the announcement, on New Year's Day 1916, that he had been awarded the Order of Merit, at six o'clock on 28 February of that year, Henry James died.

THREE

HG Wells at Sandgate

HG Wells and Jane, his wife, had come from Italy in the summer of 1898 to their home at Worcester Park, but decided almost immediately on a bicycling holiday to the south coast despite HG's 'general sense of malaise' which was in fact due to an old football injury when, ten years earlier, he had injured his left kidney. Wells attributed his lassitude to lack of exercise and was determined to master not only his physical discomfort but also the 'sense of physical inferiority [which] was a constant acute distress . . . which no philosophy could mitigate.' On the road he caught cold and settled in lodgings at Seaford at the end of July. He was struggling to finish a new novel, *Love and Mr Lewisham*, 'because while a book unfinished would have been worth nothing, a finished book now meant several hundred pounds.' A medical friend of George Gissing, the novelist, lived at New Romney where he was medical officer of health for Romney Marsh; Wells consulted Dr Hicks who diagnosed kidney trouble, put Wells to bed, recommended an operation, and put him on a diet. Thereafter, according to Wells, there was no further trouble. An operation became unnecessary when it was discovered that 'the offending kidney had practically taken itself off and . . . there was nothing left to remove.' Jane and HG moved first to Sandgate, thence to a small furnished house nearby called Beach Cottage, after Hicks had advised against a return to Worcester Park. 'I had to reconcile myself to complete exile from London, and contrive to live in dry air with no damp in the subsoil and in as much sunshine as possible.' Beach Cottage was far from dry ('in rough weather the waves broke over the roof'), so they moved to Arnold House, an unfurnished property, and began to think about building a house in Sandgate – which they did, though they stayed the full term of their three year lease at Arnold House.

There, through a neighbour, Wells met the Fabian Graham Wallas who, like his fellow political idealists, 'took the idea of getting a living as something by the way; a sort of living was there for them anyhow; and the real business of life began for them only after that had been settled and put on one side.'

A greater contrast than Wallas to Wells could scarcely have been found, which is perhaps why he so interested Wells. Wallas walked, talked, theorised, dissected and reformed ideas, but 'was under no inner compulsion to get things positively done . . . Somewhere between my own tendency to push on to conclusions and Wallas's interminable deliberation, lies I suppose the ideal method of the perfect student working "without haste and without delay".' Among the further Fabian contacts Wells made in Romney Marsh at this time were Hubert Bland and his wife, the novelist E Nesbit, who had a house at Dymchurch. E Nesbit is described by Wells as 'a tall, whimsical, restless, able woman who had been very beautiful and was still very good-looking.' She, and her husband, 'dramatized life . . . They loved scenes and "situations". They really enjoyed strong emotion. There was no such persistent pursuit of truth and constructive ends in them as in their finer associates. It was not in their imaginative scheme.' E Nesbit was a poet, a writer of children's stories, and 'she earned the greater part of the joint income.' Hospitable, bohemian, with a 'touch of aloof authority', she entertained regally at the Dymchurch house to which came 'the Chesterton brothers, Laurence Housman, Enid Bagnold, . . . Berta Ruck, Jack Squire, . . . Monsignor [Hugh] Benson, Frederick Rolfe (Baron Corvo), a multitude of young writers, actors and aspirants in an atmosphere of talk, charades, mystifications and disputes. And there also I and

Jane visited and learnt to play Badminton and gossip and discuss endlessly.' The dramatic household of the Blands contrasted, sometimes agreeably, sometimes disturbingly, with HG's familiar world of his own family: 'It was a world of rôles and not of realities.' Quite contrary to the simple- or the scientific-minded people Wells was used to, the Blands 'were fundamentally intricate . . . had no primary simple idea. They had brains as active and powerful as most other brains in my world, but . . . they had never taken them down to any sort of philosophy; they had never focussed them on any single objective, and they started off at all levels from arbitrarily adopted fantasies and poses.'

Meanwhile, Wells was busy 'getting on in the world', 'concerned in questions of "rights" and royalties and "price per thou" in a manner that was altogether ungenteel.' But certainly he managed his life more successfully than Conrad or Crane or Hueffer or Henry James: 'I was full of mercenary "go"; "price per thousand" and "saleable copy" were . . . present in my mind . . . My commercialism is not, I think, innate, but my fight with the world for Jane and myself and my family, had set a premium upon money making. I was beginning to like the sport. I was beginning to enjoy being able to pay for things. I was getting rather keen on my literary reputation as a saleable asset.'

He set about finishing *Kipps* and then making notes for *Tono Bungay*, 'a novel, as I imagined it, on Dickens-Thackeray lines.' 'Scientific' works followed, a stream of lectures, essays, books such as *Anticipations, A Modern Utopia* and a novel, *The Food of the Gods* published in 1904, followed by *In the Days of the Comet*, 1906, in which 'an impalpable gas from a comet's tail sweeps into our atmosphere, does the work of centuries of moral education in the twinkling of an eye, and makes mankind sane, understanding and infinitely tolerant.' Wells, working in pious expectation of the progress towards perfection of man, horrifying Henry James by his involvement in the wider, grosser world, and deeply puzzling Conrad with his scientific notions of the purpose of novels, was simultaneously beset by particular problems of his private, emotional life.

In *Experiment in Autobiography*, HG Wells reflects upon the influence of the Blands upon his sexual nature. Hubert Bland 'was, he claimed to me at least, not so much Don Juan as Professor Juan. "I am a student, and experimentalist," he announced, "in illicit love".' Wells remarks, 'In those days I would have made illicit love impossible – by making almost all love-making licit. . . . He [Bland] was sincerely disgusted at my disposition to take the moral fuss out of his darling sins. My impulses were all to get rid of the repressions of sexual love, minimize its importance and subordinate this stress between men and women as agreeably as possible to the business of mankind.'

Towards 1900, Wells established what he was pleased to call a *modus vivendi* with wife Jane. He and Jane had been living together since 1893, and they married, he at the age of twenty-nine, in 1895 after his divorce from his first wife Isabel. 'I have never been able to discover whether my interest in sex is more than normal,' Wells wrote in a memoir unpublished until 1984, but he did not think it excessive. Circumstances, he admitted, might have been in favour of a full expression of his libido: 'Most other men probably have as much or more drive, I suspect, but less outlet. Their sexual lives are forced to be more furtive than mine, and they are in consequence more subject to complexes.' Wells was an early admirer of Freud. Sexual relations with Jane were adequate, so long as they were struggling together to make a place in the world. When that place was assured, Wells felt his interest wandering and his intimacy with Jane unfulfilling: 'with success, an ampler life and more vigorous health, our close strict partnership was relaxed. I began to think of lovelier sensual experiences and to ask "why not?" ' Wells philosophized about a concept he called 'the Lover-Shadow' – a 'continually growing and continually more subtle complex of expectation and hope; an aggregation of lovely and exciting thoughts; conceptions of encounter and reaction picked up from observations, descriptions, drama; reveries of sensuous delights and ecstacies; reveries of understanding and reciprocity.' These mental reveries excite, and are made concrete, as books, poems and pictures – 'it is for the Lover-Shadow that they are written.' The Lover-Shadow 'is the inseparable correlative to the *persona* in the direction of our lives.' The *persona* is the male aspect of the individual, the Lover-Shadow, the female, so in the social conditions of 1900 the *persona* was the man of action in the outside world. Wells's *persona* was developed and consolidated 'as a devotee, albeit consciously weak and insufficient, to the evocation of a Socialist World-State.' The *persona* was dominant in Wells's character: 'With me the Lover-Shadow never became . . . a sought-after saint or divinity. My innate self-conceit and the rapid envelopment and penetration of my egotism by socialistic and politically creative ideas was too powerful ever to admit the thought of subordinating my *persona* to the Lover-Shadow' – though the Lover-Shadow, 'so largely feminine, stood over me' while the *persona* was developed and Wells became 'a man of science, a leader in human affairs.'

The great Lover-Shadow fell, like the intimation of a storm, over many women including Violet Hunt who was later to be Ford Madox Hueffer's mistress. Violet, who was a novelist and a little older than Wells, introduced him to 'the mysteries of Soho and Pimlico,' without much disturbance to their literary work. Dinners and lunches in private rooms in out-of-the-way restaurants, assignations in anonymous lodging houses, were thrilling and satisfying, leaving time for 'the broader interests' of Wells's life and, naturally, amatory entanglements with other women – 'the latent adventurousness between Dorothy Richardson and myself was consummated.' He also developed the 'kindliness' that Ella D'Arcy (who wrote one or two vivid stories in the *Yellow Book*) felt for him. Dorothy was difficult. She was a 'glowing blonde.' They made love in the bracken between Eridge and Frant, but she 'wanted some complex intellectual relationship . . . She wanted me to explore her soul with wonder and delight.' But Wells was in no mood for mental adventures for he was more preoccupied with the literary lady's 'adorable dimple' and 'interestingly hairy' body. Wells was responsive to such sensual details – an Australian woman, who wrote him a fan letter about *Kipps* and invited Wells to her lodgings, was memorable for 'her ruddy sunburnt skin and straw-coloured hair.' It may be doubted whether *Kipps* was much discussed. Occasionally, the Lover-Shadow got Wells down: 'I am half disposed to sympathize with Origen, and scream for peace and chastity at any price.' Though to 'make love periodically, with some grace and pride and freshness, seems to be, for most of us, a necessary condition to efficient working, it admits of no prosaic satisfactions. It is a mental and aesthetic quite as much as a physical need. I resent the necessity at times as much as I resent the perpetual recurrence of meal-times and sleep.'

Dorothy Richardson might have longed to spice lovemaking with a little intellectual stimulation, but Wells would have none of it – lectures 'on philology and the lingering vestiges of my Cockney accent, while there was not a stitch between us' were not much to Wells's taste. But intellectual communion might lead to love. Wells's involvement with Fabianism resulted in him being 'almost assigned as the peculiar interest of Rosamund, the dark-eyed sturdy daughter of [Hubert] Bland and the governess, Miss Hoatson.' Rosamund hinted at incest, of Bland's unpaternal interest in her, and Wells, rather winningly, writes that 'I conceived a great disapproval of incest, and an urgent desire to put Rosamund beyond its reach in the most effective manner by absorbing her myself.' Miss Hoatson, Rosamund's mother, says Wells, was not much perturbed by the liaison, but E Nesbit, Mrs Bland, was affronted. Jane was informed, in an abusive letter, and Rosamund was married off to an ambitious young Fabian, Clifford Sharp. 'It was a steamy jungle episode,' says Wells, 'a phase of coveting and imitative desire, for I never found any great charm in Rosamund. I would rather I had not to tell of it.' But, like Boswell, Wells continued to be obsessively self-charmed, and presently he is divulging another 'steamy jungle' episode, this time concerning young Amber Reeves, the daughter of Pember Reeves, the Agent-General for New Zealand. Amber fell in love with 'great vigour and determination' and Wells was 'stirred . . . to a storm of responsive passion.' Amber is described as 'a girl of brilliant and precocious promise' in 1904. 'She had a sharp, bright Levantine face under a shock of very fine abundant black hair, a slender nimble body very much alive, and a quick greedy mind. She became my adherent and a great propagandist of Wellsism at Newnham College.' Mrs Reeves was a Christian Scientist of the most dedicated type – Wells considers that her feminism drew her to Christian Science, since she 'hated the admission of inferiority implied by the periodic disablement of women, and she denied its physical reality.' Amber and her sisters were regularly driven out into the rain for healthful bicycle rides and walks and, says Wells, 'I never knew a household so firmly convinced that windows were made to be opened.' Like Bland's mistress, Miss Hoatson, Mrs Reeves was not disconcerted by the intimate friendship between Wells and her daughter: she considered 'all love, romance, and, above all, desire, as a kind of unaccountable silliness that could not affect the kind of people one really knew and lived with.'

The affair began on a high plane of intellectual companionship: 'For a time I maintained our relationship of a great and edifying friendship at an austere level. We went for walks discussing social philosophy and suchlike questions with considerable earnestness and sincerity.' They called one another 'Master' and 'Dusa' (short for Medusa) but presently the austere philosophical basis of the relationship broke up into 'the business of making love with the greatest energy.' Their 'insatiable mutual appreciation' coincided with Amber's Cambridge examinations for Part II of the Tripos and 'did not in the least impair her success with the Mental and Moral Science examiners.' It would have been a surprise to Dorothy Richardson, perhaps, to learn that Wells and his new inamorata lay on the beach discussing Amber's thesis and planning her future career at the London School of Economics after making love in the bushes at twilight near Hythe or embracing in a church bell tower.

According to Wells, Amber's intellect was still that of a

student, as yet incapable of going 'into the thickets of fact with an interrogative hatchet and hewing out the frame of an answer.' She became discouraged and unsettled, and, concentrating less on her work, gave herself more fully to the affair with Wells. She developed a wish to want her lover's child and to live 'more closely and continuously' with Wells who had taken some trouble to 'maintain a triangular grouping' with his wife Jane and his young mistress. Jane and Wells and Amber 'all understood each other, we asserted, beautifully.' Amber began to spread the glad word among her friends, family, and the dons at Newnham. Amber's desire for his child, however, did not suit Wells's 'obsession to "get on with the work", and my disposition to treat love as an incidental refreshment in life.' There was some conflict between the *persona* and the Lover-Shadow, which he had not expected, having been careful to separate them in his own mind. They were very confused in Amber's brain. He did not in the least want to leave Jane for Amber. Inevitably, the affair was bound to be exposed and, when it was, through gossip (Amber having been as discreet as a town crier in her own and Fabian circles), 'Pember Reeves became all that an eighteenth-century father should be. He made the affair public, threatened to shoot Wells, and "saw red" with zealous thoroughness.' Mrs Reeves kept her acquiescent head down and Amber was married off to an admirer, 'Blanco' White, who had betrayed her to her father.

But before the marriage, there were earnest talks between Amber and Wells who slipped off to Le Touquet where the prospect of 'wandering about the Continent, a pair of ambiguous outcasts', appealed to neither of them. 'We wanted to have London and all its activities.' And Wells wanted Jane, who came out to Le Touquet with the two Wells sons after Amber had been shipped back to England from Boulogne, and Wells took up the threads of an energetic family life again, racing and bathing with the boys on the beach, and walking for miles on his own. Then he sat down to write *The History of Mr Polly* in the peaceable company of Jane who 'betrayed no resentment, no protesting egotism . . . Presently we were talking about my case as though it was someone else in whom we were both concerned.' A result of these seemingly objective, reasonable discussions was the decision to leave Sandgate and 'the all too healthy, all too unstimulating life we led there. . . . We would sell the house and go to a new home in London. I should see more people and vary my personal excitements. She [Jane] had been starved for music, and there she could go to concerts – and the picture- and other art-shows that attracted her. We should both be taken out of ourselves. I should be taken out of physical jealousy in an unobtrusive promiscuity.' As a *modus vivendi*, it would suit very well, and in 1909 the Wells family – HG, Jane, Gip and Frank, together with the governess, Fraulein Meyer, moved to 17 Church Row in Hampstead.

'When the sexual obsession was uppermost in me,' says Wells during his discussion of the affair with Amber, 'all my theorizing about the open-living Samurai was flung to the winds. I wanted to monopolize her.' The order of the Samurai had been developed from Plato's *Republic*, and in *A Modern Utopia* Wells suggested the division of society into four classes or types of character, rather: the poietic, the kinetic, the dull and the base. The kinetics would be the executive and administrative arm of society, the poietic would suggest, criticise, and take a part in promulgating legislation. The base would be controlled and the dull given incentives to support the kinetics. The qualifications for membership of the order of the Samurai were high and subject to the discipline that they could not be abandoned. Honour was the byword and personal freedom sacrosanct. 'We want the world ruled, not by everybody, but by a politically-minded organization open, with proper safeguards, to everybody.' Wells particularly admired Communists and Italian Fascists. He envisaged using the Fabian Society, 'reconditioned', as the instrument of change towards his Samurai utopia. The 'Modern Utopia' would not come about of its own accord – 'an Order of the Samurai . . . must be realized as the result of very deliberate effort.' Wells began 'a confused, tedious, ill-conceived and ineffectual campaign to turn the little

Fabian Society, wizened already though not old, into the beginnings of an order, akin to these Samurai in *Modern Utopia*, which should embody for mankind a sense of the State.' However, Wells has the grace to admit, 'I can be quite silly and inept; I was wrong-headed and I left the Society, at last, if possible more politically parliamentary and ineffective than I found it.' He gives a fast, lively, satirical and amusing sketch of a Fabian meeting at Cliffords Inn and the energetic, verbose, well-meaning results. 'We typed and printed and issued Reports and Replies and Committee Election Appeals and Personal Statements and my original intentions were buried at last beneath a steaming heap of hot secondary issues.' As a result of this excited effort, 'The order of the Fabian Samurai perished unborn.' But the political battles continued. Ford Madox Hueffer, much later, remembers Wells in full flight 'when he left off being primarily an imaginative writer and became a politician or something of the sort, . . . why then I really used to see him as another Mr Chaplin of the days when that hero used to attack an enormous, a gigantic black-bearded villain – flying from the top of the kitchen sink at the giant's neck, being thrown through the windows, plunging down the chimney to kick his foe in the rear, being thrown through the ceiling, flooring the giant with tiles from the roof. And so on for ever and ever.'

Wells became a man of substance and was recognised as such by his neighbours in Romney Marsh: 'I became a Borough magistrate and stability and respectability loomed straight ahead of us. I might have been knighted; I might have known the glories of the OM; I might have faced the photographer in the scarlet of an honorary degree. Such things have nestled in the jungle beside my path. But *Ann Veronica* (bless her!) [a later novel] and my outspoken republicanism saved me from all that.'

He was famous as the author of *The Time Machine*, published in 1894, and in 1898 wrote *When the Sleeper Awakes*, 'essentially an exaggeration of contemporary tendencies . . . It was our contemporary world in a state of highly inflamed distension.'

In 1899, he began to write *Anticipations*, published in 1900, 'a book . . . which can be considered as the keystone to the main arch of my work. . . . It was the first attempt to forecast the human future as a whole and to estimate the relative power of this and that great system of influence.' It was 'a comprehensive attempt to state and weigh and work out a general resultant for the chief forces of social change throughout the world, sober forecasting, that is to say, without propaganda, satire or extravaganza.' Sales were encouraging. His book, 'crude though it was and smudgily vague . . . sold as well as a novel.' He was 'writing the human prospectus,' in short, and he became his own first disciple. 'The fact that in 1900 I had already grasped the inevitability of a World State and the complete insufficiency of the current parliamentary methods of democratic government is of more than merely autobiographical interest,' says Wells in *Experiment in Autobiography*. He considered himself outside and apart from established systems of 'electoral and parliamentary methods, the prestige of the universities and the ruling class, the monarchy and patriotism, because I had not the slightest hope or intention of ever using any of these established systems for my own advancement or protection. For a scientific treatment of the theory of government my political handicap was a release. I had the liberty of that irresponsible child in the fable of the Emperor's Clothes. I could say exactly what I thought because it was inconceivable that I could ever be a successful courtier.'

'In the early Sandgate days not only was I being attracted more and more powerfully towards the civil service conception of a life framed in devotion to constructive public ends *à la Webb* [Fabianism], but I was also being tugged, though with less force, in a quite opposite direction, towards the artistic attitude,' wrote Wells. 'I have never been able to find the artistic attitude fundamentally justifiable but I understand and sympathize with the case for it.'

Wells's scorn extended in particular to the aesthetic philosophy of art and literature held and practised by Henry James.

James had taken an early interest in Wells, when he and

Edmund Gosse had ridden over to New Romney from Rye, on bicycles, to visit in 1898. Wells and Jane were flattered by the attentions of these two considerable literary eminences, and chatted sociably over tea. Then, later, JM Barrie took it into his head to visit them at Beach Cottage at Sandgate, and talked, unprompted, of the financial difficulties a writer might sometimes experience when 'down'. Only later did it occur to Wells that the Royal Literary Fund had been making discreet inquiries as to whether he might be temporarily strapped for ready money. Nothing of the kind, writes Wells: 'I was now some hundreds of pounds on the solvent side and thinking of building a house with my balance. I knew nothing of investment and having a house of my own seemed as good a use for savings as I could imagine.'

Spade House, at Sandgate, was designed by Charles Voysey, 'that pioneer in the escape from the small snobbish villa residence to the bright and comfortable pseudo-cottage.' Voysey had wanted to adorn the front door with a heart-shaped letter plate, but Wells 'protested at wearing my heart so conspicuously outside and we compromised on a spade. We called the house Spade House. The men on the lift beside my garden, which used to ascend and descend between Folkestone and Sandgate, confused my name with that of another Wells, "The Man who Broke the Bank at Monte Carlo" – and they told their passengers that it was "on the ace of spades that the trick was done".'

The house was begun in 1899, and the Wells family – which later included two boys who were born to them – lived at Sandgate until 1909 when they moved to Hampstead, to live in a house in Church Row.

Wells puzzled and interested Henry James. Hueffer describes, in the tones of James (if not the words), how Wells's interest and involvement in the grosser affairs of the world agitated James: ' "You don't suppose . . . it has been whispered to me . . . you know swift madness *does* at times attend on the too fortunate, the too richly endowed, the too altogether and overwhelmingly splendid. You don't suppose then . . . I mean to you too has it been whispered? . . . that . . . well, in short . . ." And very fast indeed: "That-he-is-thinking-of-taking-to-politics?" ' It was all too likely; and, if not on that ground alone, then certainly on the vexed question of literature and its dignity as art, James and Wells remained opposed. Hueffer says of himself, being a partisan of James, that 'Mr HG Wells and I must have been enemies for more years than I care now to think of . . . in the kingdom of letters Mr Wells and I have been leaders of opposing forces for nearly the whole of this century.'

Wells in the 1930s described the cause of the enmity and the concern he caused to James: 'I find myself worrying about various talks and discussions I had with Henry James a third of a century ago. He was a very important figure in the literary world of that time and a shrewd and penetrating critic of the technique by which he lived. He liked me and found my work respectable enough to be greatly distressed about it. I bothered him and he bothered me. We were at cross purposes based . . . on very fundamental differences, not only of temperament but training. He had no idea of the possible use of the novel as a help to conduct. His mind had turned away from any such idea. From his point of view there were not so much "novels" as The Novel, and it was a very high and important achievement. He thought of it as an Art Form and of novelists as a very special and exalted type. He was concerned about their greatness and repute. He saw us all as Masters or would-be Masters, little Masters and great Masters, and he was plainly sorry that "Cher Maître" was not an English expression. One could not be in a room with him for ten minutes without realizing the importance he attached to the dignity of this art of his. I was by nature and education unsympathetic with this mental disposition. But I was disposed to regard a novel as about as much an art form as a market place or a boulevard. It had not even necessarily to get anywhere. You went by it on your various occasions.'

On 5 July 1915, long after Wells had left Sandgate in 1909, Henry James picked up a book, wrapped and addressed to him by Wells at the Reform Club. It was entitled *Boon, The Mind of the Race, The Wild Asses of the Devil, and The Last Trump*. It was an elaborate, pseudonymous joke by Wells who satirized many contemporary writers in the guise of one George Boon, whose literary remains, selected and edited by one Reginald Bliss, were prefaced with 'An Ambiguous Introduction' by HG Wells who disingenuously described the book as 'indiscreet and ill-advised'. It was pretty clear that Wells himself was author, editor and only-begetter of *Boon*, though he could not say so directly. James objected strongly to the critique and parody of his work, and Wells confessed that it was 'just wastepaper basket' stuff. By way of consolation, he also said that James's stature as a novelist made it inevitable that he should have been the target: 'there was no other antagonist possible than yourself.' James was very deeply offended.

If the contents of *Boon* were indeed words salvaged from the wastepaper basket, wrote James in reply to Wells, there was no excuse for publishing them. It was the end of a long friendship, in which there had been mutual respect, though no agreement, in literary matters. They had been polite and tolerant one with the other and Wells at least had had 'a queer feeling that we were both incompatibly right.' That he did not, or was unable to, dismiss James out of hand is clear from his final judgement that no other antagonist presented such a suitable face for having a pie pushed in it. James was the Goliath who, in Wells's view, had to be brought low before he himself could assume a place in the front rank of literature and ideas. James, in a real sense, was literature for most of his contemporaries. He was the Master to whom, if they did not defer, they at least felt bound by ties of some respect and against whom they could sharpen their arguments.

James's feelings were hurt, and he said so. Wells felt obliged, not to retract his views, but to attempt to salve the wounds. He wrote, 'I had rather be called a journalist than an artist, that is the essence of it . . . But since it [*Boon*] was printed I have regretted a hundred times that I did not express our profound and incurable difference with a better grace.' Wells had written that James 'splits his infinitives and fills them up with adverbial stuffing. He presses the passing colloquialism into his service. His vast paragraphs sweat and struggle; they could not sweat and elbow and struggle more if God himself was the processional meaning to which they sought to come. And all for tales of nothingness . . . It is leviathan retrieving pebbles. It is a magnificent but painful hippopotamus resolved at any cost, even at the cost of its dignity, upon picking up a pea which has got into the corner of its den.'

The image is witty and, what makes it worse, fills the mind's eye as if Max Beerbohm had sketched it. Its subject found it 'very curious and interesting, after a fashion – though it has naturally not filled me with fond elation.' James regarded *Boon* as 'bad manners', a joke in poor taste 'at the expense of your poor old HJ.' Wells was embarrassed, but his defence did not mitigate his error. James refused to be mollified. He could not regard *Boon* as a prank, as a *jeu d'esprit* by a 'warm if rebellious and resentful admirer' with cause to be grateful and affectionate towards the subject of the critical satire. James believed too deeply in his own view of art to be able to treat it lightly or have it impertinently attacked without coming sternly and passionately to its defence. 'I live, live intensely and am fed by life,' he wrote to Wells, 'and my value, whatever it be, is in my own kind of expression of that.' Formerly, James had, as a writer himself, criticised and playfully remonstrated with Wells in letters more or less reviewing Wells's novels – but it had been, until now, a professional exchange of views. There had grown up between James and Wells 'some common meeting ground,' taken for granted between them, 'and the falling away of this is like the collapse of a bridge which made communication possible.' James attempted to see objectively what Wells was saying about his work, but in the end the man took precedence over the critic and was affronted by Wells's 'cheek'. James had seriously and affectionately attempted to help Wells – he had even, improbably, suggested collaboration at one point. He had attempted to persuade Wells to accept election to the Royal Society of Literature. Wells had refused the offer more than once, no doubt because he would not take any part in an establishment organisation. He kept himself very carefully outside all that Henry James enjoined upon him. There was a fundamental difference between the two men that only literature could have bridged, and when that common ground was removed, there was nothing between Wells and James and they were obliged to fall to fighting.

The attack on James in *Boon*, in 1915, marked the final, most wounding analysis of James's literary integrity by the younger man – last, that is, save for the self-defence that turned into attack in Wells's *Experiment in Autobiography*, published in 1934. The literary battle had been waged for forty years, since January 1895 when Wells, as a tyro drama critic, had seen and reviewed the disastrous first night of James's play, *Guy Domville* at the St James's Theatre in London. Hueffer attributes the failure of the play to a claque in the audience who, incensed at having been charged for their programmes, howled it off the stage. But Wells provides a full, excruciatingly embarrassing account of the performance which goes on to animadvert upon the character of James:

> It was an extremely weak drama. James was a strange, unnatural human being, a sensitive man lost in an immensely abundant brain, which had had neither a scientific nor a philosophical training, but which was by education and natural aptitude alike, formal, formally aesthetic, conscientiously fastidious and delicate. Wrapped about in elaborations of gesture and speech, James regarded his fellow creatures with a face of distress and a remote effort at intercourse, like some victim of enchantment in the centre of an immense bladder. His life was unbelievably correct and his home at Rye one of the most perfect pieces of suitably furnished Georgian architecture imaginable. He had always been well off and devoted to artistic ambitions; he had experienced no tragedy and he shunned the hoarse laughter of comedy; and yet he was consumed by a gnawing hunger for dramatic success. In this performance he had his first and last actual encounter with the theatre.

Guy Domville was one of those rare ripe exquisite Catholic Englishmen of ancient family conceivable only by an American mind, who gave up the woman he loved to an altogether coarser cousin, because his religious vocation was stronger than his passion. I forget the details of the action. There was a drinking scene in which Guy and the cousin, for some obscure purpose of discovery, pretended to drink and, instead, poured their wine furtively into a convenient bowl of flowers upon the table between them. Guy was played by George Alexander, at first in a mood of refined solemnity and then, as the intimations of gathering disapproval from pit and gallery increased, with stiffening desperation. Alexander at the close had an incredibly awkward exit. He had to stand at a door in the middle of the stage, say slowly "Be keynd to Her . . . *Be* keynd to Her" and depart. By nature Alexander had a long face, but at that moment with audible defeat before him, he seemed the longest and dismallest face, all face, that I have ever seen. The slowly closing door reduced him to a strip, to a line, of perpendicular gloom. The uproar burst like a thunderstorm as the door closed and the stalls responded with feeble applause. Then the tumult was mysteriously allayed. There were some moments of uneasy apprehension. "Author" cried voices. "Au-thor!" The stalls, not understanding, redoubled their clapping.

Disaster was too much for Alexander that night. A spasm of hate for the writer of those fatal lines must surely have seized him. With incredible cruelty he led the doomed James, still not understanding clearly how things were with him, to the middle of the stage, and there the pit and gallery had him. James bowed; he knew it was the proper thing to bow. Perhaps he had selected a few words to say, but if so they went unsaid. I have never heard any sound more devastating than the crescendo of booing that ensued. The gentle applause of the stalls was altogether overwhelmed. For a moment or so James faced the storm, his round face white, his mouth opening and shutting and then Alexander, I hope in contrite mood, snatched him back into the wings.

That was my first sight of Henry James with whom I was later to have a sincere yet troubled friendship. We were by nature and training profoundly unsympathetic. He was the most consciously and elaborately artistic and refined human being I ever encountered, and I swam in the common thought and feeling of my period, with an irregular abundance of rude knowledge, aggressive judgements and a disposition to get to close quarters with Madame Fact even if it meant a scuffle with her. James never scuffled with Fact; he treated her as a perfect and unchallengeable lady; he never questioned a single stitch or flounce of the conventions and interpretations in which she presented herself. He thought that for every social occasion a correct costume could be prescribed and a correct behaviour defined. On the table (an excellent piece) in his hall at Rye lay a number of caps and hats, each with its appropriate gloves and sticks, a tweed cap and a stout stick for the Marsh, a soft comfortable deer-stalker if he were to turn aside to the Golf Club, a light-brown felt hat and a cane for a morning walk down to the Harbour, a grey felt with a black band and a gold-headed cane of greater importance, if afternoon calling in the town was afoot. He retired at set times to a charming room in his beautiful walled garden and there he worked, dictating with a slow but not unhappy circumspection, the novels that were to establish his position in the world of discriminating readers. They are novels from which all the fiercer experiences are excluded; even if their passions are so polite that one feels that they were gratified, even at their utmost intimacy, by a few seemly gestures; and yet the stories are woven with a peculiar humorous, faintly fussy, delicacy, that gives them a flavour like nothing else in the language. When you want to read and find reality too real, and hard storytelling tiresome, you may find Henry James good company.

At the turn of the century Wells had met Stephen Crane whom he describes as 'one of the earliest of those stark American writers who broke away from the genteel literary traditions of Victorian England and he wrote an admirable bare prose.

. . . He was lean, blond, slow-speaking, perceptive, fragile, tuberculous, too adventurous to be temperate with anything and impracticable to an extreme degree. He liked to sit and talk, sagely and deeply. How he managed ever to get to the seats of war to which he was sent I cannot imagine. But he got deeply enough into them to shatter his health completely.' They did not meet often, and they did not find one another influential in their work but both Crane and Wells liked to air their views about literature to an appreciative listener and competent practitioner of the art, and to that extent they found a common interest.

At about the same time, Conrad and Hueffer swam into Wells's ken: 'my first impression of Conrad was of a swarthy face peering out and up through the little window panes [of the Pent]. He talked with me mostly of adventure and dangers, Hueffer talked criticism and style and words, and our encounter was the beginning of a long, fairly friendly but always rather strained acquaintance.' Conrad and Hueffer shared the Jamesian view of literature to which Wells was fundamentally opposed, but it was nevertheless a pleasure to see Conrad approaching, with his wife and son, Conrad riding a little pony carriage like a droshky and shouting to his Kentish pony in Polish, when they came to visit Jane and Wells at Sandgate. Despite determined efforts to investigate him, Conrad was at a loss to understand Wells, finding him perhaps 'Philistine, stupid and intensely English; he was incredulous that I could take social and political issues seriously . . . The frequent carelessness of my writing, my scientific qualifications of statement and provisional inconclusiveness, and my indifference to intensity of effect, perplexed and irritated him. . . . "My dear Wells, what is this 'Love and Mr Lewisham' *about*?" he would ask. But then he would ask also, wringing his hands and wrinkling his forehead, "What is all this about Jane Austen? What is there *in* her? What is it all *about*?" ' To confound Conrad, says Wells, one only had to say 'humour': 'It was one of our damned English tricks he had never learned to tackle.' Lacking, perhaps, a thorough sense of English humour, Conrad also lacked English forbearance: an insult was an insult, and an offhand remark by GB Shaw or Wells might unaccountably and instantly infuriate Conrad whose honour could only be redeemed by a duel. It had to be explained to him that satisfaction of blood was neither the custom nor the 'done thing'. Conrad stimulated Wells by his persistent inability to understand Wells's scientific approach to literature, and usefully concentrated the younger man's mind, helping to form opinions directly antithetical to those held by Conrad, Hueffer and James. For Wells, the aesthetic valuation of literature was 'at best a personal response, a floating and indefinable judgement. All these receptive critics pose for their work. They dress their souls before the glass, add a few final touches of make-up and sally forth like old bucks for fresh "adventures among masterpieces". I come upon masterpieces by pure chance; they happen to me and I do not worry about what I miss.' During the years in Sandgate, the 'definition and confirmation of my mind was the principal thing that was happening' to Wells, whose mind veered further from what he called 'conscious artistry', away from 'self-dramatization' and towards 'social purposiveness'.

To Ford Madox Hueffer, Wells 'always seemed to me to resemble one of those rather small British generals who were so unlimitedly beloved by their men - a Buller or a Bobs. Blond, rather stocky, with a drooping cavalry moustache and with eyes always darting about, I fancy he would have been happy as a general, commanding bodies of men to do things and they doing it. . . . But in those days, when he was already in the saddle and had glimpses of all the worlds that he might conquer, what struck one most was his tough, as it were Cockney, gallantry of attack – upon anything.'

Wells's sojourn in Romney Marsh had been very productive. Like an enthusiastic little general, he was full of promise and plans and fairly itched to prove himself in heroic victories. He had come to Romney Marsh, trailing behind him some fame as an author of works of imaginative fiction dealing with man and his place in a wider universe that might be his through the application of science and technology. A new order was, perhaps, about to be born with the new century. He began to make creditable political and literary acquaintance in Romney Marsh and in London, he built a house and he established a family. He fell violently in love several times, and still managed to keep the love of his wife. He recovered his health, and felt fit for anything. Wells was never passive; he threw himself upon life as he did upon women, and generally life, like women, responded favourably to his attentions. In the eight years he spent with Jane and his sons at Spade House, Wells joined and abandoned the Fabian Society and turned out books – sometimes with a large element of autobiography in them – expounding his ideas for a new world. *Anticipations*, *Mankind in the Making*, *A Modern Utopia*, *Kipps*, *The Sea Lady*, *The Food of the Gods*, *In the Days of the Comet*, *Tono Bungay*, and finally *Ann Veronica*, established his reputation not only as a theorist but as a popular, saleable author and public figure.

Romney Marsh proved, as it proved with other writers, too small a continent in which to flourish adequately. With health restored, with a world to reform, in 1909 Wells gave up the oppressive solidity of his fine house and moved to the less claustrophobic atmosphere of London.

FOUR

Joseph Conrad in Kent

'Inveni Portam' is a characteristically vivid piece of writing by the romantic, swashbuckling, Scottish adventurer, politician and writer, Robert Bontine Cunninghame Graham. It describes the funeral of Joseph Conrad in Canterbury in the week of the cricket festival, on 7 August 1924. Just three months before, in May, Conrad had been offered a knighthood – an honour he chose to decline, perhaps because he and Ford Madox Hueffer, twenty-five years or so earlier, had derided decorations as inappropriate for an artist, though they would not, perhaps, have summarily refused the Nobel Prize or the Order of Merit as more seemly rewards for endeavour and achievement in the lists of literature. Conrad and Cunninghame Graham had first exchanged complimentary letters in 1897 and met soon afterwards, through Edward Garnett at Limpsfield, when Conrad was living at Stanford-le-Hope in Essex. At that time, Cunninghame Graham was the better-known writer and public figure and Conrad responded gratefully to his commendations. In retrospect, Cunninghame Graham remembered:

> His cheek bones, high and jutting out a little, revealed his Eastern European origin, just as his strong, square figure and his walk showed him a sailor who never seems to find the solid earth a quite familiar footing after a sloping deck.

His feet were small and delicately shaped and his fine, nervous hands, never at rest a minute in his life, attracted you at once. They supplemented his incisive speech by indefinable slight movements, not gestures in the Latin sense, for they were never raised into the air nor used for emphasis. They seemed to help him to express the meaning of his words without his own volition in a most admirable way. Something there was about him, both of the Court and of the quarter-deck, an air of courtesy and of high breeding, and yet with something of command. His mind, as is often the case with men of genius – and first and foremost what most struck one was his genius – seemed a strange compact of the conflicting qualities, compounded in an extraordinary degree, of a deep subtlety and analytic power and great simplicity.

As he discoursed upon the things that interested him, recalled his personal experiences, or poured his scorn and his contempt on unworthy motives and writers who to attain their facile triumphs had pandered to bad taste, an inward fire seemed to be smouldering ready to break out just as the fire that so long smouldered in the hold of the doomed ship in which he made his first voyage to the East suddenly burst out into flames. His tricks of speech and manner, the way he grasped both of your hands in his, his sudden breaking into French, especially when he was moved by anything, as when I asked him to attend some meeting or another, and he replied, "*Non, il y aura des Russes*," grinding his teeth with rage. . .

Cunninghame Graham's literary reputation, once so high among his contemporaries, has long since been consigned to the backwaters of biography, fiction and *belles lettres*, while Conrad's has been raised almost to the cult status that his friend once enjoyed among his peers. Cunninghame Graham's masterpiece, in the opinion of Sir John Lavery, was himself: in the art of personality he was a master. But he was also a selfless, generous friend and in Tschiffely's biography of Cunninghame Graham, *Don Roberto*, it is alleged to Cunninghame Graham's credit that, in the period July 1898 to February 1899, he was actively assisting Conrad in his efforts to gain command of a ship. This assistance was directed more towards Conrad the writer than Conrad the sailor, since Tschiffely also claims that Cunninghame Graham had secretly asked Sir Francis Evans of the Union Line and Sir Donald Currie of the Castle Line to receive Conrad but, on no account, to employ him, 'for, should they do so, a great writer would be lost to the world.'

Whatever the truth of the matter, and Cunninghame Graham's intervention is denied by Jocelyn Baines, Conrad's biographer, on the ground that Tschiffely gives no source for the story, it would appear that Conrad was at least thinking, in some desperation, of returning to seafaring as his principal profession. But, too, he had begun a novel, *Lord Jim*, early in 1898. In that year he met the young writer Ford Madox Hueffer with whom he determined, only a couple of weeks after, to collaborate. Seafaring was put aside as a thing of the past, when no offer of a ship was made, and Conrad wrote to Cunninghame Graham: 'the fact is from novel-writing to skippering *il y a trop de tirage*. This confounded literature has ruined me entirely. There is a time in the affairs of men when the tide of folly sweeps them to destruction.'

Conrad was to spend the next eleven years, from 1898 to 1909, at Pent Farm which he would then leave for a mere fourteen months to go to The Someries near Luton before returning to Aldington, first for a short time to a cottage near Pent Farm and then to Capel House at Orlestone. It was Hueffer, with whom he was to collaborate, who introduced him to the Marsh.

Hueffer was twenty-four years old in contrast to Conrad's forty years when they met. The young man's effortless fluency and his distinction as a garrulous, ambitious, determined junior member of the literary and social establishment, with wide contacts and persistent use of them, seemed to offer hope to Conrad who considered his own writing halting and slow. Collaboration was the thing. He had already considered a collaboration with WE Henley, a journalist and writer who had collaborated with RL Stevenson, and Henley had perhaps dropped Hueffer's name as a likely substitute. Hueffer claims that Henley had described him as 'the finest stylist in the English language of today . . .' Henley had said nothing of the kind to Conrad; indeed, Henley had difficulty even remembering Hueffer at all, at one time turning on him and asking, none too kindly, 'Who the hell are you? I never even heard your name!'

On the question of collaboration, Conrad had had some initial doubt. He admitted to Hueffer that he had consulted with eminent men of letters, speaking frankly of his difficulty with English, a language he had acquired rather than inherited as a native tongue, the slow pace at which he wrote, and the 'increased fluency that he might acquire in the process of going minutely into words with an acknowledged expert.' When Conrad and Hueffer were first introduced, by the Garnetts at The Cearne at Limpsfield, in the first week of September 1898, Hueffer says, 'I must have told him I was writing a novel about Cuban pirates.' Evidently, this colourful piece of literary information stuck like a barnacle in Conrad's mind, so that two weeks later Hueffer 'had a letter from Conrad asking that he might be allowed to collaborate with me in the novel about pirates.' Hueffer had not been, at first, overly impressed by Conrad who was known to him as the author of *Almayer's Folly*, 'a great book of a romantic fashion, but written too much in the style of Alphonse Daudet, whom the writer [Hueffer] had outgrown at school.' Besides, Hueffer felt that Edward Garnett had been showing him off 'precisely as if one had been a mangy lion in a travelling menagerie' to a stream of visitors who included not only Conrad but Stephen Crane, Lord Olivier, Mrs Pease and Edward Pease, Secretary of the Fabian Society. Much as Hueffer liked to be stroked, he felt some resentment, perhaps, which rubbed off on Conrad as a tourist who had come to poke through the bars of his cage.

But he was aware of Conrad's reputation as an author who had already published three books (*Almayer's Folly* in 1895, *An Outcast of the Islands* in 1896, and *The Nigger of the Narcissus* in 1897). 'He stood absolutely in the front of English authors, yet the great public was extraordinarily slow to hear of him.'

Reputation but few sales, in short. 'I suppose it did not really do so until the publication of *Chance* fifteen years after that date. And they were fifteen years of agonized labours and the most fell anxieties, the most desperate expedients.' Away from Limpsfield, Conrad was less the visiting celebrity. Hueffer recognised that he toiled at his work in the most difficult and dispiriting conditions, 'living in the rather lugubrious village of Stanford-le-Hope, on the estuary of the Thames, amongst the Essex marshes. His poverty was like a physical pain, but his reputation as an author was already enormously high.' By early October it had been arranged that Hueffer and his wife Elsie would move out of the Pent Farm near Postling in Kent and sublet it to Joseph and Jessie Conrad, who took possession on the 26th of the month. The novel Conrad and Hueffer were intending to write together was *Seraphina*, a tale of smugglers that was to be aimed at the public which had so much admired Stevenson's *Treasure Island*. With Borys, their eight-month-old baby son, Conrad and his wife Jessie moved to 'the dear old place,' taking over also a good many items of Hueffer's furniture, including such literary relics as a writing desk that had belonged to Christina Rossetti, a large table designed by William Morris, and a picture cupboard that had once been the property of the Pre-Raphaelite painter Ford Madox Brown, Hueffer's grandfather. Jessie Conrad also remembers, 'hanging above the couch in the front room, a death mask of Dante G [abriel] Rossetti and one of Oliver Cromwell, gruesome relics that held for me a good deal of awe, especially in the dusk or firelight. There was a great deal of dignity in these pieces of furniture, and when in the course of time these heirlooms were removed, our efforts to replace them according to our means, fell very short. I believe my husband rather missed these things. By that time we were the real tenants, having taken the place over from FMH.'

Conrad 'was small, rather than large in height,' remarks Hueffer, confirming and elaborating Cunninghame Graham's description; 'very broad in the shoulder and long in the arm, dark in complexion with black hair and a clipped beard.' Jessie

Conrad was proud of her husband's shoulders and insisted, when Sir William Rothenstein made a drawing of Conrad, that he should be given his due shoulders rather than an insignificant scribble below the portrait head. 'He had the gestures of a Frenchman who shrugs his shoulders frequently. When you had really secured his attention he would insert a monocle into his right eye and scrutinize your face from very near as a watch-maker looks into the works of a watch. He entered a room with his head held high, rather stiffly and with a haughty manner, moving his head once semicircularly.' This last characteristic may have been open to misinterpretation as arrogance, but Hueffer declares that it was not Conrad's intention thereby to dominate the occupants of the room, rather to master the room itself, to express it and its occupants to himself, the better to come to terms with it, and them. Though perhaps sometimes shabby in his dress. Conrad 'wore his old clothes with the air of a Prince,' Hueffer admits, and Jessie Conrad certainly took infinite pains to turn out her husband in a respectable light, despite their poverty. 'My husband, I claim, had the appearance of a man whose garments are whole and in good condition all through.' She was seriously annoyed with Hueffer when, on one occasion, she discovered that he, as an overnight guest, had carelessly piled all Conrad's neatly cared-for clothes on top of the bed for warmth.

Neither Hueffer nor Conrad were particularly easy men, and even the loyal Mrs Conrad has, occasionally, to give Hueffer the benefit of the doubt, if not quite the palm: 'The small house seemed at times full to overflowing and there were days when the two artists with their vagaries, temperaments and heated discussions made it seem rather a warm place. Still, to give FMH his due, he was the least peppery of the two, being a native of a less excitable nation and his drawling voice made a sharp contrast with the quick, un-English utterances of his fellow-collaborator.' According to Hueffer, he and Conrad would sit up half the night, after their wives had gone to bed, and until about half past two in the morning they would talk – about Flaubert and Maupassant and Turgenev – and Conrad would become more and more excitable, progressing from low, slow and intimate talk to quick, staccato and heavily accented speech, with an inaccurate command of his adverbs. Hueffer would thump the oak beam of the ceiling, and Conrad would throw himself about excitedly in his chair or pace the patterned border of the carpet in his agitation. Conrad and Hueffer were to be intimate for a decade, more or less, and in that time they supported one another's work wonderfully. But not everyone was so sure that their collaboration was useful and appropriate to Conrad.

When a joint venture, *Seraphina*, a novel later called *Romance*, came to the ears of HG Wells, the rumour caused anxiety and anguish sufficient to prompt Wells to mount his bicycle and pedal from Sandgate to Postling to nip the collaboration in the bud. He earnestly pleaded with Hueffer not to spoil Conrad's style: 'The wonderful oriental style . . . It's as delicate as clockwork and you'll only ruin it by sticking your fingers in it.' Hueffer countered with the claim that Conrad wanted collaboration and that he would get what he wanted. Wells rode dispiritedly back to Sandgate. Later, he changed his mind about the collaboration, evidently, since in his autobiography he declares: 'I think Conrad owed a very great deal to their early association; Hueffer helped greatly to "English" him and his idiom, threw remarkable lights on the English literary world for him, collaborated with him on two occasions and conversed interminably with him about the precise word and about perfection in writing.'

One result of the Conrad/Hueffer association was to make Wells think seriously to consider and define his own literary position: 'All this talk that I had with Conrad and Hueffer and James about the just word, the perfect expression, about this or that being "written" or not written, bothered me, set me interrogating myself, threw me into a heart-searching defensive attitude. I will not pretend that I got it all clear at once, that I was not deflected by their criticisms and that I did not fluctuate and make attempts to come up to their unsystematized, mysterious and elusive standards. But in the end I revolted altogether and refused to play their game. "I am a journalist," I declared, "I refuse to play the artist" . . . So I came down off the fence . . . and I remain definitely on the side opposed to the aesthetic valuation of literature.'

Firmly on the side defending 'the aesthetic valuation of literature' was Henry James, in Rye, who, when informed by Elsie Hueffer that her husband and Conrad were collaborating on a novel, *The Inheritors*, could not forbear from declaring that, 'To me, this is like a bad dream that one relates at breakfast. Their traditions and their gifts are so dissimilar. Collaboration between them is to me inconceivable.' James, writes his biographer Leon Edel, 'continued to marvel at the collaboration; he had a certain sense of the unsounded depths of Conrad; he could not reconcile them with the shallows of Hueffer.' Conrad impressed Wells, as Wells says he also impressed James, 'as the strangest of creatures . . . he reminded people of Du Maurier's Svengali and, in the nautical trimness of his costume, of Cutliffe Hyne's Captain Kettle . . . he had set himself to be a great writer, an artist in words, and to achieve all the recognition and distinction that he imagined should go with that ambition, he had gone literary with a singleness and intensity of purpose that made the kindred concentration of Henry James seem lax and large and pale.'

Wells has something to say, too, about Ford Madox Hueffer, since he met both men when they were associates in literature. 'Ford is a long blond with a drawling manner, the very spit of his brother Oliver, and oddly resembling George Moore the novelist in pose and person. What he is really or if he is really, nobody knows now and he least of all: he has become a great system of assumed personas and dramatized selves. His brain is an exceptionally good one and when first he came along, he had cast himself for the role of a very gifted scion of the Pre-Raphaelite stem, given over to artistic purposes and a little undecided betwen music, poetry, criticism, The Novel, Thoreauistic horticulture and the simple appreciation of life. He has written some admirable verse, some very good historical romances, two or three books in conjunction with Conrad and a considerable bulk of more or less autobiographical unreality.' At the time of his association with Conrad, Wells admits that Hueffer was still 'very much on the rational side of life; his extraordinary drift towards self-dramatization – when he even changed his name to Captain Ford – became conspicuous only later, after the stresses of the war.'

Conrad needed Hueffer, and Hueffer needed Conrad. Conrad was the better known, and the more saleable, author with a colourful past behind him and a fund of stories and experience upon which to draw. Hueffer delighted to draw out Conrad's reminiscences: 'I would . . . walk up and down in front of Conrad who would groan, extended in a steamer chair. I would say: "Well now, what about the *Tremolino*," or "What about the diamond mine you owned in the Transvaal?" and, after exclaiming a dozen times: "Nonsense, no one will want to hear about that," he would begin to talk about the Ukraine of his Uncle's day and Palmerston's Emissary with a sledgefull of gold or about Venice when he was a boy or about his exile in Siberia or, of course, if I suggested that he should talk about the Ukraine or Venice or Siberia, he would insist on telling anecdotes about the *Tremolino* or his Transvaal mine. In any case, once he started, he would go on for a long time and as I wrote shorthand very fast, I could take him down without much trouble.' Hueffer, as Boswell to Conrad's Johnson, thus coaxed Conrad to believe that it was possible for him to narrate and therefore write in English with a decent fluency. Jessie Conrad corroborates Hueffer's usefulness in this respect: '*The Mirror of the Sea* owes a great deal to [Hueffer's] ready and patient assistance . . . that book would never have come into being if Joseph Conrad had had no intelligent person with whom to talk over these intimate reminiscences. The book is absolutely built upon personal experiences.'

Conrad is said, by Hueffer, to have complained to Henley that his 'intimate, automatic less expressed thoughts are in Polish; when I express myself with care I do it in French. When I write I think in French and then translate the words of my thoughts into English. This is an impossible process for one desiring to make a living by writing in the English language.' Conrad had the imagination, which Hueffer could draw out like a thread, and he was a painstaking stylist. But he despaired of his natural command of English. Hueffer perhaps exaggerates Conrad's wail to Henley, but Wells confirms Conrad's occasional uncertainties with the language and his accent. Conrad 'spoke English strangely. Not badly altogether; he would supplement his vocabulary – especially if he were discussing cultural or political matters – with French words; but with certain oddities. He had learnt to read English long before he spoke it and he had formed wrong sound impressions of many familiar words; he had for example acquired an incurable tendency to pronounce the last *e* in these and those. He would say, "*Wat* shall we do with *thesa* things?" and he was always incalculable about the use of "shall" and "will".' Ford Madox Hueffer talks of Conrad's eccentric, excitable misuse of adverbs, and Henry James's nephew William remembers the regular use of French when James and Conrad conversed during a walk: 'Hueffer babbled and I didn't listen. I wanted to hear what the great men were saying up ahead, but there I was stuck with Hueffer. Occasionally a word or two would drift back and what I always heard was – French!'

Hueffer made no claim to the 'legend that I had any part in teaching Conrad English, though, on the face of it, it may well look plausible since he was a foreigner who never till the end of his life spoke English other than as a foreigner. But when it came to writing it was at once quite a different matter.' Conrad wrote letters, with no thought of publication, with a 'speed, a volubility and a banal correctness' that astonished Hueffer. 'On the other hand, when, as it were, he was going before the public, a species of stage-fright would almost completely paralyse him so that his constructions were frequently very un-English.' It was precisely this slow, halting, solitary and professional struggle with literature that Conrad hoped Hueffer could help speed up and refine.

Hueffer and Conrad had 'confessed that each of us desired

one day to write Absolute Prose,' but their collaboration, according to Hueffer, produced a vehicle that both of them could comfortably control in tandem until the moment arrived at which a fusion of styles was achieved and Conrad could declare, delightedly, 'By Jove, it's a third person who is writing!' Hueffer remarks, 'The psychology of that moment is perfectly plain . . . Conrad interrupted with a note of relief in his voice. He had found a formula to justify collaboration in general and our collaboration. Until then we had struggled tacitly each for our own note in writing. . . . We had to find at least an artistic justification for going on. We were both extremely unaccepted writers, but we could both write. What was the sense of not writing apart if there were no commercial gain? He found it in the aesthetically comforting thought that the world of letters was enriched by yet a third artist. The third artist had neither his courage nor his gorgeousness; he himself had none of his collaborator's literary circumspection nor verbal puritanism. So the combination was at least . . . different.'

Henry James had some stylistic reservations about Conrad's work which he expressed in a two-part article in *The Times Literary Supplement* in the Spring of 1914. The two men had met in 1897, after an exchange of books – Conrad inscribed a copy of *An Outcast of the Islands* to James in 1896, and James responded by addressing a copy of *The Spoils of Poynton* to Conrad in February 1897. They lunched together later that month in London, and initiated a friendship that continued when they found themselves neighbours, more or less, in Romney Marsh quite soon afterwards. When the two men happened to meet, they conducted their conversation with the utmost diplomacy and politeness. As Hueffer remembers it, 'their phrases could not have been more elaborate or delivered more *ore rotundo*. James always addressed Conrad as "*Mon cher confrère*", Conrad almost bleated with the peculiar tone that the Marseillaise get into their compliments "*Mon cher Maître*." . . . Every thirty seconds.' This ceremoniousness perhaps disguised or compensated for the 'state of malaise', as Leon Edel describes it, that Conrad induced in James. 'James honoured the craftsman but was uneasy about the man . . . he couldn't quite fathom the gifted Pole.' On a professional and literary basis the two men met as equals. Socially, it was a different matter. At Lady Ottoline Morrell's suggestion that James might introduce her to Conrad, 'Henry James held up his hands in horror and was so perturbed that he paced up and down the grey drawing room. I remember best some of his exclamations and expostulations: "But, dear lady . . . but dear lady . . . He has lived his life at sea – dear lady, he has never met 'civilised' women. Yes, he is interesting, but he would not understand you. His wife, she is a good cook. She is a Catholic, as he is, but . . . No, dear lady, he has lived a rough life, and is not used to talk to –" an upward movement of the arms to describe who – and it was, of course, myself.'

James underestimated Conrad's social graces. He was a punctilious host, correct in his manners, and careful to observe social conventions. He insisted, in sea captain's fashion, on regularity and discipline. It was a tremendous matter to him that tea should be served at a precise moment every day, and that the meal should conform to the expectations that afternoon tea excites – mere bread and butter was not an adequate spread. His social standing may not have ranked high in the estimation of Henry James, but his literary reputation was second to all but a handful of other contemporary writers. By August 1899, Conrad was persuaded that it would be in his interests to employ an agent and he was adopted as a client by JB Pinker, who had established his literary agency in 1896. HG Wells and Oscar Wilde were among his first clients, while Arnold Bennett was perhaps the client who brought him most profit. Crane, Hueffer and James also joined Pinker's stable of thoroughbreds. Conrad represented prestige rather than profit to Pinker who found himself constantly advancing money to cover Conrad's debts and expenses while waiting for the financial success that Conrad would surely, finally, make. Meanwhile, Conrad worked, sometimes with Hueffer, sometimes alone. On 20 July 1900 Conrad wrote to John Galsworthy to announce: 'The end of L J [Lord Jim] has been pulled off with a steady drag of 21 hours. I sent wife and child out of the house (to London) and sat down at 9 a.m. with a desperate resolve to be done with it. Now and then I took a walk round the house, out at one door and in at the other. Ten-minute meals. A great hush. Cigarette ends growing into a mound similar to a cairn over a dead hero. Moon rose over the barn, looked in at the window and climbed out of sight. Dawn broke, brightened. I put the lamp out and went on, with the morning breeze blowing the sheets of MS. all over the room. Sun rose. I wrote the last word and went into the dining room. Six o'clock I shared a piece of cold chicken with Escamillo [his dog] (who was very miserable and in want of sympathy, having missed the child dreadfully all day). Felt very well, only sleepy: had a bath at seven and at 1.30 was on my way to London.' That same day, Conrad and his family were off to Bruges to join the Hueffers for a holiday in Belgium for a month. *Lord Jim*, when Conrad returned to Pent Farm, was a disappointment. To Edward Garnett, who had criticised the novel acutely, Conrad wrote on 12 November: 'I've been satanically ambitious, but there's nothing of a devil in me, worse luck. The *Outcast* is a heap of sand, the *Nigger* a splash of water, *Jim* a lump of clay. A stone, I suppose, will be my next gift to impatient mankind – before I get drowned in mud to which even my supreme struggles won't give a simulacrum of life . . . Like the philosopher who crowned the Universe, I shall know when I am utterly squashed. This time I am only very bruised, very sore, very humiliated.'

Humiliation or no, Conrad was not yet extinct. The Garnetts 'stand by me so nobly that I must still exist.' So he continued to work – on 20 June, from The Bungalow at Winchelsea, he wrote to Galsworthy to announce: 'I've finished "Falk" and I've written another story since ['Amy Foster', set in Romney Marsh]. Now I am here working at *Seraphina*. There are 10,000 words which I am going to write in *manu propriae*. I reckon to be done on Sunday sometime.' Writing at such a rate, it is surprising that the friction of pencil against paper did not set the manuscript alight – though something else did. An oil lamp exploded, utterly consuming the story 'The End of the Tether' in June 1902. As a disaster, the conflagration could not have been worse. It had to be rewritten quickly, since it was being serialised in Blackwood's 'Maga' – four thousand words by 2 August at least, and the rest in monthly instalments for the rest of the year. Then, in 1903, there was *Nostromo* to fret over. To HG Wells, Conrad wrote: 'I, my dear Wells, am absolutely out of my mind with the worry and apprehension of my work. I go on as one would cycle over a precipice along a 14-inch plank. If I falter I am lost.' But *Seraphina* was coming along, though the comparative failure of *The Inheritors* had to be set against its chances of success in the balance sheet. Altogether, Conrad was going through one of the blackest patches: on 22 August 1903, he was writing to Pinker to complain, 'But it's a miserable life anyhow' and that he no longer dared draw any cheques for lack of money. 'Moreover, my salvation is to shut eyes and ears to everything – or else I couldn't write a line. And yet sometimes I can't forget – I remember the tradesmen, and all the horrors descend upon me. Damn!' The same day, to Galsworthy, Conrad wrote that *Nostromo* was half done (some forty-two thousand words) and that he felt 'half dead and imbecile . . . I feel myself strangely growing into a sort of outcast. A mental and moral outcast. I hear nothing – I think of nothing – I reflect upon nothing – I cut myself off – and with all that I can just only keep going, or rather keep on lagging from one wretched story to another – and always deeper in the mire.' Not only financial and artistic worries bothered him – he also had gout to contend with.

To HG Wells, on 30 November 1903, Conrad wrote in despair: 'Things are bad with me – there's no disguising the fact. Not only is the scribbling awfully in arrears, but there's no "spring" in me to grapple with it effectually. Formerly in my sea life, a difficulty nerved me to the effort; now I perceive it is not so. However, don't imagine I've given up, but there is an uncomfortable sense of losing my footing in deep waters.' Conrad admitted, 'it comforts me to worry you a little.' Despite the gout, the worries, the tiredness, the slowness of his work, a yell goes up on 1 September 1904 when, writing to John Galsworthy, Conrad exults, 'Finished! finished! on the 30th in [G F W] Hope's house in Stanford in Essex, where I had to take off my brain that seemed to turn to water.' He had completed *Nostromo* under appalling conditions which he fully describes: 'For a solid fortnight I've been sitting up. And all the time horrible toothache. On the 27th had to wire for dentist (couldn't leave the work) who came at 2 and dragged at the infernal thing which seemed rooted in my very soul . . . I went back to my MS. at six p.m. At 11.30 something happened – what it is, I don't know. I was writing, and raised my eyes to look at the clock. The next thing I know I was sitting (not lying) on the concrete outside the door. When I crawled in I found it was nearly one. I managed to get upstairs . . . and slept till 7.' The next day he was driven to Hope's house with Jessie and Borys, and 'That night I slept. Worked all day. In the evening dear Mrs Hope (who is not used to that sort of thing) gave me four candles and I went on. I finished at 3. Took me another half hour to check the numbering of the pages . . . I have survived extremely well. I feel no elation. The strain has been too great for that. But I am quite recovered and ready for work again. There can be no stoppage until end of November when the Sketches [*The Mirror of the Sea*] will be finished.' To Edward Garnett, he wrote, '*Nostromo* is finished; a fact upon which my friends may congratulate me as upon a recovery from a dangerous illness.'

Conrad's relations with his family were loving but tetchy. Borys, as a young boy, learned quickly that 'my farver's a very furious man', and even in the soothing matter of making knots, which Borys was slow to learn, Conrad's 'small stock of patience was soon exhausted and it always ended in a burst of exasperation out of all proportion to the matter in hand.' He was impatient that Borys was slow to read: 'Disgusting! I could read in two languages at his age. Am I a father to a fool?' But when Borys did learn to read, the delighted Conrad had a pedal car made for him as a reward. In August 1906, the

Conrads' second son, John, was born. John Galsworthy had loaned them his house in London for the period of Jessie's confinement, and a car was hired to take them from the Pent to Addison Road. A few days after settling in, Conrad was bedridden with a sharp attack of gout which irritated him beyond endurance. Jessie always suspected that gout lay at the bottom of her husband's crankiness, but she was partial in her judgement. Suddenly, it was imperative that Conrad should have a particular book that had been left behind at the Pent and nothing would do but that Jessie should return to retrieve it. It was a Sunday. Trains were infrequent, and Jessie got back to London after a long, troublesome, tiring journey with the book which she had found under a towel on the bathroom floor. Dr Tebb was seriously annoyed: 'You came up to town in every comfort and when I come three days later to see you, I find you have taken yourself off by train, and on a Sunday too. You will go straight to bed, or I won't be answerable for the consequences.' Conrad, says Jessie, 'was full of compunction', at least at first, but in the end he finished up by declaring: 'Of course, Tebb doesn't know you, my dear. You're not one of these frail, hysterical women, who go to pieces at the mere idea of a little exertion. Bless you.' He could be cavalier in his demands on others, and irritable if disturbed. He flew, on one occasion, at Hueffer who had interrupted him in close examination of some proofs on a long train journey, when startled by the announcement that they had reached their destination.

Four months later, the Conrads and the two boys set off for France for a holiday, and on their return in August 1908, after an absence of some eight months from the Pent, they decided to look for a better house. Impetuously, and disastrously, Conrad decided on a farmhouse in Bedfordshire. The Someries, as it was known, came as a shock to Jessie who had not seen it until she arrived with the children and the furniture. 'That was an adventure that nearly robbed me of all my philosophy . . . My husband had assured me that there was a fine drove of cows on the farm. My consternation can well be imagined when we arrived to find the vans already half unpacked, things strewn everywhere, pigs in the kitchen, the well in the process of being cleaned out – which meant there was no water available – and the fine drove of cows, every one a bullock. There was not a cow on the place. My provisions included a half bottle of champagne, and some tinned milk. . . . I don't think I was prejudiced against the house unduly, but the fact remains that I was not very happy there.' Conrad, during these initial alarms, was staying peacefully with John Galsworthy. When he arrived, at about six o'clock on the day Jessie had moved in, he was 'all excitement and anxiety to start work at once. He first of all made what he declared was the most reasonable demand – his dinner, it was nearly seven o'clock. Time any decent man was fed. And, I smile now at the recollection – his dinner he had, and a hot one at that. "Not as well served as usual, my dear. You must see to it. Put your foot down at once!" ' Generously, Jessie adds that 'It was easier to say nothing, and he could not see that he was being desperately unreasonable. By twelve the next morning he was able to take possession of a room in which he began to write at once.' The house was not satisfactory, and the Conrads spent only fourteen miserable months in The Someries before returning again to Kent which, they felt, was their home county. In the time they had been away, Conrad had begun a novel, *The Secret Agent*, which had at first been intended as a short story but, as he had reported to Pinker, 'Alas, it'll be longish.' It was published in the autumn of 1907 and Conrad sent a copy to Henry James with a nervous letter saying little beyond commenting on the fact that the 'covers are deep red I believe. As to what's inside of them I assure you I haven't the slightest idea. That's where Hazlitt's Indian Juggler has the pull over a writer of tales. He at least knows how many balls he is keeping up in the air at the same time.'

In December 1907, Conrad was fifty years old. *The Secret Agent* fell, like the rest of his novels, into the world noiselessly and without, apparently, exciting any significant interest on the part of the book-buying public. On 6 January 1908, he wrote to Galsworthy to complain about The Someries, about gout, and the indifference of Blackwood's towards his work:

'Ah! my dear, you don't know what an inspiration-killing anxiety it is to think: "Is it saleable?" There's nothing more cruel than to be caught between one's impulse, one's act, and that question, which for me simply is a question of life and death. There are moments when the mere fear sweeps my head clean of every thought. It is agonizing, – no less. And, – you know, – that pressure grows from day to day instead of getting less . . . things are not well with me. *The Secret Agent* may be pronounced by now an honourable failure. It brought me neither love nor promise of literary success. I own that I am cast down. I suppose there is something in me that is unsympathetic to the general public, – because the novels of Hardy, for instance, are generally tragic enough and gloomily written too, – and yet they have sold in their time and are selling to the present day. Foreignness, I suppose.' Additionally, there was the acute anxiety that, though his expenses amounted annually to not more than six hundred and fifty pounds, Conrad was deeper and deeper in debt to Pinker – near enough fifteen hundred pounds or more.

The thing now was to make money, and Conrad turned to resurrect *Chance* which he had begun in 1905. But *Under Western Eyes* was a more immediately exciting project and he abandoned *Chance* again – it was, after all, something that had been conceived merely to please the public, and *Under Western Eyes* was not, like *Chance*, 'a jaded horse' that could no longer be spurred into a gallop. In 1909, the Conrads rented a small cottage at Aldington. The move was, as usual, complicated by Conrad who refused to have carpets taken up, pictures taken down, or any furniture moved (some of it, already in the removal van, was taken back into the house) before he himself moved out to stay with friends, leaving Jessie to supervise the move. He intended to finish *Under Western Eyes* and then take up *Chance*, with the additional possibility, as he confided to Galsworthy on 30 April 1909, that 'at the same time shall write enough to complete a vol: of *Reminiscences*.' Not that Conrad was any more cheerful: the gout was bad, and 'the horrible depression worst of all. It is rather awful to lie helpless and think of the passing days, of the lost time. But the most cruel time is afterwards, when I crawl out of bed to sit before the table, take up the pen, – and have to fling it away in sheer despair of ever writing a line. And I've had thirteen years of it, if not more. Anyway, all my writing life. I think that in this light the fourteen vols. (up to date) are something of an achievement. But it's a poor consolation.

The way was long, the wind was cold,
The minstrel was infernal old:
His harp, his sole remaining joy,
Was stolen by an organ boy, —

That's how I feel.'

Before completing *Under Western Eyes*, Conrad submitted a short story, 'The Secret Sharer', to Pinker, accompanying it with the request for a further advance. Pinker had advanced enough, and did not feel inclined to stump up more money until *Under Western Eyes* was completed. However, he did offer a wage of six pounds a week in return for 'regular supplies of manuscript', a suggestion which deeply offended Conrad who wrote indignantly to Galsworthy: 'It is outrageous. Does he think I am the sort of man who wouldn't finish a story in a week if he could? Do you? Why? For what reason? Is it my habit to lie about drunk for days instead of working? I reckon he knows well enough I don't. It's a contemptuous playing about with my worry . . . this gratuitous ignoring of my sincerity of spirit and also in fact is almost more than I can bear . . . I wouldn't finish the book in a week if I could – unless a bribe of six pounds a week is dangled before me – I sit twelve hours at the table, sleep six, and worry the rest of the time, feeling the age creeping on . . .'

In 1904, enraged by a piece of gossip, Conrad had written to Edmund Gosse to defend Pinker's reputation and attitude towards Conrad as his client: 'I have no taint in my character either of vice, indolence or subserviency which could ever make me the victim of such a situation as is implied in that piece of baseless gossip. [It had been said that 'Pinker deals harshly with Conrad.'] . . . He [Pinker] has known me for six years. He has stepped gallantly into the breach left by the collapse of my bank: and not only gallantly, but successfully as well. He has treated not only my moods but even my fancies with the greatest consideration . . . his action, distinctly, has not been of a mercenary character. He cannot take away the weariness of mind which at the end of ten years of strain has come upon me; but he has done his utmost to help me to overcome it by relieving the immediate material pressure . . . How much can he expect in return for these services? I don't know. But I fear I am not a "profitable" man for anybody's speculation.'

Conrad counted wholly upon Pinker as a prop and a stay, and to be turned away in a period of great need was not only incomprehensible but alarming and, as it began to seem, insulting. Conrad's honour, ever his most sacred possession, had been implicitly impugned. It could not – would not – be borne. By the end of January 1910, *Under Western Eyes* was complete. The effort had exhausted Conrad and, in a considerable state of nervous agitation, he set off for London to see Pinker – but without the manuscript. Some circumstance irritated Conrad further and, digging his elbows into the sides of a chair in his publishers' office, he contrived to push the sides of the chair quite out. He departed for Pinker's office where, according to Jessie, 'my excitable husband propounded some quixotic notion to his tried and trusty friend, making use of some foreign idiom. This greatly exasperated the other [Pinker], and he turned upon him with a sharp demand that he should speak English if he could!' Conrad was still seething when he got back to Aldington from these testing encounters with publisher and agent, and began turning over the pages of the manuscript of *Under Western Eyes*. Immediately he wired to Pinker, 'Have you a complete copy of "Western Eyes"?' Pinker wired back, 'No.' Jessie was surprised to note that this reply appeared to cause Conrad great excitement and, with practiced intuition, closely watched Conrad who, she suspected, meant to destroy the manuscript: 'I knew by some intuition that some disaster hung over that mighty pile.' It was the sole existing copy. As though dealing with a superbly clever madman, Jessie watched for her moment and, 'Under the pretext of tidying the table and while he seemed absorbed in his own moody reflections, I surreptitiously removed the package, and the next moment I had the satisfaction of turning the key in the lock of the drawer containing it. I was not a little disconcerted to hear his voice the next moment speaking in smooth, level tones from the window seat behind me. "Mind what you do with that key, don't mislay it".' The calmness was deceptive – within a day, Conrad was raving against Pinker, and showed evidence of being very ill. His throat had swelled, and he was delirious. For days, Conrad raved in Polish, and fiendishly confounded three separate doctors by surreptitiously pouring their medicines down the drain. Jessie fed him hot toddies and aspirin, and nursed him for three months after which he recovered sufficiently to write to Galsworthy that the recovery of his health and senses was 'very much like coming out of one little hell into another.'

In June 1910, the Conrad's moved to Capel House, Orlestone, about eight miles west of Pent Farm. Conrad described its situation on 17 May to John Galsworthy: 'We have secured a house. I can't stay on in this (comparatively expensive) hole. It has become odious to me after this illness . . . [Capel House is] a farmhouse with biggish rooms and 1½ acres of orchard standing in the fields and surrounded by 750 acres of unpreserved woods, where I am at liberty to roam. Five miles from Ashford and only a mile from Ham Street station . . . it is a very attractive place and cheap at £45. It may be folly to take it – but it's either that or a break-down: for my nerves are just on the balance. I require perfect silence for my work, – and I can get that there. This is as cheap as almost any place we have tried for this last year and a half.' The move, as ever, was not made smooth by Conrad who, as Jessie exclaimed to him, was more difficult to shift than all the household goods. 'As before, the vans stood empty waiting while he got in and out of the car, finding first one book then another that he simply could not be happy without, even although he expected to return to his new home in a couple of days. He had portioned out what I was to accomplish in the way of placing each article of furniture, pictures and books. Everything was to be in position within the next two days. It was done. Curtains, carpets as well, even to the filling of the lamps. Only the books remained still in drawers when the master of the house arrived.'

Conrad was still suffering some after-effects of his illness. To John Galsworthy, on 26 June, he reported: 'On leaving Ashford all alone, on my first outing since the illness, I felt all of a shake and utterly lost without Jessie.' And to Norman Douglas (whom he and Jessie had met on a holiday in Capri some years previously) he wrote two days later: 'I've lost all self-respect and have abandoned myself to a debauch of illness and laziness . . . I feel like a man returned from hell and look upon the very world of the living with dread.' Idleness could not long be prolonged. The *Daily Mail* suggested he review some books for them at five guineas a column, and he accepted with some reservations. In the event, after five or six books had arrived and been reviewed, Conrad found the whole business too irritating to continue. But the *Daily Mail* had not finished with Conrad, though Conrad had finished with them. He was mysteriously disturbed at his work by the approach of an antiquated motor car. A man appeared to say that he had been sent to fetch Mr Conrad to speak on the telephone at Ashford. The *Daily Mail* had, rather improbably, summoned this gentleman from his bath and directed him to undertake this mission. Grumbling, Conrad consented to go to Ashford to speak on the telephone. He assumed it must be a matter of vital and urgent importance. Very shortly, the car, and Conrad, returned from Ashford. Conrad flung down his hat, sat down at the table, and ate his meal in silence. Finally, it was too much to bear in silence: 'The damned cheek,' cried Conrad, banging his fist on the table and rattling the cups. 'Imagine, Jess, all they wanted when I got there was an article on the books Crippen had read on his passage home, after he was caught . . . They wanted it telegraphed too, this evening. I gave them a price of £20 and the ass at the other end began to stutter, "Isn't that a bit stiff?" Then I let myself go and . . . he rang off pretty soon after that.' Conrad's career as a freelance journalist came to a swift end.

An impression of Conrad at about this time has been left by Joseph Retinger, a young Pole, who met Conrad in November 1912. What he saw at Ham Street station was 'unmistakeably Polish, even to his old fashioned sort of brown greatcoat, like the one my father used to wear when he was a child. He seemed, indeed, a typical Polish landowner from the Ukraine . . . A trifle too short in build, he was over-broad of shoulders. His head was powerfully sculptured in rough, sharp contours framed with unruly hair and a strong, wiry but short beard. His nose, almost aquiline, was somewhat broadly, one might say carelessly carved. His eyes, grey-brown and clear, slightly watering in a strong light, were underlined by wrinkles, which under his right eye had become veritable furrows from supporting a stiff monocle.' Conrad was hard at work, again, at *Chance*, turning out words at the prodigious speed (for him) of about twelve thousand words a fortnight in seasons of inspiration. And *Chance*, so long delayed, was at last the success Conrad had so long worked for and hoped for. It was finished, in the usual frenzy, at three o'clock in the morning on 25 March 1912 – seven years after its inception. In June 1913 after it had been serialized in the *New York Herald* Conrad sent a revised manuscript to Pinker with a covering letter expressing his fears that this latest novel would merely go the way of all the rest – quickly into an oblivion of indifference and neglect.

In the first two years, *Chance* sold more than thirteen thousand copies, at least three times as many as *Under Western Eyes*, and about eight to ten thousand copies in the United States. Conrad accepted success as he had accepted failure – it made a financial difference, but he was cool about a triumph that, had it come earlier, might have meant much more. He and Pinker were reconciled, and became better friends than ever. It is stretching geography to insist that Orlestone lies within

Romney Marsh, but it is pleasing to leave Conrad on a note of success. Heaped with honours, though he rejected a knighthood, he died in his adopted home county of Kent at eight-thirty on the morning of 3 August 1924, in the presence of his wife and two sons, and four days later was buried at St Thomas's, Canterbury.

FIVE

Ford Madox Hueffer in Romney Marsh

In 1898, both HG Wells and the American author Stephen Crane came to live in Romney Marsh and completed what has come to be recognised as a grouping of literary figures in a Kent and East Sussex regional landscape – Wells at Sandgate just outside Folkestone, Crane at Brede Place, Conrad at Pent Farm at Postling, near Aldington, James at Lamb House in Rye, and Ford Madox Hueffer first at Aldington and later, from 1901, at Winchelsea. Rudyard Kipling lived further away, nearer to Brighton, though within driving distance of Rye and Romney Marsh. In no sense can these writers be considered to form a group. Their attitudes, interests and styles were all very different, as were their backgrounds and the promptings that had brought them into the same neighbourhood. There was no 'Brotherhood' such as had existed between the Pre-Raphaelites, and no bed-hopping or gossip-swapping such as bound the members of the Bloomsbury Group together. But they visited one another, took an interest in one another's fortunes, occasionally told stories and speculated about one another (Hueffer being the Trickster figure who flitted between them, stirring things up from time to time) and sometimes collaborated or consulted with one another in literary matters. Contact was not – except in the case of Conrad and Hueffer – continuous; Henry James was quite likely to dive into a ditch or bolt behind a tree in order to avoid meeting Hueffer whom he had observed approaching along a country road, and Crane sometimes inveighed mightily against the constant troop of visitors to Brede Place.

Hueffer liked to be noticed by those he admired. He was particularly interested in Henry James who kept him, as much as possible, at a cautious distance. He treasured even an ironic compliment, such as that given by Stephen Crane which, with a disarming frankness, Hueffer told against and for himself: Crane had written to a friend, advising, 'You must not mind Hueffer; that is his way. He patronizes me; he patronises Mr Conrad; he patronizes Mr James. When he goes to Heaven he will patronize God Almighty. But God Almighty will get used to it, for Hueffer is all right.' Hueffer claims this reference as 'the greatest pride of my life'. It came from a writer, an artist, and that connection robbed it of any personal slight that Hueffer might have felt on hearing such a backhanded compliment. WH Hudson, Henry James, Joseph Conrad and Stephen Crane were, on his own testimony, 'all gods for me. They formed, when I was a boy, my sure hope in the eternity of good letters. They do still.'

Hueffer made this comment after all four were dead, and continued: 'For me they were the greatest influence on the literature that followed them – that has yet been vouchsafed to that literature. Young writers from Seattle to the Golden Gate and from Maine to Jacksonville, Florida, write as they do because these four men once wrote.' Hueffer believed, all his life, that 'every artist of whatever race was my fellow countryman – and the compatriot of every other artist. The world divided itself for me into those who were artists and those who were merely the stuff to fill graveyards.' The writer with whom Hueffer had most contact was Conrad. He gave Conrad firm and continuous psychological and moral support both in literary and practical, everyday matters. He had the ideas, and the dynamism to work them up and stimulate Conrad to involve himself fully in their joint art of fiction. But each man had also his own concerns, his own novels to write quite apart from their collaborative efforts. Hueffer speaks disparagingly of his own work during the decade of his association with Conrad, but he produced a respectable body of work nevertheless, including his book about the Cinque Ports, and Conrad produced, among, others, *Lord Jim* and *Typhoon*. This latter book was serialized early in 1902 in *The Pall Mall Magazine*.

Jessie Conrad did not much care for Hueffer, although she recognised his usefulness and the stimulation he provided for her husband: 'Altogether the intimate years of our connection with F M H and his family could hardly be considered dull,' she commented with some asperity in *Joseph Conrad and his Circle*, published after Conrad's death.

As for the domestic relations with Hueffer, the more intimate they became the more vexing they were to Jessie. She describes his apparent tactics: 'F M H had an uncanny way of picking out people from the point of interest, and having found anyone to his mind was extremely tenacious of them. There was also some, one might almost say, promise held out to the other, either of material gain or some intellectual reward, which cemented the acquaintance between them. Certainly very few lasted very long, but there was some kind of fascination about the man.' There is in this description an attempt to account for the hold he seemed to keep on her husband, for Hueffer's charms were unfathomable to her. That she was not, and could not be, all in all to Conrad in intellectual terms, was perhaps an irritation that found its outlet in an antipathy towards Hueffer who provided Conrad with mental nourishment while Jessie was responsible merely for the nourishment and maintenance of the body.

Hueffer's grandfather had been the Pre-Raphaelite painter Ford Madox Brown, celebrated for pictures such as *The Last of England* and *Work*. The young Hueffer had been familiar with anecdotes of the great, which he retailed in four self-aggrandising volumes of autobiography with an apparent appetite for second-hand detail that did not always very strictly accord with the facts but which made a good story better. His first-hand recollections are generally unreliable as to specifics:

he stated firmly that Carlyle had once told him how he had seen Schiller and Goethe together in Weimar, drinking coffee in a garden restaurant, and that Carlyle had given a waiter a sum of money to be allowed to put on a white apron to serve these two distinguished men who were dressed in court-dress with wigs and swords. This was quite untrue, even had it been possible, but Hueffer was unabashed: 'I have for facts a most profound contempt . . . This book, in short, is full of inaccuracies as to facts but its accuracy as to impressions is absolute.' This self acknowledged literary impressionist admitted he altered episodes when it seemed expedient to do so but claimed never to have distorted the character of episodes he had witnessed. 'The accuracies I deal in are the accuracies of my impressions. If you want factual accuracies you must go to . . . But no, no, don't go to anyone, stay with me!' And, of course, we do. We may now know the truth, more or less, about many of Hueffer's fabrications, but they remain nonetheless entertaining and the stuff of gossip.

HG Wells spoke of Hueffer's 'copious carelessness of reminiscence' which led Hueffer to believe that Lamb House was built of grey stone rather than that red brick which gives it such mellow, weathered, rosy charm. He was also persuaded that Henry James forever harboured a resentment against Flaubert for having received him *en déshabille* in Paris, wearing a dressing gown, when in fact James had been charmed by 'that long colloquial dressing-gown, with trousers to match, which one has always associated with literature in France – the uniform really of freedom of talk.' *The Legend of the Master* by Simon Nowell-Smith unravels the knotted threads of Hueffer's inspired inventions concerning Henry James, most of which began with a grain of fact, were inflated by being loosely connected with information that Hueffer had picked up elsewhere and misapplied, and garnished with an improbable but not implausible pastiche of James's magisterial, civil, and most orotund style of speech and deportment.

James, after living briefly at Point Hill at Playden, had leased the Old Vicarage in Rye in July 1896, where Hueffer first encountered his idol whom he characterised as 'well-off for a bachelor of those days, when four hundred pounds a year was sufficient for the luxurious support of a man about town. You might have thought he was in his ancestral home, the home itself one of elegance in the Chippendale-Sheraton-Gainsborough fashion. He had the air of one of the bearded elder-brother statesman of the court of Victoria; his speech was slow and deliberate; his sentences hardly at all involved.' James himself must have felt a little unnerved in Rye, with a niggling sense of *déjà vu*: he had already invented the likes of Cora Crane in his novels, and now, here, was the Colonel Capadose of 'The Liar' to the life, the character who 'lies about the time of day, about the name of his hatter,' but 'there's no harm in him and no bad intention; he doesn't steal nor cheat nor gamble nor drink; he's very kind . . . He simply can't give you a straight answer.' It is true that Ford Madox Hueffer was a romancer, a fantasist, a fabulist, and true also that he was kind, with no harm – or at least no bad intention – in him. His grandfather, Hueffer said, had told him: 'Fordie, never refuse to help a lame dog over a stile. Never lend money; always give it . . . Beggar yourself rather than refuse assistance to any one whose genius you think shows promise of being greater than your own.' 'That is a good rule of life,' says Hueffer. 'I wish I could have lived up to it.' He certainly tried to, and was generous not only to Conrad but to a host of other, younger writers in a spontaneous, sometimes eccentric, often apparently meddling, manner. His heart was good and large, and it was his text that a writer helps other writers who need or ask for assistance.

Much as he took Crane's back-handed compliment as a tribute pure and simple, so Hueffer took James's reference to himself as '*le jeune homme modeste*' as being quite without irony. He regarded himself as an intimate friend of James: 'I think I will, after reflection, lay claim to a considerable degree of intimacy.' James, on the other hand, seemed to have been hard pressed to reciprocate, now and again going to considerable and undignified lengths to avoid the company of his importunate admirer, this young man who regarded James as 'the most masterful man I have ever met,' but who acknowledged, 'I do not think that, till the end of his days, he regarded me as a serious writer.' Says Hueffer, 'It was . . . an almost purely non-literary acquaintance.' Of his claimed intimacy with James, 'I could, I think, put down on one page all that he ever said to me of books – and, although I used, out of respect, to send him an occasional book of my own on publication, and he an occasional book of his to me, he never said a word to me about my writings, and I do not remember ever having done more than thank him in letters for his volume of the moment.' At this point, Hueffer breaks off to state that James 'expressed intense dislike for Flaubert' and to embroider the dressing gown anecdote, as well as to introduce the interesting snippet that Maupassant, who had invited James to lunch, 'received him, not, to be assured, in a dressing gown, but in the society of a naked lady wearing a mask.' Hueffer committed no such improprieties and so, 'Myself, I suppose he must have liked, because I treated him with deep respect, had a low voice – appeared, in short, a *jeune homme modeste*. Occasionally he would burst out at me with furious irritation, as if I had been a stupid nephew.'

Hueffer's impressions of James were bound up with, and coloured by, his observations of Crane and Conrad. His feelings about these three men are summed up in his books, *Return to Yesterday* and *Mightier than the Sword*: Henry James 'gives you an immense – and an increasingly tragic – picture of a leisured society that is fairly unavailing, materialist, emasculated – and doomed. No one was more aware of all that then he. Steevie [Crane] used to rail at English literature, as being one immense, petty parlour game. Our books he used to say were written by men who never wanted to go out of the drawing room for people who wanted to live at perpetual tea-parties. Even our adventure-stories, colonial fictions and tales of the boundless prairie were conducted in that spirit. The criticism was just enough. It was possible that James never wanted to live outside tea-parties – but the tea-parties that he wanted were debating circles of a splendid aloofness, of an immense human sympathy, and of a beauty that you do not find in Putney – or Passy! It was his tragedy that no such five-o'clock ever sounded for him on the time-piece of this world . . .

'Crane's utopia, but not his literary method, was different. He gave you the pattern in – and the reverse of – the carpet in physical life, in wars, in slums, in western saloons, in a world where the "gun" was the final argument. The life that Conrad gives you is somewhere half-way between the two; it is dominated – but less dominated – by the revolver than that of Stephen Crane, and dominated, but less dominated, by the moral scruple than that of James. But the approach to life is the same with all these three; they show you that disillusionment is to be found alike at the tea-table, in the slum, and on the tented field.'

Hueffer also regarded HG Wells as disillusioned, as a pessimist: 'inspired with the gospel of Science, he snorted a little on the side . . . not loudly, but with meaning. We, his snorts said, we who delighted hilariously in his works, were poor idiots towards whom a dark shadow was swiftly drifting. Science was going to devour us as the underground working populations of one of his stories crept out and at night devoured the butterfly beings of the planet's surface. Good for Mr Wells; good for Science; good for everybody. Particularly good for us intelligentsia because we began to see that Mr Wells too was a pessimist. We slapped each other on the back hilariously. The note of the world of those days was hilarity. It was good to think that our pet Genius was also going to develop into an Intelligence . . . And in the days of which I am talking the rest of the personages of my young drama – Conrad, James, Crane, Hudson – dwelt in a half circle of distances of from five to thirty-odd miles round Spade House. So it was not to be wondered at if we lived rather in each other's pockets and interested ourselves in each other's affairs.'

There was much to be interested about in the case of Hueffer's own affairs. The first house Ford and Elsie Hueffer owned after their marriage on 17 May 1894 was Bloomfield at Bonnington, near Aldington, which was near enough to Romney Marsh which both of them had known as children during summer holidays. It was an unappetising house with an air of 'damp cold' which they stood for some eighteen months. They had married in dramatic circumstances at Gloucester, having eloped to confound Elsie's father, Dr Martindale, who was violently opposed to their love affair, far less their marriage. Dr Martindale was a prosperous, eminent pharmacist and he had no optimism that Ford Madox Hueffer would ever be able to support his delicate daughter Elsie, who had, as a child, suffered from tuberculosis of a vertebra in her neck and, as a result of an operation, limped slightly and was unsteady on her feet. Ford was thought to be a fortune-hunter and immoral. His advanced views about sex appeared to Dr Martindale to be a corrupting influence upon Elsie. Ford had published some fairy stories and fancied himself, on the ground that a volume of verse was about to be published, a poet. This was insufficient recommendation, and his ancestry was another difficulty. He was the grandson of an artist of rather pronounced character and views, and he associated with dangerous radicals such as the Socialists and Anarchists of Kelmscott House. These substantial impediments to his preferment were disregarded by Elsie who was about four years short of the age of her majority and, thereafter, could choose to marry whom she pleased. But the marriage would not wait and Dr Martindale attempted, after the event, to get Elsie made a ward of Chancery – but to no avail. Ford and Elsie took a holiday in Germany and began their domestic life together entertaining and living on one hundred pounds a year, an insufficient sum by about half even for the working classes who were considered adequately well off on an annual income of one hundred and fifty pounds.

Hueffer was left three thousand pounds by an uncle in 1897, and by that date he was a regular man of letters, having published a biography of his grandfather, *Ford Madox Brown*, in 1896. On October 1896, Ford and Elsie rented and moved into Pent Farm, where they stayed until Hueffer leased it to the Conrads in October 1898. 'In the ten years from 1894 to 1903 I was hardly at all in London,' says Hueffer. 'I had buried myself in the country and for three or four years hardly saw anyone but fieldworkers.' He proceeded to restore the old house 'on the most approved lines to its original antique condition of great rafters and huge ingles with rackets and crocks' with the assistance of his gardener, Wilson, who could do everything but write and apparently slept on a coffin stool in an ingle, with both hands stretched above his head still holding his tools – a hammer and a cold-chisel. For a while, Hueffer took to country and village life with the gusto he displayed in everything. Like Ragged-Arse Wilson, who worked all the hours God sent, turning from one handicraft to another like a man of parts, and was interested in everything that marked the seasons, Hueffer always found 'plenty to talk about and plenty to do.' The social centre was 'T'Shop at Aldington Corner on a Saturday night. T'Shop was the village club, the Emporium, the news centre, the employment agency, the bank. . . . From its rafters and the rafters of all the out-buildings hung a mysterious forest of unassorted objects – boots, buckets, ploughshares, strings of onions, flasks of olive oil, red herrings, corduroy trousers, baggin-hooks, bill-hooks, tool-baskets, cradles, hams. There was no imaginable thing that you could not buy there – even books. I once bought off the counter Dostoievsky's *Poor Folk*.'

Besides the more remarkable characters of the Marsh, such as Shaking Ben (liable to unnerving eldritch shrieking), the Parson (who had unwisely married his cook and was thus barred from preferment and the material joys of a house in a Cathedral Close among deans and minor canons), there was the literate Grocer Rayner who, stone deaf, read the works of Henry James, Joseph Conrad and Stephen Crane 'with the passionate engrossment of a man in deep isolation.' He had complete sets of first editions, bought as soon as published. 'When Crane and Conrad came into his shop one day Rayner's emotion was so great that he was ill for some time – a dour, bearded, Scotch-looking grocer.' The grocer, who ruled T'Shop of Aldington with a rod of iron, was a welcome figure in Hueffer's rustication: 'one day to come across a village grocer, or a bank president, or a railway porter or a doctor, accidentally to find that they support what you stand for – your friends, your point of view, your Movement – that is a great encouragement.'

The Pent was a larger house, more suitable for entertaining and for raising a family. On 3 July 1897, Elsie was delivered of a baby girl, christened Christina Margaret, after the poet Christina Rossetti, 'We've got room for a small army and welcomes for a large one,' said Hueffer to his friends who were encouraged to bring their bicycles as their situation was ideal – 'glorious country for that sport. You push up a hill – jump on, ride down – push up and so on for miles and miles.' Edward and Constance Garnett brought their son, David, from Limpsfield and the man, remembering childhood impressions of the Hueffers, recalls Ford Madox Hueffer as 'a very young man, tall and Germanic in appearance, with a pink and white complexion, pale, rather prominent, blue eyes and a beard which I referred to when we first met as "hay on his face".' Hueffer was the perfect companion for a child: 'he would suddenly squat and then bound after me like a gigantic frog. He could twitch one ear without moving the other – a dreadful but fascinating accomplishment.' Elsie Hueffer was seemingly devoted to aesthetic dress and struck the young David Garnett as something of a Pre-Raphaelite figure: she 'was tall, high-breasted and dark, with a bold eye and a rich, high colour, like a ripe nectarine. She dressed in richly coloured garments of the William Morris style and wore earrings and a great amber necklace, and I, at the age of five, was greatly attached to her.'

Elsie's dress probably inspired Mrs Edward Pease, a redoubtable Fabian, to order Hueffer to proceed at once to Cora Crane in order to teach her how to make medieval dresses. Hueffer's Pre-Raphaelite origins made him eminently suitable for this task, she considered. Cora Crane, when Hueffer arrived at Brede Place on this improbable errand, declared that she 'had never had any idea of abandoning coats and skirts. We worked out that Mrs Pease had determined that I should get together with the Cranes. Mrs Pease wanted to see the countryside covered with ladies in medieval attire.' The Pent was more accessible to friends of the Hueffers than the house at Bonnington, and perhaps a more continuous and intense exposure to literary men and literary talk and literary work stimulated Hueffer to reconsider the style of country life he had adopted. Writing an eclogue was one thing – living it quite another. In 1897, he had been involved in preparing a retrospective exhibition of Ford Madox Brown's work at the Grafton Gallery. He was obliged to travel more often to London and to be in touch with old friends. London, if not as sustaining as the Kent countryside, was certainly a good deal more stimulating and in 1898 Hueffer rented the farmhouse to the artist Walter Crane and moved with his wife and daughter to Gracie's Cottage, near to Limpsfield and the Garnetts. It was there, two months later, that Conrad and Hueffer met for the first time.

By mid-September 1898, the Hueffers were living again at the Pent, but a month later they had ceded it to the Conrads and took over a nearby house, a labourer's cottage called Stocks Hill near Aldington, where Hueffer began work on his book about the Cinque Ports while Conrad worked at *Lord Jim*. They collaborated on *Romance* and also laboured together on another novel, *The Inheritors*, which on 16 March 1899 was despatched to the publishing firm of Heinemann. It was accepted and published in 1901 to general critical hostility and public disregard – sales were pitifully low. *The Inheritors* had been Hueffer's idea: Conrad had asked to see what he had already done of this 'extravagant' novel, and despite some anxiety that the book should fairly be credited to Hueffer alone, he agreed to collaboration. 'Heinemann (and McClure too I fancy) [McClure was an American publisher] are waiting for our joint book and I am not going to draw back if you will truly consent to sweat long enough. I am not going to make any sort of difficulty about it. I shall take the money if you make a point of that. I am not going to stick at that trifle. Do come when you like. Bring only one (or at most two) Chapters at a time and we shall have it out over each separately . . . I've been – I am animated by the best intentions. I shall always be.'

The work had not been without difficulty. To Edward Garnett, Conrad wrote that he had at first considered *The*

Inheritors 'as a sort of skit upon the sort of political (?!) novel, fools of the N.S. sort do write. And poor H. was in dead earnest! Oh Lord. How he worked! There is not a chapter I haven't made him write twice – most of them three times over. This is collaboration if you like! Joking apart the expense of nervous fluid was immense. There were moments I cursed the day I was born and dared not look up at the light of day I had to live through with this thing on my mind. H. has been as patient as no angel has ever been. I've been fiendish. I've been rude to him; if I've not called him names I've *implied* in my remarks and the course of our discussions the most opprobrious epithets. He wouldn't recognize them. 'Pon my word it was touching. And there's no doubt that in the course of that agony I have been ready to weep more than once. Yet not for him. Not for him.' After such travail, the reception given to *The Inheritors* was very disappointing. To Hueffer, in 1903, Conrad wrote that *Seraphina* (the novel *Romance*) had been sent, in part, to JB Pinker, the literary agent, and confided that 'Heinemann means to work up *The Inheritors* . . . there is nothing against the book's success but the general slump in the trade. Of the slump, alas, there can be no doubt.'

Seraphina, or *Romance* as it came to be known, was written in a state of terrific frenzy shortly after publication of *The Inheritors*. By this time, the Hueffers had moved to Winchelsea in April 1901 at the behest of Elsie's father, Dr Martindale. The Bungalow was a small house, an imitation Canadian or New England frame house with white clapboards, its back to the sea a little way distant. Hueffer added a large drawing-room at the back of the house, thus extending and improving the accommodation which was needed since Elsie Hueffer had again given birth to a daughter, Katherine, who had arrived a year earlier, in April 1900. The Bungalow faced towards the monumental ruins of the parish church (uncompleted) of St Thomas of Canterbury where Wesley had once preached in his best manner to the unpersuaded people of Winchelsea. Martindale had bought The Bungalow for the Hueffers so that they might be family neighbours and, in close proximity, more intimate. An intimacy certainly developed between Hueffer and Elsie's sister Mary Martindale. They became lovers, the affair lasting five years until 1906. In 1901, Hueffer was twenty-seven, and Elsie twenty-four. They had had a reasonably happy married life, allowing for Hueffer's capricious, gadfly temperament. Elsie discovered the affair by accident in 1904, inadvertently opening a telegram that had been addressed to Mary. Ford Madox Hueffer had spoken, at the time of his marriage, of the likelihood that he would be unfaithful – a warning that Elsie had probably paid little heed to in the complicated circumstances of their courtship.

Possibly Hueffer was feeling marooned in Winchelsea. The intensity of life with his family, with his own work and the collaboration with Conrad, with financial pressures, with his own physical ailments and those of his associates and family, probably required some romantic relief that would ease the pressures upon him. Winchelsea, beautifully situated and possessing a tranquil, charming appearance, is not the gayest or the most stimulating place in England. Hueffer was beginning to feel irked with country life. He was busy with Conrad, with his own writing, with cultivating good and intellectual acquaintance, with domestic life and unpredictable servants, and with the disappointing rejections he suffered from magazines and publishers. Blackwoods turned down *Romance* which had to be rewritten. The writing of it continued until the summer of 1902, and finally it was published in 1903 to better reviews and sales than *The Inheritors*. It had been a difficult time: Hueffer, besides slogging away at this, had been in difficulties with a book about Dante Gabriel Rossetti for Duckworth's Popular Library of Art, and on 2 February 1902, Dr Martindale died suddenly, possibly suicide, from an overdose of drugs. Ford Madox Hueffer had increasingly liked and respected his father-in-law, and he took Elsie to Germany for a holiday to restore their morale.

Late in 1903, Hueffer was hard pressed for money. He had counted on *Romance* to mend his pocket, but it failed to sell in any significant quantity, and he was obliged to apply to Robert

Garnett for a loan of one hundred and fifty pounds and again in 1904 for one hundred pounds. These sums settled only his debts, leaving little over for everyday and occasional expenses. Edward Garnett suggested that Hueffer should write about Holbein for Duckworth's and off his own bat he considered writing a novel about Katherine Howard – the research for the one would be useful for the other. It seemed, suddenly, imperative that he should move to London, to his brother Oliver's house at 10 Airlie Gardens, a cul-de-sac off Campden Hill Road in Kensington. Hueffer, Elsie, and the two girls moved early in January 1904 and the Conrads came too, renting a couple of rooms nearby at 17 Gordon Place. They settled to a literary and social life, Conrad working on *Nostromo*, Hueffer on *The Soul of London* (which, since he had failed to place this book about London, modelled on his book about the Cinque Ports, he was obliged to write without advance commission), and together working on *The Mirror of the Sea.* It was a disastrous interlude. Jessie fell and wrenched both her knees painfully; Conrad was depressed and beset by financial and practical difficulties: everyone came down with influenza, and Christina's hair caught fire.

The literary effort was intense: Conrad, writing to HG Wells, said he could dictate *The Mirror of the Sea*, which he described as 'that sort of bosh', at the rate of three thousand words in four hours. Generally, he dictated from 11 to 1 am, devoting the day to *Nostromo.* Hueffer knew he had overstretched himself by taking on an expensive, large London house and was desperate to make some money. He decided the best way to do this was to write 'a dozen fairy stories' and churn out articles 'on Jap.; French Literature and German subjects.' He acquainted Pinker with these proposals. Meanwhile, there was the job of steering Conrad through *Nostromo* – an urgent task, since the novel had already begun serialisation in a magazine and the episodes were written to deadlines. Conrad was not easy. He would climb innumerable stairs to Hueffer's 'small, dreadful study' and, having arrived, would 'sit for hours motionless and numb with a completely expressionless face.' His sole utterances would be expressions of the direst despair, disclaiming any possibility that the work could be done. Then, late at night and into the early morning, Hueffer would sit scribbling assiduously as Conrad dictated *The Mirror of the Sea*. Then the cook, Johanna, keeled over, plunging her head into a great sieve of flour, felled by influenza, and Hueffer was obliged to cook, nurse, and take care of most of the household chores.

Despite all inconveniences, he worked away, completing all but a few thousand words of *The Soul of London* by mid-April, and completing it by May. *Nostromo* was a struggle for Conrad. To meet one of the deadlines, Hueffer 'had to write the part of the serial that remained to make up the weekly instalment. Our life was like that.' This apparently simple statement has been violently disputed by scholars and partisans who consider that Hueffer's memory of the composition of *Nostromo* was faulty and dedicated to bolstering his own vanity. The first few months of 1904, in London, were 'the most terrible period of Conrad's life and of the writer's [Hueffer's], and in late March Hueffer bolted, leaving Elsie to close up the Airlie Gardens house. He first made for the New Forest where he took two cottages at Winterbourne Stoke where Elsie and his daughters joined him in May. In April, he published his third book of poetry, *The Face of the Night*, which was virtually ignored by the press and the public. Winterbourne Stoke was a fiasco – no better, and somewhat worse, than anywhere else. He was unable to write anything other than letters to friends, and early in June he left England for Germany in search of a cure for his nervous troubles. Domestic life had become as intolerable as the prospect of solitude, and he developed severe agoraphobia. It was a struggle to walk up the ship's gangplank unaided. In Germany, he landed himself upon two aunts who lived in a small town near Coblenz and who were kind to him – 'Here I am treated as a sort of demi-god,' he wrote to Elsie, and his agoraphobia somewhat abated. But another symptom raised its Hydra-head: he was homesick, and longed for Romney Marsh.

God, to be in Romney Marsh
And see the ships above the wall —
I'd give these lakes and alps and all
For just an hour of storm and shower,
And just a glimpse of Lydd church tower,
And just to hear the wind in the thorns —
Just not to hear the cowbell's din,
Just not to hear the cowmen's horns —
But just to mark the tide come in,
Dear God by Romney Wall

Elsie returned to Winchelsea, embarrassingly short of money. Hueffer, conscious of his parlous financial condition, somehow found the will and ability to resume writing, and began to work at his study of Holbein. *The Soul of London* and a novel, *The Benefactor*, had not yet found publishers, and it was now that Conrad found the relations between himself and Hueffer reversed. Conrad was obliged to find within himself psychological strength to support Hueffer morally and practically. He was unable to send Hueffer money, but he offered to speak to Pinker and suggested that Hueffer should write letters that he could arrange to get published. In *The Saddest Story*, a biography of Ford Madox Hueffer, Arthur Mizener summarizes Hueffer's financial position at this time: 'Ford's investments consisted of two properties in London that had been purchased in 1896 for £779.17.6, the Hurst Cottage [in Aldington] which had been purchased in 1896 for £150 invested at 5 per cent. The income from these assets was £75.17.0 a year, but this income was offset by the interest on debts of £425 to Mrs Hueffer, Martha Garnett, and Miss Wanostrom; this interest amounted to £27 a year and reduced the interest on their investments to under £50, none of which was, for the moment, available, despite Ford's hopes. In addition to these assets there was what Ford had lent Conrad, which, together with the arrears of rent on the Pent, came to nearly £200.' Conrad, of course, was in no position to offer anything but a token contribution towards redemption of this debt. Hueffer wandered around Germany for a while, working on the book about Holbein and subjecting himself to cures at the hands of nerve specialists, but at last he returned to England at Christmas – but not to Winchelsea. William Rossetti loaned him his house at 3 St Edmund's Terrace, and there Hueffer secluded himself. He kept mainly to his bed and filled the bedroom with exotic birds. Conrad urged the merits of a Dr Tebb who, when Hueffer consulted him, lugubriously gave the prognosis that Hueffer would be dead of his agoraphobia within a month. Hueffer claims that this verdict stimulated him to get up, dress, and take a hansom cab to Piccadilly where he walked back and forwards for an hour and a half, saying to himself, 'Damn that brute, I will not be dead in a month.' At the end of the month, Ford again consulted Tebb and presented himself as very much alive. 'If I hadn't told you you would be dead you would have been dead,' said Tebb, justifying his oblique approach to Hueffer's interesting condition.

Hueffer immediately returned to Romney Marsh – first to Sandgate, and then, in February, to Winchelsea, whereupon Elsie fell ill with a complaint that was eventually diagnosed as a tubercular kidney. The household removed itself to Mrs Martindale's house at 93 Broadhurst Gardens in London so that Elsie could be properly cared for. Thereafter, Hueffer was in a constant state of motion between London and Winchelsea, continuing to labour at the Holbein book which, when it was finished, Pinker managed to place and thus relieve Hueffer's chronic depression. *The Soul of London* was also taken, by Alston Rivers, and quite unexpectedly Hueffer found himself with a success on his hands after enthusiastic reviews. He had become, in the summer of 1905, a noted author. He was not slow to capitalise on 'SUCCESS at last' by cultivating creditable literary and social acquaintance, particularly at Edward Garnett's Tuesday luncheons at the Mont Blanc restaurant in Gerrard Street.

If things were looking up for Hueffer on the literary front, domestically his life was at a low ebb. Elsie had discovered the affair with her sister in 1904, and in 1906 the Hueffers were living apart. Elsie was at her mother's house, Ford was living with his mother at Brook Green, Hammersmith, and the two girls were boarded at La Sagesse Convent in Rye for their education. Hueffer spent school holidays with his daughters in Winchelsea and spent some weekends there. In early March, Conrad completed *The Mirror of the Sea*, and when they returned to England, having gone to Montpellier in the spring of 1906, they were offered the use of The Bungalow in Winchelsea on the understanding that Hueffer could spend weekends in the house. The arrangement was not a success. Jessie Conrad, alarmed at being in closer proximity to Ford Madox Hueffer than necessary, but anxious that Conrad should have a change of scene from the Pent, agreed (privately hoping that prolonged exposure to Hueffer on his home ground would show him to Conrad in his 'true' light) to the plan, but 'I think every conceivable thing happened that fortnight to make me regret coming to Winchelsea. The two long week-ends that F M H had stipulated he should come down were the longest I have ever known, and a fit punishment for any sins I might have ever committed, or even contemplated.'

Hueffer had made a hash of the travelling arrangements, and had locked up the family plate. He had lost the key to the cupboard. Hueffer washed his Panama hat and placed it tenderly in the oven, over Jessie's Sunday roast, to dry. 'It was a real Panama, but his washing had been confined to the outside only, there was too much grease inside the lining for my liking . . .' Then Conrad, quite unexpectedly, asked his wife to sew a new black ribbon on the offensive Panama. 'I dutifully sewed it on the hat.' On Monday, entering the dining room for breakfast, Hueffer noticed a small cut in the tablecloth. 'Look at that,' said Hueffer. 'Elsie will be furious.' Jessie murmured, 'I don't suppose she will ever see it.' Hueffer bounced to his feet in a temper '. . . I must say that when I lent the house I expected ordinary care . . .' Jessie triumphantly informed him that it was her own tablecloth. 'Are you satisfied?' Hueffer had hardly gone a yard out of the house before Jessie majestically informed him that she had brought all her own linen and put away all of

Hueffer's '*without using it.*' The next weekend was equally fraught with domestic difficulties and ended with Hueffer strewing Conrad's clothes over his bed for lack of a blanket which he had chosen to hang over the window to keep out the early morning light.

'Conrad and Jessie go on Wed.,' Hueffer wrote to Elsie in London, '– and I've not pressed them to stay: they're rather exhausting.' Elsie had been feeling neglected, but she was not yet ready to forget or forgive her husband's misconduct with her sister. They were partly reconciled and took a flat in Holbein House, near Sloane Square, as a London base and spent weekends in Winchelsea. Their financial state was shockingly bad – a cheque to the American publisher McClure had bounced, Pinker was owed more than six hundred pounds, a debt that increased to eight hundred, and Hueffer was struggling to complete two novels – *Privy Seal* and *An English Girl*. They abandoned the London flat and settled back in Winchelsea, Hueffer using his mother's house as a London residence. But it wouldn't, and didn't, do. In 1907, Hueffer decided, finally, that 'the country is not the place for intellectual contracts.' He had tired of Winchelsea, to which ' "genteel families" come . . . in search of health and quiet, which they find in abundance.' Literature might be created in such circumstances of health and quiet, but not a fullblown literary career. He retrieved Christina Rossetti's writing desk from the Conrads at the Pent, and exchanged Romney Marsh for 'the shop fronts, the artificial stone facades, the electric light standards and the faint smell of horse dung and dust of the centre' of London. He moved to 84 Holland Park Avenue, a set of rooms over a poulterer and fishmonger, which was to be not only home but also the offices of his literary magazine, *The English Review*. Elsie remained at Winchelsea, but in September she fell ill with a recurrence of her kidney complaint. She was operated upon, and afterwards went to stay with her husband at Holland Park Avenue. But she did not care for life in town, and returned to Winchelsea where Hueffer visited her at weekends until she decided to give up The Bungalow because life at Winchelsea had become 'artificially fashionable'. In December, Hueffer wrote to his mother, 'We have definitely unfurnished The Bungalow and stored the furniture – so there's an end of Winchelsea. I'm sorry myself but E. never liked the place and was always more or less ill there. We are going to tidy up the cottage at Aldington and use that as our country abode.' Hurst Cottage was prepared, and Elsie moved in at the beginning of March 1908. The Bungalow was sold and the proceeds applied to the refurbishment of the house which was re-named Kitcat. When Elsie fell ill again in May, and her complaint was at last correctly diagnosed, she refused to return to London. In due time, and after Hueffer had set up a ménage with Violet Hunt, Hueffer and Elsie were permanently estranged, though she consistently refused to divorce him. His life in Romney Marsh was at an end.

In Romney Marsh, with Conrad, Hueffer had laid a solid foundation for a literary career. After he left, he worked indefatigably. 'I fancy that for ten years – say from 1904 to 1914 – I never took a complete day's rest . . . My record in the British Museum Catalogue fills me with shame; it occupies page on page with the mere titles of my printed work . . . I do not imagine that any one not a daily journalist has written as much as I have and I imagine that few daily journalists have written more. I am not proud of the record. If I had written less I should no doubt have written better.' But so, too, thought Arnold Bennett about his own prolific work, and though a great deal of Ford Madox Hueffer's writing may now be out of print, and likely to remain so, his masterpiece – *The Good Soldier* – is still read and reprinted in every generation.

SIX

Stephen Crane at Brede

On 16 January 1899, having driven out from Hastings, Stephen and Cora Crane set eyes on Brede Place, a relatively noble pile built by the Oxenbridge family in the fifteenth century. It is described by Augustus Hare as 'one of the best existing specimens of the small country-houses of the time of Henry VII . . . It is of stone, with foliated windows, and two fine chimneys with diagonal shafts battlemented. Additions in brick with stone dressings were made under Elizabeth.' Writing in *Sussex*, published in 1896, Hare gives particulars of the peculiar internal economy of the house as the Cranes would have found it: 'The house is strangely ill-arranged internally. The hall, which once rose to the whole height of the building, has been subdivided into an upper and lower floor. The present porch leads at once into the principal chamber. South of this is another large but low room, with an arched chimney. Hence a door opens into a chapel, divided by an oak screen. The staircase is dark. The Place was long a satisfactory resort of smugglers, as the legends attached to Sir Goddard kept people away, and accounted to them for all the strange sounds which were heard there.' Sir Goddard died in February 1531 with the reputation of being an ogre, a cannibal giant, who ate local Sussex children for dinner. The story goes that the children, in self defence, invented beer and gave it to Sir Goddard who drank himself into a stupor, whereupon they sawed him in half, the children of

West Sussex on one end of the saw, the children of East Sussex on the other.

Crane was not married to the thirty-four year old Cora, whose life, filled with incident, had already included two husbands. The first had been a dry-goods vendor called Thomas Vinton Murphy whom she had met, married, and abandoned at the age of twenty-one in 1886. Her second marriage, to Sir Donald Stewart, a baronet and son of the former Commander-in Chief in India, gave her the title Lady Stewart; but it had been an unsatisfactory bargain since Cora claimed she had left Captain Stewart because he had rapidly spent all her money (perhaps the divorce settlement from Murphy). Stewart felt strongly that Cora had been responsible for the failure of the marriage and afterwards bitterly described himself in *Who's Who* as 'unmarried' though he refused to divorce his wife.

Cora was an enthusiast. She was proud of having always packed five years of living into one, and wrote, 'I have never economized in sensation, emotion. I am a spendthrift in every way.' In this sense, she suited Stephen Crane who discovered a heightened sensibility in the testing conditions of war as a newspaper correspondent and writer of fiction. They had met, Crane and Cora, late in 1896 at the Hotel de Dream, a Jacksonville Sporting House where Cora was the madam. Her biographer, Lillian Gilkes, is at pains to euphemize Cora's profession which she describes as proprietress of an establishment which 'was primarily a place for the enjoyment of superior food and entertainment.' This subtle understatement could place Cora as anything from 'Diamond Lil' to a common brothel-keeper. But, 'Nothing at the Hotel de Dream was vulgar,' says Lillian Gilkes. 'As long as certain standards of propriety and taste were maintained, it seems never to have occurred to her that she could not defy with impunity the governing mores in sexual matters.' Cora had ideas in advance of any conventional, contemporary social morality. She 'pursued her own unconventional theories of "rescue" and from diary entries it is at least inferable that she felt she was performing a worthwhile philanthropy in also furnishing to the clients of the Hotel de Dream, if they wished to avail themselves of it, a trysting place among civilized surroundings. It is important to keep in mind that, in her view, such associations had nothing in common with debauchery – though she later extended this rationale to include prostitution.'

Cora fell instantly in love with Stephen Crane when he presented himself in 1896 at the Hotel de Dream, and became proprietress, manageress, lover, and wife in all but the eyes of the church and the law, of Crane, who was waiting out the months of November and December in Jacksonville in hopes that he would be sent to Cuba to report the rebellion there. To Cora, he wrote in November: 'Brevity is an element that enters importantly into all pleasures of life, and this is what makes pleasure sad; and so there is no pleasure but only sadness.' Whether this refers to larger things, or passing pleasures with sporting girls is not apparent, but Crane was at least frequenting night clubs in Jacksonville to while away his time.

Ford Madox Hueffer describes Cora as 'large, fair and placid,' and gives no information about her past other than that she 'came from Jacksonville, Florida.' HG Wells confidently says that Cora and Crane had met and married in Greece, Cora having 'been sent out by some American newspaper as the first woman war correspondent.' She and Crane had certainly been in Greece together, Cora adopting the name Imogene Carter as her journalistic nom-de-plume, covering the Greco-Turkish war in 1897. It is conjectured that Crane may have arranged for Cora to join him in Greece, as a correspondent for the *Journal* to which he also contributed despatches. Since Stewart had refused to divorce Cora, it seems unlikely that they were married in Greece, as Wells claims. They did not disabuse his assumption.

Early in June, Crane was in London. Reviewers had been praising the British publication of *The Third Violet* and the celebrated author was looking for some peaceful, quiet spot in which to write. He had not come to England, says his biographer John Berryman, for cultural reasons. 'We must distinguish Crane's expatriation from the expatriation of James and Whistler and others . . . Crane's indifference both as a man and as an artist to "culture", in the ordinary sense, was absolute; nor was he interested in English society.' There were reasons of celebrity, of personal animosities, and of his liaison with Cora, to detain him in England. A return to the United States, to New York, was for the time being imprudent. Crane and Cora settled first at Ravensbrook at Oxted in Surrey, not far from Limpsfield where the Garnett family lived at The Cearne. Joseph and Jessie Conrad, living then at Stanford-le-Hope, met the Cranes at The Cearne and the two men met, also, in London where they tramped the streets and talked in October 1897. At Ravensbrook, Crane was in touch with Paul Revere Reynolds, an American literary agent who had taken him on as a client after publication of *The Red Badge of Courage* in 1896. In this letter of October 1987, Crane discussed two stories, 'The Monster' and 'The Bride Comes to Yellow Sky', both of which he had written since coming to England in the early summer. He was writing, then, and making friends. First, Harold Frederic, an American writer in London and correspondent for *The New York Times*; and an invitation to tea at The Pines, Putney, with Swinburne. And a luncheon with Edmund Gosse. An American lawyer with an introduction to Crane visited him at Ravensbrook in November and described, in a letter, Crane's 'quiet, boyish way' and 'how young he is.' Crane was just twenty-six years old: his birthday had been on 1 November. Cora seemed 'to be six or seven years older than Mr Crane with big blue eyes and reddish hair.' Harold Frederic arrived with four or five friends, in the middle of the luncheon, quite unexpectedly. 'Mr Frederic is not at all agreeable. He is funny in a sarcastic way about politics and people but he kept interrupting everybody else and was downright rude to Mr Crane several times. They made Mr Crane shoot with his revolver after lunch and he is a fine shot.' Crane's tricks with a revolver were regular diversions for guests – and guests came tumbling in by the score. 'We have been overwhelmed with callers,' wrote Cora on 29 November, while Crane was then desperately trying to finish the story 'Death and the Child'.

1 Henry James at Lamb House

2 Henry James at Brede Summer Fete in 1899, gazing rather quizzically at a doughnut: 'I look as if I had swallowed a wasp … and I tried to look so beautiful.'

3 *HG Wells in 1905: 'rather stocky, with a drooping cavalry moustache and with eyes always darting about.'*

4 *The exterior of Lamb House 1912*

5 Joseph Conrad in 1904: *'very broad in the shoulder and long in the arm, dark in complexion with black hair and a clipped beard.'*

6 Ford Madox Hueffer: *'what he is really or if he is really, nobody knows now and he least of all.'*

7 Stephen Crane: 'lean, blond, slow-speaking, perceptive, fragile and tuberculous.'

8 Henry James and Cora Crane at Brede Summer Fete in 1899

9 Painting by Mary Aiken in 1939 of the view across the Marsh towards Winchelsea from the studio at Jeake's House

10 Conrad Aiken and Lorelei One (Jessie) in 1922

11 Studio portrait of EF Benson

12 EF Benson working in his 'little secret garden' at Lamb House

13 Radclyffe Hall in 1932: 'ivory clear and pale, the exquisite line of the jaw, the pure aquiline of the nose, the beautiful modelling of eyelids and brow.'

14 EF Benson leaving Lamb House with his dog in the 1920s.

15 Noel Coward in 1945: 'everything in the jardin is couleur de rose.'

16 For Russell Thorndike 'happenings were never enough on their own. Being a writer he turned every event in his and other people's lives into a romantic adventure.'

This story was sent to Reynolds in December, and in January 1896 reviewers were enthusiastic about publication of *The Red Badge of Courage*. 'Over here,' Crane wrote from England, 'happily, they don't treat you as if you were a dog, but give every one an honest measure of praise or blame. There are no disgusting personalities.' Crane and Cora had arrived in England with *carte blanche* to be what they chose to be, and had found the English credulous: 'They will believe anything wild or impossible you tell them and then if you say your brother has a bathtub in his house they – ever so politely – call you a perjured falsifier of facts. I told a seemingly sane man at Mrs Garnett's that I got my artistic education on the Bowery and he said, "Oh, really? So they have a school of fine arts there?" '

Crane was poor. In January 1898 he was writing that 'My English expenses have chased me to the wall,' but he acquired an agent in London, the miraculous James Pinker, and when some money came across from the States he rejoiced with Ford Madox Hueffer, whom he found waiting with Cora at Ravensbrook, after a visit to London. Things were looking up – presently there was a war in Cuba, which he attended. He was absent from England for nine months, but returned in January 1899, first to Ravensbrook and thence to Brede Place on 12 February. The house belonged to Moreton ('Mortal Ruin') Frewen, a friend of the Garnetts, who rented it to the Cranes for forty pounds a year. There Crane rested for a winter, writing very little but reading a great deal. Debts had followed them from Ravensbrook even to this remote retreat, and it was to be a constant struggle to live despite the generous hospitality the Cranes dispensed to all and sundry – report had it that barons of beef were roasted and kept outside the kitchen door for passing tramps to appease their hunger. There might also be a barrel of beer so that they could wash down the victuals. Ford Madox Hueffer's first reception at Brede was ambiguous: the Cranes at first took him for a tradesman or a bailiff demanding payment and were reluctant to let him in. Leon Edel, in his biography of Henry James, appears to imply that James knew, or conjectured, something of Cora's past: 'but there was no failure of courtesy on James's part when she became his neighbour. He had known bohemianism in all its forms from the days of his studio hauntings in Rome, Paris, London. He had chronicled the lives of dissolute artists in his novels and tales. . . . James had invented her long ago; indeed, everything she did seemed to have been told in his early "international" tales.' Cora, described as 'an egotist, a woman slightly overblown, proud of her blonde hair and fleshly charm, and energetic pursuit of pleasure and society' was not wholly to James's taste. Crane interested him more, as an artist, and partly as a fellow-expatriate and neighbour, while for Cora he retained a hard place in his heart and was 'unavailable' when after Crane's death and her remarriage, she attempted to call on him, though he had been generous to her in the immediate aftermath of Crane's death.

Crane and James had met at an uncorseted party in London, an occasion elaborated by legend which has it that a lady called Madame Zipango had poured champagne into James's top hat, to the considerable affront of his dignity. Crane had led her away and returned to salvage the hat and the discomfiture of Henry James. It was the sort of incident to fluster and confound James very thoroughly, but a minor incident to be taken in Crane's bohemian stride. Writing to Harold Frederic, Crane described the incident as an example of James making 'a holy show of himself in a situation that – on my honour – would have been simple to an ordinary man.' But, Crane adds, 'it seems impossible to dislike him. He is so kind to everybody.' Frederic had rudely spoken of James as 'an effeminate old donkey who lives with a herd of other donkeys around him and insists on being treated as if he were the Pope.' He added, 'he has licked dust from the floor of every third-rate hostess in London.'

Despite Frederic's estimation of James's social sensibility, it was certainly sufficiently acute to nose out Cora as not quite top drawer, but that did not stop him being gentlemanly and generous to the Cranes or, indeed, to the memory of Frederic himself when, after Frederic's death, James contributed fifty pounds towards the maintenance of his legitimate and illegitimate children, two of whom were fostered by Crane and Cora at Brede Place. On Crane's death, James forked out a further fifty pounds to defray some of Cora's expenses – a not inconsiderable sum from a man who constantly felt the pinch in his own purse.

Leon Edel explodes the fiction that James and the Cranes saw one another more or less constantly. 'So far as we know, the Cranes came to Lamb House for tea on two, perhaps three, occasions during the rest of that summer [of 1889, James having returned from Italy in July]; and James in turn visited them at Brede the same number of times. In a word, the deep and "intimate" friendship between the Cranes and James of which so much has been made never existed: and this in part because James had little opportunity that year to be neighbourly.' James was at least preoccupied by an infatuation for Hendrik Andersen, the young, handsome monumental sculptor; by a visit from his brother William James; and by the purchase of Lamb House when the lease was offered for sale. To pay for the house, James was obliged to write to earn money for the down payment. Edel also dismisses the myths that the fifty-six year old James sent his manuscripts to Crane for the twenty-seven year old author's criticisms, and that James turned up on the doorstep of Brede Place with a party of 'stuffed shirts', unannounced, for lunch. Harold Frederic was liable to do such a thing, but James, says Edel, never.

Crane had enough to do for himself without reading the work of Henry James, and James was impatient to place his own writings without the delay of submitting them for criticism to another writer. Neither of them could have spared the time for the other. In August, however, James had leisure to accept an invitation to a garden party at Brede Place where he was photographed with Cora and, later, snapped while gazing rather quizzically at a doughnut. Writing to Cora, he observed that the 'strange images' formed a 'precious memento of a romantic hour. But no surely, it can't be any doughnut of yours that is making me make such a gruesome grimace. I look as if I had swallowed a wasp or a penny toy, and I tried to look so beautiful. I tried too hard, doubtless. But don't show it to anyone as HJ trying.'

Ford Madox Hueffer's picture of relations between Crane and James is of an adolescent tormenting a bewildered schoolmaster. 'Crane, in those days [at Oxted], and for my benefit, was in the habit of posing as an almost fabulous Billy the Kid, just as later, to *épater* Henry James, he insisted on posing as, and exaggerating the characteristics of, a Bowery boy of the most hideous type.' But, Hueffer must admit, 'I never heard James say anything intimately damaging of Crane and I do not believe he ever said anything of that sort to other people. But what made the situation really excruciating to James was the raids made by Crane's parasites on Lamb House. No doors could keep them out, nor no butler. They made hideous the still levels of the garden with their cachinnations, they poked the old man in the ribs before his servants, caricatured his speeches before his guests and extracted from him loans that were almost never refused. There were times when he would hang about in the country outside Rye Walls rather than make such an encounter.' This is all exaggerated, and Hueffer fails to add that James would make determined efforts, also, to avoid Ford Madox Hueffer. The 'parasites' were certainly a plague to Crane who complained on at least one occasion, after an invasion of friends, children, and journalists, 'If you don't tell some of these lice that Cora and I aren't running a hotel I'll have to advertise the fact in *The Times*!'

Crane was conjured by James as, 'oh, heavens, received, surrounded and adulated . . . by, ah, the choicest, the loveliest, the most sympathetic and, ah, the most ornamental . . .', but nevertheless Crane remained for James 'as if you should find in a staid drawing-room on Beacon Hill or Washington Square or at an intimate reception at Washington a Cockney – oh, I admit of the greatest genius – but a Cockney still, costermonger from Whitechapel.' Hueffer describes the marvellous boy as 'the most beautiful spirit I have ever known. He was small, frail, energetic, at times virulent. He was full of fantasies and fanaticisms. He would fly at and deny every statement before it was out of your mouth. He wore breeches, riding leggings, spurs, a cowboy's shirt, and there was always a gun near him in the medieval building that he inhabited seven miles from Winchelsea. In that ancient edifice, he would swat flies with precision and satisfaction with the bead-sight of his gun . . . He would put a piece of sugar on a table and sit still till a fly approached. He held in his hand a Smith and Wesson. When the fly was on the sugar, he would twist the gun round in his wrist. The fly would die, killed by the bead-sight of his revolver. That is much more difficult than it sounds.'

Hueffer, like most people, had a soft spot for Crane: 'There are few men that I have liked – nay, indeed, revered – more than Crane. He was so frail and so courageous, so preyed upon and so generous, so weighted down by misfortune and so erect in his carriage. And he was such a beautiful genius.' Hueffer contrasts Conrad as representing 'Man – humanity as it should be. Crane, on the other hand, was like the angels. He did not seem to have the motives of common clay. Conrad produced with agony and you saw how it was done; Crane hovered over his foolscap sheets using a pen as a white moth uses its proboscis. His work had for me something of the supernatural. He comes back to me always as joyous.' Hueffer knew Conrad better than, perhaps, he knew Crane: certainly he was not constantly in Crane's company.

Conrad had shown an immediate interest in Crane since his arrival with Cora in London in 1897. On 9 November of that year, Conrad inscribed and sent a copy of *Almayer's Folly* to Crane and, before it had time to reach Crane, Conrad received a letter from him with an invitation to a Sunday luncheon and referring enthusiastically to their recent meeting: 'Did we not have a good pow-wow in London?' In his introduction to Thomas Beer's biography of Crane, published in 1923, Conrad wrote: 'He had a quiet smile that charmed and frightened one. It made you pause by something revelatory it cast over his whole physiognomy, not like a ray but like a shadow . . . It was the smile of a man who knows that his time will not be long upon this earth.'

But, with foreknowledge or none, Crane enjoyed life and the living. He took fondly to Conrad's son Borys who stayed a fortnight, with his parents, at Brede Place and there took his first steps. Jessie Conrad remembers the house as 'only partly furnished, just a few bedrooms and the drawing room and dining room. The study only just habitable as regards necessities. Cora Crane was of a somewhat monumental figure and affected a statuesque style of dress. The house, even the unfurnished part of it, was occupied. Harold Frederic . . . was there a great deal, not long before he died. There was also a lady whom we all knew as Mrs Frederic and three young children, two girls and a boy, who lived the simple life tucked somewhere out of sight under the roof, and who only appeared for a short time in the evening in the drawing room. All day long these three intelligent little folks ran about barefooted, but every evening saw them clothed in some coarse bronze plush frocks, terribly ornate, their socks mended with weird cobbled darns in some colour that swore violently with that of those pitiful little garments.'

In turn, the Cranes would visit the Conrads at Pent Farm, where Borys and Crane would lie for hours on a blanket on the grass gazing gravely into one another's eyes until Crane would burst into laughter. The admiration Conrad felt for the younger man, whose work he admired above his own, increased. While at Stanford-le-Hope, Conrad had written to Crane: 'You are an everlasting surprise to one. You shock – and the next minute you give the perfect artistic satisfaction . . . You are a complete impressionist. The illusions of life come out of your hand without a flaw. It is not life – which nobody wants – it is art – art for which everyone – the subject and the great – hanker mostly without knowing it.' To Edward Garnett, Conrad wrote: 'He is *the only* impressionist and *only* an impressionist.' In February 1898, Conrad inscribed a copy of *The Nigger of the Narcissus* to Crane, and there was some talk, unfulfilled, about collaboration on a play. In October 1898, Harold Frederic died and Cora instantly took in his mistress Kate and her three children at Ravensbrook. Two of the children, Héloise and Barry, with a governess, followed Cora to Brede Place, when Crane arrived back in England from Cuba and, together with Cora's companion Mrs Reudy, a relic of the days of the Hotel de Dream, formed the household.

In his absence, a story, 'The Price of the Harness', had appeared in *Blackwood's Magazine*, and on 13 January 1899 Conrad wrote to congratulate Crane on 'the best bit of work you've done (for its size) since the *Red Badge*. . . . Several fellows wrote to me about it as soon as it came out. Lucas [EV], Hueffer, Graham [HB Cunninghame] and others you don't know.' That was something to give Crane heart, but despite the gaiety on moving into Brede, and Hueffer's memory of him 'always as joyous', the image of Crane at Brede Place is of a man pressed and depressed by debt, mechanically trying to write himself free of financial anxiety, fatally consumed by malaria and tuberculosis (about which he had consulted the eminent Dr Trudeau at Saranac Lake who had diagnosed and recommended treatment for RL Stevenson), and saddled with a large, inconvenient, insanitary house filled with dependents. 'Crane was at twenty-seven the author of seven books besides three or four others written but unpublished, several of which would live – at this age Chekhov was just emerging from humorous journalism, and Maupassant was still a poet,' writes Crane's biographer, John Berryman. 'Crane though had no future. Did he know it? He did not act as if he knew it.' Some inkling of possible disaster must have been in his mind, since he was careful to keep as much of the truth about his physical condition as possible from Cora. But Cora, no fool, knew something and wrote to James Pinker, Crane's agent: 'I am so glad that you wrote him *not* to go to the Transvaal. His health is not fit for it. He had a return of Cuban fever while we were in Paris and he is in no physical condition to stand a campaign, no matter how short.' She added a postscript: 'Please don't let Mr Crane know I've said a word against the Transvaal.'

Cora was concerned to protect Crane against her anxiety, just as he hid his own from her. In a note, in the spring of 1900, he warned off a meddling acquaintance: 'Please have the kindness to keep your mouth shut about my health in front of Mrs Crane hereafter. She can do nothing for me and I am too old to be nursed. It is all up with me but I will not have her scared.'

HG Wells, in a laboriously optimistic letter of 22 April 1900, wrote: 'I have just heard through Pinker that you are getting better and I rejoice mightily thereat. I was hugely surprised to hear of your haemorrhaging for you're not at all the hectic sort of person who does that with a serious end in view.

'As an expert in haemorrhages I would be prepared to bet you any reasonable sum – I'll bet an even halo only I'm afraid of putting you on that high mettle of yours – that haemorrhages aren't the way you will take out of this terrestrial tumult.

'From any point of view it's a bloody way of dying, and just about when you get thirsty and it bubbles difficult and they inject you with morphia, I know few more infernally disagreeable.

'And confound it! What business have you in the Valley? It isn't midday yet and Your Day's Work handsomely started I admit, is still only practically started. The sooner you come out of that Valley again and stop being absolutely irrelevant to your work, the better!'

Some others take the view that Crane, through his illness, was being wholly relevant to his work – or, at any rate, to the spirit of it. Berryman theorises that he set himself up for death more than once, more or less courting suicide during his adventures as a war correspondent, and reference has been made by critics to Crane as a latter-day Edgar Allan Poe, careless of his own safety and preoccupied, in a literary sense, with death. Willa Cather regarded Crane as having 'the precocity of those doomed to die in youth. I am convinced that when I met him he had a vague premonition of the shortness of his working day, and in the heart of the man there was that which said, "That thou doest, do quickly".'

Crane was certainly trying to do as much as he could, under trying conditions. He wrote in an upstairs room, facing over the park, and for exercise he rode a horse around the hundred or so acres of the property. Thomas Beer considered the Brede household as an odd and *ad hoc* blend of formality and bohemianism. The English, he says, noted the bohemian ways – rushes on the floors, assorted pieces of furniture that Cora had picked up cheaply and at random (including four-poster beds retrieved from a chicken house) while American visitors were astonished to see the Cranes dress formally for dinner served at a long refectory table. Dinner was often uncertain as to time and the quantity and quality of the food. The cook drank, and so did Heather, the serving man. The gardener, Mack, was as old as Adam. The Frewens had insisted on the Cranes retaining these ancient, alcoholic and inadequate servants. The cook was, however, occasionally brilliant though prone to giving instant notice which she would retract only on being supplied with a brandy bottle, whereupon she would return to her kitchen and turn out a delicious dinner for as many as could be expected to dine – and visitors were frequent. A friend, Sanford Bennett, nicknamed Crane 'Baron Brede', and Cora called him 'Duke'. Cora slept in a queenly bed, raised on a dais in the ballroom. These airs caused some local ill feeling, and Henry James did not approve. Jessie Conrad did not approve of Cora's 'slatternly' maidservants, and it was said the dogs (five in all – Sponge, Flannel, Powder Puff, and two Russian poodles) foraged for bones under the table. 'Our affairs', Crane wrote to Pinker shortly after moving to Brede, 'are in a woeful condition.' There was little enough money to pay for all this – even the moderate rent of forty pounds a year was to be in arrears, though that was the least of the worries.

He began writing more of his successful Whilomville stories, and for the *Anglo-Saxon Review*, run by Lady Randolph Churchill, mother of Winston Churchill, he prepared his war memories of Cuba. Money, cash on delivery and often before, was demanded constantly of James Pinker. He was not always fair to the hard-working Pinker. In February 1899, he was dealing with Mr Collis, proprieter of The Author's Syndicate agency, asking whether a story, 'The Blue Hotel', had sold in

England and asking for a typed copy of the manuscript and a record of the papers and magazines to which it had been sent by Mr Collis. The next day, Crane was sending a Whilomville story, 'whacking good . . . 4000 words', to Pinker and begging for one hundred and fifty pounds within ten days. The Whilomville tale, Crane reckoned, already represented forty pounds of that sum, and he would quickly earn the balance. Crane and Cora eternally counted each word written as pence in the pound to be paid directly on submission of such material to Pinker. 'If you can stick to your end,' wrote Crane on or about 26 February, 'all will go finely and I will bombard you so hard with ms that you will think you are living in Paris during the siege.' Collis, meanwhile, was being instructed to submit 'The Blue Hotel' to the *Westminster Gazette* and sell it for fifteen pounds – 'whenever I have to sacrifice myself upon the alter [sic] of copyright, I have found them good priests.' Cora now and again wrote on Crane's behalf to the long suffering Pinker, fulminating against blockheaded editors: 'I cannot understand what can be the reason for the English publishers refusing such stuff as those children [sic] stories and "God Rest Ye". They seem to fancy themselves as judges of literature but to me they appear to be a good set of idiots to refuse really clever and artistic stuff and to print the rot they do.' Ticking off Pinker, in tones she would be ill-advised to use to her cook, Cora advised him that 'Mr Reynolds has pleased us very much by his prompt placing of these stories [in America]. We hope that you will be equally successful in placing the serial rights of *Active Service* and in also, perhaps by pointing out to London publishers that Harpers have not only thought "Lynx Hunting" and "The Angel Child" good enough but have asked for *all* the Whilomville stories that Mr Crane may write, that they have a lot to learn and that the firm of Pinker are the people to teach them.'

Much of this imperious imperative tone stemmed from anxiety, but also from a firm faith in the value of Crane's work. To judge by the royal 'we' in the letter, to refuse it would be *lèse-majesté* by an impertinent publisher unaware of the sterling worth of Baron Brede. Pinker, in milder tones, replied: 'In condemning English editors for their want of appreciation, one must remember that Mr Crane's reputation is not established on this side as it is in the States, so that his name does not carry so much weight with the readers of sixpenny magazines, which are, after all, what one has most to depend on.'

Crane was pressing ahead with his novel *Active Service* and had great hopes of it: 'I expect to get in the neighbourhood of £600 for the American serial rights.' On 17 March, he was able to report to Pinker that 'the novel is now at 48000 words . . . I am confident that it will be the most successful book that I have ever published.' Each new piece of work, remark the editors of Crane's letters, was thought by Crane and Cora to be an artistic and financial improvement over the previous one. And haste, as ever, was of the essence. Cora, on 25 April, wrote minatorily to Pinker asking him to 'give editors to understand that two weeks is the limit to keep Mr Crane's copy. Please make this your fast rule for all of Mr Crane's work. Editors have always subscribed to this for me, when I have been disposing of Mr Crane's stuff.' She enclosed, with this note, twenty-two chapters of *Active Service*. Cora, though deficient in principles of domestic economy at Brede, and a self-confessed spendthrift of money, energy, and emotion, still retained a sufficient grasp of business efficiency to urge it upon others.

But still the Crane's income was small and inadequate. In August, a letter from Cora to Pinker advised him that 'The wine man must be satisfied and Mr Crane must have a change or I fear he will break down and we can't have that.' Appeals to the charity of the Cranes fell on deaf ears: a subscription for Oscar Wilde did not move them, since, apart from a disinclination to aid Wilde at all, 'I owe my brother too much money to bother about helping with subscriptions for a mildewed chump like Wilde . . . All I ought to do right now is pay some of my debts. My charities begin in the right pants pocket.' The wine man's bill, for thirty-five pounds, was more pressing than the trials of a fellow author. Working constantly, Crane had begun another novel – *The O'Ruddy* – thirty-six thousand words of which he despatched to Pinker on or about 7 November, a week after his twenty-eighth birthday, and then he began to interest himself in the preparations being made for the Brede Christmas party, writing to HB Marriott-Watson, a contemporary author, about the free play he proposed to give to the villagers: 'I have written some awful rubbish which our friends will on that night speak out to the parish.

'But to make the thing historic, I have hit upon a plan of making the programmes choice by printing thereon a terrible list of authors of the comedy and to that end I have asked Henry James, Robert Barr, Joseph Conrad, AEW Mason, HG Wells, Edwin Pugh, George Gissing, Rider Haggard and yourself to write a mere word – any word "it", "they", "you", – any word and thus identify themselves with this crime.' This 'distinguished rabble' was invited to attend the festivities.

It was on 22 April 1900, some four months after the events of Christmas, that Wells wrote his letter about the probability of Crane recovering from his latest haemorrhage. Wells cannot have been as surprised as he professed to be about the spring haemorrhage, since Cora sent him 'in a drizzling dawn along a wet road to call up a doctor in Rye' on 29 December when Crane fainted and haemorrhaged after the Christmas party and the play at Brede Place. Wells remembers the events, in which he and his wife participated, very vividly: 'We were urged to come over and, in a postscript, to bring any bedding and blankets we could spare. We arrived in a heaped-up Sandgate cab, rather in advance of the guests from London. We were given a room over the main gateway in which there was a portcullis and an owl's nest, but at least we got a room. Nobody else did – because although some thirty or forty invitations had been issued, there were not as a matter of fact more than three or four bedrooms available. One of them however was large and its normal furniture had been supplemented by a number of hired trucklebeds and christened the Girls' Dormitory, and in the attic an array of shake-downs was provided for the men. Husbands and wives were torn apart.

'Later on we realized that the sanitary equipment of Brede House dated from the seventeenth century, an interesting historical detail, and such as there was indoors, was accessible only through the Girls' Dormitory. Consequently the wintry countryside next morning was dotted with wandering, melancholy, preoccupied men guests.' Eight people sat down to an elaborate American-style Christmas dinner, and the rest of Crane's guests arrived on Boxing Day to rehearse the play while servants, beds, an orchestra, seasonal foods, and candle sconces, ordered specially in advance, were disposed about the house in preparation for the ball and the play which was performed in the Brede Hill schoolhouse on 28 December to the immense amusement of the participants and the gratification of an audience that had toiled through dreadful weather to attend.

Henry James elected to remain at home, advising AEW Mason to beware of rapacious American beauties. Absentees also included Robert Barr, Conrad, Rider Haggard and Gissing, but things went very well without them. Wells remembers 'that party as an extraordinary lark – but shot, at the close, with red intimations of a coming tragedy. We danced in a big oak-panelled room downstairs, lit by candles stuck upon iron sconces that Cora Crane had improvised with the help of the Brede blacksmith. Unfortunately, she had not improvised grease guards and after a time everybody's back showed a patch of composite candle-wax, like the flash on the coat of a Welsh Fusilier. When we were not dancing or romping we were waxing the floor or rehearsing a play vamped up by AEW Mason, Crane, myself and others. It was a ghost play, very allusive and fragmentary . . . We revelled until two or three every night and came down towards mid-day to breakfasts of eggs and bacon, sweet potatoes from America and beer.' The provision of American victuals was a novelty. Wells had been given some kernels of corn by Crane and Cora, and was asked how he had liked the stuff. Wells had enjoyed it very much, but was puzzled when asked to describe how he had cooked it. 'Cook it! We didn't cook it. We cut it when it was six inches high and ate it for salad. Wasn't that right?' Wells, in his innocent ignorance of the social conventions of American manners, further disgusted Crane when he sat at the card table gossiping with an old friend while Crane attempted to teach some of his guests the finer points of poker. 'In any decent saloon in America,' he shouted, 'you'd be shot for talking like that at poker,' and gave up trying to instruct them.

'That was the setting in which I remember Crane,' says Wells. 'He was profoundly weary and ill, if I had been wise enough to see it, but I thought him sulky and reserved.' Wells, asking Crane whether he was writing anything, got the joyless answer, 'I got to do them, I got to do them,' speaking of some stories Pinker had fixed for him to write. 'He was essentially the helpless artist,' in Wells's view, 'he wasn't the master of his party, he wasn't the master of his home; his life was altogether out of control; he was being carried along. What he was still clinging to, but with a dwindling zest, was artistry.' That night of 29 December 1899, Crane was standing, after the party, strumming a guitar – or, some say, a violin. A guest approached, as he crooned softly with his face close to the strings. Crane fainted against his friend's shoulder, haemorrhaging from the lungs.

Robert Barr, hearing of the party and its gory aftermath, thought it was 'all over with the boy, he might last two years.' Crane was twenty-eight, and he had barely six months left to him. On 2 January, Cora reported that he was 'in bed but is still keeping at his work.' She begged Pinker, asking again for money, 'please do not get out of patience with these constant requests for money "*at once*".' She and Crane were very much distressed by the constant pressing of creditors. *The O'Ruddy* was being sent to Pinker, chapter by chapter, together with instalments of Crane's work on *Great Battles of the World*. Cheques were being returned by the Crane's bank at Oxted, and Cora was in constant agitation to salvage her credit there. On 5 January, Crane rashly wrote to Pinker, 'I must have the money. I cannot get on without it. If you cannot send £50 by the next mail, I will have to find a man who can. I know this is abrupt and unfair, but self-preservation forces my game with you precisely as it did with Reynolds.' Cora, two days later, rushed to reassure Pinker that 'Mr Crane intended no threat and will keep all engagements with you.' Pinker was too valuable a man to lose through a fit of anxious irritability. Pinker had been a bulwark against the deluge, but even he had his limits as a generous businessman and friend: 'I am sure it is not necessary for me to tell you that you and Mr Crane may always count on all the help I can give, but as you know, the demands on my help have been greater in extent and persistency than was ever contemplated . . .'

On 9 January, despite Pinker's muted warning, and the recent call for fifty pounds, Cora was obliged to write again to Pinker, prefacing a request for one hundred and fifty pounds with the assurance that 'Mr Crane is very faithful to any agreement and he appreciates the fact that you have advanced money upon stories before you received payment for them yourself.' Cora offered her own services as a go-between, to prise money out of Methuen who had not yet contracted for *The O'Ruddy*. That was a desperate shot, and Cora, at her wit's end, even suggested that Crane might drop *The O'Ruddy* altogether and concentrate on short stories for instant cash. She resorted to stratagems to avoid local creditors knowing the precise state of their finances: on 8 February, she asked Pinker, 'Please wire me on Friday night but state the words rather ambiguously because my post-master is my grocer.' On 24 March, bailiffs were threatening, and cheques to the amount of sixteen pounds had been returned by the bank. Crane hoped that *The O'Ruddy* would pull him out and ahead of debt, but 'I only question the wisdom of my abandoning my lucrative short story game for this long thing which doesn't pay (much) until the end.'

On 31 March, Crane haemorrhaged again, very severely, and Cora, who was in Paris, immediately wired Moreton Frewen and a friend, Mrs Hoyt de Friese, to obtain from the American Embassy the name of London's best lung specialist. The Embassy introduced her to Dr JT McLaglen and, with two nurses, McLaglen proceeded immediately to Brede Place. Cora arrived on 3 April, and three days later wrote to Pinker to say that the specialist's fee was fifty pounds. She had paid it by cheque, and required that sum to be deposited at her London bank to meet it. Sanford Bennett, who hurried from France when he heard of Crane's collapse, found Cora 'lashing her skirt with one of his [Crane's] riding crops. She broke into frantic denunciation of herself for allowing so much entertainment at Brede. It was a ghastly quarter of an hour. She finally sank into a chair, sobbing . . . She had no real hope of his recovery. But she showed her courage, and cheered him up. . . . There was something very fine about her.'

Ready money was essential: the nurses cost two pounds, four shillings and sixpence each per week, and their expenses and medicines had also to be paid for. Crane was dictating copy for 'The Battle of Solferino' from his bed. To Wells, Cora admitted, 'I fear that we shall have to give up Brede Place and go to a more bracing place on the sea.' Doctors gave Cora some hope that Crane might pull through, and according to Cora the local doctor, Dr Skinner, was of the opinion 'that the trouble seems only superficial; not deeply rooted.' On 23 April, Crane was able to be moved downstairs to sit in the sun the next day. Cora had resolved to rent Brede Place to any likely tenant 'at a reasonable figure'. Pinker was asked to look out for a prospective taker. Dr Skinner had meantime amended his view and had all but given Crane up. He advised immediate removal to Bournemouth, or a sea voyage. McLaglen dissented. He advised that Crane should not be moved for at least two months, though later a change of air might be advisable. He did not give much for Crane's chances: 'I would not readily take a hopeless view of his case.' A letter from Wells had cheered Crane, since it spoke bracingly of his imminent recovery, but privately Cora advised Wells that, although the lung trouble seemed over and the right lung was 'entirely unaffected,' an abscess 'which seems to open from time to time in the bowels – or rectum, makes him suffer the most awful agony. And it takes away his strength in an alarming fashion. The abscess seems to have upset the bowels too. So he is very weak. Then the *fever* (Cuban fever) comes for an hour or two each day. The chills seem to have stopped the past week.'

RL Stevenson had benefited from Bournemouth and from sea voyages, and had experimented with the climate at Davos in Switzerland which was also recommended by the Duchess of Manchester, a friend of Moreton and Clara Frewen. She offered to intercede with a Dr Doughty there, to try to have Crane admitted to his Sanitorium. But Cora favoured the rigorous Nordracht treatment and on 8 May she outlined her plans to Pinker: 'He is carried on an air bed on a stretcher to *Rye*. There an invalid carriage will take him, the nurses one doctor and myself, to Dover. Here we rest for one or perhaps two weeks at the Lord Warden Hotel to have sea air and rest then a deck cabin to Calais and there an invalid carriage awaits us. *It* costs *sixteen* first class fares and there is no change to the Black Forest. . . . With expenses at the Hotel at Dover it will mean £100 – to get there and I must have this within the week. Now you know the situation . . . This is a matter of life and death so please do your best. The lung has healed over and he has a chance to get well and live for years if we can get him out of England.'

Cora also appealed for money to Conrad, who confessed himself, miserable, as 'a man without connections, without influence and without means. The daily subsistence is a matter of anxious thought for me. What can I do? I am already in debt to my two publishers . . . it is not even in my power to jeopardize my own future to serve you . . . my future, such as it is, is already pawned. You can't imagine how much I suffer in writing thus to you.'

By 12 May, Pinker had still not come up with ready money, and Cora again appealed to him. Crane had Conrad on his mind at this time, and took time to write to Sanford Bennet, asking him to assist as best he could: 'Garnett does not think it likely that his writing will ever be popular outside the ring of men who write. He is poor and a gentleman and proud. His wife is not strong and they have a kid. If Garnett should ask you to help pull wires for a place on the Civil List for Conrad please do me the last favour.' Conrad was of the opinion that Moreton

Frewen paid most of Cora's expenses of moving Crane to Dover and the Black Forest. However it was done, Cora was writing from the Lord Warden Hotel in Dover to Wells on 15 May. Crane was too ill to see anyone, she reported.

Jessie Conrad has an affecting account of the last, mad dash to Calais – though she did not see it except, on her own evidence, vicariously in a dream. Her vision accorded very well with the facts 'of dear Stephen lying on a stretcher being placed in an ambulance with two nurses in attendance and Cora Crane, and of the ambulance being driven to the coast as quickly as possible . . . When the post arrived an hour later a letter told us the exact substance of my dream and begged us to go that morning to the "Lord Warden" in Dover where the poor fellow lay awaiting a calm sea to cross and try to reach the Black Forest in search of health. For poor Cora it was a pitiful business, she had not the means to pay for meals in the "Lord Warden". The nurses were fed outside, but I know the wife often went without.'

Moves to relieve Crane's financial difficulties were afoot. Moreton Frewen had asked Cora for a list of Crane's debts and had approached the American banker JP Morgan, who indicated on 18 May, three days after Crane reached Dover, that he would be glad to see Frewen about Crane at any time. On 5 June, the day Crane died at Badenweiler, Henry James – without having been asked for his help – spontaneously sent Cora fifty pounds asking her to 'dedicate it to whatever service it may best render my stricken young friend. It meagrely represents my tender benediction to him.' James, says Ford Madox Hueffer, 'suffered infinitely for that dying boy.' He invented a fiction, perfectly credible, that James had telegraphed to Wanamakers in the States for New England delicacies – 'from pumpkin pie to apple-butter and sausage meat and clams and soft-shell crabs and minced meat and . . . everything thinkable, so that the poor lad should know once more and finally those fierce joys.' James had sent a case of champagne to RL Stevenson when he and his wife Fanny had set off for America, so it was not improbable that James had sent, perhaps, for American delicacies for Crane – but he did not. The invention was, says Leon Edel, a product of Hueffer's shaky ego to give legendary form to James whom he revered.

The Cranes reached Badenweiler on 28 May and installed themselves in a room on the second floor of the Villa Eberhardt, one of the buildings of the Sanitorium which was run on principles much like those of Dr Trudeau's celebrated Sanitorium at Saranac Lake in the Adirondacks. It was fiendishly expensive and Cora, to keep Crane's mind at rest, had to lie to him, saying that she had three hundred pounds in cash. He dictated notes for *The O'Ruddy* to Cora who also corrected proofs by his bedside. Crane was not restful: 'He lives over everything in dreams,' Cora wrote to Moreton Frewen, 'and talks aloud constantly . . . I nearly went mad yesterday and the nurse gave me some drug that made me sleep for hours, so I'm fresh again today. He worries so about his debts and about our not being able to live here.' On 4 June, Crane was given an injection of morphine and slipped into a coma from which he never wakened. On 5 June 1900, at three o'clock in the morning, Stephen Crane died. His body was taken back to London, at some expense, where it lay open to view in the mortuary before being shipped to New York where Crane was buried in the family plot at Elizabeth, New Jersey.

SEVEN

Conrad Aiken at Jeake's House

In 1920, on a visit to England, the American poet Conrad Aiken wrote to his wife, Jessie McDonald Aiken, to ask: 'How *do* you feel about the winter here? I consider quite seriously Oxford, London, and Rye.' Rye, he was assured by friends, 'is lovely; it is where Henry [James] lived.' Aiken's friend and contemporary, TS Eliot, who had been two years senior to Aiken when they had both been students at Harvard, had settled permanently in England and, though Aiken did not 'know how well I could work here . . . it might be just worth trying. Even if it failed, it might have been worth doing.' He was just thirty-one years old, the author of five books of poems, the father of two children – John and Jane, who had been born in 1913 and 1917 – a third child had died at birth in 1915 – and had been living, since 1919, in the village of South Yarmouth, on Cape Cod, Massachussets. Two children having begun to strain their modest resources, he and Jessie had been obliged to live as cheaply as possible. His first visit to England in 1914 had been intended as a fishing trip, an attempt at 'deliberately widening one's circle,' while the 1920 trip was intended as a reconnaissance of the educational system for the children, an attempt to find a publisher for his fifth book of poems, and to renew acquaintance with friends.

He returned, not reluctantly, to Cape Cod in August 1920 and in the next month published his sixth book of poems, *The*

House of Dust: A Symphony. He was reviewed regularly and seriously by American critics and fellow-poets, and had achieved a promising reputation that had not crossed the Atlantic to any notable extent. Aiken himself found the English literary scene unsympathetic: '*The Times* is goodish, but somewhat sclerotic, and certainly none of the *Mercury* critics is satisfactory: they whet one's appetite for the analytic and the wise but give one little to chew on.' But England offered a good education for the two children, and Rye beckoned ineluctably. In *Ushant*, Aiken's coded autobiography, he writes: 'And wasn't Saltinge [Rye], symbolically now, that country, the essence of it, the very *Ding an sich* of D's [Aiken] lifelong search – wasn't this perhaps the very center, so that, although he didn't yet know it, he had at last come home, and all the more fittingly guided thither by a tutelary genius, the *genius loci*, who had himself made his way to it by a lifelong process of need, and analysis of need – the need, too, of an American?' Here Aiken is referring to Henry James who had lived at Lamb House 'where he had wrought those fabulously involute symphonies of his, those multiple palimpsests, in which, as in the changeable signs of one's childhood, each new angle of approach revealed a different shade or nuance of moral, or immoral, meaning?' Aiken, considering that his natural curiosity to see the house of the Master was perhaps 'merely tantamount to a return, a revisitation – a renewal of inspection of an area, a province, which . . . he had long been possessed of, or had been put in possession of, by the old Master himself,' looked upon 'the soft red brick of the quiet facade and the little white stone urns above the cornice.' To look thus was 'merely to read again . . . one of those lucid masterpieces of exploration which in every generation are the gift of a great writer – the gift, indeed, of a new country.'

Rye was going to be home: 'it had been home from that very moment, on the bedroom floor at Savannah, when the poet of White Horse Vale had first beckoned to him . . . everything was at once familiar: the mysterious familiarity of the *déjà vu*, but this time on a transcendental and overpowering scale. The tiny blossoms of the Mother of Thousands in the crannies of the churchyard wall: the jackdaws circling the Tower . . . the pint of beer at the King's Head, or the Ship Inn, and the narrow cobbled street that took him, down the hill, past the house that was still invisible, still under the snow of the future, but already, for all that, his own – all this, under the *ting-tang* of the golden Quarter-Boys, and in the center of the immense Marsh, that vast and intricate map of green, with its numberless canals and dykes and tree-bordered fields, where, as far as the eye could see, grazed the numberless sheep, all this had been here all his life, to be sure; but now, by some miracle of temporal transformation, it was as if all his *own* life, every instant of it, had been spent at Saltinge; for as long as he could remember, he had been leading a double life.' This sense of *déjà vu* on coming to Rye can be partly accounted for, in the opinion of Aiken's son John, by the sense of having returned to scenes of his childhood. Aiken had been brought up in Savannah, Georgia, and 'Rye reminded him of Savannah in microcosm. There were a lot of local similarities, and photographs of Rye and Savannah point up these similarities quite remarkably. Then, too, Jeake's House, the house my father bought in Mermaid Street, reminded him of the house he had been brought up in.'

In the spring of 1922, Aiken and his family moved from London, where they had wintered, to Lookout Cottage in Winchelsea, a couple of miles from Rye. Secker had brought out his narrative poems, *Punch*, in October 1921, but by December it had had 'no sale and no reviews . . . Other papers haven't even listed it as among books received.' *The Times* had noticed it, briefly, but only to note, wrongly, 'that it's mostly in *rhymed decasyllabics* (there's not one in the book); . . . O grief, frustration, and thoughts of suicide! Why on earth did I come here to begin all over again this abominable and hopeless struggle for *some* sort of recognition! What an idiot I am, what a preposterous biped wearing spectacles and an air of melancholy, a walking lamentation, a grief clad in a union-suit.' It took time for Aiken to become accustomed to English provincial life.

In March 1923, he was writing to Malcolm Cowley that life in the country was to be preferred to life in the city but that, 'As for myself, I really dont [sic] know what I shall do. We are comfortable here, it's a lovely place, rent is cheap, views and walks and tennis and beer are plentiful, it isn't far from London (only resemblance to Kew), the scrotumtightening sea is only a mile away, and it agrees with John and Jane even better than S. Yarmouth Mass. Still I don't feel settled here, yet, at any rate, and though I have been able to resume the deadly agonies of verse, thanks to its charm and peace, for the first time in several years, I am restless, feel a little cramped and repressed . . .' He missed American everyday detail – a slap on the back, or a peanut stand – and was feeling isolated in a country whose literary folk did not interest him (though America's literary folk didn't much interest him either) and Eliot, he complained, kept him at arm's length. But he was working, and in 1923 he published *The Pilgrimage of Festus* in the United States. The English edition appeared in February 1924, by which time Aiken had bought Jeake's House in Mermaid Street in Rye for seventeen hundred pounds (seven thousand dollars, approximately).

To Robert Linscott, he gave details of the house and his considerable alarm at such a tremendous undertaking: 'beams and panels and studios and views and a hotelful of bedrooms . . . Poverty from now on forever will be our lot. We scorn delights and live laborious days. Reviews must be written as by a syndicate, potboiler short stories delivered like bullets from a machine gun, plays turned out once a week, novels elaborated at magniloquent length, poetry alas eschewed world without end amen. I don't know why we did it. Nobody knows. We felt miserable when we were trying to make up our minds: we bought it without minds: we have been miserable to the point of unconsciousness ever since. We feel as if we had bought the Crystal Palace or the Taj Mahal. So vast, so tall the establishment that we are sure that at the end of a year we shall encounter, here and there, rooms unnoticed before, filled with mice and foul with bats, squealing with rats and roped with webs, littered with bones and stinking of ghosts.' The house had been built by the Jeake family in 1689 as a woolstore, but had been converted to domestic use, which partly explains its quaint internal economy largely unchanged today. The Aikens had moved in by early May 1924, and on 4 September 1924 their second daughter, Joan, was born in the house. Simultaneously, he had begun only a few weeks before to 'set myself manfully morning after morning in turning out costive pages of novel.' The novel was *Blue Voyage*, a project that had simmered in his mind for two years. The narrator of *Blue Voyage*, Demarest, a young, literary man on his way to Europe, later became the hero 'D', of *Ushant*, a code letter indicating Aiken himself. Aiken was beginning to feel more acclimatised, more acculturated. To GB Wilbur, on 21 September 1924, he wrote: 'I wish I could make out why it is that I am so much freer to *write* here (in England) than at home – freer, that is, to write verse or fiction, while not nearly so free for careful or spontaneously vigorous and assured *criticism*. The latter I find extremely painful and difficult; . . . To write verse or fiction, on the other hand, is perhaps easier for me than it has been since the delightful years 1916-7 in Boston . . .'

In May 1924, Aiken was suffering from an anal fistula which necessitated an operation in London. That being unsuccessful, a further operation was carried out in December 1925. When he returned to Rye on or about New Year's Day 1926, he discovered himself to be 'weak and fat, fatter than ever, unable to button clothes or see feet except in mirrors . . . no money in the bank, but two weeks food supply and half a bottle of Irish whisky. Joan had a sty in the corner of the left eye, the stovepipe in the study had rusted shut, damper immovable, and trying to repair same I removed epidermis from index finger (said finger of vital importance for morning and evening rites relating to rectum; painful now to both rectum and finger). Floods on all marshes, rove the jaded eye where it will . . .' To recuperate, Aiken went with a friend, Martin Armstrong, to Spain in the spring of 1926 for a couple of months, but when he returned to Rye there was still no money in the bank. On 13 May 1926,

Aiken wrote to George Wilbur, 'Both Jessie and I have got to the point where we worry *all the time* about making both ends meet, our expenses increase hourly, and the more anxious I get the less I write, and the less saleably.' They tried to sell Jeake's House, but in the end it seemed more likely that the financial situation might be retrieved if Aiken returned to the United States to visit his publishers in New York and Boston. In the autumn of 1926, Aiken set sail.

This visit was not fruitful in terms of increasing income, but it was fateful in one respect – in November 1926, in Cambridge, Boston, a young woman – Clarissa Lorenz – arrived at the house of Aiken's aunt, Edith Potter, to interview the poet for the *Boston Evening Transcript*. She was working, intermittently, as a freelance journalist specialising in literary profiles, moonlighting from a secretarial job. Aiken had been represented to her as 'a major American poet grossly neglected,' and Clarissa immediately fell in love with the subject of her article. 'What magic!' she wrote in her autobiography, *Lorelei Two: My Life with Conrad Aiken*. 'My heart swelled. I had an elaborate set of defenses against poetry, but none against poets.' She was twenty-seven, Aiken was thirty-seven. In that interview, they both flirted a little with one another, and arranged to meet again. In all, in that week before he sailed for England, Aiken and Clarissa met five times. Clarissa 'became increasingly entangled and bewitched . . . caught in a silken net of eloquence.' She had just freed herself from one man, to become enslaved by another at a point when she had no firm bases in her life: 'I had little to offer any man beyond an unformed character. A fugitive from school, church, and life, I had renounced my German heritage, neglected my talents, and lost God in the shuffle. To quote a contemporary psychiatrist, I had one foot in schizophrenia and the other on a banana peel.' Aiken, in *Ushant*, describes his encounter with Clarissa as a 'shattering disequilibration' and their first courtship as a 'magical moment when their every most random movement was that of the dance . . .'

Aiken returned promptly to Boston, and Clarissa, two

months later, in January 1927, and took up where letters between them had left off. He was tied to Jessie, his wife, and to the children, but, according to her account in her autobiography, Clarissa – known to Aiken as Jerry – refused to be merely a mistress, a casual affair. She suggested, in December 1926, a clean break: 'You must put me out of your life.' But by 'mid-January 1927 my high-flown intentions crumbled. . . . Jessie had consented to a divorce, if he still wished to marry me after a year's trial.' In November 1928, Conrad Aiken returned to Rye to negotiate a divorce from Jessie who, meanwhile, had decided to marry Aiken's friend Martin Armstrong. They had been unhappy for a while: in *Ushant*, Aiken refers to 'the anguish of Lorelei One [Jessie], alone there [at Jeake's House] with her sense of betrayal and shame, her grievously wounded pride, waking every morning, as Aunt Sibyl [Edith Potter] had said to him, to find there was no longer any floor beside her bed, no floor at all to step upon, nothing, nothing to sustain her.' This reference to the philosophy of Bishop Berkeley, that nothing is real, is followed by the reflection that life becomes beautiful when the element of death at its core is appreciated. There had been a death in Jeake's House, a death of love, that gave the house 'dignity, the requisite echo or overtone of sorrow, of sadness, the reference to Virgil's *lacrimae rerum*; the far-off sound, barely audible, of the axe striking its first musical but murderous blow in the doomed orchard.' In the memory of John Aiken, 'the separation was rather a gradual process. I was old enough to notice that my mother was increasingly unhappy, and Conrad was more and more in the States. Joan was very young. But I don't think it affected us profoundly – the children continued to see him, and he continued to be the stimulating and loving, but carefree, parent he had always been.'

In February 1930, at Rutherford, New Jersey, Aiken and Clarissa (Jerry) Lorenz were married and they arrived in Rye in August of that year. They were accompanied by a young man, Malcolm Lowry, who had visited Aiken in Boston in August 1929 after having written him a letter on 13 March 1929. This almost irresistible letter of self-recommendation would perhaps have remained unanswered, like the first one Lowry had sent to Aiken in 1928, had it not held out the bait of a regular weekly income to the harassed poet:

> 'Well, I am a boy and you (respectfully) are a man old enough to be my father, and so again I may not talk of love in the way that Russell Green intended, but all the same, I may here substitute love for – shall we say – *filial affection* . . . The point is this.
>
> I suppose there are few things you would hate more than to be invested with any academic authority. Well, this I shall say. Next October I am going to Cambridge for three or four years to try and get an English Tripos and a degree. Until October I am more or less of a freelance and a perpetual source of anxiety to a bewildered parent. The bewildered parent in question would be willing to pay you 5 or 6 guineas a week (I should say six personally, but tacitly) if you would tolerate me for any period you like to name between now and then as a member of your household. Let me hasten to say that I would efface myself and not get in the way of your inspiration when it comes toddling along, that my appetite is flexible and usually entirely satisfied by cheese, that although I can't play chess and know little of the intricacies of gladioli, I too have heard the sea sound in strange waters, – sh-sh-sh like the hush in a conch shell – and I can wield a fair tennis racket. . . And I want to be in Rye at twilight and lean *myself* by the wall of the ancient town – *myself*, like ancient wall and dust and sky, and the purple dusk, grown old, grown old in heart. Remember, when I write like this, remember that I am not a schoolboy writing a gushing letter to Jeffrey Farnol or somebody.'

Lowry now interjected some flattery, and a fairly perfunctory line or two anticipating Aiken's possible rejection of the idea that he should act as Lowry's 'guardian and/or tutor', but continued: 'I do want to learn from you and to read your earliest and most inaccessible works and perhaps even your contributions to the *Dial*.' To Theodore Spencer, on 24 July

1929, Aiken wrote: 'My young genius arrives this week.' On 8 August, to Maurice Firuski, Aiken reported that 'Last Thursday there was a wildish party in celebration of young Lowry's arrival: . . . A wrestling match between L [owry] and me, at one in the morning, for possession of the porcelain lid on a w.c. tank, (!) ended with me in possession, but unconscious on my hearth, having slipped, fallen, cracked my head on hearth-and-shattered-porcelain simultaneous-like. I bled for 48 hours.' Lowry, nevertheless, seemed to Aiken to be 'a nice chap, but incredibly dirty and sloppy and helpless. Writes exceedingly well, and undoubtedly should do something.' He had arrived in Cambridge, Boston, according to Jerry's letter from Aiken, in a grimy state, 'dilapidated, wearing dirty tennis shoes and carrying a broken suitcase. He was penniless, having spent all his cash in Antigua on a young mulatto girl.' Aware of Aiken's own excitable career as a college man, Jerry took stock and decided, 'now I had to worry about an irresponsible young dipsomaniac.'

'Lowry was perfectly easy,' says John Aiken. 'He got drunk, of course, but so did Conrad. He was very good company and easy to talk to. A father and son relationship developed between Lowry and Conrad.' The first thing, almost, that Lowry and Aiken did when they got to Rye was to fall into the river. 'Around 9 p.m. a pair of muddied, bloodstreaked apparitions staggered into Jeake's House. In their alcoholic euphoria they had staged a javelin-throwing contest across the narrow inlet where the Rother, Brede, and Tillingham rivers converged. Conrad, failing to release his weapon, fell in while launching it. Malcolm then tumbled in after him. Fortunately the tide was low. How they managed to scramble up that slimy wall remains their secret,' says Clarissa.

They were back at Jeake's House, rented from Jessie at a rent of one hundred and twenty-five pounds a year. 'The ghosts make it a bargain,' remarked Aiken to his wife who looked, appalled, on 'a bat's cave smelling of dust, mold, mice, and ghosts, the vestibule festooned with cobwebs, wallpaper in shreds. A dark passageway led to the kitchen, the only window over the sink looking out on the garden, a jungle of weeds. No heating unit in the L-shaped dining room adjacent, or in the rooms above except a wee potbellied stove in Conrad's spacious study. Leaded windowpanes, buckled floorboards, one bathroom for eleven rooms. How had Jessie managed?' Much later, after Clarissa had gone, to be replaced by Lorelei III, Aiken thought of the house in terms described in *Ushant*: 'That house, and its rituals, that wonderfully but so lightly intricate continuum of living and loving – in which their tutelary genius, or *genius loci*, the benign inquisitive ghost of the great astrologer and mathematician [Samuel Jeake] (with his zenzicubes and zenzizenzicubes and zenzikes!) had become quite indispensably the symbol of the family – all this was now established by their communion as something which they would share forever: it would die when *they* died, but not before.'

Jeake's House was a site where friends foregathered: Aiken was not a man who displayed himself willingly as a public figure. His son John remarks, 'as a young man he had been very shy. As he grew older, he remained shy about two things – big parties and speaking in public. He would not speak in public, though he was perfectly prepared to talk about his work with his friends and read it aloud to them. He didn't much like gatherings of friends – he liked people in ones and twos, and he liked to have a proper conversation with them. . . . He knew a lot of the artistic people of Rye – particularly the painters Paul Nash and Edward Burra. Burra and Aiken did one another rather a lot of good, swapping ideas, and I think Ed talked more freely to Conrad than to almost anyone else.' Another painter, Laura Knight, and her husband, the literary critic Harold Monro, were among regular visitors to Jeake's House. Visits there were recalled in *Ushant*: 'by how many noble or beautiful or delightful spirits had it been lighted and blessed! Lighted by love, lighted by laughter, the kind of light that never goes out; . . .' Clarissa, recalling the early 1930s in Rye, remembers 'a host of memorables whose lives touched ours – the Knights [Laura and Harold], GB Shaw, Arthur Bliss, HD [the poet Hilda Doolittle], Thomas Hardy's widow, Phyllis Bottome [the novelist], . . . and among local celebrities EF Benson, Edward Burra, and Radclyffe Hall. . . . A mixture of retired Indian colonels, working classes, and creative artists made up the population that remained roughly at 3,500 over the centuries, with a sprinkle of "gliglis", bridge-playing gossips (who were currently blackballing Conrad for his wickedness)' Then, too, 'Conrad's six-o'clock pub-crawls with Malcolm set tongues wagging.'

John Aiken remembers the coolness of two old ladies, the Misses Jane and Mary Findlater, authors of lively but moral Victorian novels who, in their Scottish Presbyterian rectitude, disapproved of Aiken and his second marriage. It was difficult for the Aiken children to re-establish previous good relations with the two old ladies. And Clarissa, when shopping in Rye, was sensitive to the shopkeepers who would be sure to advise the shop assistant to put her purchases on the account of the *second* Mrs Aiken. The distinction, she considered, was made rather too pointedly. Rye did not take warmly to breaches of social propriety. *Ushant* contains a sharp observation of the atmosphere of Rye: 'the Vicar, Mr Birdlime, [Fowler] stopping D. one night on the Marsh, had somewhat intensely indicated, with a wave of his clawlike hand, "You can hear its little heart beat!" But also, as D. had refrained from replying to that gaunt figure, which was forever flapping about those windy streets like a jackdaw, you could hear its little tongue wag. The window-curtains stirred as one passed, stirred and were still again, and one was aware of the watchful eyes behind them. Hadn't the Mayor [EF Benson] himself, living and writing in the Old Master's house [Lamb House] – and what a desecration! – had his own satirical fling at its inordinate propensity to gossip and snobbery and social backbiting? [a reference to the Mapp and Lucia novels] All too true: and D. had often thought that it bore a sinister resemblance to that dark little walled town, in a story of Algernon Blackwood's, which was haunted by cats; where, every night, as soon as the moon was up, and its golden swale of light on the vast marsh, the inhabitants all came out on the walls in the form of cats. It would not have been in the least surprising to find this so at Saltinge [Rye] – there was undoubtedly a sense of evil in it . . .'

Yet Rye was irresistibly attractive – in the magnetic sense: 'Was it this curious combination of beauty and evil that perpetually drew to it such extraordinary people? so that the variety of its characters, whether well-known, or simply encountered by chance in the narrow streets, was as extravagant as that in any Elizabethan play?' Among the variety, Aiken numbered Nash, Burra, 'the Bengal Lancer' [Francis Yeats-Brown], and 'the Roaring Girls, [Radclyffe Hall and Una, Lady Troubridge] that astonishing pair – and extremely entertaining, too – who could be heard almost every morning bawling out the wretched little tailor in the High Street, or flinging back at him, all publicly, a badly made pair of breeches.' Edith Potter, from Boston, wrote that the Aikens 'seem always to enjoy life there so much, you seem always to be having such a good time, and to see so many people! I don't know how you do it, and with so little money!' But 'Aunt Sibyl' did not know of Rye as 'a cheese full of mites' and 'the devious and Daedalian ways of Saltinge' – though, had she known of the true nature of Rye society, she would have been entranced and in her very element.

Clarissa was less enchanted or fascinated. Not only had she Aiken to deal with and battle with, but Lowry's 'presence complicated life at a time when I had to simplify it somehow.' There was a constant shortage of money, and she felt her own career as a journalist was increasingly secondary to Aiken's writing. She grappled as best she could with the difficulties of Jeake's House, and with the cooking: 'I found myself catering to a gourmand [Lowry] and a gourmet, finicky Conrad expecting a Cordon Bleu cuisine. His breakfast egg had to be coddled three minutes exactly. His dislikes included "promiscuous salads", stews, casseroles and that unholy trinity of cabbage, cauliflower, and Brussels sprouts.' Though Malcolm Lowry 'tried hard not to be a nuisance,' and although Clarissa felt maternal towards this rumpled, tousled, none-too-clean, but obliging and admiring devotee of her husband, she regarded him largely as 'a caged lion . . . never been housebroken . . .

Definitely no mixer . . . How much longer will Conrad put up with this madman? . . . Between the two of them I'm fast going dotty.' Both Lowry and Aiken were drinking hard and regularly, though, according to Clarissa, Aiken denied that he was becoming alcoholic: 'Don't try to change me . . . A poet without alcohol is no real poet . . . To say I'm a heavy drinker is just one of your neuroses. I'm a normal drinker.' But he later admitted 'that he was never sober while writing the Preludes.' During the early 1930s, in Rye, with Clarissa, Aiken worked hard and regularly. John Aiken can remember, nigh on fifty years later, how his father 'worked in the big top floor room, with a view over the Marsh,' and that he would work 'often all morning. Then to the pub at lunchtime, and in the afternoon he'd take it easy – perhaps sleep for a while, or go for a walk, or play tennis. His output was enormous. When he was at his most unhappy, disoriented, when he was married to Jerry in the mid-1930s, that was almost the cream of his output. That was when he finished *Great Circle* and wrote many of the "Preludes".'

In 1932, Aiken attempted suicide. He became more conscious of the history of violence in his father, and of his dependence on 'the tray on the sideboard' as a means of escape from the knowledge of how much he had provoked and had to cope with in his own and other people's lives. 'He had experienced, and was experiencing, the shock as of an enormous exposure:' he wrote in *Ushant* '. . . was there to be no anaesthetic? no refuge, at intervals – from that self-imposed glare of isolation, which so burned the eyes and heart, – or from the more normally human and social problems in which his departure from Saltinge, and return to it, had so pressingly involved him? . . . The half-quarterns of White Horse – and how appropriate *that* had been – or Booth's yellow gin, were the libations for the god of forgetfulness . . .' Paul Nash and Malcolm Lowry were bulwarks against despair – they shared it, transmuting it through their own perceptions of it – but Clarissa could not share in his vision or save him from its consequences. When she had gone out one evening to the cinema, Aiken took a moderate drink and, according to the account in *Ushant*, 'sat himself down to read Wyndham Lewis, under the electric light in the little subterranean kitchen, with the gas-rings and gas oven fizzing softly behind him. He was perfectly serene: he had made up his mind with absolute calm: it seemed to him that he had no, or few, regrets: he thought he had done what he could, with his volatile oddment of a share of life - that trick on the roundabout – and that he had now had perhaps as much of the vision as he could bear, and more than – obviously – he could find any adequate expression for. The flies dropped one by one from the ceiling, fell to the floor, spun, and died.' Suddenly, he remembered a letter in his bedroom. It was urgent that he should destroy it, and he managed to haul himself from the gas-filled kitchen, drag himself upstairs to retrieve the letter, and return to the kitchen and the article by Wyndham Lewis. The next thing he knew, he 'was lying flat on his back on the dining-room floor, and trying to sit up for the drink of straight gin which Lorelei [Clarissa] had poured for him.' Aiken, as he himself admits, had wanted to live – he had, in fact, attempted to crawl to the kitchen door in order to open it, but had been overcome and unable to do so. Clarissa had come back from the cinema an hour earlier than intended, and had found him collapsed against the door. It had been an episode that opened up a 'second existence' for Aiken – 'a whole dazzling and unexpected existence. Release, yes:' the past was finished with and he felt an obligation to the future. The past held ghosts: old friends had passed away – John Fletcher had been certified insane and committed, Harold Monro was dead, John Freeman had died, and Eliot was 'estranged.' To Henry Murray, in November, Aiken wrote, 'What next? London has become a city of ghosts for me, and I find myself almost, but not quite, too weary to set about the sad labour of making new friends, contacts, which will presumably suffer the same fate. I *have* the impulse, however, and more so now that I'm posthumous, and have begun to reach out here and there, and to find that it warms and wakes me to do so.'

One result of the attempt at suicide, aside from having given Aiken 'a comforting contempt of death' was, as he remarked in a letter of 24 October to Henry Murray, that 'it has brought J [erry] and myself much closer together, and in a better way than before – everything is more real.' Clarissa had been given a hard time: Aiken was intensely jealous of her previous relationships with men, and he conceived the notion that she and Paul Nash were flirting with some serious intent. In *Lorelei Two*, her autobiography, Clarissa gives this account of one of her set-tos with Aiken:

> 'And what did Paul give you? The glad knee?'
>
> 'No, just the glad eye.'
>
> 'I daresay you played right along with him, probably dissecting me in the bargain. If only I could believe you had a sense of honor,' Conrad said. 'God knows I want to, but I'm becoming more and more paralyzed with suspicion. Your whole history is one of promiscuity.' Oh God, I thought, here we go again. 'From infancy to adultery?'
>
> 'Never mind the wisecracks.' His eyes narrowed. 'Do you wonder that I dream about your sex orgies?'
>
> 'That's your problem, not mine,' I said. 'Punishing me for your dreams will boomerang.' I took the vegetables out of the cold box. 'Why do you get so upset if I smile at a man? Are you so mean and prudish that you can't bear to see me enjoying myself? Do you condemn every woman who flirts with you?'
>
> 'No, but I wouldn't trust her if she was my wife.'
>
> 'You make no distinction between flirting and fornicating?'
>
> 'None. One leads to the other,' Conrad said.

This last statement, in Aiken's case, was very often true. 'He was fairly promiscuous until his declining years,' says John Aiken, and Aiken himself makes no bones about his passion for women in *Ushant*. 'Clarissa was unhappy,' John Aiken says. 'She would go off to France on a bicycling tour without Conrad; she wrote interviews with literary people, but she was not on an intellectual level with my father. She used to make social gaffes, and Conrad would point them out. He was rather free-spoken about the quality of her cooking.' But Clarissa got on well with the children, and Aiken took a good deal of time to stimulate them. Joan, at age seven or eight, began to write what her brother describes as 'a lot of very adult poetry,' and John himself was an expert chess-player (he played matches at Lamb House with EF Benson) and a gifted piano-player. These quick and clever children needed to be inspired, and Aiken was the father to take the duty seriously and imaginatively. The children took to Clarissa, and they enjoyed Lowry when he visited from Cambridge. 'I can't remember ever seeing him conspicuously drunk while the children visited,' says Clarissa in *Lorelei Two*. 'Gentle, shy, diffident, he seemed rather wistful about their prior claim to Conrad's affections. They in turn treated him with the cautious manner one would a natural phenomenon like Vesuvius . . . The children came and went. A smokescreen rose around us, sadness and tension went underground only to reappear when farewells were said.'

Aiken was not unconscious of his irritability. In a letter to Theodore Spencer on 20 May 1931 Aiken wrote in a miasma of despair about domestic conditions and his depression, a continuous note of anxiety focussing on the trivia of life that buzzed round his head like gnats, too many to be lightly brushed away as temporary discomforts. Nine months later, in February 1932, he was still complaining, 'Life is just one goddamned thing after another,' and Clarissa felt that her 'inner landscape was almost as murky as his.' Aiken, she felt, was a genius, but that she was there in his life and his house only as a prop to Aiken's ego and that her 'drawbacks only reminded him of his own. I still hadn't the faintest idea what made a poet tick. The care and feeding of a bard was beyond me.' The summer of 1932 was fraught with tensions: Clarissa's diary read, 'The walls begin to crumble. Scribner's magazine rejected G. C. [*Great Circle*] for serialization. If only I were some use. Kemp [Kempton Potter Aiken Taylor, Conrad's brother] cabled, "Sorry, bust" to C's request for another loan. We're mired in petty quarrels and can't let off steam until we're in bed. I hadn't expected to cope with such a large house, or cater to so many boarders, juggling menus. . . . Explosions are inevitable.' Life was marginally complicated by the presence of Malcolm Lowry who outstayed his welcome and quarrelled with Aiken, though he tried to efface himself. Clarissa responded to his troubles - his 'fear of homosexuality' and his 'deep guilt about masturbating. . . . Malcolm never looked so alone as when part of a group – the isolation of an alcoholic on sufferance with society. His blanket was his ukelele. He strummed Negro spirituals on that long-necked instrument . . . I sometimes accompanied him at the piano.' The summer of 1932 was, says Clarissa, 'turbulent', and 'Everything seemed distorted out of kilter, like a bad photograph. Conrad could handle physical danger but not the prolonged stress of an indifferent public, strained finances, or reliving his childhood while working on *Great Circle*. Everything was an ordeal – . . . Malcolm's problems and Oedipal obsessions, my hallucinations and nightmares, with Paul's untimely overtures.' Clarissa's hallucinations and bad dreams were the result of doses of ergot. This, then, was the situation leading up to Conrad's suicide attempt.

In April 1933 Aiken, Clarissa and Malcolm Lowry sailed to Spain for six weeks, and in that month *Great Circle* was published, a novel that was shown to Freud by Hilda Doolittle who suggested Aiken should be psychoanalysed in Vienna and offered one hundred pounds towards his expenses. On 6 December Aiken was still seriously considering the idea, and the prospect that analysis might lead him to become an analyst himself, but Aiken and Freud never met and the prospect of analysis or becoming an analyst failed to develop further. Clarissa and Aiken were in Boston from September 1933 to May 1934 when they returned to Rye with journalistic commissions including a regular 'London Letter' for *The New Yorker*. As his *nom-de-plume*. Aiken adopted Samuel Jeake Jr., the name of the builder of Jeake's House.

Immediately Aiken began work on a new novel. To Winifred Bryher, the poet, he wrote on 4 June 1934: 'the countryside is lovely, much too inviting, it's not so easy to keep a studious eye turned down on the page when to lift it shows a mile of green

Romney Marsh and the blue edge of the channel – but the temptation is being resisted, and I'm making progress with a scandalously potboilerish little horror of a novel, which I hope to be able to finish before autumn. That is, if it "comes out," which it's a little too soon to say. If it doesn't, I shall groan and go to work on the one I had really *intended* to write, but which I've postponed partly because of its difficulty and partly because of its obvious predestined unsaleability.' The novel, the 'potboiler,' was to be *King Coffin*, and the novel he was postponing was finally to be written and published as *Ushant*. By 1 November, when he was writing to Maxwell Perkins, *King Coffin* was half-completed, but his 'heart isn't really in it. I don't feel very close to it, and it's difficult for me to judge of its interest or success.' Despite the novel's 'oddity', Aiken hoped it would be 'the kind of thing which will catch the Great Public Eye.' John Aiken remarks that 'as regards his writing, Conrad was well supported by most reviews and criticism. But he knew very well when he had made some sort of failure – for example, *King Coffin* was intended as a potboiler, but it didn't turn out like that: but on the other hand, it wasn't very good, either.' Financial difficulties made it necessary to achieve a success with a novel aimed not only at the 'Great Public Eye' but, equally, at the Great Public Purse. The *New Yorker* commission, the regular 'London Letter', was proving troublesome. After only a year of it, Aiken was writing to GB Wilbur on 23 June 1935 that 'it doesn't bring enough to live on by half, but at the same time swallows up so much time and energy that I can't do anything else, it's a nice metaphysical problem which as yet I haven't solved.'

There were other, pressing problems to be solved. In *Lorelei Two*, Clarissa writes, 'Our marriage was on the rocks, according to his [Conrad's] court jester, Ed Burra.' Conrad, meanwhile, according to Clarissa, had been telling friends that his attempted suicide had brought him closer to Clarissa. But in Boston in mid-December 1933, Conrad had discussed divorce. They were reconciled after recriminations and a bout of weeping, and Clarissa discovered that she was pregnant. 'It was a happier homecoming this time,' she writes. 'We saw Rye through a rainbow – red-tiled houses higgledy-piggledy, gulls flying from the church spire as the gilded quarter-boys struck the hour, Mermaid Street cobbles sprouting new grass, the Virginia ivy blanketing Jeake's House up to the chimney, the brass knocker shining on the scarlet door.' But Clarissa miscarried and lost the baby after a strenuous bicycle ride and 'I'm sure Conrad expressed sympathy, though I don't recall any special tenderness. Perhaps he felt secretly relieved.'

'Christmas [1934] was bleak, even with the children sharing part of it. John had passed his scholarship exams and would continue at London University College.' There had been trouble about that. John Aiken remembers his father's ambitions for him: 'He was very dictatorial about ways of life. He would tell people how abominably their children behaved, and instruct them. But he was very seldom cruel to me or to Jane or Joan. He thought I was comparatively feeble and anti-social when young, and he tried to correct this – when the split-up with Jerry was developing, he desperately wanted me to go to his old school, Middlesex School, and then to Harvard. When he had been there, it had been one of the most desperately unhappy periods of his childhood, so that I felt rather cross that he should have expected me to experience that too. I wouldn't have any of it, and went to London University in the end.' Aiken was working on *King Coffin*, the theme of the book being about 'a cuckolded husband bent on killing a stranger at random, then taking his own life on finding the victim's wife having a stillborn baby. "We're all murderers at heart," he once said.'

The theme of *King Coffin* was pretty close to his distrust of his own wife whom he still considered liable to promiscuity and who now realised that 'Docility only inflamed Conrad the more. Each scene dimmed the glow of romance. He was trapped; the man had fallen in love, the poet found marriage intolerable.'

By June 1935, Aiken was feeling 'that America is my home and what I need and want . . . increasing difficulties with John and Jane, perhaps just the inevitable marking off of generation from generation, but I think more complicated than that, complicated of course by Jessie and Martin, by England, by money or the want of it – increasing distance from Jerry, on the whole amiably traversed, but just the same with its violences and its ultimate loneliness – and increasing dislike of myself.' He was forty-six years old, 'in a queer in-between state, with feelings of latent fertility mixed up with the blankest of despairs, so the lord only knows . . .' Jeake's House was let for the summer, and Aiken, with Clarissa, went to stay with Laura Knight and her husband at Malvern. On their return to Rye, they resumed quarrelling and Clarissa states that several times she packed her bags to leave, but 'Unhappy wives stick it out, fearing abandonment, change, and the unknown, or because of financial-emotional dependence.' By December, she says, they were sleeping in separate rooms.

Malcolm Lowry turned up early in the summer of 1936, his marriage on the rocks. Conrad, according to Clarissa, was furious that Lowry should be 'mooning and fretting over that hardboiled little bitch. Meals were eaten in strained silence, angry dialogues echoed through the house. Their "beautiful friendship" had worn threadbare.' From the first, when Lowry had arrived in 1929 to work with Aiken on his novel *Ultramarine*, which owes a great deal to Aiken's *Blue Voyage*, they had been thick as thieves together. John Aiken's opinion, corroborated by most critics, is that Aiken 'had an enormous influence on Malcolm Lowry who was bowled over by *Blue Voyage*. Conrad in later life didn't think too much of *Blue Voyage*. Lowry was inevitably influenced: although Conrad was ostensibly trying to get rid of over-Aikenising of *Ultramarine*, all that he did was make it even more Aikenised.' It was perfectly natural: Aiken felt he knew how any particular writing should be done, and naturally he told Lowry, and naturally Lowry listened to him. In an interview with Robert Hunter Wilbur, published in *The Paris Review Interviews* series, Aiken describes 'an interesting specimen of his [Lowry's] deliberate attempt to absorb me . . . there was a page recounting the dream of eating the father's skeleton which comes into my own novel *Great Circle*. He was going to put this in his book and it didn't seem to matter at all that *I'd* had the dream and written it out . . . I said, "No, Malcolm, this is carrying it *too* far." . . . he didn't miss a trick. He was a born observer.' What Arthur Calder-Marshall calls Lowry's 'mutual admiration' with Conrad Aiken lasted a lifetime. It is sometimes disputed what Lowry might have become had he 'grown out of Aiken,' but the influence, for better or for worse, is there and it was Lowry who sought it and continued to cultivate it.

The summer of 1936 was enlivened by Aiken's leasing a nearby workmen's club and organising an exhibition of the work of local artists. The work of Paul Nash and Edward Burra caused some consternation in Rye, and Clarissa took on the job of treasurer and receptionist. Looking one day for some money in Conrad's wallet, she discovered a letter from a woman, evidently his mistress. Confronted with evidence, Aiken admitted the affair and an argument developed. It ended, according to Clarissa, with Conrad saying, 'I may have flirtations, but I'll never fall in love again. I'm too old. Divorce would break up my life.' For the sake of the children, says Clarissa, she and Aiken agreed on a temporary truce, a superficial cessation of hostilities during the school holidays, but the children nevertheless sensed the tensions and reacted to them. In retrospect, John Aiken feels, with hindsight, that his father was wholly to blame for the break-up of his second marriage. Aiken had been cruel to Clarissa, though 'he was sensitive to the cruelties he had inflicted: he agonisingly remembered the cruel things he had done to people and was often forgiven – though not always, and not by all his victims. He did a great deal of thinking about how he should act, but his emotions were also very powerful, and they changed the course of his life from time to time.' In August 1936 Conrad Aiken sailed for New York where he met Malcolm Lowry and revisited Savannah after thirty-five years' absence. He was in Boston where, on 22 August, he wrote to Edward Burra: 'I fear my days at Rye are numbered, though it looks possible I may have one last winter there. Not much money to be squoze out of the publishers, alas.' He had intended to be back in England towards mid-September, but, writing again to Burra on 18 October, he was still in the United States, at Charlestown, Mass., 'living in a wonderful slum, a stone's throw from the harbour . . . a very nice old georgian (sort of) brick house, circa 1780, occupied by a very gifted and charming artist named Mary Hoover, who lets me have a room at what you might call a nominal rent. Lots of fun . . . I shall probably stay here for at least half the winter – I even foresee that I may stay forever. Sad as it makes me feel, for I genuinely and dreadfully miss Rye.'

So much for the disclaimer to Clarissa that he was never likely to fall in love again or tear himself apart by a divorce. On 24 November, he was again writing to Burra to say, 'You may have gathered from Sundry Signs and Portents that things weren't any too merry between Jerry and myself lately – in fact, they've become so bad that I'm asking for a divorce.' Clarissa thought his first request for a divorce was not serious, but when Aiken wrote to tell her about Mary Hoover she realised that any hopes of holding her marriage together were vain. There was an exchange of acrimonious letters between them, and Clarissa finally agreed to return to America to negotiate the divorce.

To Margaret and Robert MacKechnie, two artist friends in Rye, Aiken wrote on 6 December 1936, 'that in all likelihood my Rye days are over. Gosh, the way of life or circumstance or fate or folly just grabs us up and flings us to the edge of nowhere – ! And the way we hurt each other when it happens . . . divorce seemed to me the only way out – and while I was in that state of anger and despair I had to go and meet just the kind of woman I could fall in love with, and proceeded, quite unaware of what I was doing, to do so. And there I am, and there we are, blown to smithereens.' Jeake's House, 'in spite of everything, had much to commend it. It makes me miserable to think of it, for I loved the life there despite the fact that Jerry so hated it: and to feel that I shall probably never be able to live there again just cores my solar plexus as if it were an apple . . . To bring back a *third* Mrs Aiken to the same house, even such a delightful and gifted one – she's a painter, and a very good one – would perhaps be inviting disaster. Do you think it could *possibly* be done? I wish with all my heart it could and hope with all my heart it can. And Mary herself is *determined* to. Though I tell her that she doesn't know Rye, and hasn't, like the vicar, heard its little heart beating.'

Conrad and Mary were married, after the divorce, on 7 July 1937 and sailed for England ten days later. In early August, they were settled in Jeake's House and, by 22 August, Aiken wrote to Henry Murray, 'everything here is a huge success – Mary, wonderful great gal that she is, simply loves the place, the house, the life, the smells, the landscape, everything – even John and Jane and Joan, who are all here at the moment. No ghosts hover over us, as I somewhat feared – nary a ghost, it's all serene and good, and if there's any work left in me, as in darker moments I doubt, I feel I can here get down to at least an attempt at it.' Aiken's friends were agog to see Mary – Paul Nash and Laura Knight and any number of local artists. 'What I try to dare to foresee for us is a life in which we could stay here for six or eight months at a time, and then raid Boston, so that Mary could take on a handful of commissions, at the same time arranging for a show of her latest work . . . Anyway, as the novelist said we go forward with caution reverence and hope. And o baby it's so good to be here and to be so happy.'

In John Aiken's view, his father's third wife – Lorelei Three – put up with no nonsense from him about his promiscuity. 'Mary was tougher than his previous two wives, and wouldn't stand for it. Mary was the wife who was most of a match for Conrad – she was more sophisticated than Jessie or Jerry, and could out-drink him, too.' At first, Aiken indicates in *Ushant*, John had 'formed a somewhat sinister alliance with Lorelei Two [Clarissa], there was a definite attachment there . . .' but John 'in due course recovered his balance; recovered, too, from the hostility to D. [Aiken], or disapproval, and the indifference and condescension towards Lorelei Three [Mary] which had led him so profoundly to underestimate her. It had been hard on dear Jed [John]: harder, perhaps, than the previous divorce had been . . .' Mary, set on continuing her artistic career, was encouraged by Aiken. He had not taken Clarissa's literary efforts seriously, but Mary's painting was different – he invited TS Eliot to Rye, and thought it likely Julian Huxley and 'one or two other literary celebrities' might be persuaded to sit for their portraits.

To make some money, Conrad and Mary began a school at Jeake's House for American writers and painters. On 25 July 1938, Aiken reported to Henry Murray that 'The school is a huge success, a continuous revel of good nature and good juices, a wonderfully homogeneous lot, who mix well and clash well, so that the harmonics and discords that arise from it are a joy to us.' He took morning conferences with the students, 'individually, as often as they need, recreate their creations for them, an exhausting job, but fun. In the evenings, four or five times a week, we read their works and discuss, over beer, and this has proved an enormous success – I try to keep still, and let *them* do it, but now and then take a hand, and any visitors are pressed into service as well.

'Mary, of course, when she does say something, hits the nail on the head, and is wonderful as always – besides running the house, cooking gargantuan meals. . . . But alas her own work (and of course mine) has had to go by the board – pro tem to be sure, but it's a pity.' It was an exhausting schedule, frustrating in some respects, but they both seem to have been buoyed up by a sense of euphoria. 'We're both perpetually tired, and financially we won't clear even as much as we hoped, but we're both enjoying it hugely, learning a lot, and at least feel that we have a future!'

Aiken's new novel, *A Heart for the Gods of Mexico*, was published in London in January 1939, but he was vexed by what he considered to be bad reviews – 'very bitter from the highbrow and leftwing quarters . . . the sheer malice which has been spat upon it has taken me aback.' He doubted that it would make any money. This was a setback, but still he could write to GB Wilbur on 8 February 1939 that Mary's success as an artist made him happy: 'boy what fun I have, with a genius at work under my own eyes. Life has certainly been good to me.' When, in the spring of 1939, Mary accepted a commission to paint portraits in Oxford, and left Aiken alone in Rye for seven weeks, he composed a series of sonnets which he sent to her, in letters, almost daily. He also found energies and inspiration to complete another novel, *The Conversation*, by 1 June, which he despatched to Maxwell Perkins at Scribner's in New York. Letters to Mary alone should have absorbed his creativity in time alone – though not the full span of his literary ability, since they tend to be hopelessly sentimental and gossipy. 'I've missed Mary terribly,' he wrote to Henry Murray on 30 May 1939: 'pari passu with finishing the novel I've reopened a poetic vein, and bled myself of 22 sonnets, which has been good for me in more ways than one – though I'd be hard put to it to try to tell you why.'

Maxwell Perkins turned down *The Conversation*, despite a letter from Aiken eagerly recommending it as 'much the most saleable book so far????'

Aiken's hope that 'we've really got now a very nice little line of hard-wearing fiction which an astute campaign might start selling' was dashed. He was certainly disenchanted. To Perkins, he wrote on 6 July: 'you were disappointed in *Great Circle*, and went about publishing it sadly and reluctantly, and you did the same thing only more so with *King Coffin* – and of course the short stories, as well. I didn't feel, to be candid, with any of these books, that they were really *published* – rather, that they were merely *allowed* out.' Aiken's own feelings about both novels was that they were better than anything else Perkins was publishing and that they 'were perhaps by way of being classics.' His letter went on to defend *The Conversation* and to rail against Perkins's blindness and addiction to 'shallower ideals'. He was disappointed and saddened 'more than I can possibly tell you – to have to end this long and friendly collaboration.'

Another disappointment was the summer school – only one

student had enrolled for the 1939 season, though principally because of the threat of European war rather than any shortcomings on the part of the Aikens. It seemed likely they might be stranded as aliens in a country at war, that they might be in some danger in a coastal town like Rye, and the prospects of earning enough money to support them, if they were not able to travel regularly and freely to America, were slender. The Aikens, reluctantly, decided to sail for America to live at Cape Cod. On 29 September, they embarked for New York. A final letter from Jeake's House to Henry Murray announced their departure: 'Well, Harry, we're a-coming, and if the SS Washington, star-spangled and floodlit, can whisk us past the mines and torpedoes, we'll be in New York about October 6th . . . Gosh, what a world, what a world. How fascinating, how terrible, how everything. England is astonishing – the simplicity, absence of rancour, calm and stoical *indifference* with which they're going about it is something to have witnessed: a great people. We hate to leave them . . .'

For Aiken, writing in *Ushant*, 'England itself, of course, all these years had been a window, the window which it had been his imperative need to find and to open: the window which looked into his own racial and cultural past, and thus bestowed upon him the sense of belonging, of being part of a moving continuum, the evolving series of civilized consciousness. But had that function now been, at last, performed? . . . the truth was, that he had been walking in this new country, which was his America, and with possession, for many years of the stay at Saltinge. Those periodic returns, for the purpose of "touching base", and that pressing need for a kind of revitalizing in its more electric air, and for renewed draughts of its racier idioms, and the sense of its wilder violences, not to mention the need for contact with the friends and the family . . . hadn't these, and very soon after his installation in the house, meant that he was already embarked – although unconsciously – on the return?' The Great Circle had, since his first arrival in England, made at least one complete revolution in Aiken's life.

EIGHT

EF Benson at Lamb House

On a hot Sunday in July 1884, shortly after having taken his degree at Cambridge, Arthur Christopher Benson met, at a luncheon party, a 'small, pale, noticeable man, with a short, pointed beard and with large, piercingly observant eyes. He was elegantly dressed in a light grey suit, with a frock coat of the same material, and in the open air he wore a white tall hat.' This personage was Henry James, who 'had not yet acquired, or he did not display, that fine conversational manner of his later years.' James 'talked little and epigrammatically' and bent his attention, 'indulgently and benignantly' upon Arthur who willingly, upon being kindly pressed, gave up 'the data, so to speak, of a little personal problem which he deigned to observe. The sense of this was deeply and subtly flattering, combined as it was with a far-reaching sort of goodwill. He never lost touch with me from that hour.'

AC Benson was the second son of the Archbishop of Canterbury, Edward White Benson, appointed in 1882. His first son, Martin, had died young, and, as his father's favourite, was sorely missed. Hugh (later to be a friend of 'Baron Corvo'), was born in 1871, following the third, Edward Frederic, known as Fred, in 1867. On a visit to the Bensons in 1885, James not only had occasion to meet the rather eccentric family but was rewarded too, with a story by the Archbishop which, as he later confided to Arthur, 'was the germ of that most tragical and even appalling story, "The Turn of the Screw." My father took a certain interest in psychical matters,' continues AC Benson, 'but we have never been able to recollect any story that he ever told which could have provided a hint for so grim a subject.' On the death of Archbishop Benson in 1896, Arthur began to write his father's biography, aided by his sister Maggie whose obsession with the memory of her father resulted in deep depressions and, finally, insanity which took the alarming form of 'violent homicidal mania,' directed possibly towards her mother. Mrs Benson's relationship with her friend Lucy Tait, with whom she habitually shared a bed (though probably in all innocence), was the wedge driven between Maggie and sanity. She anxiously desired to be mothered and taken care of like a child, but in Maggie's madness it appeared that Lucy stood between her and her mother. 'We are in very deep waters,' wrote Mrs Benson to Fred, shaken by Maggie's extremes of violence.

When war broke out in 1914, Arthur, who had been a schoolmaster at Eton, was Vice-Master of Magdalene, at Cambridge, and in full literary spate, turning out a continuous stream of sentimental essays, books of beautiful piety, quietist tracts and daily entries for a diary which, in sum, finally amounted to four and a half million words of private reflection. His published works 'appealed to a vast multitude of readers,' remarks EF Benson. 'He knew himself that these books were not of any high intellectual or philosophical value, but through the medium of his lucid and beautiful style they awoke in many thousands of simple and thoughtful readers the perception of the beauty of a withdrawn and untroubled and unambitious life.' Such a life was devoutly to be wished for Arthur who suffered dreadfully from fits of depression. To relieve his distress, he 'stuck to his jobs and particularly to his writing as a means of diverting his thoughts from himself, but he could not have adopted a more disastrous régime, for his books, built up of introspection, only focused his attention on himself.'

His fans, however, noted only a beautiful spirit: 'These admirers, his feminine tea-party audience, whom he had never seen, assured him that he had marvellously expressed for them what they had always thought but had never been able to formulate, and had given them the key to many problems of life which had always baffled them. More mundanely, a daring spinster told him in strict confidence that he would make a lovely husband and enclosed her photograph, to show, I suppose, that she would make a lovely wife.' But as EF Benson, in *Final Edition*, rather indulgently implies, Arthur would have not made an ideal husband: 'like Henry James he prized above all achievements of his own, signs of affection spontaneously offered him. He never sallied out of his own fortress to seek friendly invaders, but, so to speak, he left its walls ostentatiously unguarded, for them to enter and find welcome. As well as contemporaries and old friends there were among these many young men up at Magdalene and other colleges. He contrived – or rather it was natural to him – to associate with them, on equal terms. The quality of youth called to him, and though sometimes he moaned to himself that they looked on him as an amiable old buffer, that quality and its attraction for him bridged the gulf of years.' EF Benson himself was very likely of a similar turn of mind when it came to the question of matrimony and sexual interest in women. Certainly, he was not overtly homosexual and would have closed his eyes in holy dread at any specific homosexual advance, but it can hardly be denied that he was at least homoerotic and found young men aesthetically pleasing. In *EF Benson* by Cynthia and Tony Reavell, the authors extract a short passage from Benson's novel *Travail of Gold*, published in 1933, and suggest that the substitution of 'he' for 'she' 'probably sums up his own attitude fairly closely:' 'It was quite true . . . she delighted in the company of young men, but as for [the] notion . . . that she laid siege to their moral rectitude, nothing could have been falser . . . She liked young men because they were, if of the right sort, pleasant to look on and lean and clean in movement, but to have been embraced by one would have caused her agonies of outrage and embarrassment.' Sir Steven Runciman, quoted in the Reavell's book, suggests that Benson was virginal and continued in that state of sexual innocence.

In October 1919, EF Benson was a prolific, facile author with more than fifty books to his credit. His first published novel, *Dodo*, in 1893 had provided him, at the age of twenty-six, with a nickname he was to bear for the rest of his life. He was regarded by his serious, pious brothers as a lightweight, but in the event *Dodo* Benson is nowadays a more substantial figure than either of them.

He had been to Rye once or twice since he had first visited Henry James at Lamb House in 1900. On these subsequent occasions he had stayed with Lady Maud Warrender, a local notability and friend of James, who is remembered in Rye as 'about six foot four, bosom like a shelf, and singing "Land of Hope and Glory" at the top of her voice.' The patriotic words had been written by Arthur Benson and set to music by Elgar, also a friend of the monumental Lady Maud. Fred Benson had sent *Dodo* to Henry James in 1893 or 1894 for criticism. 'He wrote me two or three long and kindly and brilliantly evasive letters about it.' The style of his letters must have been reminiscent of his kindly but cautious observations to Ford Madox Hueffer on that young author's first book of poems. 'He called it "lively", he called himself "corrosively critical" though he made no criticism, except that he did not find it as "ferociously literary" as his taste demanded. "Hew out a style," he said, "it is by style that we are saved," and I drew the obvious conclusion that, for the present, I was not.'

EF Benson was never a 'bright young thing', in the days before that phrase was invented, but he was brighter and gayer than his brothers. At the turn of the century, in his mid-thirties, 'I had, like Homer's dawn, many dancing-places. I was attached to London, where I had a small flat and numerous friends, I spent a winter month or so skating in Switzerland, perhaps another month in Scotland, and yet another in Italy, and there was my mother's home, deep-buried in the country near Horsted-Keynes.' In 1916, when Henry James died, Benson was approaching fifty and inclined to settle into quiet middle age.

'With Henry James's death I supposed that Lamb House itself would concern me no more, but in the preordained decrees of fate, or, alternatively, in the fantastic hazards of a fortuitous world, it began at once to concern me more closely,' wrote Benson in *Final Edition*, his autobiography, completed just ten days before his death in 1940. Lamb House had been let to an American lady who passed the lease to Robert Norton. He, being a close friend of Fred Benson's, asked him to share the tenancy and Benson, occupied with war work in London, began to use the house as a weekend retreat. He was offered the remainder of the lease, but was unable to take it – he hoped to return to a villa in Capri after the war – but in October 1919 he took a six months sub-lease of Lamb House after he discovered the property in Capri would no longer be available to rent. Lamb House had begun 'faintly to assume a home-like aspect'. The solidly entrenched citizens of Rye, as embedded as the cobbles, perhaps regarded him as a transient visitor, but Benson, rather a sociable man, decided to stay. He kept on his flat in Brompton Square in London and divided his time contentedly between his two properties, regularly renewing the lease of Lamb House until his death.

Nothing had changed radically since James lived there: an ancient mulberry tree had been split and destroyed by a gale, but otherwise all was the same and Benson made the pleasing discovery 'that I could be very happy all by myself, not speaking a word, for days together, to anyone but my small household.' He shared the house with Arthur until his brother's death in 1925. Arthur, deeply depressive, was at first merely an occasional visitor, spending most of his time in Cambridge. At one point he suffered a nervous breakdown but, recovering, took to spending his vacations at Lamb House, filling the place with handsome and intelligent undergraduates, among them the young George Rylands. He was again, after a period of despair, hard at his literary obsession, his diary. Fred Benson remembers coming upon Arthur after tea in Cambridge 'with the writing-board across the arms of his chair, and the floor littered with scribbled sheets, incredulous that it was so late already, and beaming with literary accomplishment . . . The pencil raced on in that firm clear hand-writing, and another sheet fluttered to the floor . . . This exuberant extempore production never slackened: now it was an essay, now an article for a magazine, now the diary, the pages of which, bound in thin blue paper-covered volumes, had passed the mark of three million words: now a fresh chapter of a novel.' And his correspondence: 'an infernal morning,' Arthur might say, 'Twenty-seven letters and there are several more I must write before we go out.' Out, indeed, they would go, whirling round the countryside to call on Kipling, to gaze upon Bodiam Castle, to walk from Camber to Lydd, and return to another punishing bout of literary effort: 'I haven't touched my novel for two days,' Arthur might remark, 'and I don't believe I shall finish it before I go back to Cambridge.' He had only begun it a few weeks before. It was a nuisance that his publisher, John Murray, declined to issue more than three books a year by Arthur Benson, since there were several already in stock waiting to be published.

In terms of literary industry Fred Benson was, by comparison, a sluggard and a laggard. During the years 1919 to 1940, he published a mere forty or so novels, biographies and volumes of short stories. In all, at his death, the total amounted to one hundred books, including seventy-seven pieces of fiction, and twenty non-fiction. Three are still unclassified by those Benson aficionados, Cynthia and Tony Reavell, who also state that two plays by Benson may also have been published. Few of these books stand up to modern scrutiny. Most have dated badly and cannot now be resurrected, though in recent years The Hogarth Press have published *Mrs Ames*, *Paying Guests*, *Secret Lives*, *As We Are*, and the early autobiography *As We Were*. Most of the revival of interest in Benson stems from the continuous popularity of his six novels featuring Miss Mapp and Lucia which so enchanted Nancy Mitford and WH Auden.

The Mapp and Lucia sequence of novels germinated in Fred Benson's mind when, one day in Rye, 'the son of an old friend of my father's asked me to tea. His wife had not come in at the appointed hour, and it was not permissible that tea should be brought up till she arrived. So we admired her budgerigar which flitted screaming round the room, and after we had talked very pleasantly for some while about Henry James, I went back to Lamb House. This little incident pleased me immensely: somehow I felt it was Rye, the inner life of Rye. And what a setting, I thought, Rye and its cobbled streets and its gables and red brick, so profusely immortalized in the water-colour sketches of visitors, would make for some fantastic story! I could people it as I pleased, for I knew nothing of its inhabitants apart from this pleasant talk I had had with one of them.' Since *Queen Lucia* was published in 1920, Fred's inspiration must have come very shortly after October 1919. Evidently he had not long been in Rye, having had time only 'as an external observer . . . [to see] the ladies of Rye doing their shopping in the High Street every morning, carrying large market baskets, and bumping into each other in narrow doorways, and talking in a very animated manner.' *Miss Mapp* appeared in print in 1922.

However, Benson says, 'Lucia I knew.' The first novel is set in Riseholme, a village some two and a half miles from Lincoln, where Fred spent some happy times as a child, and Lucia does not come to Tilling (Benson's name for Rye) until the fourth novel, *Mapp & Lucia*, published in 1931. The third novel, *Lucia in London*, published in 1927, concerns the driving social ambitions of an upwardly mobile Lucia in high society. Rye, as the little town of Tilling, does not become the permanent *mise-en-scène* until Lucia moves from Riseholme to Tilling and begins her intense rivalry with Elizabeth Mapp in *Mapp & Lucia*. Benson, in 1919 and 1920, gazed wonderingly at his gossiping neighbours 'as ignorant of them all as people as a man from Mars, and I vaguely began to meditate on some design.' By the time that design had become apparent, he was very well acquainted with his fellow citizens and, despite the usual disclaimers about fiction having been in any way based upon fact, those Bensonphiles Cynthia and Tony Reavell have had very little difficulty identifying the originals of the characters created for the Mapp and Lucia novels, though not all were denizens of Rye. Fred drew equally upon the characteristics of friends and acquaintances in London, in Italy, in Cambridge, and placed them in recognisable locations in Rye.

Taking his own house as the central focus of intrigue, Benson 'outlined an elderly atrocious spinster and established her in Lamb House. She should be the centre of social life, abhorred and dominant, and she should sit like a great spider behind the curtains in the garden room, spying on her friends, and I knew that her name must be Elizabeth Mapp. Rye should furnish the topography, so that no one who knew Rye could possibly be in doubt where the scene was laid, and I would call it Tilling because Rye has its river the Tillingham . . . Perhaps another preposterous woman, Lucia of Riseholme, who already had a decent and devout following, and who was as dominant as Mapp, might come into contact with her some day, when I had got to know Mapp better. I began to invent a new set of characters who should revolve round these two women, fussy and eager and alert and preposterous. Of course, it would all be small beer, but one could get a head upon it of jealousies and malignities and devouring inquisitiveness. Like Moses on Pisgah I saw a wide prospect, a Promised Land, a Saga indefinitely unveiling itself.'

Much as Benson enjoyed his 'frivolous way with the preposterous adventures of Lucia and Miss Mapp, for there was nothing faked or sentimental about them, and I was not offering them as examples of serious fiction,' he began to feel a gnawing dissatisfaction with his work. His first novel, *Dodo*, 'had sold enormously, it had furnished a theme for discussion in alert circles for many weeks, it had aroused serious as well as amused attention.' Edmund Gosse, no less, had astonishingly and generously pronounced *Dodo* to be a 'work of high moral beauty' and indicated that, with application to life and work, young Fred might expect to set his mark on English fiction. Hard work had certainly resulted in an uncommon number of words on a very large number of pages, 'but the mark was not quite so conspicuous as one might have wished.' Early success, a brilliant début, he now saw, with a pang, had been a disaster. He had dashed off book after book with enormous industry and pleasure, but: 'Imperceptibly to myself, I had long ago reached the point at which, unless I could observe more keenly and feel more deeply, I had come to the end of anything worth saying.' Writing was still fun, Benson could still knock out a light, lucid, agreeable story and clap it between hard covers with a facility even Arthur might envy, but he felt he was 'only turning over and over the patch of ground I had already prepared, and setting in it cuttings from my old plants.' His characters, he felt, rushed about in predictable grooves, talking cleverly and plausibly, and went through the motions of life – but they were simulacra, 'they lacked the red corpuscle.'

Modern critics will not deny the acuity of this distressful insight by a prolific writer who finds, suddenly, his Muse transformed into Nemesis. 'I despised sentimentality in other writers. I looked upon it as a deliberate fake yet whenever I got in a difficulty I used it unblushingly myself.' He could look into his books with some interest, however – not for the joy of their style, but because he had perfectly forgotten their content: 'they roused not the faintest gleam of recollection.' He had forgotten, too, how inadequate they were. Clearly depressed by his situation, Benson salvaged several he considered passable – *Sheaves*, *The Luck of the Vails*, *The Climber*, and *David Blaize* – but it was time to change. Serious fiction was not, clearly, his forte: on his present showing, he would not fill a niche beside Henry James in the Hall of Literary Immortality.

He determined to launch himself afresh upon readers and critics, with whom his credit as a serious novelist was by now quite beyond redemption, as a serious biographer. 'There, at any rate, one had to do some honest work before one began writing at all.' He would be saved by industrious application to facts and psychology. His high-mindedness promptly took a lofty stand, despising the cluttered contents of the Benson brain. In *Final Edition*, Benson employs an extended metaphor in which his mind is described as 'furnished lodgings' filled with other people's stuff, with ideas not his own. A ruthless inspection of his cranial cupboards revealed things that had 'dustily survived in the dark,' toys of youth, truths with which he had never come to terms, falsities carefully stored like treasures, all covered with the cobwebs of regret. These, at least, belonged to Benson, and must be thrown away in middle-aged manhood. It was not a pleasant or an easy task, and Benson tackled it piecemeal, 'like a charwoman', because 'it is a mistake to take oneself too seriously.' A spirited spring clean, thorough and once and for all, might well have resulted in deep depression, and Fred Benson was too sensible a man to permit himself to be debilitated to the point of mental disorientation he had observed in his sister Maggie and his brother Arthur.

In 1925, Benson published a biography of Sir Francis Drake, smartly followed by a book about Alcibiades the next year. Ferdinand Magellan was marked for treatment, then Charlotte Bronte, King Edward VII, Queen Victoria, The Kaiser Wilhelm II of Germany, and Queen Victoria's Daughters, concluding with the story of his own life in 1940, the year of his death. They were carefully researched, as carefully researched as the art of biography itself which Benson had resolved to undertake and master. He discarded the hagiographical mode of Victorian biographers who had idealised the eminent dead into 'miracles of wisdom and virtue'. That path led not merely to 'De mortuis nil nisi bonum' but, ultimately, to 'De mortuis nil nisi bunkum.' Benson's condemnation of these blinkered biographers, purveyors of little more than pious tracts, extended even to Edmund Gosse who, he considered, had whited the sepulchre of Robert Louis Stevenson, and applied some tactful whitewash to Swinburne, reserving painful frankness and filial honesty for the celebrated study of his father, Gosse senior. On the other hand, Benson recognised, shying somewhat from the nothing-*but*-warts tendency of contemporary biography, that there was a case to be made for the middle path on which travellers through life might be portrayed as ordinary, fallible human beings. 'I was not so antiquely-minded as to wish to go back to Victorian modes, but the delving for belittlement seemed to produce results which were equally wide of the truth.' Gosse on the one hand, Lytton Strachey on the other, were not models to be scrupulously imitated. Taking care to be wary of his 'facility with which I could write readably,' Benson carefully wrote his study of Drake. His reward was the admiration of Gosse, who had first recommended *Dodo* so extravagantly more than thirty years before, and who now wrote to say 'that novelists alone should be allowed to write biography.' He explained this enigmatic compliment by pointing out that 'biography was primarily a study of character' and that Benson 'was far more concerned with what people were than what they did,' that he had got behind the facade of plain facts so misleadingly presented as the important events in the lives briefly chronicled in the Dictionary of National Biography. In his biography of Charlotte Bronte, Benson claims, he is true to primary sources – Charlotte herself in her letters and writings, rather than to gossip and libels. By a process of trial and error, involving the scrapping of a first draft of his Bronte book, Benson was able to feel that he achieved an approach and style of his own that involved both the scrupulous researcher and the imaginative novelist.

In his youth, Fred Benson had been a sportsman, playing rugby, squash, lawn tennis, and winter sports such as curling and skating. He had been awarded a gold medal by the National Skating Association for his skill in the difficult English Style, but he had put these things behind him by the time he came to Rye. He began to be bothered by arthritis of the hip, and set about trying to discover a cure. An adhesive plaster round the hip joint, applied by a distinguished general practitioner, came off in the bath. More thorough-going methods were clearly indicated: 'I went alike to notable regular physicians and to quacks. I returned to my friend of the sticking-plaster, who now advised tonics and a liberal consumption of oranges.' Others recommended atophan, or 'colonized my colon with hordes of the Bacillus Bulgaricus . . . Another doctor injected something radio-active into my thigh; another some potion of dead bacilli into my arm. Another drove iodine into the hip by means of an electric current . . . Another prescribed massage, another a system of physical exercises.' X-Rays, mud baths, cups of disgusting mineral waters at Bath, immersion in the salt waters at Droitwich, herbal teas, tepid baths, a necklace of small crystals, hip pads of radio-active flannel, Christian Science and faith-healing: all these nostrums produced little or no alleviation of the irritating pain. Golf and long walks became impossible – the X-Rays had shown irreparable, irreversible osteo-arthritis.

Until incapacitated, Benson tended to spend as much time at his flat in London as at Lamb House in Rye; but as middle age tended perceptibly towards old age, he spent more time pottering about his Rye garden and taking an interest in its, and his, passage towards final maturity. 'I found that growing old was in itself quite a pleasant process. All that was required of one was to keep reasonably young and the years did the rest. I had expected that it would be a burdensome and joyless task, but it resolved itself into a pastime. As energy diminished, so did also the desires that called for it . . .' He 'had not got the true Cockney heart', and he felt 'now more solidly and substantially at home in Rye than in any other of those delightful abiding-places outside London where my life had been passed.' Addington, Cambridge, Capri, Switzerland, and Tremans, the old family house, had all passed away and 'Rye had so firmly persuaded me that I never even said to myself as I stepped out of the train, "Here we are at home again".'

He sunbathed in a little secret garden he made for himself in the grounds of Lamb House and, in a sort of gazebo he had built there, worked at his writing. Here, one day, sitting with the local vicar, he 'saw the figure of a man walk past this open doorway [to the secret garden]. He was dressed in black and he wore a cape the right wing of which, as he passed, he threw across his chest, over his left shoulder.' It was gratifying to have seen a ghost. Like his character Lucia, he played Beethoven and Chopin on a Bechstein, morning and evening, after writing. Friends visited – 'Francis Yeats-Brown [a resident of Rye] sprawled on the grass busy with *Bengal Lancer*, and refreshed himself with Yoga postures and deep breathing. Dame Ethel Smyth recalled some strangely erroneous impressions she had formed about my father and mother for her sequel to her enthralling "Impressions That Remained": Clare Sheridan came over from Brede Place, and we discussed reincarnation (for which doctrine I had no use): the place was impregnated with the commerce and conversation of many friends.'

Benson took care not to bore his friends with his arthritic pain, but it was inevitable that, considering the family history of depression, he would sometimes sink into low spirits. First, he got about with the aid of one stick, but later two became necessary if he were to walk any distance. He rallied his spirits when in company, but when alone would fall back into despair at his inability, particularly in the last two years of his life, to walk or do much for himself. Charlie Tomlin, Fred Benson's manservant, talked to Cynthia and Tony Reavell in 1978 about his former employer and provided a wealth of detailed information about Benson's daily life in London and Rye. Benson had particularly enjoyed a visit to Rye by Queen Mary, the wife of George V, who toured the antique shops of the town, beady-eyed to spot a bargain, with Benson in tow. She graciously accepted an invitation to return to Lamb House. It was a high point in the life of a man who, though willing to be sociable with all types and condition of humanity, 'was inwardly proud of his aristocratic connections, his social position and of his father having been the Archbishop of Canterbury.' According to Tomlin, 'He mentioned the King's College Choir and he said, "Of course you know what makes them so wonderful is they're all gentlemen's sons – they know how to speak, they've got the right pronounciation!" He was rather keen on that sort of thing.' Benson was hardly a Fabian, and was delighted to be honoured by being elected Mayor of Rye in 1934. The previous year, he had been appointed a JP - but the Mayoralty of Rye was a tremendous thing. The office carried with it dignities appropriate to the chief officer of an Ancient Town associated with the Cinque Ports, and Benson became the 'six hundred and forty-fifth of my dynasty'. He was twice re-elected, continuing in his distinguished office until 1937, supported by his Mayoress, Mrs Jacomb-Hood, a Rye neighbour.

Before accepting his office, there was a little matter, of some delicacy, to be negotiated. Benson had just completed a new novel about Tilling, in which Lucia was elected Mayor of Tilling, 'and Tilling, as Rye knew very well, *was* Rye . . . Surely it would be very unseemly that the man whom the Town Council were proposing to honour should presently publish a piece of farcical fiction in which the Mayor of Rye was the most prominent and ludicrous figure.' No objection was made, and Benson's other polite doubts about his ignorance of municipal affairs and the pressing claims of his literary profession were magnanimously swept aside. The hesitations were courtly, merely: 'I was not like the Victorian young lady who, when asked to play the piano, only needed a little pressing. I did not need to be pressed at all for I was perfectly well aware that I was going to be Mayor of Rye.' Mrs Jacomb-Hood having consented to live with Benson in 'municipal sin' as his Mayoress, 'I started on this unlooked for adventure.' The robe was gorgeous, the ceremony of investiture was distinguished by quaint, immemorial customs and dignity, and Benson thoroughly 'liked pomp and ceremony and the due observance of ancient tradition, and being prayed for in church on Sunday morning without the disadvantage of being seriously ill.' Though perhaps the ardent prayers of the congregation might do his osteo-arthritis some good.

The excitements and longueurs of municipal meetings and duties did stimulate him, certainly. 'Sometimes I secretly and insincerely moaned over what I called these "incessant interruptions" to my work; and sometimes I thought that I was terribly tied at Rye, having to be there for a part of every month in the year. But I was aware that these incessant interruptions were actually rekindling my interest in writing again.' He was at work on a life of Kaiser Wilhelm II of Germany – a subject he found amusing and personally interesting. London remained a glamorous, beckoning lure, while Rye appeared, after a visit to the capital, 'a little backwaterish, a little provincial. After all, was it not the centre of Suburbia?' Well, yes: but by 1936 he was permanently in residence in Lamb House, apart from a week or two, at the most, away from Rye's provincial charms. These were substantial: 'many days of pellucid blue and brightness, and the knowledge . . . that in London there was a choking fog, with trains running hours late . . . On the shortest day of the year with the noon sun at its lowest, there was still a patch of brightness in the secret garden.'

His brilliant, colourful career as Mayor at an end, Benson settled back into his own life: 'I had a good appetite for my own prospects; they wore a friendly aspect, and still the masterpiece beckoned, and still I pursued.' He could not, to the end, be content with municipal distinction; literary fame still animated his desire. But he was consoled, perhaps, by a mark of distinction conferred upon him by Magdalene College to which he was elected an Honorary Fellow. The Town Council of Rye followed up smartly by conferring upon their erstwhile Mayor the Freedom of the Borough. The Magdalene Fellowship had been held previously by Thomas Hardy and Rudyard Kipling and the last Freeman of Rye had been an Archbishop: good and honourable company.

On 29 February 1940, loaded with these honours and tokens of academic and municipal esteem, Edward Frederic Benson died, of throat cancer, in University College Hospital, London. He was buried in Rye Cemetery. The 'masterpiece' had eluded him – most of his novels, and all his biographies, sold well enough but they were of passing interest. He had been depressed when even the circulating libraries ceased to carry the full corpus of the Benson literary effort over the years. An article by Beverly Nichols had said he did not care, but he did care, deeply, about the fate of his work. He would have been charmed to know that, forty years after his death, he would be back in vogue with the six novels featuring Miss Mapp and Lucia. These, being constantly reprinted, and selling in quantity (thanks in large part to the television series based on the novels), are perfect little masterpieces, minor period gems, adored by aficionados of their rather camp comedy. Though he himself regarded them as frivolous, and part of him would regret that his more substantial, more seriously-intended work has been overlooked, he would possibly regard the breeze of fashion, blowing across his most memorable creations, as a friendly wind.

NINE

Radclyffe Hall in Rye

On 9 August 1928, Marguerite Radclyffe Hall and her lover, Una, Lady Troubridge, motored down from London to Rye at the invitation of Anne Elsner, an acquaintance, to spend a day or two at her cottage in Hucksteps Row. They loved Rye instantly, as a refuge from the modern world, and it seemed a good place to start looking for a house. Radclyffe Hall's fifth novel, *The Well of Loneliness*, had been published on 27 July and looked set for a steady success. She had published four previous novels – *The Forge, The Unlit Lamp, A Saturday Life*, and *Adam's Breed* which, in 1927, had been awarded the Prix Femina and the James Tait Black prize for the best novel of the year against some stiff competition in the form of *Lolly Willowes* by Sylvia Townsend Warner and *The Informer* by Liam O'Flaherty. *The Well* received some good reviews, tempered by some reservations about it being a polemic in favour of lesbianism. It was considered to be less a novel than a piece of special pleading. The controversial nature of the book ensured that several London bookshops quickly sold out and a second edition was swiftly issued by the publisher, Jonathan Cape. Ten days after their brief stay in Rye, on August 19, the Sunday Express devoted almost a full page to an article about *The Well* under the banner headline, 'A Book That Must be Suppressed.'

The editor of the Sunday Express demanded that the publisher withdraw the book which, he alleged, was 'unfit to be sold by any bookseller or to be borrowed from any library.' The novel and its subject amounted to a plague, a contagion 'stalking shamelessly through great social assemblies. I have heard it whispered about by young men and young women who do not and cannot grasp its unutterable putrefaction . . . I would rather give a healthy boy or a healthy girl a phial of prussic acid than this novel. Poison kills the body, but moral poison kills the soul.' The editor, James Douglas, insisted that if it was not voluntarily withdrawn, the law should suppress *The Well of Loneliness*. Other papers took up the carefully manufactured and orchestrated scandal and Radclyffe Hall became a nationally known figure, through newspaper photographs of her wearing apparently a man's jacket, a tie, smoking a cigarette, and looking (so far as these signals were understood by readers) sexually ambiguous.

Radclyffe Hall was shocked and angry. The attack had caught her unawares, and the seriousness of her book threatened to be overwhelmed by these un-Christian allegations of pornography. It was not a titillating book, and she deeply resented the suggestion that homosexuality was a particularly nasty, contagious disease. Meanwhile, sales soared. But Cape was worried. On 20 August he wrote to the Daily Express offering to submit the novel to the Home Secretary. Indeed, he did just that, without consulting the author. John, as Radclyffe Hall was known to her intimates, was enraged. To mollify her, Cape offered to despatch the moulds of the type to Paris where the book might be safely reprinted, the Home Secretary having more or less instructed Cape to stop printing the novel or face legal prosecution, since he himself had no authority to ban publication. From France, the book might be imported into England on receipt of orders from booksellers and subscribers. There was no shortage of demand.

Eminent writers in England were rallied to protest about the Home Secretary's displeasure, John's postbag was full of supportive letters from readers, and she was determined, more than ever, to continue her literary struggle on behalf of her fellow inverts. Paris bookshops were full of copies of the book, and there was to be an American edition published by Knopf. But Knopf 'ratted' (Una Troubridge's word), and Knopf's wife Blanche explained that the book's reputation in England as a pornographic work meant that it would be seen, bought, and read in the United States only as a 'dirty' book. Publication would do neither Knopf nor Radclyffe Hall any good in these circumstances. On 18 October, the Customs and Excise seized a consignment of the novel being imported from France into England, and Cape's office was raided a few days later. John was ecstatic. The trial would be an opportunity to defend the cause not only of the book but of sexual inversion. There was no doubt she would win a heroic victory. The book was not, after all, obscene, and homosexuality was not a sin or a symptom of degeneracy.

But she was advised against going into the witness box to testify on her own behalf, since she herself was not being arraigned. Only Cape and a bookseller were being prosecuted. But she had her way in that no denial or apology was made of her own homosexuality. Both Cape and the bookseller Leopold Hill, who had imported the novel, were found guilty. Notice of appeal was filed on 22 November, and again the court found against the defendants. *The Well of Loneliness* was declared 'a disgusting book . . . prejudicial to the morals of the community.' It was decided that further appeal would be useless. The Paris presses kept turning out copies of the book, however, and it became an underground best-seller. It was sold, in the banned Cape edition, for considerable sums. In all, by the end of 1928, the novel had sold seven thousand five hundred copies outside America, more than half having been bought after the publicity given to it by James Douglas and other newspapers.

Radclyffe Hall had agreed to share the expenses of the trials with Cape, and she found herself in financial difficulty. Income tax had risen, and she had lost a good deal of money in the Depression. She decided to sell 37 Holland Street, in London, where she and Una had lived for four years. On 18 October, in the middle of the legal excitements, they had returned to Rye where they had taken a six-month lease of the cottage in

Hucksteps Row. Named The Forecastle, it 'was very ugly,' according to Una. 'Its Tudor charms were disguised almost beyond recognition by masses of heterogeneous junk and it rocked and swayed in the great souwesterly gales while Mabel hung up blankets to keep out the draughts. The bath-water was temperamental and we had only oil lamps, but to us it was a heavenly haven of peace in which we pulled ourselves together for the next round before plunging back into the battle.' Mabel was Mabel Bourne, who came with the cottage, a housekeeper who could be relied upon to 'greet us with blazing fires and her genius for cooking.' Despite its inconveniences, The Forecastle, at the end of the narrow passageway leading off Church Square at the crown of Rye, was pleasingly romantic and atmospheric. 'There was something jovial and carefree about that cottage, something that suggested "Yo, ho, ho and a bottle of rum!" It seemed pleasantly haunted by lawless shades and its view of the Marsh was peerless. From my bed in the little room where I slept I could see the Gris Nez lighthouse on clear days and from the windows three other lighthouses flashing.' Una Troubridge cuts short her raptures about Rye and Romney Marsh: 'why should I attempt to write again what John has immortalized in *The Sixth Beatitude?*'

This novel, which followed *The Well of Loneliness* and *The Master of the House* in 1936, is set in Hucksteps Row and concerns Hannah, the thirty-year-old daughter of the working-class Bullen household who live in Crofts Lane – the lane that ended abruptly in The Look-Out. The Look-Out is The Forecastle. Crofts Lane, in real life Hucksteps Row, stands 'well above the Marsh on a hill having Crofts Lane as its highest point, and the crazy old houses with their rotting walls, their cracked weather tiles and their sagging roofs, must huddle together rather helplessly; unable any more to withstand the winters.' The winters were liable to be cold and treacherous. Radclyffe Hall and Una Troubridge spent the Christmas of 1928 in The Forecastle, and *The Sixth Beatitude* describes the meteorological conditions of that year, the climate that might be experienced during a severe winter (very like that of 1984/85) in Rye: 'Snow blowing thickly over the Marsh and piling itself into drifts along the high road. The sheep pressing close to the roadside fences in an effort to contact themselves with the Lookers – in an effort to contact themselves with man the destroyer and man the protector. Ice on the dykes, and an icy wind sweeping across the Marsh into Rother [Rye], and Rother as white as a bridal veil with soft folds of snow on its roofs and cobbles. Anchor Street [Mermaid Street], whose steep hill once led down to the sea, grown as perilous now as the Cresta Run. And everyone throwing logs on his fire, and rubbing his hands, and cursing the weather.'

John and Una deeply loved Rye which had, in other seasons, its gentler aspect. Rother, as Rye is called in *The Sixth Beatitude*, 'would sometimes seem more than a town of old, decaying black-and-white houses huddling inside an ancient town wall – Rother would almost seem like a person. Rother could draw unto itself lovely colours: soft greys and soft browns and soft, dark purples; and at sunrise and sunset its red roofs would blaze, and so would the leaded panes of its windows; and after a storm all its cobbles would shine . . . while the grass in between them would look as bright as though it had just had a coat of fresh paint. And then there were the tall, straight masts of the ships that lay at the bottom of Anchor Street where the sea had once washed against the Strand, and where now there was only a tidal river. Masts of ships among houses – that looked queer. Rother would seem to stare down at those ships with old, thoughtful eyes very full of affection.'

Hannah Bullen's are the eyes through which Radclyffe Hall saw Rye as it 'stood peacefully dreaming, sleeping and dreaming above the Marsh . . . it would become something more than a town, especially on the warm July evenings when the dusk lay folded along its streets, and the ships lighted port and starboard lanterns, and the past . . . came wandering craftily into the present . . .' But the winter of 1928/29 was appalling: even the palm trees in Monte Carlo were frostbitten and snow fell on the Croisette in Cannes. After Christmas in Rye, with friends, John and Una returned to London on 30 December to show themselves as fearless and unbowed in public, and on 5 February 1929, they arrived in Paris. Radclyffe Hall had been exhausted by the trials, and she had been ordered by her doctor to take a complete rest in the sun. Una accompanied her to the South of France on 17 May. They did not return to England until October, and almost immediately they set out for Rye where they had decided to buy a house and to establish themselves permanently away from London.

They had planned to live abroad, but a troublesome legal matter had brought them back to the England they had vowed to renounce for ever, and it became quickly apparent that exile was not the answer. John was now comfortably off – the sensations over *The Well* had stimulated sales of her other novels, and she had begun a new novel, initially entitled *The Carpenter's Son*, in Paris. On 28 December 1929 they bought The Black Boy, a house in Rye's High Street, which fitted their desires for a place described by Una as 'not only convenient but beautiful and not only beautiful but also ancient and unspoiled.' Charles II was said to have stayed in the house, hence its name, derived from Black Charles. It was bought in Una's name, as a gift to her from John. First of all, it had to be restored to its former condition: original walls and ancient oak beams had to be uncovered, and a firm of local builders was employed. Meantime, the two women put up at The Mermaid, a hotel in Mermaid Street.

They 'were perfectly happy there in antique discomfort. It was then in an extreme state of neglect and dilapidation. It was dirty, badly heated and when fires became necessary, the chimneys smoked. The ancient windows let in arctic draughts and we were reduced to stuffing cracks and holes with stockings. But we camped in a large and beautiful room with a big log fire in a lovely old grate, and we tolerated a stinking supplementary oilstove and a host of other inconveniences with equanimity, and John was able to work because of the fulfilling atmosphere of the place. We also liked the inefficient old Irish manageress. Our attitude can best be gauged by John's reactions when we lunched one day at another and at that time decidely better equipped hotel. She was told that in deference to certain old maids of both sexes it was not permitted to smoke in the coffee-room and she remarked very audibly to me: "Let's go back to our Mermaid, shall we? At any rate there I'm allowed to spit on the floor!" '

Una, fondly remembering The Mermaid in her memoir of Radclyffe Hall, *The Life and Death of Radclyffe Hall*, published in 1961, might have been surprised to learn that the staff of The Mermaid were less than delighted with her. In *Una Troubridge* by Richard Ormrod, published in 1984, the housekeeper remembers her as 'rather "superior",' while the waiter shared the housekeeper's dislike: 'She only spoke when she had to.' A chambermaid's lasting impression of Una Troubridge was that she 'was very much the Lady and was finicky . . .' But Radclyffe Hall was a different matter. She had a natural grace and good manners, and, though 'Proper mannish, she was, . . . you respected her.' To the chambermaid, John seemed 'very nice, although she was always calling me "You fool!" as though that was my name!' Her appearance was 'very mannish' and her relationship with Una was 'like a husband, always asking for things for Lady Troubridge. "Lady Troubridge must have more fires," and so on.' When they came down to dinner, 'quite stunning Radclyffe Hall was when she was dressed – frilly shirt, man's suit . . . always very smartly dressed. Lady Troubridge, she wore evening dresses . . .' There was often a claque of young women, in late 1929, desperate to meet the celebrated author, some of whom had to be forcibly restrained from rushing up the stairs to burst into Radclyffe Hall's room. The chambermaid 'formed the impression that "Radclyffe Hall was not allowed by Lady Troubridge to give autographs", and that "Lady Troubridge kept people away," being both protective of her and "very domineering in a subtle way".'

By March 1930, the Mermaid had become too inconvenient and a little house in Watchbell Street, Number 8, was rented while the work went on at The Black Boy. Number 8 had a distinct advantage: it was directly opposite the Catholic church and 'From its sitting room, when the church door was open, we could look right through it up the nave and see the statue of the Sacred Heart softly illumined in the darkness by the votive candles that burned before it.' Radclyffe Hall was a deeply religious Catholic and, while working on her new novel, which was based on the life of Christ and was to be published in 1932 as *The Master of the House*, she disquietingly experienced severe pains in the palms of her hands. Then 'an angry looking red stain' appeared 'in the centre of both palms.' A dermatologist in London was consulted, and radiological treatment was recommended. But the pain, and the bruise-like stains, persisted. John was obliged to wrap her hands in bandages, and to continue writing as best she could. Gradually the marks and the pain disappeared – but the effect of the phenomenon was very great. Una thought John had been visited by stigmata, particularly since the theme of the book John was working on was patently religious. *The Master of the House* 'was written,' said Una, 'as an amends for that insult to her Lord and to her faith' which *The Well of Loneliness* had caused. Whether or not that was the case is certainly open to dispute, but Radclyffe Hall was at this time living, very consciously, an austere and celibate life. She worked, devotedly and intensely, twelve hours at a stretch on most days, and Una, according to gossip among the servants, was now and again to be found lying outside her lover's door weeping and pleading to be let in.

Radclyffe Hall and Una Troubridge had become lovers after meeting in August 1915 (an earlier social encounter had, unaccountably, been unfruitful). At the time, Radclyffe Hall was living with a singer, Mabel Batten, known as Ladye, and Una Troubridge was the wife of Admiral Sir Ernest Troubridge. Soon after, Ladye died and Una was divorced from Troubridge. There was a difference of seven years in age between Radclyffe Hall and Una. In 1915, Una was twenty-eight, and Radclyffe Hall was thirty-five, the former a pretty woman, the latter a strikingly handsome woman. John, as Radclyffe Hall liked to be known, was a congenital invert. There was no doubt that, as she herself considered, she had never been anything but lesbian. Una, however, probably had the capacity to be bisexual – but Radclyffe Hall provided the love and security she so much desired and which she had not found in her husband. In company, Una was very feminine, and played the little woman, whereas Radclyffe Hall was by far the more masculine not only in appearance but in mind. While Una continued to love John, John – as was to become evident – had fallen out of love with Una, however much it appeared that the two women were inseparable and relied upon one another.

Meanwhile, before the storm was to break over Una's head, they were content in one another's company in 1931. John was working long and hard at *The Master of the House*, while Una busied herself with The Black Boy, making it comfortable, and socialising in Rye. They had moved into the house in August 1930, excited by having found 'a secret room, a priest's hole, and about a dozen Jacobean shoes and clay pipes among other relics' during the course of refurbishing the property. Rye was an idyll: 'par excellence the home of history, you can't dig in a garden without finding old coins and other trophies, and it is the place in all England where you can get away from this hideous age of progress – that is why we have come to it,' wrote Una ecstatically to a friend. The house was blessed by Father Bonaventura from the Catholic church in Watchbell Street, and friends were invited to admire the work that had gone into The Black Boy. Noel Coward, who had a country retreat at Goldenhurst, came over with his secretary and Lord Amherst: 'howls of laughter. Noel *adored* "The Black Boy." Lady Maud Warrender, a daughter of the Earl of Shaftesbury, sixty years old, arrived with the singer Marcia van Dresser with whom she lived at Leasam, and "Dodo" Benson visited fairly regularly.' But he was regarded with some reserve: Lady Maud had said he had 'one-way pockets' and, as well as being tight with money, he was reticent about his own homosexuality – a grave disservice to 'the cause' in the eyes of John and Una who believed that anyone in a position to do so should stand up and be counted as they themselves had done. Then, too, they suspected that the inoffensive Benson tippled on the quiet.

Their closest friends in Romney Marsh lived in Smallhythe – Edy Craig, the elderly daughter of the actress Ellen Terry, and her two companions, the writer Christopher St John (actually Christabel Marshall) and the artist Clare Atwood (known generally as 'Tony'). Edy and Christopher had lived together for thirty years; Tony was a relative latecomer, having arrived during the war at Edy's behest. They lived fairly amicably together, running Smallhythe Place as a memorial museum devoted to Ellen Terry. John and Una visited Paul Nash at Iden, an excursion which provided them with an opportunity to take a swipe at modern art and Surrealism in particular. And they entertained the writer Francis Yeats-Brown, author of *Bengal Lancer*, who had taken a house in Rye and professed to be in love with a young woman named Rosalind Constable. John and Una looked with profound disfavour on this proposed match. It seemed most improbable: Yeats-Brown, they were convinced, was homosexual, and so was Rosalind. There were other homosexuals to be met with in Romney Marsh – notably Commandant Mary Allen (who liked to be called 'Robert') and her friend Miss Taggart who lived at Lympne with two St Bernard dogs. Robert, once a militant suffragette, had helped found the Women's Volunteer Police Force (from which she derived her proud title) during the war. On its disbandment after the war by the Home Secretary, it survived unofficially, held together by the determination of Robert who was loath to give up her uniform and gleaming boots. 'They are fine citizens,' wrote Una, warmly.

Lovat Dickson, in *Radclyffe Hall at the Well of Loneliness*, published in 1975, comments that, after all the initial excitements of moving to Rye, fitting out The Black Boy, and establishing a circle of sympathetic friends in Romney Marsh, a change came over John and Una. Some of their London friends, too enthusiastically enraptured with Rye at the beginning, dropped away. They took the relationship between John and Una for granted. 'Many of them, the majority in fact, were homosexuals or artists leading vagabond lives, or simply jolly forty-year-old girls, left-overs from the war, liberated but not free in a class-striated society like England's, where morals were often what your own kind approved of, or did not openly disapprove of.' John and Una were, in the '30s, says Lovat Dickson, becoming period pieces of the '20s. Outrageous behaviour was no longer quite so fashionable – there were other, more serious matters to engage people's attention. Then, too, John had an uncertain temper and Una was exclusive and possessive in her relationship with her beloved: 'too often they were by themselves night after night, weekend after weekend, in this charming home they were making out of The Black Boy.' Friends, now, tended to be local, though proximity and constant contact tended to breed strife and dissension. The novelist Sheila Kaye-Smith, married to Penrose Fry, was at first a welcome guest. She and her husband were invited to a successful, small, select dinner and made a good impression. Una, on account of their short stature, nicknamed them 'the small Fry'. All went swimmingly until 1932, when little Mrs Fry attempted, according to Una, to steal some of John's thunder at a Foyle's lunch at which John was guest speaker on 17 March at Grosvenor House. John's novel, *The Master of the House*, had been published on 29 February and sales, though good, were not spectacular.

Sheila Kaye-Smith had 'wangled' herself and her own new novel into the occasion, and John ended her talk on The Great Adventure of Fiction by congratulating her literary colleague on the birthday of her book and wishing it the best of luck. A generous, though probably unavoidable gesture towards another writer and friend, one might have thought, but Una gloated that 'Sheila went a deep crimson as the coals of fire descended on her head.' This was John's day and occasion, and nothing should detract from it and its potential, in the company of seven hundred literary guests, to boost sales of *The Master of the House*. Worse, ten days later Sheila and Penrose Fry visited John and Una at The Black Boy and unaccountably, in Una's view, failed to give an opinion on John's book. They made some token comment on John's research, but John did not appear vexed by what Una perceived to be Sheila's cattiness. John, on the contrary, was generous in her praise of Sheila's book and presented the Frys with a signed copy of *The Master of the House*. Una wisely restrained herself from tearing the gift from Sheila's 'mean little hands'. The Fry's were doomed: not only limited in height, they were small-minded in Una's eyes and all their minor faults and social shortcomings were instantly magnified – their house was falling down in disrepair, Penrose was wet and weedy and a terrible driver, Sheila was unsuitably dressed for life in the country, and her books were mere pot-boilers written for American magazines to sate her greed for money. Una, indulging a natural aptitude for spite and gossip, cloaked her baser nature in her noble and constant crusade to protect John against the malicious slights and snipings of an ignoble world.

Una took considerable offence at a disapproving review in *The Times Literary Supplement* which, she considered, 'went for' *The Master of the House* and its author alike. There were difficulties with American publication. Cape's subsidiary, Cape-Ballou, was going bankrupt and rights to the book had hastily to be transferred to another publisher. John had put heart, soul, and considerable dogged energy into her new novel, but it had not caught on with the public. By mid-March, *The Master* had sold nine thousand copies, but by April not more than ten thousand. *The Well*, by comparison, had sold one hundred and fifty thousand copies world-wide. To John, *The Master* was as important a book as *The Well* and she was depressed by its reception. Una could not fail to share John's dejection. In the summer of 1932, Una was forty-five years of age and menopausal. She was alarmed by recurrent bouts of heavy bleeding – menorrhagia – and was recommended to undergo a hysterectomy at a London clinic. The operation was carried out on 5 July 1932, and two days later she became seriously ill. Radclyffe Hall stayed by her bedside throughout the crisis, an act of devotion and generosity which was not lost on Una who, in her memoir of Radclyffe Hall, remarks: 'Physical pain and discomfort are so easily forgotten, but not the ceaseless and loving care that made them not only endurable but of little consequence. . . . The warm, happy consciousness of being absolutely essential to the one being on earth who is all in all.' On 2 August Una was able to leave the nursing home, and John took her to Brighton to convalesce. Dutifully, John pushed Una about in a bath chair at the height of a heatwave – temperatures in the high 80s and low 90s Fahrenheit – for three weeks until 23 August when they returned to Rye, 'glorious Rye and our own "Black Boy" for tea and found flowers from . . . Smallhythe and roses from Dodo.' Almost immediately, Una was bedridden with shingles, and an abscess, followed by influenza and severe headaches.

John, meanwhile, was busy revising a collection of short stories, to be published under the title, *Miss Ogilvy Finds Herself*. She had been offered a contract to visit Hollywood to write scenarios for three or six months, but – whether because of Una's illnesses or her own disinclination – John did not accept the offer and remained in Rye, though the remote and refined, romantic and historical charms of the little town were beginning to prove faintly stultifying. John fell ill with 'flu in January 1933 and was nursed devotedly by Una who also succumbed to the virus so that they were laid up together for ten days in the same bed. Then, longing for some metropolitan stimulation, in March John bought a London flat, 17 Talbot House in St Martin's Lane, despite medical advice that she should have three months' complete rest for nervous exhaustion. It had been a difficult time, and it had made them both restless. John, in particular, could rarely settle to a quiet life except when circumstances of work demanded it. Now, part of their life was in London, part in Rye. In *The Tyranny of Home*, Radclyffe Hall admits that a house in London and the country ended up as a home in neither. Henry James and Fred Benson had both experienced the same dilemma as John described: 'The book sought in the Country will always be in London and vice versa. A summer season spent in London will mean missing the fruit blossom, the cuckoo, the bluebells, the nightingale; a season in the Country will mean no Russian Ballet, no Opera, no Wimbledon.' John wanted both – to be a writer who found peace to write in the country, and to be a literary lion, a celebrity, who enjoyed the applause of London society and her peers. She was in demand as a lecturer, having spoken effectively to audiences at the Oxford University English Club and at the London University Literary Society. She attended literary gatherings where, gratifyingly, she was considered quite a personage, a prominent literary figure. This, in view of the modest success of her last novel, was heartening. On 5 March 1934, she published her volume of short stories, *Miss Ogilvy Finds Herself.*

The five stories make up rather a depressing book. The work that Radclyffe Hall had put into writing and revising them for publication had seemed to Una like a reprise of the agonies suffered by both of them during the writing of *The Master of the House*. In *Radclyffe Hall*, published in 1985, Michael Baker considers that, 'Taken together, all five stories present an extremely bleak vision. Each of the main protagonists inhabits an introspective, isolated private world where love and friendship are almost entirely absent.' Clearly, Radclyffe Hall was depressed. Though Heinemann agreed to publish the book in the United Kingdom, Houghton Mifflin in the United States refused it on the ground that the stories were too gloomy. But it was taken by Harcourt Brace. British advance sales amounted to eighteen hundred copies, but the reviews were patchy and disappointing. 'There is no one so difficult to live with as an author suffering the pangs of being unjustly neglected,' remarks Lovat Dickson, and John was retreating more and more from what she perceived as a hostile, materialist, modern world that was not merely indifferent but actively prejudiced against everything she held dear. She retreated more and more into herself, abandoning anyone - friends, agent, publishers – who seemed in the least disloyal or not actively and constantly striving for her best interests.

The loyalty she demanded of others was, Una believed, Radclyffe Hall's greatest virtue and the gift she most unstintingly gave in return to her lover. Una relied wholeheartedly on John, but John discovered that she could rely on nobody but herself. No amount of solicitude for her welfare from Una could shake her essential isolation and loneliness. Una was apparently not strong enough for herself, to judge by the constant illnesses and minor ailments, and her consequent demands, however unconscious, for attention and reassurance were not gratified. Outwardly, John gave Una the sympathy, patience, love and devotion that she required, but the inner woman was no longer wholly engaged with her. As Michael Baker remarks, 'Una took her partnership with John for granted. John took nothing for granted.' She was profoundly unconventional, despite her public and private recommendation of the minor domestic virtues and the central importance of fidelity within a relationship sanctified by love and – where appropriate or possible – marriage.

In 1934, all appeared well to Una: the house they had first lived in and coveted in Rye, The Forecastle, was up for sale. John was pressed for money, and The Black Boy was sold. A bid of seven hundred and fifty pounds was accepted for The Forecastle and the house was put in Una's name. The sale was completed on 2 February 1934, and by the spring they moved in. Hucksteps Row was locally known as Jolly Sailor Lane after the pub in Hucksteps Row, an improvement on its earlier name of Fishgut Alley. It was owned, mostly, by a local solicitor and property speculator, James Macdonnell, known to John as 'the happy-go-lucky landlord' and referred to as such in *The Sixth Beatitude*. The little lane was more or less a slum, inhabited by fisherman and their families who paid two and sixpence to three and sixpence a week rent to the landlord for tumbledown cottages with no gardens and no internal sanitation. But John and Una loved The Forecastle and restored its Tudor character with original and imported oak. They worked on it so successfully, that the result dismayed them a little: 'in the end we looked at one another and confessed to a curious misgiving.' Had they turned it into 'something of a museum piece?'

John was keen to get back to work. Renovation of The Forecastle had taken up a good deal of time and energy. But an old ailment began to vex her – 'the hunting vein' in her leg – and

Una persuaded John to take a holiday at Bagnoles de l'Orne in France before settling to another novel. John opposed the idea of a rest cure with considerable earnestness. 'She told me afterwards, many times,' wrote Una later, 'that she had an almost overwhelming instinct against leaving England on that occasion and had been unable to understand her own forebodings.' On 21 June, John and Una crossed the Channel to Paris where they renewed old acquaintance with Colette, Romaine Brooks, the Comtesse de Clermont-Tonnerre, Nathalie Barney and other lesbian friends. Five days later they arrived at the Hotel des Thermes at Bagnoles where Una went down with a sudden, violent attack of gastro-enteritis. The weather was stiflingly hot, and Una was too weak to move from her bed. Since John had come to rest and be cured of her leg pain, Una insisted that a nurse be found to relieve John of constant attendance on her. A telephone call to the American Hospital in Paris resulted in the arrival of a nurse, a plain-faced, unmarried thirty-year-old White Russian woman with a fat face and spectacles, called Evguenia Souline. She appeared to be competent and agreeable, and, admits Una, 'I was never better taken care of in my life, but it never for one moment entered my mind that this young Russian woman with the curious face – the refugee daughter of a deceased Tsarist Cossack general – was to be anything in our lives but a bird of passage.'

Una identified the bird more accurately, to her extreme dismay, as a cuckoo in the nest when Evguenia arrived in England on 4 November, to be met off the boat at Folkestone by John who had conceived a passionate infatuation for her. Una fretted in the flat in London, while John and her erstwhile nurse spent three days at the Grand Hotel in Folkestone. When they came to the London flat in St Martin's Lane for three days, Una moved down to The Forecastle. When John and Evguenia decided to come to Rye, Una moved back to St Martin's Lane, dispossessed not only of her lover but of her own home. Rather understating the matter, Una wrote, 'It was not to be a happy connection for either John or Evguenia.' Understandably, and with considerable restraint, she makes no mention of the unhappiness she herself was feeling.

In the space of a fortnight, at Bagnoles, John had succumbed entirely to the nurse. In order that Una might rest undisturbed, John had moved into Evguenia's room at the hotel – but Evguenia, though she could have been in no doubt as to the nature of the relationship between Una and John, did not fully respond to John's ardent advances. Una noticed only that Evguenia displayed, occasionally, 'inhibitions and reserves which baffle one.' Una, consulting John, discussed the peculiarities of the nurse and John colluded in their joint decision that the horrors of the Russian revolution had left their mark on Evguenia's psyche and that, as a gentlewoman, her puzzling confusions were very natural. Una had no inkling that they were due to any intimate relationship initiated by John. Evguenia returned to Paris on 14 July, where she was bombarded with letters and telephone calls from John. Evguenia was not unresponsive, and they arranged to meet in Paris when John and Una passed through the city at the end of the month. Una felt a certain sympathy for her nurse: 'I am sorry for the poor child who is lonely and not happy,' but she thought they would give her dinner and that would be an end of their interest in her. In Paris, Evguenia flirted with John and allowed herself to be kissed in John's hotel room. She also allowed John to pay for meals and taxis, secure in the knowledge that John had fallen passionately in love with her.

On 28 July, John and Una left Paris for Sirmione to visit the novelist Naomi (Mickie) Jacob who had a house on Lake Garda. Here, staying at the Albergo Catullo, John admitted her infidelity to Una. Una was distracted, to say the least. She threw herself on the floor, sobbing hysterically, and in her grief berated John roundly for betraying every principle of fidelity she had advocated publicly and privately for 'inverted unions'. She had an obligation, as a champion of sexual inversion, to live a spotlessly faithful life. John's conscience was touched: she acknowledged Una's comradeship over eighteen years, her support during the struggles for *The Well of Loneliness*, and that

Una's health, so apparently precarious, might not withstand the shock. Una's love for John did not waver: she did not realise fully, perhaps, that John had ceased to love her, since so much bound them together. To Souline (as John called Evguenia, preferring the soft euphonious sound of her last name to her first), Radclyffe Hall admitted that Una 'has given me all of her interest and indeed of her life since we made common cause . . .' Una had relented so far as to allow John to write to Souline, and then, bowing to what she may have perceived as the inevitable, granted leave for them to meet later in Paris so long as John was not unfaithful 'in the fullest and ultimate meaning of the word'. Una hoped, perhaps, that John would soon discover how shallow a creature Souline really was and would tire of her.

In her memoir of Radclyffe Hall, Una is carefully generous and loyal: 'John was a sensitive, highly-evolved European utterly incapable of divorcing any emotional impulse from all that was kind and protective in her nature.' She is less indulgent towards Evguenia who is tartly described as 'a creature of impulses and violent surface emotions: she was indeed as violent and uncontrolled as a savage . . .' Evguenia did not, in Una's view, take John's work very seriously, having no conception of its importance to John and resenting it as an interference. Her hope that John would see through Souline was unfounded: Radclyffe Hall's attachment to this improbable creature was to last until the end of 1942, nine years more or less. At the beginning, John fired off daily letters to Souline from Italy. Una was appalled. She begged John to stop, but John thought she had at last met her 'soul-mate' and nothing would induce her to give up Souline. John and Una did not leave Sirmione until September. They arrived in Paris on the 22nd, whereupon John took up with Souline despite her promise to Una that she would not see her. That John felt considerable guilt over Una is evident in Una's claim on 2 October that, 'In spite of everything we are close, close: one spirit and one flesh, indissoluble and indivisible for ever. She [John] said to me yesterday: "Remain with me for ever and ever throughout eternity. Amen!" She said:"*You* are permanent!" ' John was making fairly similar declarations to Souline a few days later, after arriving back in England: 'Nothing is real but those ten days in Paris when I held you in my arms and taught you to love, when your heart beat close against my heart, and your mouth was on mine, and our arms were round each other straining our bodies closer and more close, until there was an agony in our loving . . .' Later, 'Souline, my most dear, you have suddenly grown up – I found a child and I have made you a woman.' Una was not convinced on this latter point. When Souline was ill, she made a terrific fuss, John bearing with her 'realizing always the element of childishness that was a racial component of this Cossack nature.'

Despite her dislike and distrust of Souline, Una agreed to help John gain a visa for Souline to stay in England, using her status 'as the widow of an Admiral' to vouch for her. And thus it was, through her connivance, that Souline arrived in England to continue the affair with her lover. Souline left in mid-November, leaving both Una and John emotionally exhausted. Quarrels erupted at The Forecastle, and on 31 December Una wrote in her Day Book, 'The last day of a very unhappy year'. John continued to write to Souline, and made her an allowance for rent and living expenses in Paris. She roped in Una to help get French naturalisation papers for Souline who recognised the considerable hold she had on both women, John directly, and on Una through John. Una was still not convinced that the affair was not a passing infatuation despite her gnawing despair. Then, too, Souline was having a disruptive effect on John's work.

In April 1935, however, John settled down to work on the book that was to become *The Sixth Beatitude*, the novel set in Hucksteps Row. Una was ill – heart palpitations and breathlessness worried her. Another worry was that John's passion for Souline had not diminished: she was as hungry for this 'rather under-developed type of child . . .' as Una described her, 'whose deficiences of sympathy and perception would distress one were she one's own,' as ever. Una and John visited Souline in Paris in the summer of 1935 and in August they revisited Sirmione where, at the Albergo Catullo, John visited Souline's room every night until Una protested that she might cause a public scandal. Back in Paris, John rented and furnished a better flat for Souline who took to her new, luxurious conditions like a pig to clover.

Back in Rye, Una and John found that autumn storms had flooded the older slum houses in Hucksteps Row, and that they were to be demolished to make way for new houses. 'Change, always change – how I hate it!' mused John, innocent of any regret for the changes that had been forced on Una. Souline was coming for Christmas, and lavish preparations were made to fête her. Una drew a diamond pin out of her bank to give to Souline as a present, and with unexpected goodwill she wrote in her Daybook: 'except that I deplore this affair with Evguenia as a blemish upon our complete mutual faith and as a thing that wrongs it and her integrity, there are times when I weakly feel that I have not the heart to grudge her the pleasure . . . that she gets out of it.' Despite all provocations, Una could wish happiness for John wherever she might elect to find it. She could not go so far as to like Souline, however, and it was naive of John to hope piously that they might be friends with one another.

Una could not leave John: there would be no life for her without Radclyffe Hall, in whom she had invested everything she had to give. John did not leave Una, because she was comfortable with a familiar friend and life, because she felt guilty not only towards Una but because she had been unkind (as she thought) towards Mabel Batten in her last days with her, and because she was, after all, the celebrated and newsworthy Radclyffe Hall who had become, in herself and in her apparently settled life with Una, something of a symbol, example and inspiration to other sexual inverts who took strength from her heroism and her commitment to fidelity within a lasting relationship with another woman. She would not give ammunition to her many critics by disavowing, in a public act, all that she had built up and maintained over so many years. Souline must have felt slighted and peripheral, despite John's continual passionate letters and actions, because in January 1936, in Paris, she accused John of repressing her and using her merely as a sexual convenience. John, appalled, wept bitterly at this accusation and turned to Una for comfort. Souline continued to be difficult that year: she suffered bleeding on her lung and was admitted to the American Hospital where she was treated. In March, the three of them travelled to Grasse and in the summer they went to Trois Epis in Alsace after a few days in Paris. In September, they found themselves at Merano in the Italian Tyrol. Here Souline caught her finger in a door and, when the doctor attempted to lance the blister, kicked and screeched and behaved quite in a manner that disgusted Una: 'I have never seen an adult of our class exhibit such unashamed cowardice.' In May, 1937, they were in Florence where, they decided, the air was good for Souline's lungs and they would make camp for the following winter.

Souline, however, kicked her heels and said she would rather be in Paris. She adamantly refused to winter in Florence. John was tormented. She turned upon Una, in her despair when Souline threatened to leave John rather than be forced to live even for a while in Florence, and to Una it appeared, despite John's rage with her, that the tide had turned against Souline and in favour of herself. But John and Souline patched things up between them, and Una, bewildered, recorded her feelings: 'I am simply exhausted in spirit, mind and body.' On 14 July, John and Una returned to Rye without Souline. Here, things seemed somewhat quieter and they fell back into the usual routine of old friends and The Forecastle which, however, was only approachable through the rubble of demolished cottages. The work of rebuilding Hucksteps Row had begun. John wrote to Souline, telling her that they had to mark time for a while and assured her that she would never again have to put up with a *ménage à trois*. John also agreed to allow Souline more freedom, more latitude to manage her own extravagant life, though she found it difficult to break her view of Souline as a child: 'the little child for whom I so much long – the little Chink child – our child, our most precious, spoiled and naughty little Chink.' The reference to 'little Chink' is an allusion to Souline's high cheekbones and slanting eyes – her only distinguished features, and irresistible to John.

On 25 August John fell and twisted her ankle. X-Rays confirmed that it was broken – a triple fracture which required John to spend some weeks with her foot in plaster at the London Clinic. She took a strangely long while to recover, but was determined to go to Florence as planned. With considerable difficulty, she made the trip, with Una, to Paris in October where a painful course of physiotherapy became necessary to treat a shrunken Achilles tendon. At length they reached Florence, with Souline, and settled into an apartment with a view over the Ponte Vecchio. Souline demanded a flat of her own – she was not going to live with Una again – and a suitable apartment was found on the Via dei Benci. Una had friends in Florence, and quickly began to develop a social life. John was naturally a party to this activity, and both she and Una enjoyed antiquarian excursions in search of antiques and historical sites. Souline was bored, and made no bones about it. She demanded to return to Paris, and John, anxious to placate her, made every effort to soothe her ruffled feathers. John was having troubles of her own. She had always been healthy, but now her ankle injury refused to heal completely and she was enduring a painful form of chronic conjunctivitis. She was sleepless, having begun another bout of intensive literary work, and in February she was struck down by influenza. Souline, still pressing for a return to Paris, was allowed to go with an increased allowance of three hundred pounds a year to enable her to study at the Sorbonne. She failed the qualifying exams, and immediately thereafter announced, to John's dismay, her intention to go off on holiday with a woman friend. Writing to her, John complained (with justice): 'You have not been a good woman to me, my Evguenia, not as good as you might have been. You were not a kind woman to me during my recent breakdown – you could have taken care of me but you did not.' Souline more or less demanded that John should abandon Una, and in return John hinted at suicide. It is generally acknowledged that Souline was an unscrupulous, manipulative, demanding woman who used Radclyffe Hall unmercifully for her own ends and gratification. Souline's selfishness passed all bounds of reasonable behaviour, and time and again John gave in to her. Una, recognising John's unaccountable love for this ungracious and ungrateful child-woman, was miserable to the point at which she even felt 'that the long mutual trust and confidence between John and I has degenerated, in spite of all our affection.' They were no longer lovers in the physical sense, but there was still a deep bond between them that threatened to be tested to the limit.

Despite the intimations of approaching war in 1938, and the anxiety that White Russians in France might be rounded up, John and Una travelled from Rye to Paris in October 1938 after Chamberlains's Munich Agreement with Hitler and managed to persuade Souline to come to Florence for the winter. Both Una and John were sceptical of Hitler but supporters of Mussolini. They deeply regretted 'this madness that has suddenly stricken Europe . . . these are terrible and dangerous days indeed.' In Florence, at Christmas, John kept to the letter of her agreement with Souline that there should be no sexual relations between them: the result, of course, was a period of suffocating sulks on Souline's behalf and tension caused by continual tiffs. John did not find it easy to repress her physical passion for Souline who returned to Paris, leaving John and Una to stay on in Florence until July 1939. Stopping only to collect Souline in Paris, they arrived back in Rye on 4 August 1939 with the intention of selling The Forecastle and making their permanent home in Italy.

'It was out of the question,' says Una, 'to continue keeping up a house which would only be occasionally occupied during the summer, and while the circumstances of Evguenia's illness had already led to such a procedure for several years past, that had been regarded by both of us as a temporary measure. But now it was John's health that was in question, her unfitness for the northern winters being permanent, and we must harden our hearts and let The Forecastle go.' It was a wrench to think of leaving the house that had captivated them from first sight, but 'The Forecastle was only habitable in summer. It was ruthlessly exposed to sun, wind and rain which engineered an alternate swelling and shrinkage so that its sixteenth-century plaster and timbers parted company. No amount of caulking would cope with this defect and we very soon found that in inclement weather we were driven from sitting in the parlour or study to seeking refuge in the dark little dining room. All the same, the idea of selling it was definitely painful. John had given it to me and we had both adored it, and although that had been over five years ago we had actually been able to live in it so rarely that we had not had time to get tired of it.'

Into The Forecastle, with all these inconveniences and associations, came Souline in August 1939. She complained constantly that she would prefer to be in Paris – no doubt Una heartily wished her back there. The Forecastle was tense with rising tempers, and towards the end of the month Souline and Una came physically to blows after a violent argument. John insisted that Souline apologise to Una for having pushed her, but Souline refused. Five days later, on 1 September, Hitler invaded Poland and put paid to any number of plans, including John and Una's intention to remove permanently to Italy on completion of the sale of The Forecastle. There was an immediate excitement. The air-raid sirens howled and the first alert, on the first morning of war, caught Rye on the hop: 'we never knew whether it had sounded for a raid or whether it had been somebody's unpleasant manner of finding out whether Rye's A.R.P. was alive to its responsibilities. My principal memory,' says Una, 'is of Dodo Benson's valet, Charlie, hurrying to our door in full regalia of tin hat, gasproof suit and policeman's rattle, calling out: "Miss Radclyffe Hall, Lady Troubridge, are you all right?" and of later drinking a glass of sherry with two young men acquaintances in a cottage up the lane and searching my heart as to whether I had been frightened.'

The Forecastle was finally sold on 4 January 1940 for sixteen hundred and fifty pounds, more than twice what it had cost in

1934, and Rye was put behind Radclyffe Hall and Una Troubridge when they left on 19 September, to go to Lynton in the West Country. There, Souline found herself a nursing job in Exeter and made a fairly inefficient job of a life for herself. By the end of 1942, the capricious Souline was living in London, working for a department of the Foreign Office, and – pleading the excuse that the nature of her job precluded her from keeping John informed of her whereabouts – she faded from Radclyffe Hall's life though scarcely from her memory or that of Una. The long, nine-year affair was over, trailing dismally off into darkness and silence except for one or two brief, pointless appearances at John's deathbed. Radclyffe Hall's eyes began to trouble her more in the summer of 1941, and at the end of March 1943 she collapsed with colitis and excruciatingly painful haemorrhoids. Una installed herself and John at the Ritz Hotel in London and employed nurses night and day to attend to John who, in September, was operated upon for cancer. A colostomy was performed, and John was taken to Lady Carnarvon's Nursing Home in Hadley Wood ostensibly to recuperate but – as she knew full well – in fact to die. She spent seven weeks there, before being removed to the London Clinic where, after making a will leaving everything to Una, Radclyffe Hall died at seven minutes past eight on the night of 7 October 1943. She was a rich woman: her estate was valued at one hundred and eighteen thousand pounds so that Una was not only left materially comfortable, but comforted, too, by John's last words which, in a letter found after John's death, exhorted Una to 'believe in my love which is much, much stronger than death.' To the end it had been Una who had kept faith, and her last memory of Radclyffe Hall in death was of a stranger, almost: 'It seemed a young airman or soldier who perhaps had died of wounds after much suffering. Ivory clear and pale, the exquisite line of the jaw, the pure aquiline of the nose with its delicate wing nostrils, the beautiful modelling of eyelids and brow. Not a trace of femininity; no one in their senses could have suspected that anything but a young man had died.'

TEN

Some Writers of Romney Marsh

The house in Lion Street, Rye, where John Fletcher is said to have been born in 1579, is now a teashop catering to the tourist trade taste for scones and buns and sticky cakes. Fletcher is the sole son of Rye to have achieved lasting literary reputation, though Rye did not long delay him since his father, Richard, was an ambitious and comely cleric who was soon appointed Chaplain to Queen Elizabeth I, then Dean of Peterborough, Bishop of Bristol and Lord High Almoner to the Queen and finally, in 1594, Bishop of London. Richard died in 1596 of a surfeit of tobacco, having taken to the pipe in search of comfort after falling into disfavour with the Queen who disapproved of his having married for the second time without royal consent. The Bishop, according to Sir John Harington, 'seeking to lose his sorrow in a mist of smoak, died of the immoderate taking thereof.' The seventeen-year-old John Fletcher, who had been admitted pensioner of Bene't College, Cambridge, in 1591 (there is no record of his having taken a degree), was turned out of Fulham Palace and his father's house in Chelsea, virtually penniless, and thereafter vanishes from the ken of literary historians until 1606 or 1607, when he is rediscovered as a playwright in association with Francis Beaumont. Dryden asserts that their first success, *Philaster*, performed between 7 December 1609 and 12 July 1610, had been preceded by two or three unsuccessful plays. Before his association with

Beaumont, Fletcher had written, independently, at least one play known to modern critics – *The Faithfull Shepheardesse* – and Beaumont is best known for his own early play, *The Knight of the Burning Pestle*. Neither were very well received by their contemporaries. Aside from the fact that Rye was Fletcher's birthplace, and that his father was briefly minister of the church in Rye, there is no record of any further association of the Fletchers with the town or with Romney Marsh.

Two hundred and thirty eight years have to pass before another literary and clerical connection occurs in Romney Marsh. In 1817, Richard Harris Barham was collated by the Archbishop of Canterbury to the Rectory of Snargate. At the same time, he was also offered the curacy of Warehorn, and elected to live in the Warehorn parsonage with his wife, Caroline, whom he had married in 1814 while curate at Westwell, a small parish adjoining Eastwell Park, a few miles from Ashford. According to Barham's son and biographer, Richard HD Barham, the parsonage at Westwell had been 'unhealthy and dilapidated,' and the Barhams' first two sons had died there in infancy.

The villages of Warehorn and Snargate are about two miles apart, remote on the boundary of the Marsh, and Barham's situation would not have appeared enviable to a fainter-hearted or more worldly cleric. The rustic remoteness of the villages was, nevertheless, a considerable advantage to 'desperadoes engaged in what, by a technical euphemism, was termed "The Free Trade".' The Rev Mr Barham, sensibly, paid as little attention as he could to the smugglers and their trade. The tacit compliment was returned by the smugglers, 'notwithstanding the reckless character of these men.' Barham 'met with nothing of outrage or incivility at their hands. Many a time indeed, on returning homewards late at night, has he been challenged by a half-seen horseman who looked in the heavy gloom like some misty condensation a little more substantial than ordinary fog, but on making known his name and office, he was invariably allowed to pass on with a "Good night, it's only parson!" while a long and shadowy line of mounted smugglers, each with his led horse laden with tubs, filed silently by.' The Excise was generally corrupt, so there was not much a strictly moral man could have done about the smuggling trade in any case, and very likely smuggling in itself was not regarded as a deadly sin. Parson Woodforde, in Norfolk, was not likely to deliver a sermon when 'Andrews the smuggler brought me this night about 11 o'clock a bag of hyson tea 6lb. weight. He frightened us a little by whistling under the parlour window just as we were going to bed. I gave him some Geneva and paid him for the tea at 10s. 6d. per pound.'

Doubtless some nocturnal whistling disturbed the rest of Mr Barham, since the smugglers 'extended their familiarity so far as to make the church itself a depot for contraband goods; and on one occasion a large seizure of tobacco had been made in the Snargate belfry – calumny contended for the discovery of a keg of hollands under the vestry-table. When it is added, that the nightly wages, paid whether a cargo was run or not, were at the rate of seven and sixpence to an unarmed man, and fifteen shillings to one who carried his cutlass and pistols, little surprise can be felt if nearly the whole population pursued more or less so profitable an avocation.' Mr Barham, says his son indulgently, 'possessed a disposition which readily accommodated itself to circumstances . . . A writer in *Bentley's Miscellany* speaks of him as "essentially a peacemaker" . . .' Barham 'had a natural relish' for 'the ordinary amusements of a country life,' and diverted himself with occasional verse, couching invitations to dinner in poetic form. To Dr Wilmot of Ashford, Barham addressed this irresistible parody on 'O Nanny, wilt thou gang with me':

O Doctor! wilt thou dine with me,
And drive on Tuesday morning down?
Can ribs of beef have charms for thee —
The fat, the lean, the luscious brown?
No longer dressed in silken sheen,
Nor deck'd with rings, and brooches rare,
Say, wilt thou come in velveteen
Or corduroys that never tear?

And so on for three more stanzas.

On 13 May 1819, Barham noted in his diary, 'Drove William and Dick into Ashford – overturned the gig – broke my right leg and sprained my left ancle . . .' These serious injuries confined Barham to his house for several weeks, 'a tedious seclusion which served to bring fairly into play a taste which might otherwise have died out for lack of exercise.' He began to write, at top speed, a novel, *Baldwin*, which he completed in a few weeks – 'a work faulty perhaps in style, but by no means destitute of merit as regards plot and delineation of character, but which fell still-born from the Minerva press, under the management of the matrons of that establishment.' Barham received twenty pounds for his effort, 'with additional advantages dependent on certain publishing "contingencies" which Theodore Hook used to describe as *things that never happen*. The definition was not violated in the present instance.'

Rheumatism followed the injuries to his bones, and Barham took the opportunity offered by his inability to move about to write a second novel, *My Cousin Nicholas* which, says RHD Barham, was published in *Blackwood's Magazine* with 'considerable success'. He recovered his health, but no sooner had he done so than one of his children fell ill and Barham was obliged to post to London to consult an eminent doctor, Sir Astley Cooper. Meeting a friend by chance in the Strand, a friend who happened to be carrying a letter to the post inviting a young rural clergyman to stand for a minor canonry in St Paul's Cathedral, it was immediately decided between them that Barham should himself become the candidate for the position. The letter was torn in shreds, tossed to the wind, and within two days Barham, after consulting his wife, signified his willingness to relinquish his curacy and stand for the canonry which, in due course, he acquired on 6 April 1821. The Barhams removed to London towards the end of the summer of 1821, in mid-August. Barham was thirty-three years old at this point, and entered 'the society of a highly intellectual circle'. In 1824 he was appointed a priest in ordinary of the King's Chapel Royal, and shortly afterwards was presented to the incumbency of St Mary Magdalene and St Gregory-by-St Paul. He fell again to literary work to support the expenses of his family, and in rapid succession threw off any number of articles for a variety of magazines, including *Blackwood's* which serialised *My Cousin Nicholas* in 1828. But Barham's fame rests most securely on *The Ingoldsby Legends*, published in 1837. He had not forgotten his residence at Warehorn and Snargate or Romney Marsh as a whole, since several of the 'Legends' derive their themes or are set in and around the Marsh. In 'The Leech of Folkestone', the town is neatly and succinctly characterised: 'Rome stood on seven hills; Folkestone seems to have been built upon seventy. Its streets, lanes, and alleys, – fanciful distinctions without much real difference, – are agreeable enough to persons who do not mind running up and down stairs; and the only inconvenience, at all felt by such of its inhabitants as are not asthmatic, is when some heedless urchin tumbles down a chimney, or an impertinent pedestrian peeps into a garret window. At the eastern extremity of the town, on the sea-beach, and scarcely above high-water mark, stood, in the good old times, a row of houses then denominated "Frog-Hole". Modern refinement subsequently euphonized the name into "East-Street" but "what's in a name?" – the encroachments of Ocean have long since levelled all in one common ruin.'

He describes in satirical tones the Royal Military Canal which may be conveniently taken as the northern boundary of Romney Marsh. It was, even then, hardly regarded as a wonder or a substantial impediment to invading French troops who might, for whatever reason, urgently wish to reach and occupy Ashford. 'When the late Mr Pitt was determined to keep out Bonaparte, and prevent him gaining a settlement in the county of Kent, among other ingenious devices adopted for that purpose, he caused to be constructed what was then, and has ever since been conventionally termed a "Military Canal". This is a not very practicable ditch, some thirty feet wide, and nearly nine feet deep – in the middle, – extending from the town and port of Hithe to within a mile of the town and port of Rye, a distance of about twenty miles, and forming, as it were, the cord of a bow, the arc of which constitutes that remote fifth quarter of the globe spoken of by travellers. . . . The French managed to scramble over the Rhine and the Rhone, and other insignificant currents, but they never did, nor could, pass Mr Pitt's "Military Canal".'

'Jerry Jarvis's Wig' is set mainly in Appledore, just north of the Marsh, but the description of the 'Cinque Port court-house' is derived from the court-room of Dymchurch's New Hall: 'Those who are fortunate enough to have seen a Cinque Port court-house may possibly divine what that useful and most necessary edifice was some eighty years ago. Many of them seem to have undergone little alteration, and are in general of a composite order of architecture, a fanciful arrangment of brick and timber, with what Johnson would have styled "interstices, reticulated, and decussated between intersections" of lath and plaster. Its less euphonious designation in the "Weald" is a "noggin". One half of the basement story is usually of the more solid material, the other, open to the street, – from which it is separated only by a row of dingy columns, supporting a petition of the superstructure, – is paved with tiles, and sometimes does duty as a market-place, while, in its centre, flanking the broad staircase that leads to the sessions-house above, stands an ominous-looking machine, of heavy perforated wood, clasped within whose stern embrace "the rude forefathers of the hamlet sleep" off occasionally the drowsiness produced by convivial excess, in a most undignified position, an inconvenience much increased at times by some mischevious urchin, who, after abstracting the shoes of the hapless *detenu*, amuses himself by tickling the soles of his feet.'

In 1893, intending to reconnoitre Hythe as a possible holiday resort, Mrs Hubert Bland, better known to posterity as Edith Nesbit, author of continuously popular books for children, happened to take a four-horse charabanc excursion to Dymchurch with her two children, Paul and Iris. The attractions of Dymchurch, 'then quite secluded and almost unknown to the outside world . . . so delighted her that she decided to exchange those of Hythe for them. She took rooms immediately, and sent to London for the rest of the family.' So writes Doris Langley Moore in her excellent biography, *E Nesbit*, published in 1933, nine years after E Nesbit's death at Jesson St Mary's in Romney Marsh in 1924. The rest of the family, for whom she sent, consisted of her husband, Hubert Bland, and Fabian, her second son. Fabian was eight years old in 1893, Paul was thirteen, and Iris was twelve. Also included in the family circle was a daughter of Hubert Bland's, Rosamund, adopted by Edith and raised as her own child. Bland had given Edith to understand that the mother was a former fiancée of his. Edith met this mythical 'Maggie', befriended her, and kept constantly in touch with her until 'Maggie's' death some eighteen years later. In fact, Rosamund was the daughter of Miss Alice Hoatson, the Bland children's governess who, in 1899, clandestinely bore another child, a son named John, whose father was also Hubert Bland. HG Wells, summing up the complications and intricacies of the relationship between Hubert and Edith Bland, commented: 'All this E Nesbit not only detested and mitigated and tolerated, but presided over and I think found exceedingly interesting.' At any rate, when Edith discovered Dymchurch and summoned her family, no doubt Miss Hoatson came too, and adopted her accustomed role of apparent subservience to her mistress who was used, like everyone else, to refer to Alice as 'the Mouse' – a mouse who, nevertheless, had a sharp tongue and occasionally presumed to meddle in areas Edith thought her own domain. Alice held her tongue when she could, and her discretion was rewarded by condescension and rudeness by her own two children who supposed her nothing but their governess.

The family home was Well Hall at Eltham, but the Blands acquired a cottage at Dymchurch which they visited regularly and where they hugely and uproariously entertained a large and varied company of guests who, as Wells commented, 'rushed down from town at the week-end to snatch one's bed before anyone else got it.' Wells, who lived just along the coast at Spade House in Sandgate, was, with his family, a constant, lively and welcome visitor. Doris Langley Moore tells us that 'Everyone who proved acceptable at Well Hall was invited to a Dymchurch week-end sooner or later, and no one ever stayed there without enjoyment or returned without a little store of beguiling memories. Several families whose names are associated with art and letters had seaside houses in that district. There were the Sterndale Bennetts and the Thorndikes, the Jepsons, and the Griffiths – whose son, Hubert Griffith, later well known as a writer and traveller, was then a little boy and a great favourite with E Nesbit, his godmother (*The Phoenix and the Carpet* contains an admirable little dedicatory poem addressed to him). Sybil and Russell Thorndike were among the dearest of her young companions; their mother an affectionate friend for nearly twenty years.'

Wells rather despised Hubert Bland, a 'tawdry brain in the Fabian constellation,' and was wary of Edith, 'a tall, whimsical, restless, able woman who had been very beautiful and was still very good looking.' Edith had been born on 15 August 1858 and would, at the turn of the century, have been in her early forties. 'Most of her activity,' says Wells, 'went into the writing of verse, rather insincere verse, rather sentimental stories for adults and quite admirable tales for children.' She would have been extremely vexed to hear Wells disparage her verse – she was enormously proud and pleased with it. Wells sums up the differences between Hubert and Edith rather neatly. 'In the end she became rather a long-suffering lady, but her restless needle of a mind, her quick response, kept her always an exacting and elusive lady. It was I am convinced because she, in her general drift, was radical and anarchistic, that the pose of Bland's self-protection hardened into this pose of gentlemanly conservation. He presented himself as a Tory in grain, he became – I know of no confirmation – a man of good old family; he entered the dear old Roman Catholic church. These were all insistencies upon soundness and solidity as against her quickness and whim. He was publicly emphatic for social decorum, punctilio, the natural dependence of women and the purity of the family. None of your modern stuff for *him* . . . She acquiesced in these posturings. If she had not, I suppose he would have argued with her until she did, and he was a man of unfaltering voice and great determination. But a gay holiday spirit bubbled under her verbal orthodoxies and escaped into her work.'

But Bland in fact, 'was under an inner compulsion to be a Seducer – on the best eighteenth-century lines. That, and not Tory-Socialism, was his essential preoccupation; that was what he talked to himself about when he was in his own company.' Wells also states that 'Most of us who went to them were from the first on the side of the quicksilver wife against the more commonplace, argumentative, cast-iron husband.' Visitors to Well Hall and the Dymchurch cottage were disconcerted, now and again, 'as flashes of conflict and fierce resentment, as raised voices in another room, a rush of feet down a passage and the banging of a door' appeared to indicate that not all was well between the Blands. 'At the first encounter it had seemed so extraordinarily open and jolly. Then suddenly you encountered fierce resentments, you found Mrs Bland inexplicably malignant; doors became walls so to speak and floors pitfalls.' The 'web of concealments and intrigue' that Wells found so interesting and alarming sound like nothing so much as the household in Noel Coward's *Hay Fever*. Indeed, Coward had become hopelessly addicted to E Nesbit's children's books at a very early age and met her much later when she was living, in her old age, at Jesson St Mary. It is perfectly possible that, had he based *Hay Fever* on her household, rather than Laurette Taylor's, hardly a word would have needed to be changed.

Wells, until he met E Nesbit in 1902, was convinced that the author was a man – and Edith rather fostered this impression in her writings – so that he decided that the E stood for Ernest and, after discovering his mistake, continued for a while to address her as 'Ernest' until 'Duchess' or 'Madam' replaced the name in his fancy. Dymchurch took a dim view of Edith and her unconventional guests. One of them, a Mrs Heady, quoted by Doris Langley Moore, remembers E Nesbit 'as she sat at breakfast . . . hung with beads and jingling silver bangles, and glowing in a flowery crimson dress like a poppy: and those young men about her all talking and arguing. We had our picnic at Hythe Canal and returned home in the evening – only to learn that there was no dinner! Our hostess had forgotten to order it. Quite unperturbed even by the appearance of several extra visitors, she disappeared while we went to dress, and when we came down, there was a perfect meal ready – an omelette about a yard long and some delicious strange drink with excellent coffee to follow. At about 10 o'clock we all bathed by moonlight.' These diversions were the least of E Nesbit's eccentricities: what really confounded the burghers of Dymchurch was the sight of Mrs Bland bicycling 'down the sea front in a billowing garment bearing some resemblance to a tea-gown, and even now she could be seen holding conversation with the Vicar from a seat on her rain barrel, her long quill cigarette holder [the woman smoked!] between her lips, or walking about arm-in-arm with the humble woman who did her housework. But by degrees she prevailed over her antagonists, for she proved a useful inhabitant, and, busy as she was, helped to organise amateur theatricals for local causes, and even by strenuous efforts prevailed upon the authorities to give the little town its first dust-cart – the rubbish before her day having been dumped into the sea.' She was indefatigably cheerful: she happily embarked for a trip on a makeshift raft which some young artist friends had cobbled together out of old fencing and tar, and roared with laughter when it fell apart and dumped her in the water, ruining her new Liberty dress. She was delighted when a friend like Wells chose to present himself unexpectedly at her door and announce he had come to stay, and she thought nothing of filling a car with people and five dogs to motor to London, stopping frequently to repair the engine and mend tyres that constantly punctured themselves. It was all the greatest possible amusement.

She wrote, she played, she entertained, she recognised and encouraged new, young writers and artists (she picked out EM Forster early as a young genius), she engaged warmly in argument about the authorship of Shakespeare's work – she was an ardent and unshakeable Baconian – all the while smoking incessantly, desperately pinning up her untidy brown hair, trailing her long Liberty frocks hither and thither with a gusto and an enterprise that somewhat belied her uncertainties as to her ability as a writer. Her novels for adults are not, in truth, very good – but her fondness for children, her genuine interest in their views, and her understanding of them came across most vividly and successfully, in a creative sense, in her writing for and about children. Among her most enduring books are *The Railway Children* and the series of novels and stories that feature the irritable Psammead (an ancient sand fairy) and the tetchy Phoenix. She was not always tactful or consistent in her dealings with her own children – natural and adopted. She could be whimsical and capricious, but – when she recognised herself to have been in the wrong – she could be instantly contrite and take pains to show her repentance.

Doris Langley Moore comments, 'She was not the sort of adult who would preach to a child of virtues that she did not think it worth while to aspire to herself. Her practice often fell far beneath her aspirations, but her failures were at least as grievous to her as to those who felt the sting of her sharp tongue and the injustices of decisions made when she was out of temper . . . Ill humours came and went, but the sparkling stream of gaiety, ingenuity, generosity, was never quenched for long. Her quick anger soon melted into repentance. Her capacity for enjoyment was measureless; and when she set aside her work to play with a child, she played not as an adult pleasantly condescending, but as another child released from bondage.'

E Nesbit's real bondage was to her husband. George Bernard Shaw commented, 'No two people were ever married who were better calculated to make the worst of each other,' and, in a letter to Doris Langley Moore, Shaw described Edith as 'an audaciously unconventional lady' and Hubert as 'an exceedingly unfaithful husband'. Had divorce been possible, she would have left him. But, as the years went on, it could have been alleged that she had condoned her husband's philandering and, since he was never brutal to her in the physical sense, there were no grounds to allege 'cruelty' which, at that time, did not include mental suffering. Edith had had her own amorous flings outside marriage – Doris Langley Moore describes her infidelitites as having taken place 'under huge provocation, and must have been to some extent a way of living down the humiliation Bland inflicted on her.' She became infatuated with George Bernard Shaw, but Shaw did not respond – though he was not indifferent ('Well, I didn't say "How dare you!" '). Doris Langley Moore 'heard on good authority that she was once on the verge of eloping with the attractive young Richard le Gallienne, who was about eight years her junior but romantically in love with her.' The obsession with Shaw came in the 1880s, with le Gallienne in the 1890s, and in the period 1887 to 1895 she was the lover of Noel Griffith for a while. Later, in 1905 or thereabouts, she begged the Egyptologist, Dr Wallis Budge, to take her away. He could not, or would not, so she dried her eyes and took him as a friend. 'E Nesbit had the rather rare knack of remaining on the best of terms with ex-lovers;' comments Doris Langley Moore, 'but this was possibly because, her deepest affections being bound up with her husband, she was able to take partings lightly. Yet if her love affairs were gestures, they were vigorous and meaningful gestures while they lasted, and since she was the absolute reverse of promiscuous, they were not mere passing fancies.'

Hubert Bland died in 1914, very suddenly, and – despite the insecurity of her married life – she grieved piteously. She went to stay with friends in Paris, but soon returned after becoming seriously ill with a duodenal ulcer which all but killed her. Money was short, the War desolated her, her son Fabian had died, and her surviving children were either married or at war and thus separated from her. She was zealously patriotic, once she had come to terms with the necessity for fighting with Germany – in any case, she had always heartily detested the Germans. She became obsessed with the Bacon-was-Shakespeare notion that near enough deranged her. It took up most of her time, and little was left over for remunerative, creative writing. In sore financial straits, she applied to Shaw for money and, says Doris Langley Moore, so importunate did she become that 'he eventually warned her that she must count on him no more, but should adjust her scale of living to her diminished means. She was, he told me, "very angry" with him about that.'

War inevitably led to confusion that resulted in the breaking up of her large social circle. E Nesbit found herself, for once, lonely. But on 20 February 1917, she remarried. Her second husband was Thomas Terry Tucker, known as 'Skipper', a marine engineer, cheerful, inquiring, and – though enthusiastic – level-headed. He had been a Fabian, and had known Edith for some years. He had visited Well Hall, and he, too, had been recently bereft of a spouse. When he said to E Nesbit, 'It looks to me as if you need a tug round here!', she replied, 'I wish I had one,' and so they were married soon afterwards. 'I feel as though I had opened another volume of the book of life (the last volume) and it is full of beautiful stories and poetry,' she wrote to her brother. It turned out to be an excellent match, and she was excessively happy with Skipper. She began writing again, while her husband began making sense of her financial state, and it was possible to start entertaining again. But, by 1921, it became clear that Well Hall was an impossible drain on their finances, and the opportunity to buy a double bungalow at Jesson St Mary, close to Dymchurch, presented itself. By the spring of 1922, Well Hall had been sold and they installed themselves in the two houses, the one called The Long Boat, the other the Jolly Boat, the passage between them known as The Suez Canal. The accommodation was far from conventional – the bungalows had been requisitioned by the military during the War for use as a photographic laboratory and a storehouse for medical materials. But they converted the buildings and referred to the various rooms in nautical terms – the drawing room was the saloon, the bedrooms were cabins, and the kitchen was the galley. Old and new friends descended upon them, including Sybil and Russell Thorndike (the one by now a famous actress, the other a prolific writer of adventure stories) and their mother, and Athene Seyler.

Something of the former gaiety and life had gone out of E Nesbit, perhaps unsurprisingly, since she was now in her early sixties. She recognised the onset of bronchial illness, though she managed still to be bright and wilful when occasion demanded. Her last illness was very painful. To the novelist Berta Ruck, she wrote, in June 1923, 'I suppose I shall not get well again, but, like Charles II, I take an unconscionable time over the business. You would not know me – I am so thin. Once a Rubens Venus in figure, but now more like a pre-Raphaelite Saint Simeon.' To the writer Angus MacPhail, on 18 November 1923, she dictated a letter saying that the experience of dying 'is a long business and very tiresome . . . I fear I shall never write anything again though I feel now as though I had never written anything comparable in importance and interest to what I could write now if I could hold a pen.' In December 1923, she wrote to complain to Berta Ruck that she had nearly died a week previously, 'and I assure you the hitch in the arrangements was no fault of mine.' To Mavis Carter, in the same month, she wrote, 'I have everything to make me happy except health, kindest and most loving nursing and care . . . A four-post bed like a golden shrine and a view of about eight miles of marsh bounded by the little lovely hills of Kent.'

She reviewed her working life and decided, quite inappropriately, that 'Poetry . . . is really what I should naturally have done, that and *no* prose, if I had not had to write for a living.' We may be thankful that it had been imperative she should have had to make her living and that poetry did not pay as well as prose. Death came to her too soon: 'What things there are still to see and to do, and to think and to be, and to grow into and grow out of!' On 24 May 1924, she died. She was buried in the churchyard of St Mary's in the Marsh. Her last written words had been a poem, inspired by the view over the Kent hills. Mrs Thorndike had contrived to have her bed raised up level with the window.

"Mother of Stars! enthroned I lie
On the high bed of your kindness sent,
And see between the marsh and sky
The little lovely hills of Kent;"

Whether his acquaintance, as a child, with E Nesbit influenced the young Russell Thorndike to start writing cannot now be known – but he had 'begun writing when he was quite small. He had a hen-house he turned into his "study",' according to Daniel Thorndike, Russell's son. 'It had all started on the nursery table. He and Sybil wrote their own plays, as children, and roped in all the local villagers to help act them out.' Thorndike was born at Rochester, where his father was a minor canon at Rochester Cathedral, on 6 February 1885. Both he and his sister Sybil, avid to become actors, applied to audition for the Ben Greet Academy after they left school. 'Sybil did her little bit,' says Daniel Thorndike, 'and was judged to have the makings of an actress. Russell hadn't been able to attend, so Sybil was asked if he was any good as an actor. "Oh, he's *far* better than I am", she said loyally, "he's absolutely frightening. He could make your flesh creep". He got the job, and they both joined Ben Greet's Academy and toured America with him, visiting every state of the Union. He was a mercurial actor – he was wonderful. He had eyeballs that stood out like organ stops. One of his marvellous roles was Death in *Everyman*, and he absolutely riveted audiences with his eyeball acting and the wonderful cadences to his voice.' Writing was, generally, secondary to acting as Russell Thorndike's occupation. Daniel Thorndike inclines to the view that his father's novels 'were written for love *and* money. He was never very good with money. We were always short of it – he earned a decent amount, but always contrived to get through most of it. But he worked as much for love as for money – he was underpaid for a lot of things he did as a writer and as an actor.'

The character who dominates Thorndike's seven best-known novels is the smuggler-parson Dr Syn. He was conceived in dramatic circumstances, if we are to give full credence to the tale told by Russell and Sybil who, before the War, happened to find themselves on tour in Spartanburg, Carolina. 'We arrived on the Sunday,' writes Russell in his biography of Sybil Thorndike, 'and had to rehearse *The Tempest* that evening in the hotel. During our rehearsal a revolver shot sounded outside the window. That shot turned out to be a momentous one in my life, as you shall hear. Following the shot came a great shouting and the noise of many feet. We heard the word "Murder!" called by the gathering multitude on the side-walk. I dropped the prompt-book and dashed to the window followed by Sybil and the Company . . . Well it was a murder. A young man had shot his stepfather dead for being unkind to his mother . . . The murdered man was left lying on the side-walk and when we went up to bed, the corpse, with a bullet hole in its hard-boiled shirt, was still gazing with glazed eyes up at Sybil's window. Sleep for Sybil was impossible. She asked me to go and sit with her. I kept having another look out of the window. Sybil kept making another pot of tea. And we talked, and that night the first idea of Dr Syn . . . was born. That dreadful night we piled horror on horror's head, and after each new horror was invented, we took another squint at the corpse to encourage us.'

Doctor Syn may have been inspired by a glassy-eyed corpse on an American street, but he was set firmly in Romney Marsh for his piratical and freebooting activities. Like EW Hornung's sophisticated and civilized crook, Raffles, Dr Syn was a thoroughly gentlemanly anti-hero. He was brought to literary life in one of two coastguard cottages that Mrs Thorndike had bought at Dymchurch on the sea wall. That first novel created a future difficulty for its author – he killed off his hero at the end, and the six novels had, therefore, to be set backwards in time. But that was a minor inconvenience for a man who was a natural storyteller. In *Lewis and Sybil*, the biography of his parents by John Casson, Russell Thorndike is described as 'a great favourite . . . He had such wonderful stories to tell us of his own Munchausian adventures . . . to Russell happenings were never enough on their own. Being a writer he turned . . . every event in his and other people's lives into a romantic adventure.' The holiday house at Dymchurch was kept on by the Thorndikes until 1930, and Russell brought his own family to live in a house in Sycamore Gardens at Dymchurch, 'a big rented house,' as Daniel Thorndike remembers, 'on the corner of a field. He loved the place and we loved the house. We could look out to sea, and my father could dream up pirates and all manner of smuggling adventures.' Russell Thorndike also loved the pub, where – when he was not working as an actor – he could be sure of an audience for his tall tales. 'We had the greatest difficulty getting him out of the pub and back home for lunch. He wasn't a great one for parties, but he loved to rivet cronies in the pub with a story when he could.'

Unfortunately, the Dr Syn novels did not make his fortune as they ought to have done. He appears to have had little head for business, and the legend has it that he sold the film rights for twenty pounds which he spent in the Pier Hotel, Chelsea. Life was a stage, and the stage was life to Thorndike – it was difficult to tell where reality began and ended. The tales he conjured might just as well have been true – perhaps a little dressed up to make them more entertaining and perhaps the emphases were different in the telling than they had been in real life, but the tale and its delivery were what mattered after the event. Indeed, Thorndike's Dr Syn stories were so popular that an annual Day of Syn is held at Dymchurch and it is difficult to convince some participants and observers that Syn is merely a fictional character. He fits the mythology of the Marsh perfectly, so that he might have been true enough as a composite figure compounded from many a smuggler of Romney Marsh. Like his creator, Dr Syn is the last of the great romantic barnstormers.

Noel Coward's earliest reading had been the stories of E Nesbit in the *Strand Magazine* where they were serialized. His devotion to her was so compelling that he even stole and pawned a coral necklace to buy one of her books, *The Magic City*, for four and sixpence. It is pleasing to know that his last reading had also been a Nesbit book – *The Enchanted Castle* – which was found open on his bedside table when he died. Just before Christmas 1956, in Jamaica, he wrote: 'I am reading again through all the dear E Nesbits and they seem to me to be more charming and evocative than ever. It is strange that after half a century I still get such lovely pleasure from them. Her writing is so light and unforced, her humour so sure and her narrative quality so strong that the stories, which I know backwards, rivet me as much now as they did then when I was a little boy . . . E Nesbit knew all the things that stay in the mind, all the happy treasures. I suppose she, of all the writers I have ever read, has given me over the years the most complete satisfaction and, incidentally, a great deal of inspiration.'

According to his biographer, Cole Lesley, Coward re-read the works of E Nesbit annually, and he visited her after the War when she was living in Jesson St Mary in the Long Boat: 'there was something in her character which made him think of her as one of the most truly bohemian persons he had ever met. Although she was now an old lady within sight of the end of her life and with a severe code of behaviour, Noel found to his joy that there was no generation gap between them; she read his plays and listened to his "modern" views with equanimity, encouraged him and advised him as though to a writer of equal status. They at once took to one another and Noel visited her often, but she by no means took to everybody; when his mother accompanied him on one occasion she met with a cool reception and from then on referred to Miss Nesbit as stuck-up.'

Coward was, at this time, living in a cottage 'nestling up against the Star Inn' at St Mary-in-the-Marsh. It was a weekend retreat, where he came to write and where he could install his beloved but difficult mother. Athene Seyler, a friend of E Nesbit's, had loaned Coward her house in Dymchurch for a fortnight in 1921, when he was twenty years old, and he had bicycled the countryside in search of a suitable place for himself. 'On his walks and bicycle rides in early spring,' says Cole Lesley, 'arose Noel's long love-affair with Romney Marsh, a silvery green flatland laced with lazy canals, huge skies, clouds ever-changing and spectacular sunsets often as red as a blood orange. ("Too red. Very affected," Noel would say.)' The cottage was 'small and tender,' with four bedrooms and an outside privy. One result of this infatuation would be, a few years later, Coward's purchase of 'the farmhouse, woods and verdant fields from Aldington Knoll, his favourite cycling objective, down to as far as the Military Canal, this vista stretching before him as he sat and rested.' The farm was Goldenhurst, bought in 1926, where he lived at irregular intervals until 1956 when he retired to Bermuda. It was not, initially, promising – no bigger than a villa, with a 'lopsided new wing', and a tin roof. Coward had had successes with his play *The Vortex*, with *Easy Virtue*, *On With the Dance*, *Fallen Angels*, and he was very much in demand. *The Vortex*, which had had its first night in November 1924, had been the beginning. By 1926, Coward was able to travel stylishly in a Rolls Royce, and there was money enough to lavish on Goldenhurst which was remodelled. It was extended by running a passage from the house to a barn, by building a guest room off the passage, by converting the barn into a suite of rooms for his own use, and by adding on a large drawing-room. Hythe, Deal, Folkestone, and the villages of the Marsh were combed from end to end for antiques – even Herstmonceaux Castle was rifled – and the fashionable interior designer Syrie Maugham was commissioned to do her 'costly best to supply what else was needed in the way of furnishings . . .' The drawing-room housed two grand pianos, back to back, where Coward played double piano improvisations with friends who could be relied upon to match his own skill. Here, at Goldenhurst, he would spend weekends and retire to write in peace, escaping from an increasingly vivacious social life with his lover and manager, Jack Wilson. Though he filled the house with theatrical friends more often than not, he had decided that 'People . . . were the danger. People were greedy and predatory, and if you gave them the chance they would steal unscrupulously the heart and soul out of you without really wanting to or even meaning to. From now on there was going to be very little energy wasted, and very little vitality spilled unnecessarily.'

The old seventeenth-century farmhouse having been made ready by 1927 – oak beams exposed, walls painted white, Grinling Gibbons carvings installed – Coward imported his mother and Auntie Vida who squabbled constantly and took offence at any seeming incivility or slight. When her son gave over the new part of the house to her, she complained that she was being kept out of the way. When he gave her the old part instead, she complained it was poky. She was very deeply jealous of Vida whom she excoriated in letters of intemperate rage. Nevertheless, Goldenhurst was a place to which Coward came to work, to get away from London, and much of his work in the thirty years he owned Goldenhurst owes much to the love he had for Aldington and the Marsh. There, he composed *Present Laughter*, *This Happy Breed*, the scores for *Conversation Piece* and *Operette*, the songs for *Tonight at Eight-Thirty*, and worked at most of his best-known and most often revived stage successes. Coward did work, constantly and indefatigably, wherever he happened to be at any point in his international career as playwright, composer, songwriter, and entertainer, so that it is difficult to say exactly what was written where. Goldenhurst, though, remained the focus and the house to which he constantly returned. Nine years after he had installed himself at Aldington, in his mid-twenties, it might have been supposed that the locals would have become a little blasé about the sophisticated cosmopolite star and his friends but, according to Cole Lesley, they could still be awestruck by the sudden irruption of glamour into their lives: 'One peaceful Sunday evening, the village postmistress, who also worked the tiny switchboard, telephoned; Noel could tell from her voice that she had been frightened to death by a call from California. It was Marlene Dietrich, whom he had never met, and he always marvelled at the trouble she must have taken to track him down to that little village six thousand miles away.'

Cole Lesley 'loved the drive down in the Rolls on the London-Dover road . . . and I loved the drive up on Mondays, the back of the car stacked with branches of roses, huge peonies, delphiniums and lilies . . . Then the weekends themselves, the house filled with jolly guests . . . Rebecca West came that year, Owen Nares, Binkie Beaumont, Alexander Woollcott, Alice Duer Miller, Zena Dare, Adrianne Allen, Bobby Andrews, GB Stern – the visitors' book goes on for pages.' But Mrs Coward, too, was there: 'when we arrived at Goldenhurst, often very late at night, to see the light still on in Mum's window, we knew there had been trouble and the ebb and flow of the week's battles were to be recounted and the recounting, exhausted as we were, had to be endured.' Mum always had the last word: even at Vida's funeral, looking at the corpse in the coffin, she couldn't resist a last dig: 'Doesn't she look pretty, like a little snowdrop. It's a pity she looked so disagreeable when she was alive.'

During the Second World War, Goldenhurst was requisitioned by the Army, which omitted to tell him, after the War was over, that he could have it back. They had left it clean and in reasonable condition, but had not bothered to do any gardening beyond minimal maintenance. Coward did not return to Goldenhurst until 1951, when he set to the work of restoring the thirty or more rooms to a condition as good as, or better than before the Army had moved in and out again. It was, decoratively, in a sorry state. The day after his fiftieth birthday, on 16 December 1951, he moved back into a Goldenhurst that had been freshly painted, hung with pictures again, stocked with books, and furnished with the antiques and Syrie Maugham furniture that had been stored for many years. 'Probably the nicest birthday I have ever had,' he wrote, ' – the house and land seemed to envelop me in a warm and loving welcome.'

But he would be at Goldenhurst only five years longer: 'Noel was . . . too old at fifty-six to be living solely on the income from his royalties, and the fees from Las Vegas and the TV shows. Something had to be done, and it was in 1956 that Noel had to make his "Great Decision".' Cole Lesley comments on the burden of taxation that is imposed upon the rich, and Coward's annual tax liability had risen to something like twenty-five thousand pounds, up to fifty thousand pounds. His expenses were great: there was a house in Gerald Road, SW1, to be kept up, staff salaries, and Goldenhurst was not cheap to run. He decided to leave England, though not without regret: 'Goldenhurst of course I mind dreadfully about, but only sentimentally dreadfully, because after all I did without it quite comfortably for ten years and have only been back in it for five and I am certainly in a far less painful position than people who have had, owing to the tax situation, to give up the ancestral homes they were born and brought up in . . . It is quite startling to receive so much more admiration, respect and enthusiasm in America at ten times the money and as I propose to appear less and less as time goes on I really think I might as well do it for more than double the appreciation and ten times the lolly. Another important point is that I am in no way saying goodbye to England, I would never become an alien citizen and am only going on being as British as I can be in two British colonies . . . apart from a very few small pangs, everything in the jardin is couleur de rose.' In January 1956, Noel Coward arrived in Hamilton, Bermuda, to take up residence. He died, in March 1973, in Jamaica.

Besides E Nesbit, another favourite author of Coward's was Sheila Kaye-Smith, who was Sussex-born. 'She and her novels contributed greatly to Noel's . . . love for the Marsh, for Dymchurch and Dungeness, for the peace of the little village of St Mary-in-the-Marsh in which he wrote his early plays, and eventually . . . for Goldenhurst Farm,' writes Cole Lesley. Coward had written fan letters to Sheila Kaye-Smith who, despite her reclusive nature, replied and later, after an animated exchange of correspondence, met him in London and at Goldenhurst. Most of her novels are set, if not in Romney Marsh, in Sussex and as a regional novelist she is coming back into favour after a period of comparative neglect. The famous satire on novels of rural life, *Cold Comfort Farm*, by Stella Gibbons, was a hilarious and brilliant swipe at novels such as Sheila Kaye-Smith's *Joanna Godden* and Mary Webb's *Precious Bane*; but satires pass or are remembered for their own qualities as much as for their targets, while a good novel re-surfaces in time and is re-appreciated for its style and content. Auden remarked that there are no novels that are undeservedly remembered or forgotten, since all novels can be faulted in one respect or another. Sheila Kaye-Smith will be remembered, at least, for *Joanna Godden* when others in her large body of work are still unread in their last editions.

By the time she had left school, legend has it, Sheila Kaye-Smith had written thirteen novels and carried several more in her head, to be recited on demand. She was born in 1887 at Battle Lodge, Dane Road, St Leonards, the daughter of a doctor, and educated at Hastings and St Leonards Ladies College. *The Tramping Methodist*, her first novel was published when she was twenty. Her second, *Starbrace*, drew upon the exercise-book novels she had written in longhand as a child. The novel that made a first impression on the reading public was *Sussex Gorse*, her fifth, published in 1916. By now she was known as 'the Sussex novelist'. In 1924, Sheila Kaye-Smith married the Rev Penrose Fry, a Hastings curate, and in 1929 both were received into the Roman Catholic church. Soon after, they returned from London, where they had been living, to a fifteenth-century farmhouse, known as Little Doucegrove, at Northiam, a few miles north west of Rye. Northiam, like Brede, lies a little way west of Romney Marsh and Sheila Kaye-Smith, though she cannot be claimed as a writer in Romney Marsh can certainly be adopted as a writer of the Marsh. In *Joanna Godden*, she writes lyrically of Rye and the surrounding area, drawing upon the happiness that she so powerfully drew from three things: 'the country, my writing, and my religion. The country and my writing are really two different parts of the same thing . . . They are so interwoven that I cannot separate them. As for religion, that is the third strand in the shining cord.' *Joanna Godden*, published in 1921, precedes her religious conversion, and, though it deals sympathetically with religion, does not so much concern itself with 'the third strand.'

Readers of *The Times Literary Supplement* might have read, on 18 October 1985, David Cecil's recommendation of an unjustly neglected novel, *Crossriggs*, by Mary and Jane Findlater. Since his previous recommendation of the neglected novels by Barbara Pym rocketed that lady to late literary fame, David Cecil may be taken to have a nose for the recondite and an uncanny sense of timing. Victorian novels, or novels of a later date set in Victorian times and reflecting Victorian values, have a certain current political vogue. Since *Crossriggs* is published in paperback by Virago, it may be that the Findlaters' time has come again. They were, for a while, residents of Rye and two redoubtable Scottish dames who thoroughly disapproved of Conrad Aiken's divorce from his first wife in order to marry a second. They were neighbours of EF Benson and Radclyffe Hall and their story is told in *The Findlater Sisters: Literature and Friendship*, by E Mackenzie, published in 1964. Mary and Jane Findlater were born, respectively, on 4 November 1866 and 26 March 1865, daughters of a minister of the Free Church of Scotland at Lochearnhead. In 1896, the success of Jane's first novel, *The Green Graves of Balgowrie* enabled the family, after the death of the father, to move first to Devon, later to London on the outbreak of War, and thereafter to Rye. Eventually, they moved back to Scotland, to Comrie in Perthshire.

The sisters were devoted to one another. They were pious, moral, and excellent storytellers. Their post-war collaborations included the novel, *Beneath the Visiting Moon*, published in 1923, but, says Trevor Royle in *The Macmillan Companion to Scottish Literature*, 'By the 1920s the artificial Victorian world – similar to that created by Margaret Oliphant, whose work that of the sisters resembles – was a thing of the past, and the Findlaters' novels, rooted in the forgotten manners of that age, passed with it into obscurity.' Literary reputations do, occasionally, undergo a sea change and David Cecil comments favourably on the 'mixture of comedy and drama, satire and pathos' in *Crossriggs*, noting also a 'strain of imaginative poetry in it . . . which also reinforces and colours the tragedy of the drama, dignifying it by a sense of inevitable fate.' But *Crossriggs* was not written in, or about, Rye – though the little town, and Romney Marsh, do not lack the material for domestic novels of the traditional type, or for such fateful tragedies.

In the London Library, *The Orchid Trilogy* by Jocelyn Brooke is to be found on the autobiography and biography floors. Comprising three books, nominally fictional, the trilogy – *The Military Orchid* (1948), *A Mine of Serpents* (1949), and *The Goose Cathedral* (1950) – is, in fact, an almost wholly autobiographical account of the life of the author who was born on 30 November 1908, the third child and second son of Henry and May Brooke of Sandgate. Henry Brooke was a wine merchant in Folkestone. His establishment was known as The Office and is described by Jocelyn Brooke in *The Goose Cathedral*: 'To have called it the "shop" would have been a solecism not easily forgiven. And indeed, when one entered it, one would have supposed it to be a bank or an estate-agent's office, rather than a wine merchant's. Severe counters with grilles; a bevy of neatly dressed clerks: etchings on the walls – it seemed highly unlikely that one could enter these grandiose premises and buy a bottle of ginger-beer: not only buy it, for that matter, but take it away under one's arm! Yet such, indeed, was the case. In point of fact, nobody ever did anything of the kind – except for a few misguided "trippers" in August (and these were not encouraged); the correct procedure was, of course, to "order" one's wine (or, possibly, even one's ginger beer) which was, in due course, "delivered" . . . "Going to the Office" was rather a solemn business altogether: I was unpleasantly reminded of going to church.'

Brooke was not long in Sandgate: he was sent to King's School, Canterbury, from which he bolted after a few days. He was sent back, and the next week he ran away again. But he settled down more happily, and to his surprise, at Bedales. He went on to Worcester College, Oxford, and afterwards worked for a couple of years in a bookshop in London before being adopted into the family business in Folkestone. Brooke had been, as a child, 'more interested . . . in flowers than in people,' and this led to an early, obsessive interest in botany, an interest that, together with a fascination with fireworks, engrossed him for the rest of his life. 'No psycho-analyst so far as I know, has yet attempted to explain the love of flowers in Freudian terms . . . the botanophil – the unscientific lover of flowers, as opposed to the professional botanist – remains a mystery . . . Doubtless the matter will be cleared up before long; but – happily, perhaps for its adherents – the cult of botanophily has been so far neglected by investigators. Often, but not always, the botanophil is precocious. A family legend relates that myself, at the age of four, could identify by name any or all of the coloured plates in Edward Step's *Wayside and Woodland Blossoms* . . . Why, without any particular encouragement, should flowers, rather than stamps, butterflies or birds' eggs, have become my ruling passion? True, I flirted throughout my childhood, with butterflies, tame grass-snakes, home-made fireworks; but flowers were my first love and seem likely to be my last.'

Bondage to 'The Office' resulted in a nervous breakdown, and it was not until the outbreak of war in 1939, when Brooke enlisted in the Royal Army Medical Corps, that he found his vocation. He loved the regular, disciplined life of a soldier and, after the war, to the astonishment of other conscripts, re-enlisted. The success of *The Military Orchid* in 1948 gave Brooke the opportunity to buy himself out of his engagement to the military, and he settled at Ivy Cottage, Bishopsbourne, his mother's house, to write and botanise. Between 1948 and 1955, he published fifteen books – drawing largely on notes and writings he had stored before the war – and in 1966, at the early age of 58, he died.

In the spring of 1947, returning from a holiday in France, Patric and Sheila Dickinson 'landed unforeseenly at Folkestone, so that we approached Winchelsea, where Mrs Shannon [Sheila's mother] was living, across the marsh from Brookland. Rye was silhouetted against the west: Sancerre *dégonflée* . . . Eastward there is a great vista of new land – new since the Romans built the Rhee Wall and Romney Marsh began to grow grass. Below, the last Tudor-rose castle: Camber Castle, a defence work for a silted estuary no one would invade. In Rye we had seen a small derelict house, a tiny eighteenth-century façade painted old-meat red. We peered through a dirty window into a room which had two wooden columns painted chocolate brown. We wanted to see more. There was no key, though the house was for sale. It looked ghastly, what we could see, yet we craved to see more. Often when we were in Rye we were drawn to Church Square to try the door. One afternoon it opened.' The Dickinsons were able to buy the house in Church Square for the palindromic figure of £2855.8s.2d. It hadn't been the highest bid, but it had been the most intriguing.

The question of living in Rye and working in London was solved by the award of an Atlantic Award in Literature which was given to Patric Dickinson on the sole condition that he gave up his job as a producer of literary propaganda programmes at the BBC. 'For some while the BBC did not accept what appeared to be a monstrous folly, nor were the builders eager to evacuate, though Spring was coming. The only way to expel them was to move in. We moved on the day of the Grand National.' One of the runners in that race was Sheila's Cottage: they put five shillings on this fifty-to-one outsider which won. With the proceeds, the Dickinsons bought a coveted clock. That night, 'The church clock struck. We were together in our own house,' wrote Patric Dickinson in 1964 in *The Good Minute*. 'As she lay in my arms I did not think it possible to love her more. So far, I am seventeen years wrong and more wrong year by year.'

As a published poet, Dickinson had in effect been Poetry Editor at the BBC, though his title has been Producer (Drama) and he had been Producer (Features) after joining the Corporation as a trainee after the War. 'I had two selves, my private poetic self and my public self as an Editor and a producer. From the moment I began, I knew that these two selves would be in opposition. I have never been eager to join groups or movements. My "editorial" position made any such identification impossible, even had I wished it . . . I kept all the more outside a literary world I had not really been in. By choice I made myself immune. I cannot say whether this has had any effect upon the reception of my own poetry.'

Nevertheless, perforce, he was increasingly involved with the literary world before settling in Rye: 'In the three years I was "Poetry Editor" I met or corresponded with nearly every poet. I went to Edith Sitwell's levees at the Sesame Club. It was inevitable that I should mostly be dealing with poets older than myself.' – Patric Dickinson, thirty years old in 1945, had been born on Boxing Day 1914 – 'Any good contemporary anthology of poetry up to 1948 will give their names. I do not want to list them like some football league table. I met them not as a poet but as an editor-producer. I did not always find it easy to efface my private poetic self, when it was clear that my companion had no idea that I too wrote poetry. But I am certain the dichotomy made no odds to the poetry I wrote, however it affected my character.'

Ian Parsons, an editor at Chatto & Windus, who crops up constantly in literary biography of the twentieth century, became a close friend of Dickinson and publisher of *The Sailing Race*, Dickinson's third book of poems which followed his first two, *Theseus and the Minotaur*, and *Stone in the Midst and Poems*. He continued as Dickinson's editor, publishing *The Scale of Things*, *The World I See*, and *This Cold Universe*. Parsons and Dickinson had golf in common – 'In the cellar were my clubs . . . The chromium was flaking off the rusty shafts, the grips were rotten. I had never told Sheila that I had played golf. She thought of me as a poet. Although we *knew* each other through and through, we did not know all *about* each other. She was startled to discover that I had once been a "Blue". So Ian gave me back a part of my life I had thought gone.'

Rye's magnetic attraction for eccentrics had not diminished in the late 1940s. They were still there, as full-blooded as ever. On the golf course, Dickinson first caught sight of the Brigadier who had been amusing himself by taking pot shots at Dickinson's golf ball from the window of the secretary's room in the golf club. 'There he was, iron-grey, bullet-head, gold-rimmed monocle in maroon face, laughing his head off, leaning out revolver in hand. Clearly the Brigadier was a good shot, how good we did not wait to see as he took aim again . . . He was six foot four square, he had been left for dead, at sixteen, in 1917, he had survived. He was larger than life or death. A Japanese sniper had killed two of his best men. The Brigadier had gone out, tracked him down, killed him and beheaded him. His gramophone played *fortissimo* Bach or Sullivan. He hated women, but he asked us to dinner.'

As an example of unusual hospitality in Rye, it is useless to resist quoting Dickinson's account of dinner with the Brigadier in full:

> 'Sherry was served in white china pint-mugs. He had had every burner of his gas cooker on for some hours. He went out to see to the soup. Sheila quickly passed me her mug. It was a mistake, for when he came back he was so impressed with this hard-drinking daughter of the regiment that he filled her up. *The Yeoman of the Guard* rocked the room. We managed to swop mugs. When they were empty they were removed and soup was served. This subtle recipe consisted of half a pint of Bovril to half a pint of sherry. By now the haze was considerable. The volume of smoke from the kitchen almost quietened *The Gondoliers*. "How do you like your chops," he asked Sheila, "black and blood? black and blood?" . . . A roar summoned us through to the glories of *cordon noire et sangle*. I thought of Vachel Lindsay's Simon Legree
>
> *He eats de meat he drinks de wine*
> *Burnin' blood and turpentine*
> *Down down with the devil.*
>
> Then there were slices of well-trained Stilton; the pint mugs were washed and filled with port. Bach thundered, the skull seemed to vibrate. The Brigadier dropped his mug (which was empty), said the most ladylike word in his vocabulary, and looked at Sheila like a little boy brazening

out a clear conviction. All was well. We left to the sound of the Brandenburg No 2. In his bathroom was a swan he had humanely shot some weeks before. When its flesh was black, he had it cooked, and survived. He was of a race of Titans who fell with Saturn. To find him in Rye in the twentieth century seemed odd, till I knew Rye better.'

There were less noisy or noisome neighbours to interest the Dickinsons in Rye. 'The inhabitants within earshot of the ungovernable sea grow set in their ways . . . which are often eccentric. A rich man going daily to the Bank to read, free, the *Financial Times*; a lady whose first thought when a garage was burnt out was for the dear cars: "What I keep telling myself is that they didn't suffer, they didn't *suffer*"; a great painter [Edward Burra] ambling out in gym-shoes to go shopping with a BOAC hand-grip and writing next from America; our antiquarian other neighbour [Leopold Vidler], whose house dates from the fourteenth century to the stairs he made out of fish boxes to please his wife. "Used to go up on a rope myself".'

On 14 March 1949, Sheila Dickinson gave birth to their son, David, and soon after a daughter, Virginia, was born. David entered the world at the same time as Dickinson's first freelance work – a literary feature on the poet Ernest Dowson – was being broadcast on BBC radio. Dickinson has supported himself since, mainly by freelance broadcasting and by his work as a poet: 'In our "freedom as freelances" Sheila and I have shared only one misfortune. The cost of living has increased in the years 1948-1964 faster than our capacity to earn from the work we are qualified to do . . . Always I hopefully imagine I can work about twice as fast as I do. I am a slow worker. I write in 2B pencil, with a rubber, and though it may not always seem so, I leave every sentence clean and finished. As in hurdling, one sometimes knocks down a hurdle but can regain stride and rhythm.'

There are compensations: 'It is a liberation for a poet to know that he is very unlikely to earn subsistence by writing poetry . . . A poet is free from the temptation of "writing for money'' as a poet. My attic study at No 38 Church Square looks out over the Marsh, a wide and seducing view. I keep a telescope on the window-sill.' Rye itself, the little town, is peaceful in winter: 'Sometimes I have seen the ground mist cover the marsh, so that Rye Harbour and South Undercliff disappear; the town is alone on its conical hill, the church at the top ''holding to the east its hull of stone''. In summer the visitors wash round the Square like flotsam on the tideline. When they see the town on the telly they will recognise where they have been. They caw like rooks, ''Quaint, quaint, quaint'', and ask for Woolworths and the Catholic church.' Dickinson's poem, 'Tourists of a Sort,' in *Poems from Rye*, published by The Martello Bookshop, sums up the constant despair of Rye residents when the tourists summer season begins just after Easter every year:

Through our streets the morons shamble
Asking for Woolworths,
Waiting for the Quarter Boys
To strike at the hour.

They pile our streets with litter and fag-ends,
Too-fat adults and kids
Slurping ice-cream as they lurch on the cobbles,
Gawping and peering.

Poor flatulent boobs, they're only doing
What the God Teev bids.
If they should see the date on the exquisite
Queen Anne weathercock,

They might have heard she's dead, but precious
Little else. I have been asked
About equally for the way to the Catholic
Church and to Woolworths.

But once, an ace-moron, a master-shambler,
Stopped me and angrily
Snarled 'Where's the town?' And one's overheard,
Crossing the churchyard,

'We've half an hour to spare, whatever shall we
Do? We had better
Go back to Woolworths, dear.' Oh indeed yes
They better had.

The weathercock glints in the moonlight,
The winds blow through its date,
And in the moonlight river and sea
Perpetually meet.

His is not a unique distaste for the usurpation of Rye by trippers. But Rye and Romney Marsh have attracted incomers, permanent or temporary, for long ages. Some, like Aiken and James, have recognised it immediately as home: Dickinson admits, in 'Henry James and Lamb House.'

Telegrams bought it: this somewhat impecunious
Cosmopolitan genius from fashionable London
Saw veritable home, and came and put his roots in
This exquisite backwater.

And what came up was exotic and yet native,
An American — almost-Ryer, a curious
Equation, but he was. The first tourist to settle,
Also the greatest.

Rye, smug and serene on her little hill, surveying the Marsh at the hem of her skirts, smiles like a siren and is used like a whore by her customers, literate or illiterate. She is a *hôtel de passage*, a narrow bed on which to lie for a while, for her customers who come and go, leaving her somewhat the richer and more attractive to those who will, inevitably, sight and be seduced by her in their own time.

BIBLIOGRAPHY

Aiken, Conrad: *Great Circle*. Arbor House 1984.

Aiken, Conrad: *Ushant*. Duell, Sloan & Pearce, and Little, Brown & Co 1952.

Baker, Michael: *Our Three Selves*. Hamish Hamilton 1985.

Barham, RHD: *Life and Letters of the Rev Richard Harris Barham*. Richard Bentley & Son 1870.

Barham, RHD: *The Ingoldsby Legends*. Frederick Warne & Co 1843.

Beer, Thomas: *Stephen Crane*. Knopf 1927.

Benson, AC: *Memories and Friends*. John Murray 1924.

Benson, EF: *As We Are*. Longmans, Green & Co 1932.

Benson, EF: *As We Were*. Longmans, Green & Co 1930.

Benson, EF: *Final Edition*. Longmans, Green & Co 1940.

Benson, EF: *Our Family Affairs*. Cassell 1920.

Berryman, John: *Stephen Crane*. William Sloane Associates 1950.

Brooke, Jocelyn: *The Orchid Trilogy*. Penguin 1981.

Casson, John: *Lewis and Sybil*. Collins 1972.

Church, Richard: *Kent*. Robert Hale 1948.

Conrad, Jessie: *Joseph Conrad and His Circle*. Jarrolds 1935.

Delbanco, Nicholas: *Group Portrait*. Faber 1982.

Dickinson, Patric: *Poems from Rye*. Martello Bookshop 1979.

Dickinson, Patric: *The Good Minute*. Gollancz 1965.

Dickson, Lovat: *H.G. Wells*. Faber 1984.

Dickson, Lovat: *Radclyffe Hall at the Well of Loneliness*. Collins 1975.

Edel, Leon: *Henry James Letters*. Bellknap Harvard 1984.

Edel, Leon: *The Life of Henry James*. Penguin 1977.
Edel, Leon & Ray, GN: *Henry James and HG Wells*. Rupert Hart-Davis 1959.
Ellman, Richard: *Golden Codgers*. OUP 1973.
Ford, Ford Madox: *Joseph Conrad: A Personal Remembrance*. Duckworth 1924.
Ford, Ford Madox: *Memories and Impressions*. Penguin 1979.
Garnett, David: *The Golden Echo*. Harcourt, Brace & Co 1954.
Gayley, CM: *Francis Beaumont: Dramatist*. Duckworth 1914.
Gilkes, Lillian: *Cora Crane*. Indiana University Press 1960.
Hare, Augustus: *Sussex*. George Allen 1896.
James, Henry: *English Hours*. OUP 1981.
Jean-Aubry, G: *Joseph Conrad, Life and Letters*. Heinemann 1927.
Killorin, Joseph: *Selected Letters of Conrad Aiken*. Yale University Press 1978.
Kipling, Rudyard: *Puck of Pook's Hill*. Macmillan 1946.
Langley Moore, Doris: *E. Nesbit*. Ernest Benn 1967.
Lesley, Cole: *The Life of Noel Coward*. Penguin 1978.
Leslie, Anita: *Clare Sheridan*. Doubleday 1977.
Lorenz, Clarissa M: *Lorelei Two*. University of Georgia Press 1983.
MacShane, Frank: *Ford Madox Ford*. Routledge & Kegan Paul 1965.
Martin, Jay: *Conrad Aiken*. Princeton University Press 1962.
Mizener, Arthur: *The Saddest Story*. The Bodley Head 1971.
Nowell-Smith, Simon: *The Legend of the Master*. Constable 1947.
Ormrod, Richard: *Una Troubridge*. Jonathan Cape 1984.
Piper, John: *Romney Marsh*. Penguin 1950.
Reavell, Cynthia & Tony: *E.F. Benson*. Martello Bookshop 1984.
Stallman, RW & Gilkes, Lillian: *Stephen Crane: Letters*. New York University Press 1960.
Tennant, Roger: *Joseph Conrad*. Sheldon Press 1981.
Thackeray, William: *Denis Duval*. Smith and Elder 1869.
Theroux, Paul: *The Kingdom by the Sea*. Penguin 1985.
Thorndike, Russell: *Sybil Thorndike*. Theatre Book Club 1950.
Thurston Hopkins, G & R: *Literary Originals of Sussex*. Alex J Philip 1936.

Troubridge, Una, Lady: *The Life and Death of Radclyffe Hall.* Hammond Hammond 1961.
Wells, GP: *H.G. Wells in Love*. Faber 1984.
Wells, HG: *Experiment in Autobiography*. Faber 1984.
Wells, HG: *Kipps*. Collins 1952.

INDEX